PRAISE FOR THE

"*Blur* is an intense thriller with grip
and a tight storyline."
—THE CHRISTIAN MANIFESTO

"Mr. James takes us on a ride that leaves us breathless."
—THE SUSPENSE ZONE

"James cranks up the creep factor."
—BOOKLIST

"*Blur* is a masterfully crafted mystery that will keep you on your toes
and guessing throughout the book."
—LILY BLOOM BOOKS

"[*Blur*] really stretches the imagination and packs some thrilling
suspense with a hint of supernatural."
—A PEEK AT MY BOOKSHELF

"The convoluted clues make for one thrilling chase for the reader."
THE COVER CONTESSA

"A great story that had me totally immersed and enthralled."
—LIFE IS STORY

"Steven James well deserves the title Master of Suspense."
—CROSSROAD REVIEW

"If you're looking for a story that will make your heart beat a little
faster than normal, then this is your book!"
—BOOK NERDERIE

"*Fury* is a fast-paced adventure with engaging characters and great
suspense that leaves the reader impatiently waiting for the final book
in the series."
—STRAIGHT OFF THE PAGE

ALSO BY STEVEN JAMES

YOUNG ADULT NOVELS

Quest for Celestia

Blur

Fury

ADULT THRILLERS

Featuring FBI Special Agent Patrick Bowers:

Opening Moves

The Pawn

The Rook

The Knight

The Bishop

The Queen

The King

Checkmate

Every Crooked Path

Featuring escape artist Jevin Banks:

Placebo

Singularity

CURSE

CURSE

STEVEN JAMES

SKYSCAPE

Text copyright © 2016 by Steven James

Published by Skyscape, New York

www.apub.com

Amazon, the Amazon logo, and Skyscape are trademarks of Amazon.com, Inc., or its affiliates.

ISBN-13: 9781503933453
ISBN-10: 1503933458

Book design by Katrina Damkoehler and Susan Gerber

Printed in the United States of America
10 9 8 7 6 5 4 3 2 1

*For
Tom and Rhonda,
friends and family*

The markings of madness ring true in my soul.

Each day is a scream and a chore.

The echoes of bedlam won't let me be whole.

For they've eaten the dream by the door.

—ALEXI MARËNCHIVEK

PART I
TAKEN

CHAPTER ONE

Dusk.

The forest, thick on each side of the road, lies caught in the deep shadows of the coming night. Lake Algonquin sits nestled among them.

A net of darkness settles across the woods.

Though I'm driving, there's no traffic and I'm alone in the car, so I sneak a quick glance at my phone.

No texts from Kyle.

His house is exactly eight miles from the corner up ahead, so at this speed I'll be there in just under twelve minutes and forty seconds.

I don't even have to consciously think about it.

Math comes naturally to me. Sometimes it's helpful.

Sometimes it's just annoying.

We're going to spend some time planning for our upcoming trip to Georgia next Saturday.

In my headlights, I glimpse movement ahead of me on the right side of the road and I brake.

Two skittish whitetail deer stare at the car, then bound in front me. I wait for them to clear, make sure there aren't any more coming, then pull forward.

Two weeks ago when I received the invitation to the basketball camp in Atlanta, I was surprised. I'd had a good season, but it's an elite camp and usually fills up early, so just getting an invite was a big deal. But since it was half-way across the country, getting there was going to be a challenge.

Because of their work schedules, neither of my parents could take me.

Apparently, there was some anonymous donor who gave money to cover the tuition and travel costs of students from out of state to help assure "diversity."

At first we weren't sure if the camp scholarship was legit, but everything cleared, my coach told me it wasn't breaking any college recruitment rules, and I sent in my registration. But there was still the issue of getting down there.

The camp is at Northern Georgia Tech, a private university just outside of Atlanta.

Not a short trip from Beldon, Wisconsin.

Right around eighteen hours, actually.

Then Kyle's girlfriend, Mia, mentioned that she had an aunt in Atlanta whose house wasn't too far from the campus and it got us thinking.

Dad told us his college roommate lived half an hour south of Champaign, Illinois, which is about halfway down there. After he brought that up, things came together quickly. Kyle, Mia, and Nicole, the girl I was dating, would go down with me.

All of us are rising seniors, getting ready for our last year of high school. Three of us are seventeen, but Mia is eighteen and that helped our case.

Her aunt could show everyone else around Atlanta while I was at the camp. Just the right amount of freedom for us and the right amount of supervision for our parents.

Ground rules: Check in every day. No drinking. No drugs. Nothing stupid.

The first three, no problem.

That last one might take a little more work.

Now, as I come around a curve that follows the shoreline of the lake, I catch sight of some movement again, about a hundred feet away.

I slow to a stop.

But this time it's not a deer.

A little boy emerges from the woods. He's maybe five or six years old and seems distracted as he wanders to the middle of the county highway.

He stops at the centerline.

I wait to see if his mom or someone will follow after him, but after a moment it's clear that he's alone.

I let the car idle, then, stepping out, I call to him, "Hey, are you okay?"

The summer day has cooled off. There's a slight chill in the air.

Crickets chatter in the shadows.

After a quick glance toward the forest, the boy faces me. Pale complexion—even in the dim light I can make that much out. He reaches one hand toward me as if he somehow wants me to hold it from this distance, but he doesn't leave the road.

Beyond him, around the bend, headlights cut through the darkening day and the rumble of a logging truck rolls toward us from the direction of the sawmill.

I start the boy's way. "You need to get off the road."

He doesn't move.

As I get nearer, although I can't place him, I have the sense that I've seen him before.

"Hurry!"

Nothing.

The truck doesn't slow.

Now I'm running.

Its headlights come sharply into view, glaring toward me, backlighting the boy.

As it barrels toward us, I yell again for him to move. His back is still turned to the logging truck as he stands completely still with that one arm held out to me.

"Hey!" I gesture wildly. "Get off the road!"

He stays there, but lifts the other arm.

Both hands outstretched now.

He wants you to help him.

He needs you to save him.

I bolt as fast as I can toward the oncoming truck to sweep the boy into my arms and get him to safety.

My mind is calculating speed, distance.

Math.

Second nature.

There isn't time to get there and save him.

Yes there is. There has to be.

Go!

I do.

The driver blares his horn and slams on the brakes, but he's going too fast and there's no way he'll be able to stop in time. The sharp smell of burning rubber fills the air. As the cab begins to slow, the truck bed, which is loaded with logs, starts sliding sideways along the road.

When I'm just a few strides away from the boy, he finally looks over his shoulder at the truck.

I throw out an arm to pick him up, but my hand passes through empty air.

I spin to see how I could've missed him, and my back is to the truck as it clips my left side and launches me into the air toward the ditch.

Time somehow slows and slurs around me while I'm in midair. The night becomes liquid and I'm aware of the cool evening air brushing against my face, of the rich scent of pine trees surrounding the road, of the sound of the wailing brakes. The glaring sweep of the headlights. The rocky ground beneath me. Coming closer.

Time collapses.

Rips forward.

Impact.

I careen down the embankment, rolling toward the lake until I smash into a tree and come to an abrupt stop about fifteen feet from the road.

Breathe, breathe, breathe.

You're okay. You're going to be okay.

It should hurt. It will hurt, but right now adrenaline is blocking the pain—during all my years of playing football I've taken my share of hits. I know how this works.

But right now, I don't care about any of that.

All I can think of is the boy.

You didn't get to him. You missed him. He's gone.

My left arm hangs loose and useless from a dislocated shoulder.

It's happened to me before in football and every time it does, seeing it like that is pretty shocking, but the pain hasn't quite registered yet.

I get to my feet and scramble up the bank toward the pavement.

The logging truck has skidded past me and finally come to a stop. One of the straps holding the logs in place must have snapped because the logs have spilled sideways off the bed and are strewn across the road, blocking it.

Terrified of what I might see, I scan the pavement, but can't find the boy. No blood. No sign of a body. I gaze into the ditch I landed in.

It's shrouded in lengthening shadows, but from where I'm standing I can't see the boy—or what might have been left of him if he was hit by that truck.

My ankle got wrenched when I landed and as I take a wobbly step forward to study the other side of the road, it buckles. I collapse and the driver of the logging truck comes hurrying toward me.

"You okay?" he shouts.

Using only one arm, it's tough to push myself to my feet again, but I manage. "Did you hit him?"

"Who?"

"The boy. The little boy."

"What boy?" He stares at me dumbfounded. A mixture of confusion and fear. "We're the only ones out here. You came running at my truck. What happened to your arm?"

"No, no, no. The boy who was in the road."

"Listen, I'm telling you, there wasn't anyone else. Just you. What'd you think you were doing?" He offers a hand to steady me. "You could've been killed. Are you okay?"

I take a step, but lose my balance again and barely catch myself from falling by grabbing his arm.

"We need to get you to a hospital. Is your shoulder . . . ?"

"Dislocated. I'm okay."

"You shouldn't be walking around."

"We have to find the boy."

The pain is finally tightening around me. I gaze at that left arm. By the awkward angle, anyone could see that things aren't right. The last time this happened the physical therapist told me it might sublux again.

So.

His prediction came true.

Either I get it back in place myself or I wait for a doctor to do it—and it's going to hurt just as much then. And in the meantime the tissue will continue to swell, so it'll only get harder to pop back into place if I wait.

"Help me," I say to the driver. "I need to get to your truck."

He tells me once more that I shouldn't be walking around, but when I start limping forward, he joins me, supporting my good arm.

We arrive at the flatbed and I wedge my left wrist into a gap between the boards on the back.

Okay, this is really not going to feel good.

The man gasps. "What are you doing?"

"Traction. I have to get . . ."

I clench my teeth and lean backward.

A sharp explosion of pain.

I almost collapse.

But, I didn't go back far enough. The shoulder remains out of its socket.

Relax. You need to relax the muscles. It's the only way it'll go back in place.

"Give me a sec." I take a deep breath, close my eyes, ready myself, and pull back again, harder. I twist slightly and finally, after what seems like the longest three seconds of my life, the shoulder grinds as it slides back into place. There's a shot of relief but, at the same time, a wave of a heavier, duller kind of pain.

The driver's face blanches. "Did you just . . . ?"

"Yeah."

I use my right hand to support the weak arm and to keep it from swinging. Based on how things went the last time this happened, it's going to be sore for a couple weeks at least.

"You might have internal injuries." The man produces a cell phone and punches in 911. "You should lie down until help gets here."

"We need to find the boy."

Finally, he gives in. "Listen. I'll look for him. But you, rest."

When dispatch picks up, I say to the driver, "Tell them I'm Daniel Byers. They'll know who I am."

"They will?"

"Yeah. My dad's the sheriff."

CHAPTER TWO

After the driver hangs up, it's clear that he's worried about the fact that my dad is our county's sheriff.

"You're the one who ran in front of my truck. I tried to stop. I couldn't help it."

"I know. I was just trying to get that kid out of the way."

"I don't want to get in trouble for—"

I'm losing my patience here. "Just look for him. Okay?"

"Yeah. Alright. Wait here. I'll be right back."

He digs a flashlight out of his cab and starts scouring the ditch that I'd been thrown into.

I shuffle over and take a seat on the guardrail that's meant to keep the logging trucks from toppling over the side of the road if they take this curve too fast.

The smell of burnt rubber still hangs in the air.

I notice the crickets chirping from the shadows just as I did when I first got out of my car. I don't know if they've been doing it this whole time or if they were quiet for a while and have just started in again now.

It's odd how certain things at certain times attract our attention. It's almost as if our brains focus on one sense or impression at a time. You get hurt—you notice that. Then, as the pain starts to fade, you realize you're hungry. But the thing is—were you hungry that whole time and your brain just didn't tell you? Or did you suddenly start to get hungry right when you stopped focusing on the pain?

It makes it hard to tell how much of the world passes by every day in that slipstream between what's really happening and what our brains register as real.

Sometimes it can be a pretty big gap.

That's one thing I've been learning this last year, ever since the blurs started.

An ambulance siren echoes off the water, somewhere around the other side of the lake.

I wonder if my dad will be the first one from law enforcement to arrive.

I'm sure that as soon as he hears his son was hit by a truck he'll break every speed law in the county to get here.

Mom would too, but she's at a graphic design conference in Madison this week for work. Even though she isn't supposed to get back until Sunday night, I'm guessing she'll start the five-hour drive back home right away when she finds out what's happened.

The ambulance's siren swells over the other night sounds, but it's still a few minutes out.

While I wait, I watch the truck driver finish checking this side of the road and move to the other side.

Evidently he hasn't found anything yet.

Letting my attention drift away from my ankle and shoulder, I consider what he said about me possibly having internal injuries. Gently, I prod at my side to see if there are any broken ribs. I can't tell for sure, but I've got some tender spots.

Finally, his flashlight beam comes bobbing back toward me.

"Anything?"

He shakes his head. "No."

Well, if there was no boy, then you were seeing things. And that would mean—

The driver arrives by my side and asks me concernedly, "How are you doing?"

"I'm alright."

But that's not quite true.

Because I know I saw a boy out here.

I know I did.

The ambulance comes into view.

By now, darkness has nearly devoured the forest.

Because of the logs in the road, the paramedics aren't able to pull all the way up to me, so I hobble toward them as they hustle my way, rolling a gurney along the road.

As they check my vitals and give me a quick eval, they tell me that my dad was over in Pine Lake—which is on the other side of the county—but that he'll meet me at the hospital. Then, they load me up, and when they swing the doors shut it's almost like they're closing off a time in my life when things were normal again, the way they used to be before last fall, before the blurs began.

But now, it sure looks like they're back. And if I'm starting to have them again, it almost certainly means that something terrible has happened.

It almost certainly means that someone is dead.

CHAPTER THREE

I still don't know what caused the blurs to start in the first place, but over time it became clear that whenever I experienced one, whenever reality and fantasy overlapped and merged in such a way that I couldn't tell them apart, then my subconscious was piecing together clues to a mystery that my conscious mind needed to solve.

But deciphering the blurs isn't an exact science, and so far it's also been deeply troubling because nearly all of them have revolved around people who were murdered.

So that's what I'm thinking here in the emergency room as the doctor inspects me for internal bleeding: that boy in the road. And the blurs. And death and grief and the girls that I saw last fall and in the winter. That first one, reaching out of her casket and clutching at my arm. Then the second one, bursting into flames right before my eyes.

Both were dead when they appeared to me.

And now, I saw a little boy.

"Well," the doctor says, drawing me back to the moment. "So far so good. I can't find any sign of internal injuries. You're one lucky guy."

"Yeah, I guess so," I tell her.

While she's getting ready to take me down the hall for some X-rays, Dad bursts into the room.

"Dan!" He's out of breath. "Are you okay?"

"Yeah. I am."

"You were hit by a truck?" He looks from me to the doctor as if she might be able help shed some light on all this.

"Grazed," I tell him.

"Grazed enough to throw you into a ditch."

"I'm okay, Dad."

After the doctor confirms that she hasn't been able to find anything seriously wrong, Dad goes from being worried to upset. The transformation is almost instantaneous.

I've seen it before, both in him and Mom.

Concern first.

Then anger.

Two different sides of love.

Probably every parent goes through it when they find out their kid has gotten hurt from doing something that maybe wasn't the smartest thing in the world.

"The driver said you ran right out in front of his truck," Dad says.

"I thought I saw a boy there. I was trying to get him out of the way."

"Yes. He mentioned that on the phone. He didn't see anyone."

"I did. It looked like he was about five years old."

My dad is quiet.

"It really happened, Dad."

"Okay."

It's strange. I'm both hoping that there *wasn't* really a boy, because he would've likely been seriously hurt or even killed, but I'm also hoping that there *was*—because otherwise it means I'm losing touch with reality.

While I'm trying to figure out what else to say, Dad gets a call on his radio. From growing up in a home where I hear dispatch codes all the time, I'm familiar enough with them to recognize that this one is for a drug overdose or attempted suicide.

"I'll have some deputies search out there one more time," he says, but I can tell he's distracted by the call, by the address they announced. I don't know whose place it is, but it's in the next town over and for something this serious he'll probably need to be onsite. "But from what I've heard, they already went over the area pretty carefully."

After talking briefly into his radio, he tells me he has to go, then rests a hand lightly on my uninjured shoulder. "Dan, I can't tell you how glad I am you're alright. On the drive over here, I spoke with your mom. She's on her way back from Madison. I'll let her know you're fine, but you should call her yourself."

"Don't tell her about the boy."

He looks like he's going to object to that.

"I'll tell her," I say. "It'll be better if I do it."

"Alright." He turns to the doctor. "Call me the minute you get those X-ray results."

"I will."

He gives her his number, speaks with dispatch one more time, and after he leaves, she leads me to the X-ray room.

Our hospital isn't huge, so the doctor serves double-duty, taking the X-rays herself. While she gets everything ready, I try to figure out how to tell Mom about the blur.

In a way, she knows what this kind of thing is like. She's had hallucinations too and last year she had such terrifying nightmares that she actually moved out because she was afraid she might hurt me or Dad.

She's back now, we're figuring things out as a family, but she's a natural worrier and I'm not really sure how she'll react when she hears the news that I'm seeing things again.

• • •

Dr. Adrian Waxford was at home completing the prisoner transfer request paperwork when the screen saver on his computer flicked to the picture of his younger brother. The movement caught his eye, momentarily distracting him.

It was a photograph from a quarter century ago. Adrian had scanned it in and used it to remind himself every day why he did what he did.

In the photo, which had been taken when Jacob was thirty, the two of them were standing on a beach holding up the sea bass they'd caught that day. Sunlight danced on the waves behind them. Everything was perfect.

It was the last time Adrian saw his brother alive.

Less than a week later, Jacob had been murdered by a serial killer who was eventually caught and sentenced to four hundred and fifty years in prison for the nine homicides he'd committed.

However, he died after just a few years, before he'd served even a tiny fraction of his sentence.

So ever since then, Adrian had dedicated himself to justice, to the greater good.

It motivated everything he did.

Those who commit crimes like that deserve to be punished.

And they deserve to serve out their entire sentences—even if that sentence stretches hundreds of years longer than a normal lifespan.

He placed a hand on the screen, touching the image of his brother, remembering that day, all their days together, and how they'd been cut short by a man with no conscience. Then the picture flipped to a landscape shot from when he was lecturing in Scotland last year.

Adrian let his hand linger there for a moment as he thought of how our lives are like that—here for a moment, and then abruptly, without warning, and all too suddenly, they pass away.

Then he went back to his paperwork, but was interrupted a few minutes later when a text came through from his associate Henrik Poehlman: *He's on the move. Can you meet me at the Estoria?*

Adrian knew that the kinds of things they would be discussing would best be done in person. And the safest place to do that was at the old Estoria Inn, which now served as their research center.

He replied that he would be there as soon as he could.

Then, thinking of his brother and how this meeting would help honor his memory, he went to get his car keys.

CHAPTER FOUR

The X-rays only take a couple of minutes.

The doctor checks my ribcage as well as my ankle, just to confirm that it's only sprained and not broken.

She's reviewing the results in the room across the hall when Kyle and Nicole arrive.

Even though most of my friends are into basketball and football, Kyle's the one major exception. While it's true that he did go out for track this spring, organized sports normally aren't his thing. He's more into writing lyrics for his band, reading graphic novels, and making up recipes for hot sauces that will burn the taste buds right off your tongue.

Kyle is taller than me and kind of spindly. Tonight he has his surfer-style hair pulled back in a ponytail. He lopes into the room first, but Nicole is right on his heels and hurries to my side before I really get a chance to greet either of them.

"How are you?" she asks worriedly.

I've known Nicole since grade school, but only caught on last year that she wanted to be more than just friends—reading girls isn't exactly my strong suit. We've been dating since right around homecoming. Although she's usually quick with a smile, tonight I can see she's seriously alarmed by what's happened.

"I'm alright, Nikki," I tell her.

"Are you just saying that, or . . . ?"

"No, I'm good. A little banged up, but nothing worse than after a football game."

"Bro." Kyle gulps down some of the Dr Pepper he's holding. "I heard you dislocated your shoulder and then popped it back into place yourself. That is *sick*."

"Where'd you hear that?" Then it hits me: The paramedic has a son in our class. "Wait, let me guess—Gavin's dad."

"Yup." He nods. "Told Gavin and he texted me. Word travels fast in a small town. And seriously? You were hit *head-on* by a logging truck? That's gonna make for a sweet story."

Kyle's a natural taleteller and in his hands this night could easily become a campfire or road trip epic. His stories have a way of taking on a life of their own, though. By the third or fourth telling he might very well be the one who got hurt. And I wouldn't be surprised if he threw in a few extra broken bones just for good measure.

"What was it like?" he asks. "Was your arm hanging way off to the side, like in that football game last year when—"

"Can we not talk about that part?" Nicole looks a little faint. "Seriously, I don't need to be thinking about arms hanging out of their sockets."

"Fair enough." Then he says to me, "Mia would've come over, but she's watching my little sister. She said you better not die or else she'll kill you."

Yeah, that sounds like Mia.

She and Kyle have been on and off for a few months now. Things are kind of in flux and I'm not sure if they're going to make it in a relationship, but they're good for each other, so I hope it works out. Besides, the trip to Georgia will be seriously awkward if the two of them aren't getting along.

"So." Nicole goes for a chair, slides it close to my bed, and takes a seat. "How'd it happen?"

They know about my blurs, so I go ahead and lay everything out there. "I'm pretty sure I had another blur. This time it was a boy, maybe in kindergarten or so. I don't know who he was."

"Did he say anything?"

"No." I fill them in on what happened. "I need to find out what all this means."

"Well," Kyle says somewhat grimly, "then there's one thing we're gonna need to do."

"What's that?"

He pulls out his phone. "Check the obituaries."

CHAPTER FIVE

Dr. Waxford wound his way along the road, climbing higher into the Great Smoky Mountains.

He and his team had made great strides in the last couple of years, but the loss of the research facility in northern Wisconsin last December had slowed things down—that is, until they located this old hotel here in this remote part of eastern Tennessee.

Actually, the site was ideal. It was isolated and lay at the end of a one-lane road that had hardly been used in years.

Back in the 1950s when a new highway was built that wrapped around the other side of the mountain, it took the tourists and other businesses with it. The hotel owners went bankrupt and the property went into foreclosure.

Rumored to be haunted, the Estoria Inn had sat empty for decades and was being reclaimed by the forest when Adrian and his team started renovations. Most people, even those in the nearby towns, had forgotten that this place even existed.

And none of them knew what kind of research was happening there now.

Which was probably a good thing.

Fortuitously, the Estoria was also less than an hour drive for the hypnotherapist Adrian sometimes brought up to implant suggestions in the minds of his subjects after they'd been put into a deep trance.

When you pay a hypnotist enough, you can get him to implant any suggestions that you want.

Despair.

Depression.

Loneliness.

They can all be the tools you use in the service of the greater good.

• • •

We're on our phones searching Internet news sites for recent obituaries when the X-ray results come back.

No broken bones.

The ankle is only sprained. The shoulder will recover. It won't be ideal for the basketball camp, but at least it's not my shooting arm.

The doctor gives me a sling to keep the shoulder in place, then explains what I already know: It's going to be very sore for a while and I'll run the risk of it coming out of its socket again unless I'm careful. "You'll need to keep your arm in that sling for the next four to six weeks."

"Okay. Thanks," I say, but I know that's not going to happen.

This camp is a huge deal and missing it isn't an option. At least a dozen Division I coaches will be there recruiting players and it's my best chance to get the attention I need for a scholarship offer.

Although I've had some interest from a few Big Ten football coaches, honestly, I'd rather play college basketball. Way fewer injuries. Less time lifting and more time actually playing. Besides, I don't really have the size for college football—not to mention my mom worrying about me less, which is a bonus.

While the doctor calls Dad to bring him up to speed and also get permission to give me some pain medication, I touch base with Mom to make sure she knows I'm alright. I decide that it'll be best to explain about the blur in person, so I don't bring it up.

Finally, the doctor hands me the meds, along with a prescription.

On their way to see me at the hospital, Kyle had picked up Nicole from her place, so now we swing by to get my car from the road out by the lake where I left it earlier.

Somehow, the logging company has managed to get the logs far enough to one side to allow cars to get past.

Being here brings everything back again and I can't tell if it's just my imagination, but my shoulder seems to throb more as I remember what it was like to get hit by that truck.

My attention shifting from one thing to the next.

That slipstream again.

All those unnoticed slivers of reality curling right past me.

But now, the ones branded with pain are coming to the forefront.

I ride with Nicole, who drives my car so I can rest my shoulder.

Kyle follows us back to my house in his vintage Mustang.

Even though it's late, we search online again for a little while, but we still can't find anything about kids who've recently died—at least not any that match the age of the boy in the road.

However, that doesn't necessarily mean he's still alive.

He might not have died recently. After all, the girl I saw burn up in my blur back in December had actually died in the 1930s.

As it turned out, I'd learned about her story and seen her picture years ago when I was nine. Then, just before Christmas, my mind threaded some clues together and showed me what it might have looked like when the lantern she was standing next to caught fire to her nightgown and ended up taking her life.

I'd forgotten all about her.

When the memory came back, it brought a flood of other grisly images with it because the day I first saw her photo I'd been present when a killer struck, but I'd blocked it out.

They say trauma can do that, that it can rip the fabric between your conscious and your subconscious mind.

My problem is that the rip keeps getting bigger.

My friends get word from their parents that they need to take off and I tell them goodnight.

"See you tomorrow?" Nicole says.

"Yeah." I give her a quick kiss.

"Kiss me and I'll dislocate your other shoulder," Kyle tells me. Then he taps a finger thoughtfully against the air. "But at least then you wouldn't notice the first one so much. So there is that."

"Thanks, but no thanks."

"Okay, so before I go, I've got one for you."

"You've got one?"

"A riddle: I'm twice as old as I used to be when I was half as young as I am now. How old am I?"

For months he's been trying to trick me with math or logic problems. Doesn't always work out so well.

"That one's easy. It would be whatever age you are, so you're the same as me. Seventeen."

"Yes. And I'm seriously glad you're still seventeen and not dead."

"Yeah."

"It would have totally ruined my night."

"Mine too."

"Text me."

"I will."

A little while after they leave, Dad comes home and checks on me.

"I'm good," I tell him. "Anything serious with that call?"

"Call?"

"The dispatch code. I heard it at the hospital. Was it a suicide?"

"Scarlett Cordova accidentally overdosed on some over the counter drugs."

Scarlett is a year behind me at school. "Is she alright?"

"She will be. Gave everyone a scare, though."

"How do they know?"

He looks at me curiously. "How do they know what?"

"You said she accidentally OD'ed. How do they know it was an accident?"

"There were three other kids there with her when it happened. It was during some kind of drinking game. Her parents were gone. Good thing she's alright. Lucky girl."

"There's a lot of that going around tonight."

"A lot of what?"

"Luck."

"I guess maybe there is."

After telling me one more time how thankful he is that I'm okay, he heads to his room and I climb into bed, hoping that even with the aching shoulder I'll be able to get some rest.

Instead, I find myself caught up thinking about who that boy might have been and what the blur might mean.

He'd reached out to me, just like the girls in my earlier blurs had done.

It'd been too late to save them.

Maybe if we were lucky one more time, it wouldn't be too late to save him.

CHAPTER SIX

Dr. Waxford unlocked the gate, swung it to the side, and turned onto the dirt road that, by design, had no sign on it.

After locking the gate behind him, he drove the two miles up to the research facility that the Department of Defense had recently renovated for him.

He parked, then went to the front door and placed his hand on the vein recognition reader to verify his identity.

Vascular biometrics, or palm vein recognition, is even more accurate than retinal scanners or fingerprints. And, since blood flow is required, the hand has to be attached to the arm for the reader to identify you, so it's nearly impossible to fake.

You couldn't just cut off someone's hand to get their fingerprints or remove an eyeball to use in a retinal scanner—both things Henrik Poehlman had done to people in the past when the circumstances dictated.

An unpleasant business.

The door swung open and Adrian passed through the lobby, entering one of the long, narrow hallways interspersed with research rooms on either side.

Well, to his mind they were research rooms; to the men inside, they were solitary confinement cells.

Ten were currently occupied. More would eventually be filled as renovations were completed on the Estoria Inn's third and fourth floors.

Though it was the middle of the night, Adrian didn't mind being called in. Actually, he preferred coming in at this time. After meeting with Henrik, he would stay and get some work done on the new drug he was developing.

The oversight committee's meeting was coming up in less than two weeks and he needed to verify and quantify his findings before then.

His studies were going to make a profound and lasting difference.

In fact, they would transform the way the entire justice system functioned.

All for the greater good.

All in the name of providing appropriate punishment to those who deserved it.

He approached room 113, where he kept the man who'd killed eight people in the northwoods of Wisconsin.

Adrian paused by the door and peered through the one-way mirror.

Despite the time of night, the bright fluorescent lights in the subject's room were on as part of his sleep deprivation therapy.

The design of the room was based on the "white torture" techniques perfected by the Iranians.

The subject is placed in a completely white room. He's dressed entirely in white, served white food on a white plate. No colors. No exterior windows. No sounds.

The sensory deprivation and isolation help distort the passage of time.

Using these techniques you can get someone to break without beating him, without waterboarding him, without inflicting any physical harm on him at all.

Not that Adrian was necessarily against those things when they were justified, but they weren't always necessary.

Not when you had other, less intrusive but just as effective means at your disposal.

The glass on the other side was chipped, but not cracked.

During the hours when this man wasn't medicated, he'd tried desperately to break the mirror to get free, but the glass was far too thick for that.

In fact, Adrian had provided the subject with a steel chair—white, of course—just to see how he would use it to try to escape. All part of his research while he tracked the downward spiral of the man's mental ability.

Rather than removing all hope of escape, Adrian found it more effective to create the illusion that getting free was a possibility. This kept the subjects' mental capability intact and it allowed for a deeper emotional letdown when he found himself unsuccessful in his efforts to get away.

Some people might have claimed that it was cruel to taunt the subjects like that, to provide them with an object that, at first glance, appeared helpful for an escape, but turned out to be useless in the end. To Adrian, however, it wasn't a way to taunt the men, but simply a way to evaluate how the different treatment strategies affected their mental states.

And it was far less cruel than what these men had done to their victims.

Now, Adrian observed subject #832145 staring into the corner of the room, muttering to himself.

Curious, he turned on the audio feed from the room to find out what the man was saying.

Something about a boy and blood. It sounded rambling and incoherent, but it was all being recorded. He would analyze it later.

He might have to monitor things to make sure this man didn't slip too far into madness.

After you lose all touch with reality you're no longer aware of the break. You think you're fine and that everyone else is crazy. There is relief. Until then, though, things can be very terrifying.

And, really, that's what Adrian was going for.

Terror.

Suffering.

Justice.

In fact, a continual recognition of their mental states, of their situation, was essential.

It was a vital aspect of the punishment our legal system strove for.

Subject #832145 would be in solitary confinement here for decades, perhaps for the rest of his life, and because of the treatment he was receiving, it would seem like much, much longer than that.

All at once, the man turned and looked at the one-way mirror as if he could see Adrian on the other side. With the whites of his eyes completely dyed black with Henrik's special tattoo ink, it looked like two holes had been drilled into his head.

He hissed, and then went back to talking to himself.

The subject couldn't get out of that room and there was no way for him to know that anyone was watching, but still, Adrian found himself taking a slight step backward.

Of course he was safe, though. The lock on this door was electronically controlled and could only be opened from inside a secure room down the hall.

As he was reminding himself of that, he got a text from Henrik: *I'm on the lower level. By the fly room.*

There was no cell reception up here in this remote part of the mountains, but since uninterrupted communication was so vital for them, Adrian and Henrik used radios and advanced satellite phones that even allowed them to text and to have video chats.

All paid for by the Pentagon, which had a vested interest in their work.

After one more curious look at subject #832145, Adrian continued past the kitchen and descended the stairwell to the rooms in the basement.

This is where most of the actual research took place.

Henrik stood at the end of the hall waiting outside the room containing the *Tabanidae*, more commonly known as horse flies, or deer flies.

Painful bites but not deadly.

No poison, no venom, just torn skin.

Then, once they've scored the flesh, they suck out the blood that pools into the wound.

Adrian kept ten thousand or so in there—even with the computer analysis that monitored their daily population fluctuations, it was obviously difficult to keep track of the exact number.

Insects process the passage of time differently than larger species, like humans, do.

When he originally proposed his funding request, Adrian had compared things to a science fiction or action movie slow-motion sequence during which the bullets or knives are flying at the hero and he's able to watch them slice through the air and easily step out of their way before they hit him.

During the initial meeting with General Vanessa Gibbons, Adrian had told her that to the *Tabanidae*, the world appears to pass by at a much slower rate than it does for *Homo sapiens*. "That's why it's so hard to catch or swat flies—because they have, for all practical purposes, more time to respond and escape."

"And you can replicate this effect in people? This morphing of time?"

"Yes. And I'm steadily improving my techniques."

By better understanding how flies and other insects processed time, Adrian was able to design ways—through drugs, sleep deprivation, isolation, and environmental manipulation—to make it seem like more time was passing for his subjects than was actually the case.

That was the key to his research.

That was the ultimate goal.

All for the greater good.

He passed the surgery room containing the intracranial electrodes and brainwave sensors, then the room where the tattooing took place, and came to Henrik.

He was an imposing man, broad shouldered and thick chested. As a former police officer he'd seen too many guilty people get off on technicalities. He shared Adrian's ardor for justice.

"I like this room." Henrik was staring through the window at the dark swarm. "I'd have to say it's my favorite one here."

"Even more than where you do the tattooing?"

"That's a close second." He tapped the glass. "Sometimes I wonder what it would be like to be stuck in there."

"You could always find out. The door is right over there."

"I'm not that curious."

"Who would be? So, you texted me that you wanted to talk."

"We lost Zacharias."

"Where was he last seen?"

"Philadelphia."

"Hmm. That's his third visit there."

Henrik finally shifted his attention from the flies to Adrian. "My people had eyes on him when he entered an office building downtown, but he must have slipped out another door because they never saw him leave."

"And what about those young men and women who have the hallucinations?"

"Besides Daniel and Petra, it's not clear who else they've located. Although, if our sources are correct, there are two others out there."

"Four in all."

"Yes."

"It's been six months since—"

"Yes, but Zacharias has skills and whoever's funding him is good at hiding their tracks."

"And Petra?"

"I have two people in place. They're ready to take her whenever you give the word."

Normally, Adrian wouldn't have resorted to such extreme measures, but everything depended on continuing this research, and once they'd procured the senator's daughter, they would have the leverage to make sure that happened.

"Alright," Adrian said. "I'll let you know when to have them move in. Meanwhile, do whatever it takes to find Zacharias."

"I will."

"And see what businesses have offices in that building in Philadelphia. I want to know if any of them might be funneling money to him."

"We looked into it, but I'll check again."

Adrian nodded. "Good."

"By the way, I understand we have a new arrival coming in soon?"

"We'll be processing him on the sixteenth."

"Will you be trying out the Telpatine on him?"

"In time. Until then, keep your needle ready. I'll make sure we have enough ink to do both eyes."

"I always enjoy that part."

"I know you do."

After Henrik left, Adrian observed the *Tabanidae* flying into the glass, instinctively trying to get out.

Such a powerful thing, instinct.

Always, always compelling organisms to try to be free.

Just like the subjects with their steel chairs.

The readings on the counter beside the door noted a dip in the flies' population.

He tapped at the keys and lowered a slab of rotting beef into the room.

Let them feed.

Let them breed.

The maggots would rejuvenate their numbers.

The flies swarmed onto the meat, covering it almost instantly, just like they did with the subjects when he locked them in there, unclothed, as part of their treatment.

CHAPTER SEVEN

I wake up slowly, caught in a wrestling match with my dream, trying to will myself free from its clutches.

Trying and failing.

It's as if I'm reliving last night's accident over and over again.

It's all there: the boy, the truck, the headlights slicing through the forest.

But in my dream I'm surrounded by a thick blanket of darkness that comes alive and turns into thousands of bats, all winging their way around me, their leathery wings and clawed feet brushing and scratching across my face, my arms, my hands.

I duck and swing at them, trying to get them to leave me alone. But they crawl on me, get caught in my hair, bite at my skin. I cry out. And then all at once, they're gone.

It's pitch black, yet somehow I can see that boy standing in the road.

It's a dream.

It follows its own rules.

Then I'm sprinting toward him.

But I'm too late.

Here in my nightmare, the truck hits him. There's a sickening crunch and a spray of blood, and then a lifeless mass in the road.

Suddenly, I'm there beside him, kneeling over his broken body.

A few bats return and stalk across his face as he stares with unblinking eyes at the night. I brush them away and as they scatter, he tilts his head toward me.

His hollow stare unsettles me.

Even though someone with his injuries couldn't possibly have survived, he whispers to me, his voice thick and wet from the blood dribbling from his mouth, "He never meant to go. It all began right here. Follow the bats. Find the truth."

I tell myself that it's not real, that none of this is real, that all I need to do is wake up and all of this will disappear.

It's all a dream.

Just a dream.

Then the scene plays itself out again.

But this time, at the end, the boy's words become living things. They take form and turn into bats themselves, circling up past me into the night—fanged, newly formed creatures escaping into the darkness.

And at last I'm able to stir, to free myself.

I open my eyes.

Instead of sitting bolt upright in bed like people do in movies but almost never do in real life, I lie there taking short, shallow breaths, trying to relax the tight, anxious muscles in my chest.

Sweat drenches the neckline of my T-shirt.

I blink against the sharp morning light cutting through my window.

The images recede like a tide washing back from shore, but the emotions don't go away and I feel a deep, primal weight of sadness and loss.

For the boy, for myself. I'm not sure which.

My room is on the second floor, and as I get out of bed I can hear Mom downstairs in the kitchen putting dishes away.

I check the time.

8:02.

Both my shoulder and ankle are stiff, so I opt for some of the meds the doctor gave me.

As sore as I am, it's awkward getting dressed, but I manage to change clothes and snug up my left arm into the sling. Then I head downstairs toward the living room.

Mom must hear me coming, because while I'm still on my way down the steps, she emerges from the kitchen, drying her hands nervously on a dishtowel.

"Daniel. How are you?"

"I'm alright. What time did you get in?"

"Just after three. Are you really alright or are you just saying that?"

"Nicole asked me almost exactly the same thing last night."

"That's because we both know you pretty well."

"I'm fine, Mom. Really."

She wrings that towel in her hands. "Your father had to head to work. He wants you to call him this morning after breakfast."

"Okay."

She eyes me for another moment as if she's not sure if she should believe me or not that I'm okay. Then she finally puts on a smile, joins me on the stairs, and offers me a hug.

I hide the limp from my sprained ankle as much as I can as we head to the kitchen.

A bowl of fruit and a sweating glass of orange juice are waiting for me on the table.

She asks me to tell her what happened and how I ended up in front of that truck.

And, while I grab some milk and cereal to go with the fruit, I tell her about the deer I saw last night and reassure her that I'm good and that the doctor gave me the sling just to keep the swelling in my shoulder down.

Then I take a seat, snatch an apple from the bowl, and crunch into it.

But I still haven't mentioned the boy in the road.

I'm not sure how to bring that part up.

After making some coffee, she settles into the chair across the table from me.

On the surface, everything might appear pretty normal here: just the two of us having breakfast, a teen guy and his mom eating quietly together. But there are all sorts of doubts and unspoken questions lurking here between us.

As we eat, I realize it's not going to get any easier to tell her about the blur so I decide I might as well just go for it.

"Mom, I saw something out there last night. Out on the road."

"The deer?"

"No. A blur."

She pauses with her coffee cup halfway to her lips. "Of what?"

"A boy. I tried to save him. The truck was coming right at him."

"And that's why you ran in front of it?"

"Yes."

Slowly, she lowers the cup. "And were you able to save him? Were you able to get there in time?"

I shake my head. "He disappeared when I reached out to pick him up. That's when the truck hit me."

"Daniel, you could have . . . That accident could have been fatal."

I get the sense that she chooses to put it that way since it's not as blunt and doesn't carry the same weight as saying that I might have "been killed."

"I couldn't just stand by and watch him get run over, Mom. I was sure he was real."

She lets that sink in. "Did you recognize him? Do you know who he was?"

"No. He looked like he was maybe in kindergarten. Nicole, Kyle and I searched online but we couldn't find anything about boys who were killed by trucks recently."

"Your grandfather was killed out on that same road. With the deer and the logging trucks it's . . . I can't even imagine if . . ."

Huh.

I'd forgotten about that. Grandpa did die out there, right near that very spot.

That boy in my dream had said something about everything beginning there and that he never meant to go.

Was he talking about Grandpa?

"Daniel, we need to find a way for you to tell what's real and what's not. We can't have you running in front of trucks."

Last year when the blurs first started, I'd tried pinching my arm to see if I was asleep or not. Then I tried touching the people in the blurs to see if they were real, but I found that, in time, neither of those approaches was foolproof.

In fact, once, when I was in an old abandoned lighthouse on an island in Lake Superior, I saw a man hanging from the end of a rope with a noose around his neck. His body banged into my shoulder, and when I touched his boot, it felt completely real.

But it wasn't.

It was all in my head, and I still haven't come up with a surefire way of telling fantasy from reality in the things that I see or hear or touch.

"Yeah," I agree. "I'll have to figure something out."

Before it happens again, I think, but I keep that part to myself.

After breakfast I check in with Dad, then I wrap my ankle, elevate it on the couch, and ice it. When you play high school sports, you learn pretty quickly that you're supposed to treat sprained ankles with RICE—Rest, Ice, Compression, and Elevation.

Twenty minutes on with the ice.

Twenty off.

While I'm icing it, I answer texts from people in my class asking how I am. I know they care about me, but they're also curious about what I was doing out there on the road and how I ended up in front of that truck.

And those are not details I want to get into.

I tell them I was confused, that I saw some deer—which was true—but I don't bring up the boy.

I know that Kyle and Nicole wouldn't go around sharing the details of what happened, but still, in a town the size of ours, when a couple of people hear about something, it usually doesn't take long before everyone has heard about it, so keeping the blurs a secret hasn't always been easy.

Last year, one guy in particular, Ty Bell, seemed to figure out that something was going on and gave me a hard time about it—although it was never really clear how much he knew and how much he was just speculating.

However, now he's in jail for wolf poaching and for trying to physically assault Nicole, so he's out of the picture.

Even with time off for good behavior, which—knowing him—isn't very likely, he's going to be locked up for years.

And, honestly, I don't know of too many people who are going to miss him.

I'm answering a text from my basketball coach telling him that, yes, I'm still planning to go to the camp—even though I haven't actually cleared that with my parents yet—when I get a text from Nicole, offering to come over.

Sure. You want some lunch? I text her.

That'd be awesome! See you soon.

Mom is gardening out back, so I whip up some mac & cheese and slather it with BBQ sauce for Nikki—one of her favorite new meals since she gave up meat last spring after doing a report for school about what happens at meat processing plants to downed cows.

Barbecue sauce is still a yes.

Beef, not so much.

Honesty, the BBQ sauce is pretty tasty on there and when we're done, Nicole joins me in my room, but pauses just inside the door when she sees my walls.

"You put up my sketches."

"The other day I was looking through that sketchbook you gave me and I realized I didn't really want to leave them in there where I would only see them once in a while."

"And you hung them right next to your Mavs and Packers posters. I feel special."

"Yeah. You made it to the Wall of Fame."

She sits at my desk, slides my journal to the side and sets her cell phone in front of her.

I pull out my laptop, then prop myself on the bed, elevating my ankle on a pillow. "Let's see if we can figure out who that kid is. The one I saw last night."

"What are you thinking? I mean, we didn't see anything in the obituaries."

"My grandpa died out there in a car accident. In my dream, the boy mentioned something about that being where things started. Grandpa's accident might have something to do with it. Besides, maybe the boy didn't die. Maybe in my blur he disappeared right before the truck would've hit him because, in real life, he survived."

"Hmm." She contemplates that. "I guess we could look through news about recent accidents, especially anything to do with logging. Who knows how specific your blur was—and we should probably go through the Internet history on your computer, see if there's anything that might have prompted you to have that blur."

I'm not psychic, so my blurs always come from things I've been exposed to. So, figuring out what those things might be—even if the stuff has only been registering in my subconscious—has usually been a good place to start in deciphering them.

We spend over an hour searching, but don't find anything specific that seems like it would have caused me to see that boy out there.

We're able to locate the news report about Grandpa's wreck, but he just hit a patch of ice and crashed into a tree. There were no logging trucks involved.

Only as we review my search history do I realize the amount of research I did on hallucinations and the antipsychotic drugs I was prescribed but haven't been taking.

I had no idea I'd visited so many medical websites.

Last year, the doctors weren't sure what was causing my hallucinations.

One of them thought it might be a form of palinopsia, which is when you keep seeing, as she put it, "recurring images or hallucinations that reflect echoes of what you've actually witnessed or experienced." Others thought it might have to do with some sort of temporal lobe disorder, but those were all guesses. Shots in the dark.

They ruled out a brain tumor and prescribed the anti-psychotics in case it might be a form of schizophrenia, but really, they had no idea what was happening.

When I met with the last doctor, he couched everything in technical jargon and Latin terms and assured me that I could control it with medication.

I didn't want to say the word "crazy," so I put it like this: "Basically, you're saying I'm mentally ill."

He scratched at his beard for a moment. "I'm not sure it would be helpful at this point to think of yourself as *ill*. We're still not sure what's causing the hallucinations and headaches."

"But people who aren't mentally ill don't have them."

"Let's hold off judging this until we have a little more information." Then he smiled in a way that I could tell wasn't really a smile, and patted my shoulder condescendingly. "Alright?"

Still bothers me to think about that.

I don't mention any of this to Nicole.

Eventually, we put the research aside and start talking about the trip to Atlanta.

"Have you thought at all about the camp?" she asks.

"I'm still planning to go."

"Your mom and dad are cool with that?"

"I haven't exactly brought it up yet. I'm hoping to talk with them tonight when Dad gets home. I've sort of been waiting for the right moment."

"Practice on me. I'll be your mom."

"Seriously?"

"Sure. Go ahead."

"Okay. Um. Let's see . . . Hey, Mom, my shoulder's feeling better."

"Nope. No good."

"What? Why not?"

"You don't want to just jump into things like that. Talk about something safe and noncontroversial first."

"Like what?"

"Hasn't anyone ever coached you on how to talk to your parents when you want something?"

"I guess I usually just wing it."

"Alright, so start with a compliment or by talking about something she likes, or offer to do a chore. Soften things up. Ease into it. Let's try it again."

"Hey, Mom. Your hair looks nice. The vegetables you grow are quite tasty. May I skin a potato for you?"

"Skin a potato for you? Seriously?"

I shrug. "I like potatoes."

"Okay, forget all that for a second. Let's just move on to the camp."

"So, it's feeling better, Mom. My shoulder is."

"That's good," Nicole replies in a very motherly way. "I'm glad to hear that."

"I think it'll be fine."

"I'm sure it will, as long as you rest it."

"I mean for the basketball camp."

"Dan, how are you supposed to play basketball with a dislocated shoulder—and don't tell me it's not dislocated anymore. You know what I mean."

"Well, it's not my—"

"Don't say it's not your shooting arm."

I stare at her. "How did you know I was going to say that?"

"I'm your mother."

"Okay. But, Mom, there's a lot riding on this camp."

"There's a lot riding on you recovering before football season too."

Ah.

Now I have her.

"You told me last week you weren't all that excited about me playing football."

"I'm excited about you pursuing your dreams and being successful at whatever you do, and that's not going to happen if you don't take care of your shoulder and give it the time it needs to heal."

"This isn't fair. You're better at being my mom than she is."

"Just trying to keep it real." She leans over and pats my leg reassuringly. "I'm sure it'll go fine. I'll be praying for you that it does."

Considering how strong of a believer she is and how seriously she takes prayer, her comment doesn't surprise me at all.

"Thanks. I appreciate that."

After she leaves, I spend the rest of the afternoon giving more RICE to my ankle and when Dad shows up at six with an extra large pepperoni and jalapeño pizza from our favorite local pizzeria, Rizzo's, I know it's time to talk with them about letting me go to the camp.

CHAPTER EIGHT

Mom, who's normally a fan of spicy food, decides against the jalapeños tonight and is picking them off her pizza and setting them aside. Dad adds them to his slices almost as quickly as she can remove them.

It seems like they're both in a pretty good mood, so I say, as nonchalantly as I can, "This is good pizza."

Mom agrees. "Yes."

"I mean, really good pizza."

"Yes, it is."

"I like pizza."

"Rizzo's is the best."

"I like potatoes too."

"Okay."

"And peeling them makes me feel pleasant."

They're both staring at me now. "Peeling them makes you feel pleasant?"

Okay, transition time.

"Almost as pleasant as my shoulder is feeling."

"Oh. Well, that's great."

"My ankle too."

"You've been staying off it?"

"Yes, and I've been icing it all day."

"I'm glad to hear that."

We eat for a few minutes. She asks Dad about his day and he mentions that most of it was spent filling out paperwork, but I'm not really paying too much attention to that. Instead, I'm waiting for a lull in the conversation. When it comes, I say, "So, I've been thinking a lot about next week. About the camp."

"It's too bad you're going to have to miss it," Mom replies. It sounds like she really is commiserating with me. "I know how much you were looking forward to it."

I glance at Dad, who has yet to say anything about all this. I'm not sure if he's on her side or is just biding his time.

"Actually, I think I'll be good to go."

"Daniel, you were just in a serious accident. You need time to recover."

"My ankle will be alright in a couple days and it's my left shoulder instead of my right one, so it's not my shooting arm. I've dislocated it in football before—no big deal. Besides, there'll be a lot of coaches at this camp. It's a good chance to get noticed."

I wonder if Mom will bring up me pursuing my dreams like Nicole did earlier when we were practicing, but instead she just asks, "Does it hurt when you move it?"

"My shoulder?"

"Yes."

"Well, I mean it's . . . Yeah. It'll be sore for a while."

"And you should rest it in the meantime."

"LeAnne." My dad finally speaks up. "He's a tough kid. He can handle it. I think he'll be alright."

"It's not about if he can handle it or not. It's about what's best for him. Four to six weeks of rest. That's what they recommend. Not one week, and then back to playing basketball for five hours a day."

The five hours a day part is probably about right. "I'll be careful and I'll wear the sling whenever we're not on the court."

"You could dislocate it again if you're not careful."

"But I will be careful—I just said I would, and . . . " I can hear myself sounding argumentative and that's not going be good for my case, so I just stop mid-sentence.

Mom pries a tiny sliver of jalapeño off her pizza and plunks it down on the side of her plate.

During football season last fall, she was living in the Twin Cities with her sister. Her year away from Dad and me isn't something we talk about much, or at least not something they talk to me about much.

When she was gone, Dad and I had to get used to managing things on our own, and we learned to do alright. Now, with her back, finding a way for everyone to agree when we're making major decisions doesn't always work out so well.

There are cracks in every relationship. Things might look good on the surface, but there are always fault lines there where it's hard to see.

So now, I wonder if her reaction is about more than just my shoulder.

"How about we see how things go this week?" Dad suggests. "We don't have to make a decision right this minute."

She goes for another jalapeño.

"How does that sound? Take a few more days and then evaluate how it looks?"

"I can't believe you would be in favor of something like this, Jerry. Don't you want what's best for him?"

"What kind of a question is that?" His voice is steel. "Of course I do. You know that. I'm just saying that we don't need to decide tonight."

"And I'm saying we already know what's best for him. Rest. It's just a matter of whether we're going to be unified in supporting our son's recovery."

"Okay, that's not even fair."

She pushes her chair back. "If you gentlemen will excuse me, I think I'm finished." She might be talking about the meal or the conversation—it's not clear.

She rises and walks out of the room.

I wait for Dad to say something, but he doesn't. He just stares at the doorway she disappeared through.

He knows how big of a deal this camp is to me, how important it could be in getting a scholarship offer— something all three of us know I'm going to need in order to afford college.

He's silent.

The seconds tick by.

Finally, he glances at Mom's remaining jalapeños, but leaves them on her plate rather than putting them onto his own. "You better do everything you can to rest that ankle and shoulder this week."

"I will."

Then he finishes his slice, dumps Mom's unfinished pizza and jalapeños into the trash, and leaves me alone in the kitchen.

● ● ●

BILLINGS, MONTANA

Malcolm Zacharias watched as two men in their mid-twenties tossed a Frisbee back and forth at the other end of the park while, closer to him, a teenage girl tapped her white cane along the sidewalk in front of her, expertly staying on the pavement, even as it curved around the lake.

He was expecting the call, so when his phone rang, he answered right away.

An electronically altered voice said, "I understand that Daniel Byers was hit by a truck last night."

"I've been following the situation. He's okay."

"I thought you were in Montana?"

"I am."

"So how are you following the situation if he's in Wisconsin?"

"Through his phone's mic. I turned it on remotely."

"You've been listening in on him?"

"I took the steps that were necessary in order to monitor things."

Malcolm still hadn't met the person he was talking with and didn't know if it was a man or a woman. Whoever it was just went by the name Sam.

Could have been short for Samantha.

Or Samuel.

Or something else entirely.

All communication had been masked, encrypted, or done through couriers and package drops at the office in Philadelphia or the educational center in Gatlinburg. While on the one hand, Malcolm understood that that's how these things worked, on the other hand it would have been nice to know who was paying his expenses, who was heading the agency.

Ever since last September when he was first contacted, he'd been curious about it.

"Will Daniel still be able to be involved?" Sam asked.

"I believe so. He wasn't seriously injured. I anticipate that he'll be at the camp in Georgia. We'll move forward with things then."

"There are reports that he ran out in front of the truck. That he might've been trying to get hit. You don't think he's suicidal, do you?"

"Where did you hear that—about him purposely running into the road?"

"You're not the only one who's monitoring the situation, Malcolm."

He hadn't considered that Daniel might have intentionally tried to harm himself. "I don't think he's suicidal. No."

"But it's possible, yes? He hallucinates. There have been instances when he's experienced lost time and when he hasn't been aware of his actions. He might have slipped too far."

The two guys with the Frisbee disappeared over the rise. The blind girl came closer.

"Things haven't progressed to that point yet."

"Malcolm, I'm a little concerned. You remember the boy from New York and that girl from South Carolina? What happened with them? How they ended up?"

"That won't happen with him."

"But how can you be sure?"

"I've met him."

"Last December."

"Yes."

"And you haven't spoken with him since then?"

"I will next week in Georgia."

"If he goes."

"Yes."

"And if not?"

"I'll pay him a visit in Wisconsin."

"I'm counting on you here. I want all four present before we move forward."

"Don't worry. We're on the same page."

"Have you arranged for the arrival of the others?"

The seventeen-year-old girl with the cane was now less than fifty feet away. No one else was on this side of the park.

"I have eyes on Alysha right now." He kept his voice low, so that, even with her sharpened sense of hearing, she wouldn't be able to make out what he was saying.

"You know how important this is to me."

"Yes."

"What are you going to tell her parents?"

"Leave that to me. I'll take care of it."

Then Malcolm hung up, rose from the bench, pocketed the phone.

And went to get Alysha Caruthers.

CHAPTER NINE

Four days have passed.

It's Wednesday afternoon.

I've been wearing the sling, giving my ankle lots of RICE, and taking the pain meds to reduce the swelling—all the things I'm supposed to do.

Every day Mom asks me how I'm feeling and I tell her, "Better." And it's true. The shoulder is hurting less and less. The ankle is recovering.

She doesn't seem convinced by my reassurances, but she doesn't argue with me either. We don't really talk too much. She keeps to herself. So does Dad.

In the last few days my friends and I have done what we can to figure out what the blur of the boy in the road might mean, but we haven't come up with anything that seems relevant to what I saw.

I think about my dream of the boy and the bats, and recall that when I was little, I used to be scared of them. Maybe that fear from my childhood was playing into all this.

In my dream the boy said, "He never meant to go. It all began right here. Follow the bats. Find the truth."

I'm still not sure what that might be about.

Grandpa's death? And what does following the bats mean?

Still a mystery.

No more blurs since that night.

And the nightmares have been leaving me alone too.

Now, it's quarter after four and I'm in my room writing in the journal I've started keeping.

Last year when our English teacher, Miss Flynn, gave us the assignment to write some blog entries about our dreams, Kyle, who can completely kill it when it comes to English, told me to try writing by hand rather than typing.

I was skeptical, but honestly, it did help me sort out my thoughts.

Ever since the blurs started, my writing has become more imaginative. Some people say we only use ten percent of our brains. Well, if that's true, then maybe the blurs have opened up a channel for me to tap into my creativity more.

Lately, the Greek myth about Pandora's box has been on my mind for some reason. And so, I write:

The world is young and screaming its first life-breath, still so close to the womb of the gods.

Granite-gray clouds hang heavy and foreboding in the sky, lurking on the edge of the fierce storm that I see churning toward me.

Sky light still makes me tremble.

I see day and night wrestling for control of the future.

Beside me, a terrible cliff towers high above the tangled green of the jungle. Screeches echo from the unseen depths of the darkened trees—of the unmapped world just beyond the meadow. I shudder, for I have seen some of the creatures spawned by the wild imagination of the gods.

Ah, now.

The box lies at my feet. The wood is carved with divine runes. Secret letters, another tongue beyond the knowledge of my heart.

What is in this box? What futures? What possibilities?

I finger the clasp that holds it shut. The gods have given me their gift but not their secrets. Why flaunt this in front of me? Why taunt me with these things I cannot experience—yet cannot help but desire?

The sky swirls around me, deep with the shadows of the coming night.

And I unsnap the latch.

Pandora's box.

She was warned by the gods not to open it.

Because once you do, all hell breaks loose.

Pain.

Disease.

Evil.

All of them given free rein in the world.

As I'm thinking about that, I hear the sound of something behind me dripping onto the floor.

Turning from my desk, I see a small pool of blood forming.

It's coming from my ceiling, from a swollen, damp circle about two feet wide.

A blur? Is this a blur?

The center of it puckers down and releases another drop of blood.

I've been caving with Dad plenty of times over the years, and the blood coming from the ceiling reminds me of a miniature stalactite.

A grisly, red one.

Drip.

Hesitantly, I go over to the pool of blood and touch it.

Sticky. And wet.

Drip.

And warm.

Dad is running errands, so I know he isn't home.

"Mom?"

She doesn't reply.

She's with him. She's running errands too.

But I'm not sure that's true.

I wipe off my finger and go to the window. Her car is in the driveway.

Entering the hall, I call out to her, "Are you home, Mom?"

My voice echoes dully through the house.

No one replies.

I go to the end of the hallway and eye the ceiling access panel to the attic.

Something up there is the source of all that blood.

I've only been up in the attic a handful of times, mostly when Dad and I were replacing some insulation last year.

There's a small window at the far end, but I doubt it'll provide enough light for me to get a good look at the area above my room, so I grab one of the headlamps from the stash of camping gear in my closet. Then, I retrieve the step-ladder from the garage, bring it upstairs, and position it under the access panel.

With only one good arm I'm not sure how I'll be able to hoist myself up and I don't want to take the chance that I'll pull my shoulder out of its socket again, but I need to see what's up there.

I climb to the third step, slide the panel aside, and stare up into the darkness.

"Mom?"

My heart is drumming steadily in my chest and it seems like it's too large for its cage in my ribs, like it's been crammed in there and now it's pushing and pounding, looking for a way to get out every time it beats.

You have to find the source of that blood.

After securing the headlamp's elastic strap, I climb the rest of the way up, using my one good arm.

Balancing myself on the top of the ladder, I maneuver my way into the hole, then ease my butt onto the attic's floorboards and sit with my legs dangling in the hall.

It's a relatively warm day outside, but the heat up here is harsh and stifling.

Turning my head, I sweep the beam of light through the dust-speckled air.

Near the corner, over where the roof slopes down above my room, there's a body lying on its side with its back to me.

From where I am, I can't tell if it's a man or a woman.

"Mom?"

The figure doesn't move.

Despite the heat, I shiver.

For some reason it brings to mind my dream on Friday night, the one about me leaning over the boy when the bats crawled across his face.

But that was a dream.

This is not.

Maybe it is.

Maybe this is all a dream too.

The ceiling is too low for me to stand up and I can't crawl with my arm in its sling, so, carefully and somewhat painfully, I ease it off.

Two voices speak to me.

The first: *This isn't smart, Daniel.*

The second: *It doesn't matter—you have to find out who that is.*

It's a blur.

Well, even if it is, you need to see who's there. You need to figure out what it means.

I start crawling forward, but only make it a couple of feet before the pain in my shoulder becomes too much.

So, giving that up, I use my good arm for leverage and scoot sideways toward the body instead.

Blood surrounds whoever it is, and as I ease my way closer, the figure's leg twitches slightly.

I hesitate.

Wait.

My heart, thick and wild, keeps probing for a way out of my chest.

The person's leg becomes still and after a moment I edge forward again.

The heat begins wearing on me. Even in the brief amount of time I've been up here, I can already feel pinpricks of sweat forming beneath my arms.

Maybe it's not just the heat, but nerves.

A shot of fear.

As I move closer, the size of the body makes me think that it's probably a guy.

Because of how the roof angles down, I can't get around to the other side to look at his face. So, if I'm going to be able to see who this is, I'll need to roll him toward me.

I reposition myself so I'm kneeling in a way that I won't have to use my bad arm for support, then I place my hand on his shoulder.

And tip him in my direction.

His arm flops over first, the knuckles thudding roughly against the floorboards. His torso follows and, because of the momentum as he rolls onto his back, his head lolls in my direction.

I gasp and lose my balance.

It's me.

I'm looking into my own eyes, staring at my own face.

My own dead face.

Grayish skin. A blank, deathly stare.

The blood is coming from a gaping wound in his chest, visible through the torn fabric.

I reel backward as his eyes slowly dial into focus and direct themselves at me—a piercing, knowing stare.

Then, he grins and pushes himself onto all fours, and begins crawling toward me.

Scrambling as quickly as I can, I make it to the access hole and swing my legs down, but I accidentally kick the top of the stepladder, sending it toppling to the floor.

The figure hasn't slowed, his wide smile revealing wickedly sharp teeth.

That's not you. It's not you.

But it is!

With no other choice, and trying my best to avoid landing on the ladder, I drop through the hole to the floor of the hallway.

Despite my best efforts, I crash down clumsily onto the ladder's edge, then roll to the side, and smack hard against the wall.

Thankfully, it's my good shoulder that takes the impact, but still, I need a moment to assess myself. The ankle seems okay—so does the shoulder.

I can still hear movement on the floorboards above me as the corpse that looks just like me moves toward the access hole.

With my heart thundering in my chest, I stare up at the opening, expecting that at any moment that thing will appear and pitch itself down on top of me.

I wait.

The sounds stop.

A square of black.

Just a square of black.

It's a blur. It's not real. You're not dead.

I catch myself holding my breath as I wait, but nothing happens.

The creature doesn't lurch through the hole at me.

But as I'm getting to my feet, I realize that I left the sling for my shoulder up there in the attic.

CHAPTER
TEN

I can't go the next few days without wearing my sling. Mom will notice right away that I don't have it.

Which means I need to go back up there.

Keeping a watchful eye on the hole, I reposition the ladder and slowly climb it.

When I get to the ceiling, I stop before poking my head through.

Listen.

Nothing.

It might be waiting right there for you, right by the edge.

But I don't have a choice. I have to get that sling.

I take another tentative step up and peer across the attic floorboards.

I don't see anything.

But I do hear something.

Not from the attic, but from down below, in the garage.

The door rattling open.

Mom and Dad are back from running errands.

My sling lies just out of reach so I need to step onto the top of the ladder again, as I did earlier, to get it. Balancing somewhat precariously and using my good arm, I leverage myself up, edge forward, and grab the sling.

But, as I pull it toward me, I can feel something tugging at the other end. There, in the air before me, the sling straightens out as I lean back, trying to yank it free.

There's nothing there.

Yet something is pulling on it.

Below me, in the garage, the door closes.

Suddenly, whatever has snatched up the other end of the sling lets go. I topple backward, barely managing to steady my foot on the ladder.

I clamber down far enough to slide the panel back into place as the kitchen door opens and my parents come in, talking harshly with each other.

"All I'm saying is, you don't need to be so blunt with me all the time," my mom tells him.

"I'm just trying to be honest. Are you telling me that's not what you want?"

"Of course I want you to be honest; it's just that sometimes you have to look out for the other person's feelings rather than just bludgeoning them with the truth."

"I'm not bludgeoning anyone with anything."

Then they move into another room and I can't catch the rest of the conversation.

With them here in the house I won't be able to get the ladder back to the garage without being seen, and I'm not too excited about the idea of explaining what's been happening up here.

So, instead, I fold it up, take it to my room, and maneuver it into the closet, figuring I can return it to the garage tonight, after they're asleep.

Both the stain on the floor and the blood dripping from the ceiling have disappeared.

I have no idea what all of this means or what it might have to do with the boy in the road—if anything—but in a certain sense, the two blurs are complete opposites of each other.

In the first, I was trying to save that boy.

In this one, my blur was trying to attack me—and who knows what would have happened if it'd been able to get to me.

When I return my headlamp to the closet, I see my hunting knife beside my camping gear and remember the time I woke up from sleepwalking last December in my dad's bedroom holding it, staring down at him.

You're losing it.

"Daniel?" It's Dad. "You up there?"

"Yeah," I call down the steps.

"Can you come here for a minute?"

"Sure, just a sec."

I don't like the idea of that knife waiting in here when I go to sleep tonight. I'm not sure where to put it, except for maybe stowing it in the garage later when I put the ladder away.

For now, I leave it in its sheath, close the closet door, and head downstairs.

Because of their argument when they first walked in, I'm a little apprehensive about what they might want to talk to me about, but when I get to the living room Dad just asks how I'm doing.

"Good. I'm good."

"You look pale," Mom says, reading me a little too well. "Are you sure you're alright?"

"Yep." Before she can probe, I change the subject. "So, do you know when we might be having supper? I'm starved."

She doesn't answer right away. "Give me a half hour or so."

While she gets started in the kitchen, Dad heads out to work on one of his carpentry projects in the garage. I go back to my room.

I feel like I need to talk to someone about what just happened in the attic, but I figure that bringing it up with either of them might kill off my chances of going to Georgia.

After considering Nicole, but deciding that I don't want her to worry about me, I text Kyle to give me a call when he has a chance. Only a few minutes later, he does and I tell him, "I saw something again. Another blur."

"Of what?"

"Myself, actually. But I was dead. Then I came to life."

"Okay. So, that would be a ten on the creep-o-meter. Let me psychobluralize you. What scared you the most?"

"What do you mean?"

"Seeing yourself dead, seeing yourself come alive, or worrying about where things might go from here?"

"I guess I'm afraid the thread will snap for good."

"The thread?"

"The one that's right in front of me. The one that holds things together."

A pause. "The one that keeps you sane?"

"Yeah."

"So basically, you're scared that you'll go completely crazy with no chance of turning back—that you're on a road that leads off a cliff and there's no exit ramp."

"Thanks for putting it like that."

"That's what I'm here for."

"I guess if I'm going to head off a cliff, I wish it would just happen. It'd be a lot less terrifying."

"Than what?"

"Than realizing that's where I'm heading, but that I can't stop."

"Have you figured out a way yet to tell your blurs from what's real?"

"No. Not yet."

"Try filming things next time with your phone. Maybe see if, when you watch it on the screen, it's still there."

"It's worth a try."

"You cool?"

I'm not sure.

"Yeah," I tell him. "I'm cool."

"In the meantime, don't drive off the cliff. I mean, meta-phorically speaking."

"I'll do my best."

Later on, when my parents are in bed, I sneak the ladder and my hunting knife down to the garage. On the way back to my room, I overhear them talking in hushed voices in the master bedroom.

"So, you're fine with him going down there to this camp?" Mom says.

"This isn't just about his shoulder, is it, LeAnne?"

I pause in the hall.

"I was never thrilled about the four of them going on a road trip halfway across the country. You know that."

"I thought we agreed we could trust them."

"I went along with it. I didn't necessarily agree with it."

"They'll be alright. They're responsible kids. And they're staying with—"

"Yes, but . . ." Then her voice fades out and it's too soft to hear any more.

Most people get louder the angrier they get. Not my mom. She gets quieter. So typically, the less you hear, the worse things are going to be.

I don't take any of this as a good sign, but I don't want to chance having them catch me eavesdropping either, so as silently as I can, I return to my room, glancing up uneasily at the attic access panel as I do.

CHAPTER ELEVEN

All morning I've been thinking about Kyle's suggestion yesterday about me filming events to see if they're blurs, so I keep my phone close by with the camera app open, but nothing unusual or terrifying appears.

My thoughts return to Pandora's box.

In the story, when the girl opens the box, it unleashes all the terror and heartache and grief that had been sealed up so none of it would torment people.

It's a myth.

But maybe, even if there wasn't a literal box long ago, each of us has one inside us. And when we give into our temptations, when we listen to the darkness, we pry off the lid.

Metaphorically speaking.

I try writing in the journal again, but that doesn't help and I realize that if there's one person who might be able to understand what I'm going through, it's my mom.

She's seen things too.

She had sleepwalking episodes so frightening that she became concerned she might hurt someone else during them.

She might be able to help me figure this out.

However, if she gets too worried about me, she'll never let me go to the camp. So if I talk with her about this, I'll need to be careful to not give too much away, but still tell her enough for her to help me.

I'm not exactly sure how to pull that off, but after lunch, since she's taking today off from work and is here at the house, I figure I'll give it a shot.

I catch up with her in the living room where she's making her way through a mound of clean laundry.

When I sit down and start helping her fold the clothes, she stares at me oddly. "Are you okay?"

"Yeah."

"You never help me fold the laundry, Daniel. Something's on your mind. What is it?"

I straighten out a towel, flip it into thirds.

"This wouldn't have anything to do with your offer to peel a potato for me the other day, would it?" She says it lightly, and that gives me the sense that this probably is a good time to talk.

"Mom, last winter you told me that you moved out because you were afraid of what you might do to me or Dad."

"I remember."

"Afraid that you might hurt us."

"Yes."

I grab a pair of my jeans, start folding them. "But why did you think that? You never gave me the details—you just said that you were seeing things."

"You really want to discuss this now?"

"Something's happening to me. I need to understand it. I think you can help."

"Mostly, it had to do with my sleepwalking."

"But why would you think you might hurt other people?"

She lays her hand on the clothes pile, but doesn't pick up anything. "You know that your father keeps a gun by his side of the bed."

"Yes."

"Well one night I woke up while I was opening up the end table drawer where he leaves it. Then two days later I already had it in my hand when I woke up."

She pauses.

"Anything else?"

"Daniel, I—"

"C'mon, Mom. Tell me."

She's started to tap her fingers anxiously on one of our crumpled sheets, but I don't think she notices.

"I had it with me," she says at last. "I was halfway down the hall on the way to your room when I woke up. It was loaded. The gun was. That was the last straw. I put it back and I didn't sleep for the rest of the night. The next day I moved out. I couldn't stand the thought of jeopardizing either of you."

In an eerie way her story reminds me of my own sleep-walking incident last winter when I carried the knife around.

"And you had hallucinations too, right? What did you see?"

"Nothing as terrifying as the blurs you've told me about. I never saw anyone who'd died. Just shadows mostly. On the periphery of my vision, always out of the corner of my eye. It felt like they were after me."

"What's different now, though? Has all that stopped?"

"The sleepwalking stopped while I was staying at my sister's place."

"And do you still see those shadows?"

"I haven't in months. I've been taking medication."

"Did the visions start when you were a teenager?"

"Oddly enough, they did. Then they left me alone and only came back recently."

"Do you know why?"

"No."

"Do you know why they started in the first place?"

She shakes her head. "No."

"Did anything else weird happen when you were younger?"

"Anything weird?"

"Like with me. Voices. Feeling things that aren't there. Whatever."

"No, but I know that my mother had some issues. She was never very forthcoming about it, but from what I was told, she met with a therapist for a while."

"Well she must have hallucinated some pretty horrifying things—in her suicide note she wrote that she couldn't stand seeing them anymore."

"But we don't know exactly what that was referring to." She looks at me curiously. "Why are you asking me about all this now? Does it have to do with what happened when you saw that boy in the road?"

"Yes." It's true. It's just not the whole truth. I don't bring up what I saw in the attic. "What's wrong with us, Mom? Grandma got depressed and then killed herself. Her uncle hanged himself. And then you and I have these, well . . ."

"Sometimes things like this run in families."

"Things like this? You mean getting depressed? Going crazy? Killing yourself?"

She eyes me concernedly. "Have you ever thought about that?"

"About what?"

"Killing yourself. Suicide."

"No—I mean, I guess everybody does sometimes. Nothing specific, though."

"But you'd tell us if you ever had those kinds of thoughts, right? You'd tell your father or me? You can trust us you know."

"Sure. I just . . ."

"Promise me, Daniel, that if you ever think about it, about hurting yourself, you'll tell us right away."

Her word choice reveals a lot: "hurting yourself," rather than "killing yourself."

"Yeah, okay. If I ever think about it, I will. I'll tell you."

We go back to the laundry pile, and even though the conversation doesn't feel like it's by any means finished, we don't take things any further.

Then when we're done and I'm putting my clothes away in my room, I hear her down the steps.

It sounds like she's crying.

● ● ●

Earlier this week, Malcolm Zacharias had made sure Alysha Caruthers was settled in at the facility Sam had designed in Atlanta.

Now, he gazed out the window of the private jet as he flew toward California to pick up Tane Tagaloa in L.A.

Soon, it would be Daniel Byers's turn, and finally, when all was set, Petra would be joining them.

Once all four were together, Sam's plan could move forward at last.

● ● ●

Dr. Adrian Waxford sat at the desk in his office on the second floor of the Estoria Inn.

He had his twenty-five camel figurines, all carved from bone, in front of him.

Sometimes, he would pull them out and remind himself of the ancient riddle of the camels, the one his brother had told him all those years ago.

A Sufi master had three students and seventeen camels. In his will, he left instructions that upon his death, the oldest student would get one-half of them, the middle student one-third, and the youngest one-ninth.

When he died, since it's impossible to divide seventeen like that, no one could figure out what to do.

But the answer was like so many things—you had to think outside the box, and when you did, it all became clear.

Sometimes Adrian gave people the riddle to see if they could solve it. But so far, not even Henrik had been able to do it.

He slid them all aside.

Thinking outside the box.

Yes.

That's what he'd been doing lately regarding finding Zacharias and putting the right amount of pressure on the senator.

The series of events that Adrian had put into play would lead them to the agency's director, the person who went by the name Sam, and finding him—or her—was the key to everything.

He phoned Henrik. "What do we know about Zacharias?"

"We have word that he might be on his way to California."

"Anything more on the office complex in Philly?"

"Not much. We're looking more closely at an offshore holding company and a nonprofit foundation that are both located in the building he likes to visit. So far, nothing specific though."

"Your people are ready to move on the young woman?"

"Yes."

"Do it tomorrow night. And make sure the senator gets the message that he needs to act on Monday evening at nine o'clock. It's vital that things happen before that Senate hearing on Tuesday morning, but not so early that anyone suspects anything."

"I understand."

CHAPTER TWELVE

No blurs since Wednesday.

No reason yet to use the camera on my phone.

However, Mom's questions about suicide have been bothering me.

Was it possible that I'd run out in front of that truck because, somewhere in the back of my mind, I wanted to take my own life, like Grandma had? Like that distant uncle of mine had?

Mom mentioned that things like this sometimes run in families.

That's not something I want to consider, not even remotely.

Though my parents are clearly not on the same page as far as being cool with me going to Georgia tomorrow, this afternoon Mom finally gave in and I agreed to be extra careful with my shoulder and ankle.

Nicole's dad has the most reliable car, so he's letting us use that for the trip. We're scheduled to leave their house at seven in the morning.

I toss my clothes and my journal into my duffel bag.

When I lie down to go to sleep, I turn on my side so I'm facing the wall with Nicole's sketches rather than the place on the floor where that pool of blood collected on Wednesday afternoon.

• • •

ATLANTA, GEORGIA
11:41 P.M.

Petra Amundsen had just left work at the hotel where she usually stayed late on Fridays balancing the books, and was on her way to her car when it happened.

She'd parked under a streetlight just like her father had taught her to do five years ago when she was first learning to drive.

It was closing in on midnight, so the street was basically empty. A dog somewhere down the block barked and someone yelled for it to *Shut up!* Other than that, and the sound of a few cars on a nearby road out of sight, it was quiet.

Okay, so the hotel wasn't in the best part of town, but since graduating from college in the spring, Petra had wanted some independence.

So, although she didn't by any stretch of the imagination need the money, she'd taken the job. The trust fund she'd received when she turned eighteen was great, but she would rather use that to make a difference in other people's lives than just indulging herself. Added bonus: the accounting allowed her to pursue one of her biggest interests: math.

As she came to her car, she noticed that across the street, a woman in her late twenties with sandy-colored hair was standing beside a minivan, holding a bundle of blankets, shushing it with baby talk.

Petra couldn't hear the child crying, but the woman looked extremely upset.

As soon as she saw Petra, she called out, "Please, can you help me? I locked my keys and my phone in my car. I need to tell my husband we're okay and see if he can come get us. I was supposed to be home by now. He'll be terribly worried."

"Oh. Um, sure."

Petra crossed the road and drew her cell phone out of her purse.

"Can you hold my baby while I make the call?"

"Yeah. Okay."

The woman carefully handed the bundle of blankets to Petra and accepted the phone, but when Petra looked down, she realized that it wasn't a real baby wrapped up in the blankets after all. Just a doll.

"What's going—?"

But before she could finish her sentence, a man threw open the side door to the minivan, leapt out, clamped his hand over her mouth, and dragged her backward.

Petra tried to scream, but his thick hand muffled her cries.

Struggling to get free, she dropped her purse and the doll, then clung to the edge of the door, but he yanked her back hard enough to break her grip and get her inside.

The woman picked up the items and closed the door.

There weren't any seats in the back of the minivan so there was room for him to wrestle her to the floor. Then he whipped out a roll of duct tape, and covered her mouth with a strip of it.

After making sure she couldn't call for help, he ripped off more tape and bound her hands behind her.

Frantically, she tried rolling to the side to get out from under him, but it was useless.

He wrapped the tape around her ankles and then around her legs just above her knees, securing her so that she could barely move.

When he was done, he leaned down and peered closely at her face in the dim streetlight that filtered through the window. She attempted to turn away, but he pressed her head roughly against the floor.

His chiseled face was all creases and shadows, and he had only a thin slit for a mouth.

When he grinned at her, his rancid breath made her feel like throwing up, but with that tape over her mouth, she didn't dare, so she gulped and tightened her throat and managed to hold back.

He brushed a strand of hair out of her eyes. "Daddy's little girl. The famous Brad Amundsen's only child. Well, let's see how valuable to him you really are."

He patted her cheek twice, climbed into the driver's seat, rolled down the window, and called to the woman, "Get rid of her car. I'll meet you at the house."

"Alright. I'll see you there."

Then he started the engine and guided the minivan onto the street.

Petra tugged against the duct tape, but it seemed like the more she struggled to get free, the more constricting it became.

Though she tried to keep track of how long they drove, she was too scared to really have any idea how much time actually passed. Besides, for all she knew, the man might have been driving around extra just to fool her.

She told herself that they'd just taken her for ransom and nothing more.

That's what they want. Ransom. Nothing's going to happen to you.

Dad will pay it. They'll let you go. It's all going to be okay.

Finally, after what seemed like hours, they slowed and she heard a garage door open. They drove inside.

Parked.

The door clattered shut behind them.

The thin-lipped man turned off the engine.

Scared of what would happen next, Petra stared nervously at the minivan's side door, trying to keep herself calm.

Calm, calm, calm.

Just keep calm.

She could hear the man and the woman talking in hushed voices outside the minivan, but couldn't make out much of what they were saying. However, at one point, she did hear him say something about Monday night and refer to the woman as Deedee, and when she replied, she called him Sergei.

When the door slid open at last, Deedee was standing there holding Petra's phone. "Okay, my dear," she said. "Let's get you ready. We have a very important video to shoot."

PART II
DESCENT

CHAPTER THIRTEEN

Mom stays home while Dad takes me to Nicole's house to drop me off.

"So, you have that debit card for gas?" he says as we pull into the driveway.

"Yes."

"Check."

"I've got it, Dad."

"Check."

I pull out the preloaded card that the camp's registrar had sent us from the anonymous donor who'd paid for my scholarship. He didn't tell us how much money is on it, but he assured us it would be enough to cover my travel expenses.

"And some cash, just in case, for emergencies?"

"I've got everything. I'm good."

"And what are the ground rules?"

"Check in every day. No drinking. No drugs. Nothing stupid."

"Okay." He raps the steering wheel once, definitively, and I take that to mean the questions are done. "Be safe. Have fun. Be careful. And do well at the camp."

"I will."

"And don't get re-injured."

"I won't."

"And as far as your mom goes, don't worry. I know things have been a bit tense this week, but she'll be alright—we'll be alright."

"Okay."

I climb out and grab my basketball and duffel bag from the backseat.

The trunk of Nicole's dad's sedan is open and has her suitcase in it, so even though she's not out here at the moment, I figure I'm good to toss my things in there.

It's possible that Mia might have stayed the night here because, though her car is here, it has dew on the windshield.

As my dad is pulling away, she comes out of the house.

She's wearing black leggings that match her inky black hair and make her look even skinnier than she really is. Pierced lip. Studded tongue. Her tank top leaves her red bra straps visible across her bare shoulders.

Her arms are loaded with five jumbo-size bags of Fritos and a camo military rucksack that she once told us was her dad's back when he was in the Army.

"What's up, Daniel?"

"Nothing. How're you doing?"

"Smokin."

She tosses the pack and Fritos into the car. "You ready for this camp thing?"

"I think so."

"So your mom eased up on it all?"

"She agreed to let me go—so, I guess so. You think you have enough Fritos there?"

She assesses her Fritos stockpile. "Good point. We can always stop for more if we need to."

"Right."

Nicole appears in the front door wearing her pajama bottoms and one of my T-shirts that I left over here a couple weeks ago.

She's clutching an armload of pillows that she stows in the backseat where she and Mia are planning to lounge for the first part of the trip.

When Nicole sees my basketball in the trunk, she looks at me quizzically. "Are you really bringing that along?"

"I might want to shoot around when there's free time."

"It's a basketball camp. They'll have, like, a million basketballs there."

"But they won't have Alfie."

Mia blinks. "You named your basketball Alfie?"

"Yeah, I know." Nicole beats me to a reply. "It's a little troubling. That and his football."

"Fred," I tell them.

Mia speaks as if I'm not standing right in front of her. "Hashtag: hemightverywellbealostcause."

Kyle and his mom pull up, he hops out, and we collect his things.

I offer to drive first, but he shakes his head. "How are you supposed to do that with one arm in a sling?" Then he holds up an enormous travel mug. "Besides, this is my special brew. Guaranteed to keep me awake and alert for at least the next half hour."

"What is it?"

"Red Bull, Dr Pepper and two bottles of 5-Hour Energy."

"That's going to do more than keep you alert for half an hour," Nicole says. "It'll probably keep you up for a week."

"My record is thirty-eight hours. You should have seen the song lyrics I was writing at the end of that."

"I can only imagine."

The girls get situated in the back, and then Nicole, who has burned some CDs for the ride, hands them up to me.

"Okay, so this car actually does have a jack for your phone," she explains, "but it also has a CD player—which is cool, even though CDs are a little old school."

As she goes on, she sounds slightly philosophical. "It sort of straddles two ages. Like those cars they used to make that had both cassette players and CD players."

Straddling two ages.

Hmm.

Interesting.

"Like Janus," Kyle says, "that Greek god that had two faces. One to look at the past. One to look toward the future."

"So this trip is officially in honor of Janus then." Mia rips open a bag of Fritos and dives into them. "I eat this corn chip in honor of Janus."

I shuffle through the CDs, which Nicole has labeled *Awesome Tunes*, *Road Trip Mix*, and *Chill*. "I wonder what cars will be like twenty years from now, what kinds of things they'll include along with the phone input."

Kyle takes a long gulp from his mug as he pulls onto the road. "Probably wireless signals to cranial implants that pump tunes directly into your brain."

"Well." I hold up Nicole's CDs. "I think I'll stick with these for now."

"Ditto."

Since we all have pretty different tastes in music, we make a deal that the driver gets to choose the tunes and no one else is allowed to complain about the music or strangle the driver, but we all have earbuds or headphones, so we should be able to handle things either way.

Nicole is into techno and trance—anything with a driving beat but no words. Kyle goes for the alternative indie bands you've never heard of, but that seem to always make it big about six months after he starts listening to them. It's uncanny.

For Mia, it's grunge and for me, Rush. My dad had all of their albums back when I was a kid and I used to listen to them when I was going to bed. Geddy Lee sang me to sleep through the years. All those rock anthems got lodged in my mind and I've never really been able to get them out.

Not such a bad thing, actually.

"Seriously though," Mia says. "I can't believe it's June and we're driving to *Georgia*. We're gonna die from the heat."

"That's what air conditioning is for." Kyle blasts it, even though there's no need for it yet.

"No, don't do that," Nicole insists. "The Freon's bad for the ozone."

"Oh, that's just an urban legend. Like the one about the people who wedge razor blades in waterslides."

"Ew! What? No, it's not like that at all!"

"Why did you have to say that, Kyle?" Mia punches his arm. "Now I'm never gonna wanna go down a waterslide again in my life."

"That's not as bad as the one about the AIDS-infected hypodermic needles they found in—"

"Don't," Mia says. "I don't want to know."

"—those little kids' climby ball pit things."

"Kyle!" both girls exclaim.

"Okay, okay."

"And turn off the air conditioning," Nicole tells him firmly. "Save the planet."

He does.

And we head south.

• • •

Petra Amundsen pounded on the narrow window in the basement room where the people who'd abducted her had left her.

Had imprisoned her.

It was useless.

She ran her fingers along the sill for the hundredth time, searching for some way to get it open, but of course, found nothing.

Well, ninety-eighth time, but who was counting.

She didn't really expect to find anything, but it was sort of like when you misplace your car keys and you know they have to be *somewhere,* so you check your purse, and then you look around your room and when you don't find anything, you come back to your purse and look in it again.

You know the keys won't be there, but you look anyway.

Just in case.

Just to be *sure.*

And now, Petra still found no way to open the window.

And no way to break the glass.

Sergei and Deedee had provided her with food and water, as well as a wire-handled five-gallon bucket to use for a toilet. But besides that, and the cot and blanket, her room was empty.

They'd been down to check on her a couple times, but mostly left her alone in this sparse, cement-block cell with that single, thick-glassed window.

When she stood on the cot and looked outside, she could see trains rocket past just a hundred yards or so away.

So close.

Yet so far out of reach.

Every couple of hours they passed by.

There were a lot of things she didn't know, but from the video her kidnapper's had filmed when they brought her here, she did know that the ransom they wanted from her dad didn't involve money but had to do with one of the committee hearings he was in charge of.

Money would have been no big deal.

Yeah, to put it plain and simple, her dad was filthy rich—and with her trust fund, so was she. He came from family money, but also made smart investments and had a knack for choosing the right stocks. By the time he was forty, he'd more than doubled the inheritance he'd received.

But what these people wanted was a different matter altogether.

Their ransom demand involved something her dad had told her about, something vital to stopping off-the-books government research that could hurt a lot of people. So, although Petra obviously didn't want to die, she also didn't want him to give in to the blackmailing.

They'd stipulated that he comply on Monday night at exactly nine o'clock.

Going that long without her medication was not going to be good.

Not at all.

You'll be okay. With Dad's connections, there are probably a thousand cops out there right now looking for you. They'll find you before Monday night. They'll find you for sure.

That's what she told herself as she stared out the window that would not open, through that glass that was too thick to break.

CHAPTER FOURTEEN

Everyone else takes a turn at the wheel, but whenever I offer to drive, my friends tell me to just rest my shoulder.

Now, as we come up on Janesville, Mia is driving with Nicole beside her.

Nicole starts using the calculator on her phone to figure out the distance and time we need to travel today, but Kyle just shakes his head. "No need for that. Not when we have a human calculator sitting right here in the car with us."

"Kyle," I say, "really, we don't need to—"

"For instance," he goes on, unfazed, "Nikki, how far is it to Mr. Schuster's house?"

She taps at her phone's screen. "Two hundred sixty-two miles."

"So Daniel, if we're averaging fifty-nine miles an hour, how long will it take us to get there?"

"Four hours, twenty-six minutes and twenty-six seconds."

"Although, by now, the seconds part has changed just a bit."

"Yes. Just a bit."

"It's like they say: Time flies like the wind, fruit flies like bananas. And what if Mia pushes it and we average seventy-one miles an hour?"

I sigh. "Three hours, forty-one minutes and, just over twenty-four seconds."

"See?"

"I'm not a human calculator," I tell him.

"Really?"

"Really."

"How many seconds until we would get to Mia's aunt's house, if we just drove straight through?"

"I'm not even going to answer that."

"But you know, don't you?"

"That's not the point."

"Ah. I knew you did."

Man, sometimes I wish I could shut this off.

Mia, who has brought along a bottle of bubbles, asks Nicole to hold the bubble dipper-thing in front of the air vent and bubbles go shooting all through the car.

Even though she and Nicole go back and forth about whether or not to put the AC on, since Nicole loves bubbles almost as much as Mia does, she has a small moral dilemma.

The bubbles are a lot better with it on, though.

As a group, we work our way through two bags of Fritos, a can of Pringles, and a bag of black-pepper beef jerky, which Nicole politely allows the rest of us to tackle on our own.

We have to stop to let Kyle relieve himself of his forty-four ounces of thirty-eight-hour energy sludge more than once, but he doesn't learn his lesson and mixes another liter of it, still hoping to break his personal best for staying awake.

• • •

Dr. Adrian Waxford made the final arrangements with the Wisconsin Department of Corrections for the next arrival to be sent down tomorrow.

Though this convict wasn't as violent as his other subjects, Adrian had his own, more personal reasons for requesting him.

Then, when the paperwork was finished, he spent some time doing critical flicker-fusion frequency tests with the *Tabanidae* to learn more about their ability to process time more quickly than humans do.

Hopefully, it would help him determine how much Telpatine, the chronomorphic drug he was developing, he would need to administer to create the same effect in his subjects.

His research would do more than just provide a way for justice to be served; it would also save the government tens of billions of dollars a year that could then be used for job growth, social programs for the poor, and judicial reform.

Currently in the United States, there were more than 2.3 million people in prison—more than any other country on the planet. And, at the cost of over $34,000 annually to keep each one incarcerated, the total expenditures reached close to eighty billion dollars per year.

Just to warehouse people.

Adrian's research would cut that down at least sixty or seventy percent, allow people to serve their complete sentences more quickly—psychologically, at least—even if they were sentenced to hundreds of years, and as a result it would also help ease the overcrowding at prisons.

The legal reforms would be fair, just, and save the taxpayers fifty to sixty billion dollars a year. True, it would require our society to rethink its views on how convicts should serve their time, but it would be well worth it in the long run.

However, all of that depended on Senator Amundsen canceling Tuesday's inquiry—the one that would abrogate things before the research was refined enough for broader use, and before society had been primed to be ready for its implementation.

But once the senator saw the video that Deedee and Sergei had filmed of his daughter, Adrian was confident that he would make the right decision and comply with their demands.

CHAPTER
FIFTEEN

Kyle is driving as we pass into Illinois.

We twist Mia's arm until she finally agrees to read us some of the ghost story she's been writing over the last year.

"If Mary Shelley can write *Frankenstein* when she's eighteen," she told us one time, "who's to say I can't write a novel too?"

True enough.

But she's been keeping the details about the story secret.

Until now.

"Well," she begins, "first of all, you need to know about ossuaries. They're rooms where they keep bones. Or, they can be just a container of some kind—a box, a chest, something like that. A lot of times they were needed in the Middle Ages during the days of the Black Plague in Europe when thousands of people were dying off so fast that their relatives didn't have a place for all the bones or all the bodies."

"Oh, lovely," Nicole says.

"My story, it happens at a monastery where they have an ossuary. It's based on a real place, actually. A Capuchin monastery—that's an order of monks, by the way. So this place has an entire wall made of skulls. The chandeliers are made of bones. You can Google it. It's crazy."

Nicole makes an *ew* face. "Why on earth would they do that? It sounds like something out of a horror movie, some sort of inbred-backwoods-cannibal-psycho-killer-thing."

"I know. So, like I was saying, sometimes it was crowding problems, they didn't know what to do with the bodies of the monks and stuff—but mostly they used it as a reminder to visitors about how brief life is."

"That would work for me."

I wonder what it would be like to walk into a church that has its walls covered with human skulls.

Honestly, it might not be the best way to attract new members.

At least not today.

Unless it was a Satanic church. Maybe then it would work.

Nicole informs us that she's officially having second thoughts about hearing this story.

"Well," Mia asks, "do you want me to read any of it or not?"

Kyle and I out-vote Nicole, and Mia pulls out her laptop and clears her throat. "The sound of shattering glass awakens me in the night."

"That's a good opening line," Kyle notes. "I like it. Sets the tense and the point of view, has action, mystery, danger, intrigue and—"

But Nicole hushes him. "You've got me curious now, Mia. Go on."

She reads:

I rise from my mat.

The darkness in my chamber is oppressive, but accompanies the cool, damp smell I have come to know so well since entering this monastery as a novice seven years ago.

I hear no feet shuffling through the corridor, no call to prayer, only the sound, once again, of glass tinkling to the ground.

Somewhat hesitantly, I step into the hallway where two torches flicker and lick at the darkness, throwing unkempt shadows across the walls, revealing the skulls. Some are faded yellow with the years, others are clean and white and only recently added to the rows with their brothers.

A stained-glass window containing the Blessed Virgin lies at the end of the hall, but in the torchlight, even from here I can see that some of its glass sits glistening at its base.

I wonder at this, but my curiosity compels me forward.

I pass the torches illuminating the faceless grins of the dead around me, and come to the broken window.

A specter hovers outside in the night—a face drained of color, drained of life, staring at me from just beyond my arm's reach.

Its mouth opens wide, swallowing the shadows that curl around it, the tendrils of the unseen realm. Then it utters a piercing howl as from the very pits of hell and fades away from me, disappearing into the black depths of the night.

"Well, okay, then," Nicole says. "I'm good here."

"You don't want me to go on?"

"You know, maybe some music would be cool. That, and let me make one tiny suggestion: Can we not talk about razor blades in waterslides or needles in ball pits or churches made of bones for a while? Actually, like, maybe forever."

"Okay, change of subject," Kyle suggests. "How about a riddle I've been working on."

"Does anyone die in it?"

"Nope."

"Skulls? Ghosts? The pits of hell?"

"Not this time."

"Alright. Go ahead."

"What's the largest thing you'll ever see, yet smaller than a pin? You're looking into history, so let the guessing begin."

"How could the largest thing be smaller than a pin?" Mia asks.

"That's what you need to figure out."

She sips at a Capri Sun. "Is it like dark matter or quantum particles or something like that?"

"Is that your guess?"

"No." She takes another drink. "Unless it's right."

"It's not. And don't forget, sometimes the answers to riddles are concepts rather than material things," Kyle reminds us, probably just as a way of trying to throw us off track. He turns to me. "So Daniel, what do you think?"

"Not bad. I'll get back to you."

CHAPTER SIXTEEN

Later in the afternoon, I use the preloaded debit card the anonymous donor sent us to fill up with gas one last time and finally convince my friends to let me drive for the final hour of the trip.

As we're passing by Champaign, Nicole is seated next to me, with Kyle and Mia in the back. They've been texting each other for the last half hour even though they're seated less than a foot apart.

Nicole stares out the window at the flat landscape that seems to go on forever. "It would be cool if we could've done a song montage of our drive instead of having to live through it."

"What do you mean?" Mia asks.

"Let's say they were making a movie of us heading down here. They'd play a song while they show clips of us snacking, rocking out, chilling, stopping for gas, napping, playing games on our phones, whatever—shrink the whole trip down to, like, three minutes. And it'd be sung by some group no one except Kyle's ever heard of, and suddenly they'd become famous and popular when the movie comes out."

"I could deal with that—not the listening to Kyle's music part, but the part about condensing our trip down to a couple minutes. That would work."

Kyle glances up into the rearview mirror. "That's what that scientist was trying to do, right Dan? Condensing time? The guy who was at the fish management center that didn't actually study fish?"

"Dr. Waxford?"

"Yeah."

Last winter, when my dad got stabbed by an escaped convict, we found out that a place near Beldon was doing secret research on prisoners from Derthick State Penitentiary. It was all led by a scientist named Dr. Adrian Waxford.

It turns out Waxford was a chronobiologist obsessed with trying to make it seem to people like time is passing more slowly than it really is. So, if you applied his research, you could make it seem to someone like hundreds of years of solitary confinement had passed when maybe only a couple actually had.

Psychological torture of the worst kind.

After we located that escaped prisoner and saved my dad, the fish management place blew up from a supposed gas leak.

The cops looked into it, but didn't find anything suspicious.

Nicole and I did some follow-up, but we couldn't find anything more on what might've happened to Dr. Waxford. It was like he just dropped off the map.

And so did a psychopathic killer who knew that convict and had murdered at least seven people before trying to burn me to death in an old lighthouse. He disappeared from the same hospital Dad was recovering in. And as far as I know, no one has heard from him since then either.

As time went by, all of that sort of faded from the main news reports, but I heard from my dad that the authorities were still searching for that serial killer.

I wonder if anyone is out there looking for Waxford.

"Actually," I tell Kyle, "Waxford could probably do the opposite and make three minutes seem like eighteen hours. And he could probably make eighteen hours seem like a year or two. I mean, if the stuff I read about him is true."

"That's just crazy."

"It's sick, if you ask me," Nicole says.

Mia finally stops texting and looks up just long enough to agree. "I'd say it's both."

Then she goes back to her phone again.

And Kyle goes back to his.

We pull into Mr. Schuster's driveway right around suppertime.

Though my dad has stayed in touch with him since they roomed together in college, I've never met him. However, I recognize him immediately from the pictures I've seen.

He's a little overweight and has wild, Einsteinish hair that makes him look like a mad scientist and not the classic car salesman that he is.

When we arrive, he's in the garage with the door open, tinkering under the hood of a car that looks like it's in astonishingly good shape even though, by its design, I'm guessing it's decades old.

Mr. Schuster shakes our hands warmly and leads us inside where a huge, slobbery mastiff jumps on us as soon as we walk through the door.

It's a dog only a PETA member could love, but Nicole gushes over how cute it is. She kneels, and as she's lovingly scratching it behind the ears, the dog shakes its head, sending sticky globs of dog drool frothing off to each side.

Mr. Schuster watches and smiles. "Easy, Annabelle."

"Aren't you sweet, girl," Nicole tells the dog.

"Don't worry, she won't bite. She just likes to lick."

"Brilliant," mutters Mia, who is much more of a cat person. Or a reptile one, from what I've heard.

Two air mattresses lie beside each other in the living room. "In the basement there's also a pullout couch and a queen bed," Mr. Schuster explains. "You'll have to fight over those."

Even though I'm not thrilled about Annabelle lapping at my face in the middle of the night, Kyle and I offer to take the air mattresses and the girls don't argue.

After checking in with our parents, we fill up on some spaghetti and meatballs, or in Nicole's case, spaghetti and tofu—Mr. Schuster has done his homework. Then he leaves us alone while he heads to the garage again to work on the 1966 convertible that he tells us he's getting ready to take to a car show later this summer.

Annabelle decides we're more interesting than her master and makes the rounds, climbing onto and slathering on each of us we talk in the living room.

Time passes, and as it's closing in on bedtime, Kyle says, "Annabelle reminds me of a story I heard about this blind woman who lived near the town where I was born, back in Minnesota."

"Is this another one of your urban legends?" Nicole asks him somewhat skeptically.

"It's just a story my friend told me when I was in sixth grade. Anyway, the lady's husband was a truck driver and was gone all the time so he got her this dog and it was trained so that when she would hold her hand down whenever she was scared, the dog would lick it, and then she would know that everything was okay."

"Oh, I can tell already I'm not gonna like this one."

"Do you not want to hear it?"

"Well . . ." But then, just like with Mia's ghost story, Nicole's curiosity wins out. "Go ahead."

"So, one night the lady hears a dripping sound in her bathroom, but she's nervous and doesn't want to check it out. All night she keeps lowering her hand over the edge of her bed and when she feels the dog lick it, she knows things are okay. But in the morning she calls her friend over to figure out what's going on. Her friend goes into the bathroom and comes running back out screaming, grabs the blind woman's hand, and rushes her outside."

"What did she see in the bathroom?" Nicole's voice catches with apprehension.

"The dog was staked to the ceiling. Its blood had been dripping down into the toilet. And a note was left there, scrawled in the woman's lipstick on the mirror: *People can lick hands too.*"

Nicole looks from Kyle to Annabelle, and then back to Kyle. "Seriously, did that really happen?"

He shrugs. "Dunno. My friend told me it did." Then he fake yawns. "Okay, we should probably be getting to bed."

"That's messed up. I'm not gonna sleep at all tonight."

I think of the blur I had on Wednesday of the blood dripping onto my bedroom floor.

Dripping blood, just like in this story.

It seems like there's a grim connection between the things that are going on, almost as if they were planned out beforehand and are now weaving together in some mysterious, unexplainable way.

That's not exactly reassuring.

"I swear to God," Mia warns us. "If any of you guys licks my hand tonight when I'm asleep, you are dead."

I'm pretty sure she's joking, but she does carry a butterfly knife in her purse, and the way she says it, I'm not sure I would want to test things.

"And I'm not kidding," she adds.

"No hand licking," Kyle says. "Got it."

●　●　●

LOS ANGELES, CALIFORNIA

"Tane Tagaloa?"

The stocky Samoan high school senior turned and slowly removed the cigarette from his mouth. "Who's asking?"

"I'm the man who contacted you last November, Malcolm Zacharias. I'd like you to come with me. I have a plane waiting."

They stood on a street corner next to an alley dominated by a looming, reeking dumpster. The yellowish glow of the sodium-vapor streetlight overhead gave the night a sickly, washed-out feel.

But they weren't the only ones out on that corner.

It was a gang-infested neighborhood and three thugs, the oldest one looking about twenty-five or so, eyed them from across the street, nodded to each other, and started their way.

Tane watched them disinterestedly.

"You don't blend in," he said to Malcolm.

"No. Probably not."

"Well, this is the wrong neighborhood for you to be visiting at this time of night."

"Thanks for the heads-up. Now, follow me before—"

"How did you find me? I didn't tell anyone I was coming out here."

"I'm good at what I—"

"Hey." The guy in the lead interrupted Malcolm midsentence. He held a bottle tipped upside down, leaving a trail of beer behind him on the road. "That's a nice shirt."

His buddies snickered.

"Thank you," Malcolm said, then he addressed Tane again, gesturing toward a rental car waiting nearby. "Shall we?"

The man shook out the rest of the beer as he stepped between Malcolm and Tane. "I said, I like your shirt."

"To which I would say I compliment your taste. But now if you'll excuse me, I'm having a conversation with this young man and I would appreciate it if you not interrupt us again."

"Give it to me."

The other men closed in around them.

"Take off the shirt."

Malcolm studied the three of them, then—almost, but not quite under his breath—said to the gang leader who was threatening him, "Are you sure you want to do this here in front of your friends? Once you lose face, it's hard to get it back again. It might be smarter if you just walk away, before you embarrass yourself."

The man cursed at him, then, holding his bottle by the neck, he smashed the other end against the dumpster, leaving him with a jagged-edged weapon.

"Okay. We'll do it your way." Malcolm eased his shirt off and held it out toward him.

However, rather than go for the shirt, the guy lunged forward with the broken bottle, swiping it at his abdomen.

Malcolm pivoted sideways while simultaneously whipping the shirt out and encircling the guy's wrist with it. He grabbed the shirt's other end, snugged it tight, then with one fluid move, he spun toward the street, twisting his attacker's arm behind him and driving him to his knees.

The man cried out.

Malcolm put just enough pressure on his wrist to make him drop the bottle. "When I let go, you're not going to hassle us anymore, are you?"

"This is my street. This is—"

He rotated the man's wrist.

Just a few more degrees and it would snap.

"Ow! Yeah! I promise!" he exclaimed. "Okay!"

Malcolm released him, then offered his shirt to the other two men. "Anyone else looking for a wardrobe addition?"

Neither of them moved, but the guy on his knees slipped his hand into his waistband and went for a Glock.

As he was removing it, Tane punched him in the face, sending him colliding hard against the sidewalk.

While he was disoriented, Malcolm pinned his arm against the ground with his foot, and then grabbed the gun to relieve him of it, but the guy held on.

"Let go."

"Screw you."

Having no other choice, Malcolm firmed up his grip on the Glock and cranked the weapon to the side, breaking the man's index finger in the process.

He howled in pain, staring at the way the finger jutted out sideways from his hand.

"I warned you about losing face." Malcolm removed the gun's clip, pocketed it, and tossed the Glock into the dumpster, then said to the other men, "You can stand up for him or step aside. The choice is yours."

They stepped aside.

"Come on, Tane. We have a plane to catch."

"Where are we going?"

"Atlanta."

CHAPTER SEVENTEEN

I can tell by Kyle's snoring that he didn't manage to break his record and stay up for thirty-nine hours. Not even close.

I'm not sure what happens with his air mattress, but as the night wears on, mine keeps losing air, until I'm basically lying flat on the floor with just a few bulges of air left around the edges where none of my weight is.

But then, whenever I roll over, the air scooches to the other side of the mattress so it doesn't end up making any difference how I position myself.

However, at last I do manage to drift off to sleep.

And this is my dream:

I'm standing ten feet from the edge of a cliff. The wind rushing up the mountain somehow feels both fierce and calming at the same time.

A voice calls me forward: *Walk to the edge.*

I do.

As I stand there, the air swirls around me, eager and expectant and full of promise, caressing my face, tossing my hair into a wispy frenzy.

I look down over the lip of the precipice.

A river wanders past, a thousand feet below me.

I feel a sense of vertigo, an enticing lure of dizziness that taps me on the shoulder and invites me to lean forward.

The wind will hold you.

It's strong coming up over the edge.

I close my eyes and let the spinning, whirling air encircle me.

My heartbeat quickens with the thrill of the moment.

I hold out my arms as if I'm going to take a swan dive.

Then the voice returns: *You can do this. You can find the beginning in the end.*

Letting go of all restraint, I tip forward, into the arms of eternity.

I awaken with a start.

Here on the floor.

Here beside Kyle.

Here in Mr. Schuster's living room.

Here.

And not on my way to the bottom of a gorge, plummeting to my death.

When I check the time on my phone, I see that it's almost three thirty in the morning.

For a while I try going back to sleep, but that doesn't work out too well, so I decide that, rather than just lying here staring at the ceiling, I'll grab a little fresh air and clear my head.

Annabelle is dozing near the door, but I ease it open, step over her onto the porch, and gently close the door behind me.

Since there are no lights out here, and my eyes are already used to the dark, when I look up, I can see the stars.

Mr. Schuster's house is far enough in the country for me to make them out pretty well, although not quite as clearly as I would if I were back home in Wisconsin.

As I trace out the constellations that I know, I sort through the images of the dream.

The cliff and the gorge and the call to die.

Or fly.

Maybe it was an invitation to fly.

Over the last nine months as I've looked for clues to deciphering my blurs, I've read a lot about dreams and nightmares and how to figure out what they might mean.

Falling is a pretty common nightmare. So is being chased and dreaming that you're late for class or that you missed it entirely.

Those three are the big ones.

I'm not really sure why the late-for-class nightmare is so common—or so upsetting. Sure, it's a little embarrassing to miss a class, but you're not in any real *danger*. Why on earth would that scare us as much as falling to our death or being chased by a monster or an axe-wielding killer?

But for some reason it does, and it's one of those dreams that people wake up the most troubled by.

Scientists still don't have any real idea why we have nightmares. They can record the brain activity that's occurring when we dream, but they don't have a clue about why we so often dream of things that terrify us.

In studies, two-thirds of the dreams that people remember are unpleasant.

Why?

No one really knows.

So now, this one—what does it mean?

In dreams, falling and flying can mean entirely different things.

One is the loss of control. The other, an exercise in control.

One ends in death. The other leads to the most glorious kind of freedom.

So maybe this dream means that I need to trust my blurs, that I need to lean out farther into them.

Or maybe the opposite: that leaning into them will cause me to fall in ways I'll never recover from. In that case, it might be telling me that I need to pull back now, before it's too late.

But, of course, that's one of the problems with interpreting dreams—how can you ever be sure you've gotten the interpretation right?

I think of my discussion with Kyle last week about me being on a road with no exit ramp, racing toward the edge of a cliff, and I wonder if that might be what led to this dream of stepping off an outcropping on a mountaintop.

Hard to say.

My thoughts cycle back to the blur in the attic and the boy in the road and the fact that my grandpa died on that same stretch of highway.

I decide that tomorrow I'll follow up with Mom, see if there's anything from Grandpa's life that might give me a hint that'll help me figure out what's going on now, in mine.

When I go back inside, I accidentally bump into Annabelle, but thankfully she doesn't bark, just whimpers, circles around herself a couple times, and then settles down and drifts back to sleep.

Unlike her, it takes me a little while to doze off, then, when I wake up again, she's licking my face. I push her away and roll over. Sunlight washes through the room and, sitting up, I hear Mr. Schuster in the kitchen asking my friends if they want chocolate chip or blueberry pancakes.

Chocolate chips all around.

After breakfast, as we gather our things, Kyle starts riffing on candy bars—maybe because he now has chocolate on the brain. "Shouldn't fun size and party size be the same size? I mean, who came up with the idea that fun size and party size are *antonyms*? And why is the smallest size 'fun'? That makes absolutely no sense. No sense at all."

"Good use of the word 'antonym,'" I tell him.

"Thanks." He digs through his duffel bag and comes up with a can of Red Bull. "Now, time to get my energy drink ready."

"Your special concoction."

"Nothing else comes close."

"But you didn't stay up for thirty-nine hours."

"If at first you don't succeed." He cracks it open.

"Right."

I email my mom, asking her to send me any pictures she has of Grandpa when he was a boy, then we say goodbye to Mr. Schuster, and Nicole pets Annabelle, who slobberingly licks her one last time.

She jerks her hand back. I'm guessing she's thinking of Kyle's story.

I know I am.

Then, we're on our way again.

This time for Atlanta.

CHAPTER
EIGHTEEN

Malcolm's plane landed in Atlanta.

In order to keep everything discreet, he made sure Tane wasn't able to tell exactly where they drove after they left the airport.

He got him situated on level B3 at the center.

Then left to track down Daniel.

• • •

The day goes by fast.

There's a ton of traffic around Atlanta and it seems like every street is named "Peachtree" or something close to it, so that makes things even more confusing.

To get to Sue Ellen's place we have to take Peach Avenue to Peachtree Circle, before ending up in the Peach Grove Estates subdivision.

Man, they must like their peaches down here.

The traffic puts us behind schedule, but eventually, right around seven, we locate her house.

It's a nondescript, beige, two-story home with a small deck in the back.

A city park with some wooded trails lies across the street.

Two baseball diamonds radiate out from a centrally located playground and basketball court, and a man on a riding lawnmower is cutting the grass on one of the ball fields.

The smell of freshly cut grass drifts toward us as we get out of the car and step into the Georgia humidity, which Mia complains about right away.

"At least it's not snowing," Nicole says encouragingly, since Mia likes snow about as much as she likes dogs. "It could be worse."

"Snow might actually be preferable to four hundred percent humidity."

One of the neighbors must be grilling because the smell of charcoal mixes in with the scent of grass clippings and it's almost as if someone has chosen two of the most classic smells of summer and threaded them through this neighborhood at the same time.

All we need is some coconut-scented suntan lotion and we'd be three for three.

Sue Ellen swoops out to meet us in the driveway.

"How was y'all's trip?" she asks with a big smile and a sweet southern accent.

"Good." Mia isn't a hugger, but she puts up with her aunt's rather gregarious embrace without complaining. "It's nice to be here."

We all introduce ourselves, then Sue Ellen says, "You must be tired!"

With her accent it sounds like "tarred" and it takes me a second to decipher it, but, in a way, it's endearing.

She gestures toward the door. "Come in, come in. Let's get y'all settled."

• • •

Without her medication, as time wore on, Petra Amundsen began to see things in the basement that she knew could not possibly be there.

At first, she told herself that it was just from stress and lack of sleep.

But then the walls began to melt and she realized that—unless she got her pills—things were only going to get worse.

Her nightmares first began four years ago when she was seventeen and her parents were going through their divorce. The dreams kept getting more frightening for about six months, until finally, they began to invade her waking life.

That's when she started to wonder if she was going crazy.

At first she tried seeing a counselor, but she didn't like it. Then she went to a hypnotist, which was really weird and a little unsettling, since after she woke up from her trances she wouldn't remember what had happened during them.

When she watched the video recordings of her sessions, she could hardly believe some of the things she'd said and done while she was hypnotized.

In the end the sessions hadn't really helped.

In fact, in that last one when she had the hallucination about the snakes attacking her and she woke up in the middle of her trance—remembering everything—it might have actually made things worse.

Now, based on the passage of time that she was able to track from the cycles of light and darkness passing outside her window, she figured it was Sunday evening.

The deadline was tomorrow night.

You're never going to make it, a voice told her. *You haven't gone this long without medication, not since—*

"Stop," she said aloud. "I'll be okay."

No, you won't. You know how these things go, how important it is for you to—

"Stop!" she yelled, even though she knew the voice wasn't any more real than the dripping concrete on the walls that encompassed her as she walked in circles and circles and circles around her small, enclosed room.

• • •

While Sue Ellen makes supper, we each contact our parents to let them know we've made it here safe and sound.

Mom, who hasn't sent the photos of Grandpa yet, tells me she's going through some old albums, scanning in pictures, and will email me later tonight. "What are you looking for, exactly?"

"I'm not sure. I guess send them all."

After having a little too much of Sue Ellen's fried chicken, green beans, and sweet—*very* sweet—tea, we drive over to Northern Georgia Tech, which is only a couple miles away, so I can get checked in for the camp tomorrow and throw my stuff in the dorm room where I'll be staying.

Quiet, shady lanes crisscross the main part of the campus and lead past the carefully manicured flowerbeds that seem to be everywhere.

It's peaceful compared to what I imagine it'll be like tomorrow when it's overrun with three hundred high school basketball players, not to mention the kids from the band and cheerleading camps that will also be going on in other parts of the campus.

The brick buildings all have a similar design. From what I can tell, the newest one is the field house, which is located between the guys' dorms and the student center.

The residence hall director has the registration forms of all the campers with him and it only takes a minute to check in. Then, because of the rule about no girls being in the guys' living areas, Nicole and Mia wait in the lobby while Kyle and I take my things up to my third-floor room. Most everyone else has a roommate, but for whatever reason, they've assigned me a room to myself.

Since I'm going to be busy here all week, the four of us head back to Sue Ellen's house to hang out until my ten-thirty curfew on campus.

We talk on the back deck for a while, and as it gets dark, the heat and humidity ease up and it feels almost as cool as if we were back home.

Almost.

But not quite.

We decide to go for a walk, but before we leave to visit the park across the street, Nicole asks me if I left Alfie at the dorm.

"No, actually he's still in the car."

"Good. Bring him along." Then she says slightly flirtatiously, "I might want you to show me a few moves."

Okay.

That can be arranged.

There aren't any lights specifically directed at the playground or outdoor basketball court, but the nearby streetlamps toss down enough light for us to see.

Mia puts her arm around Kyle's waist and they slip off toward one of the walking trails that lead into the woods.

So far on the trip, there hasn't been any sign that things have been rocky between them. Maybe they're finally working stuff out.

Nicole heads to the swing set. "Hey, push me? Oh wait!—your arm. I wasn't even thinking."

"I should be okay."

She kicks off her flip-flops, and then positions herself on the seat, wiggling her way to being comfortable. "Okay. Ready."

I roll Alfie onto the grass nearby, and then, placing my right hand on the small of Nicole's back, I ease her forward.

Once she's moving, she pumps her legs to gain more height.

"I've always liked swings," she tells me as I push her again. "Even when I was a little girl, my dad used to push me all the time. I mean, back then, I was probably only going a few feet off the ground, but when I think back to it now, it's like I was flying over the whole world."

As she talks, she continues pumping and I keep pushing her, getting her a little higher with each swing.

"Then I'd jump off and he'd always catch me—except for this one time I when jumped before he was ready and he couldn't get to me in time. I fell and scraped my knee pretty bad—got some gravel stuck in there. I still have a scar."

"So that's where that scar came from."

"What? You noticed my scar? And when exactly were you checking out my leg, Daniel Byers?"

"Oh, I might've just happened to glance in that direction once."

"Just once?"

"Maybe twice."

"Uh-huh." She pumps. Rises higher in the night. "Anyway, Dad felt terrible. And I just remember crying and holding him and how strong he was and how safe that made me feel."

She swings back toward me.

I give her another push.

In the trees, cicadas cycle louder and softer as if they're somehow orchestrated to chirp—or whatever it is cicadas actually do—in sync with each other.

"It's weird," she says. "I haven't thought about that in years. Not until just now, when I started swinging again."

"Maybe you just needed something to spark the memory."

Like the pictures of Grandpa that Mom is sending tonight.

Like the blurs.

The boy in the road.

Your corpse in the attic.

"Maybe." Then all at once she shouts, "Okay, here goes! I'm gonna jump!"

"I'm not going to catch you."

"I'll be fine!"

She swings back one last time, and as she floats forward, she leaps from the swing, squealing and kicking her feet in the air like a long jumper launching herself out over the sand.

She lands a bit off balance, but quickly collects herself, and then throws her arms out in celebration as if to say, "*Tada!*"

"Nicely done."

She takes a bow. "Thank you. I'll be signing autographs later."

"And no scar this time."

"Not this time." She flits over and picks up my basketball. "Alright, come on. Before Kyle and Mia come back I want you to show me how to shoot."

She dribbles it onto the court using both hands at the same time.

It's a little troubling.

"Okay, now." She slings the ball to her hip. "I need to tell you something."

"What's that?"

"A ton of people have tried to teach me before, but it's never worked."

"And you never wanted me to show you before now, either. Why is that?"

"Embarrassment."

"Nothing to be embarrassed about."

"You haven't seen me shoot yet."

"Well, go ahead. Show me what you've got."

"Promise not to laugh."

"I promise."

She's standing at about where the free throw line would be if it were painted on the blacktop. She eyes up the basket and heaves the ball toward it two-handed. It drops a couple feet shy of the rim. "See?"

Okay, this might take a little work.

"Well, let's start with your form. That's the key."

I retrieve the ball and choose a spot about halfway closer to the basket from where she was.

"You must not be very confident of your teaching abilities."

"We'll work our way back." I hand her the ball. "So, first, you're right-handed, so you're basically going to use that hand to shoot, not both hands. The left one is just there to help guide the ball, to keep it straight as you release it."

I take her hands and position them on the basketball, carefully guiding them into place. Even after all these months of being together, I still feel that same electricity that comes every time I touch her hand or she grazes her fingers across my arm.

I take my time to get it right.

She doesn't seem to mind.

"Now, when you line things up, keep your right elbow in. Here." I gently tilt it in for her so it's directly beneath the basketball. "Let the ball rest on your fingertips. Imagine that we painted the palm of your hand. You want to shoot so that no paint would get on the ball. So you're going to hold it just with your fingers, not your palm."

"Fingers, not my palm. Got it."

She shoots again, but still instinctively uses both hands. The ball bangs off the backboard and bounces onto the grass. I grab it, then return to her side.

"Show me where the paint would be," she says.

"The paint?"

"On my hand."

I take her right hand in mine and draw a soft circle around the edge of her palm. "Here."

"Where else?"

I brush my finger across her palm, pretending to paint it.

"Do the other one."

I do.

"Slower."

"Why?"

"I wanna make sure I've got it."

I go slower.

"No one ever taught me the painting thing before."

"I've never taught it to anyone quite like this."

"I think I'm glad to hear that."

I hand her the ball and lead her toward the side of the basket. "Try another one. And this time, bend your knees a little as you do. Keep that elbow in, and follow through with your hand. Aim for the backboard."

"Bounce it in?"

"We call it 'banking' it."

"Gotcha."

Mia and Kyle appear, walking side by side through the wash of light from the streetlamps.

Nicole studies the basket, bites her lip in deep concentration, and then fires away.

This time, I think to the surprise of both of us, the ball kisses gently off the backboard and swishes through the net without touching the rim.

"Yah!" she cries. "I made it! I banked it!"

"Have you been holding out on me?"

"No, I swear, I suck. You're a really good teacher."

"You're a good student."

"I like the paint part."

"I wouldn't have guessed."

While Kyle and Mia are still out of earshot, Nicole looks at me furtively. "I'll be sure to practice while you're at camp. Maybe when you get back we can play a little one-on-one."

Oh, man.

"I'll look forward to it."

We meet up with our friends and head back to Sue Ellen's house.

• • •

Malcolm Zacharias stood in the shadows near the edge of the park and watched the four teenagers cross the street.

He hoped things were going to work out with Daniel once he was at the center, but really, there were no guarantees.

For instance, take Jess, that girl from South Carolina, and Liam, the boy from New York.

Malcolm had found them last year, along with Tane, even before hearing about Daniel.

Both had fought so hard to control their hallucinations, but in the end, both had lost.

Now they were in separate mental institutions and none of the doctors who were treating them were optimistic about their chances of recovery.

That could happen with Daniel.

And, probably, in the end, it would. But hopefully they could make some strides first, make a difference for a few people before it was too late.

After Daniel and his three friends were in the house, Malcolm walked quietly through the cool Georgia night to his SUV.

Things were a go.

He would make his move as soon as Daniel was alone.

CHAPTER NINETEEN

Back on campus, while we're still in the parking lot, I tell everyone, "I should be able to see you guys tomorrow afternoon for a little while. There's a break after lunch before the next session."

"Hey, listen," Kyle says, "I'm hoping to sneak a run in before it gets too hot. How about I cruise over here and catch up with you for breakfast?"

"Why not—you can use one of my meal passes. We start in the gym at eight thirty."

"Cool. So, I'll see you at what, a little before eight?"

"Sure. At the cafeteria."

"And did you solve my riddle yet?"

"Let's see . . . The largest thing, yet smaller than a pin, you're looking into history . . . Nope. Not yet."

"Time?" Mia suggests, then immediately abandons it. "No, that doesn't make any sense."

"God?" Nicole muses aloud. "I mean, God exists outside of time, so maybe that could explain the history part."

"But how is God smaller than a pin?"

"True."

"It's one of your better ones," I tell Kyle. "And you made this up yourself?"

"Yup."

"Let me sleep on it."

Once I'm in my room, I check my email to see if Mom has sent the pictures over yet. There's a message from her that she's almost done, that she loves me, and that she'll get me the photos soon.

While I wait, I process things.

Grandpa.

The boy.

The dream of the cliff.

The living corpse in the attic.

Yeah, it's that last one that troubles me the most.

Writing sometimes helps. So, pulling out my journal, I flip to a blank page.

Tonight, I can hardly get the words down fast enough. It's almost like I'm not the one holding the pen, but instead that some unseen force is gliding it across the page.

Your life flicker-wisps through your mind.

Seeing a body does that to you. Makes the moments condense and expand, the past breathing down your neck.

The grave seems to chase you, knowing that no matter how hard you run from it, no matter how hard you resist, one day it's going to win.

A grave.

A body.

The person at your feet was alive and is now dead.

Perhaps he was remembering good times or dreaming about the future or worrying about something that seemed so vitally important, but wasn't, when he died.

But now he won't remember or dream or worry anymore.

The person at your feet is you.

The skulls in Mia's ghost story come to mind, and her comment about how the monks would use them to remind people how brief life is.

I stare at the words I just wrote.

Maybe her story is working on me.

Life is brief.

Death is snapping at my heels.

The night is always trying to swallow the day.

Pandora's box is right there by our feet waiting to be opened.

Last winter when I was researching hallucinations, trying to figure out what was happening to me, I came across this thing called automatic writing. Some authors and songwriters say there are times when the words seem to be dictated to them and they simply transcribe them onto the page.

But how does that work?

Where do the words come from?

That's the big question.

Maybe the same place as your blurs.

From going to church with Mom over the years, I know enough about the Bible to know that God sometimes speaks to people in visions, gives prophets things to say, and even helps them interpret dreams and predict the future.

For example, he did that with the man I'm named after—Daniel—who's famous mostly for being thrown into the pit of lions and coming out unscathed in the morning after an angel closed the lions' mouths.

But he also prophesied about the future and interpreted dreams. One time when a ghostly hand appeared and wrote a cryptic message on the wall during a party, he was able to explain to the king what it meant.

The hand had been sent from God, and it didn't leave a very encouraging message, at least not for that king. Basically, it said that his days were numbered.

A reminder of how brief life is.

Just like those skulls lining the walls.

That very night, the king was killed.

And there it is again—an underlying congruity between the events in my life, something that's tying them all together.

A saying my dad told me one time comes to mind: "Nothing is mundane if everything matters."

Maybe everything does matter.

And maybe it's all interwoven in a way I just can't see yet.

Though I'm not at all convinced that it's God who's sending me my blurs or giving me these words here tonight, they continue to flow as if they're coming from somewhere other than my own mind as I include one last entry:

I climb up the steps and I swing shut the door
and I peer out the gate of the castle once more—
only to see that it's really a prison with
    blood seeping up
    from the floor.

I'm trying to figure out what that might mean and how it might relate to everything else that's going on when I receive the pictures of Grandpa from my mom.

CHAPTER
TWENTY

There are shots of him at the cabin he used to own near Lake Algonquin, pictures of him as a kid growing up in Milwaukee, holiday family photos where we're all crowded together in the frame, and more.

I'm not even sure what I'm looking for, but I continue to review the photographs: In this one he's a teenager kneeling beside a buck that he shot, here he's celebrating his thirtieth wedding anniversary. Some photos I recognize from seeing them before, some I don't.

Fifty-five pictures in all.

I'm especially interested in the ones of him when he was young, but none of them really look like the boy I saw in the road.

I move to the later photos, the ones taken closer to when he lost control of his car on a patch of black ice and skidded off that county highway into a tree.

Nothing grabs my attention.

Then I flip back through the pictures again from the start.

When I get to one of the family Christmas photos from the year I was in kindergarten, I pause.

This time, however, it's not Grandpa's picture that catches my eye. It's me, standing by his side.

I know I've seen this photo before tonight, but I forgot all about it.

It sparks my memory.

Just like swinging did for Nicole.

My heart begins to race.

In the photograph, I'm wearing the same clothes as the boy I saw right before I was hit by the truck.

The person in the attic—that was you.

The boy in the road—that was you too.

You were trying to save him, Daniel.

You were trying to save yourself.

My thoughts coil around themselves, taking me deeper into the moment.

Grandpa.

And blurs.

And sleepwalking.

The first time you sleepwalked was right after Grandpa's funeral.

My parents were in the living room and I simply walked past them toward the front door without even acknowledging them.

When they asked me where I was going, I said, "To find him." And then, when they took me back to bed, I told them I wanted to save him "before they came"—whatever that might mean.

But you were sleepwalking and dreaming at the time. It was nothing, it was just—

My vibrating phone jars me out of my thoughts.

It's an incoming text, but for some reason, no return number comes up. The message reads simply: *Answer this call, Daniel.*

But that's enough to unsettle me.

Because I've seen those words before.

It's the same message I received back in December from a guy named Malcolm Zacharias right before we spoke for the last time.

He was this enigmatic man who kept popping up right around the time my dad was stabbed.

He told me that he was a recruiter, apparently for teens that he thought had the same kinds of blurs as I was having. Also, he was trying to stop Dr. Waxford's research on human subjects.

Mr. Zacharias was the one who helped me escape from the mental hospital that the authorities took me to when they thought I was the one who attacked Dad.

Later, he altered the place's security camera footage to make it look like I'd gotten out of there all on my own.

In the end, I was left wondering if he really did exist or, if maybe I'd been imagining him from the start.

But then where did this text come from?

The phone rings.

Is this a blur? Is this even real? If you answer the phone, it's going to take you closer to the cliff.

It rings again.

And again.

But maybe you'll get some answers. Maybe you'll finally find out what's causing your blurs.

On the fourth ring, I tap the screen to accept the call.

"Daniel," a voice says. "It's Malcolm. We need to meet."

CHAPTER TWENTY-ONE

THE ESTORIA INN

Last winter, one of Dr. Adrian Waxford's subjects had escaped the research facility in Wisconsin, and locating him afterward had proven to be somewhat problematic.

So, when Adrian and his team opened this center here in the mountains of Tennessee, he'd started experimenting with ways of implanting tracking devices into the subjects.

Although it isn't easy, ankle monitors can be disabled and removed, so he didn't even bother with those.

At first he tried inserting GPS microchips into the backs of the men's hands, but after one subject chewed his out, Adrian decided to go a different route, using a specially engineered tattoo ink that contained nanobot geotags.

It was permanent.

It was irreversible.

It was the tracking system of the future.

However, rather than tattoo someone's skin, which could be flayed off, he decided to tattoo the subjects' eyeballs.

While it was certainly possible that someone could poke out his eyes so that he could no longer be traced, none of the men had shown that much initiative yet. Besides, they hadn't been told the real reason that their eyeballs were being tattooed, so none of them knew about the geo-trackers.

Early on, Adrian had tried doing the tattooing himself, but he kept accidentally pushing the needle in too far, puncturing several of the subjects' eyeballs.

So, he'd passed the job off to Henrik, who had proven quite skillful with the needle and quite particular about his work.

Since Adrian liked to observe the men's reaction, he preferred that they remain awake during the procedure.

Now, he watched as two guards strapped the newest subject into the chair, securing him so that he couldn't move any of his limbs, couldn't even turn his head.

The man, who'd arrived less than an hour ago, frantically begged them to stop, apparently still holding onto the hope that he would be able to plead his way out of this.

Once he was immobilized, the guards left Adrian and Henrik alone.

Time for the tattoo.

While Adrian got out his iPad to take notes, Henrik picked up a spring-loaded eye speculum that would keep the subject's eyelid from closing during the procedure.

"No, please no!" he hollered.

"Shh, now."

Henrik began with the left eye, pressing the eyelid open, positioning the speculum, and then tightening the screws to secure it in place.

He did the right one as well.

Now there was no way for the man to blink.

Since it's so common to see people blink, Adrian always found it a bit strange to look at someone whose eyes were bulging out like that, looking almost amphibian, and not blinking.

Not at all.

Henrik dipped the needle into the ink.

"Are we ready, Doctor?"

"Yes. Please proceed."

"No, don't!" the man shrieked. "I'll do anything, just stop!"

Undeterred, Henrik pressed the tip of the needle against his eyeball.

"Steady, now. Don't flinch."

"Nooo!"

Adrian watched as Henrik carefully depressed the needle, and after a moment of slight resistance as it penetrated the conjunctiva, the needle's tip penetrated just far enough into the sclera to distribute the ink.

Henrik was careful not to rupture the eye.

The ink spread out from the end of the needle and curled across the surface of subject #556234's eyeball, creating a black swirl that made Adrian think of food coloring curling out into a glass of milk.

That's what he thought of every time this happened.

A glass of cool, refreshing milk.

"There, now," Adrian reassured the man. "You're doing fine. Just a few more minutes and you'll be all set to go."

He typed a few observations into his tablet as Henrik re-dipped the needle to get more ink, and bent over him again.

Despite not being able to blink, a tear trickled down one of his cheeks.

Interesting.

Adrian noted it in his file.

When they were finished, the subject's eyeballs would be completely obsidian and he would be forever monitored, no matter where he went on the planet.

There was no hiding it, no turning back, and nothing short of removing both eyeballs that could be done about it.

He was only a young man, about to turn twenty later this summer. But such was the due and just reward for his crimes.

After all, he was a poacher and had attempted to black-mail and physically assault a teenage girl up in Wisconsin. He'd held her against her will, threatened her well being, and even tried to set him up for his crimes. He deserved the punishment he was about to get.

Every hour of it.

Every minute of it.

Adrian had no patience for those who would attack people weaker than themselves.

On a more personal front, the young man had stolen one of Adrian's rifles and used that to poach the wolves.

Unacceptable.

If all went well, this subject would be the first recipient of Adrian's new chronomorphic drug and the findings would help show the Defense Department what his methods were capable of accomplishing in only a limited period of time.

"So, Doctor," Henrik said as he went for more ink, "I have word that Zacharias is back in Atlanta. I'm heading down there tonight to personally oversee things."

"And Deedee and Sergei?"

"Still with Petra."

"Perhaps you should have them accompany you to Georgia. There's strength in numbers, and as you told me yourself, Zacharias has skills. At least take one of them."

"Alright. I'll bring Sergei along."

More entreaties for mercy from the man in the chair.

More tears.

On his iPad, Adrian deleted the name Ty Bell and typed in what this subject would be known as from here on out: #556234.

A number.

Just a number.

Part of the system, now and forever.

All for the greater good.

CHAPTER
TWENTY-TWO

MONDAY, JUNE 17
8:24 A.M.

Kyle Goessel watched as the other guys from the basketball camp made their way into the field house. At first, larger clumps of players walked past, then a few stragglers, but Daniel didn't show up in any of the groups.

The first session in the gym would start in just a few minutes. Still no sign of his friend.

They were supposed to meet for breakfast at the cafeteria half an hour ago. After waiting there for twenty minutes, Kyle had come over here hoping to at least catch Daniel before the camp began for the day.

He texted him again and waited.

No reply.

At this point it was too late for breakfast, but why hadn't he at least replied to the texts?

Kyle had a disquieting feeling when he thought of the blurs his friend had been having and how Daniel had spoken last week about his fear that the thread might snap, the one that kept him sane.

He texted Nicole to see if she'd heard from Daniel and she replied almost immediately that she hadn't.

What's going on? she typed. *Can't you find him?*

I mighta missed him, he replied. *Let me just check on something.*

Someone came hurrying out of Berringer Hall and jogged toward the gym, but it wasn't Daniel, just another kid who was hustling to get to the first session.

So, okay. Even if Daniel had just accidentally slept in, he needed to get his butt over here.

Kyle didn't like his next thought, but neither could he shake it: *There's no exit ramp on the road to insanity. Maybe he went off the cliff.*

He did his best to put that idea out of his mind as he headed for the dorm to check his friend's room.

• • •

Malcolm was on level B1 of the center getting things ready for the orientation when the call came through.

Even though he was underground, special routers allowed him to receive it. He thought it might be Sam, but surprisingly, Senator Amundsen's name came up on the screen.

"Senator?"

"Petra was taken."

"What? What are you talking about?"

"Friday night. It happened on Friday. I've tried to contact Sam but haven't been able to. I finally decided I needed to call someone. I thought I'd reach out to you. They said no police, no FBI, but you're a freelancer, right? So you're—"

"No, it's good that you did. What's her condition? Do you know if she's alright?"

"As far as I know, yes. Her kidnappers recorded a video with their demands. I'll send it to you. We can talk again after you've seen it."

"Where are you?"

"At home."

"So the police don't know? You're certain of that?"

"The people who took her told me they'd kill her if I contacted the authorities. You're the only one I've told."

"Alright, forward everything you have to me. I'll take a look. And don't worry, we'll find her."

• • •

Kyle knocked on Daniel's door.

"Bro, it's eight thirty."

Silence.

"Dan?"

He tried the doorknob, found it unlocked. Swung the door open.

"You in here?"

With the lights off and the shades drawn, only a vague smudge of daylight made it into the room. The light from the hallway wasn't enough for Kyle to tell if Daniel was there or not, so he felt the wall for the light switch.

Found it.

Flicked it on.

Daniel's bed was neatly made. His basketball shoes waited beside it. A leather-bound journal sat on the desk next to his wallet.

But he was gone.

After verifying that he wasn't in the closet or the bathroom, Kyle glanced around for Daniel's phone, but didn't see it.

Hoping for some sort of clue about what had happened, he opened Daniel's journal and found that the last two entries were all about death and blood and the loss of hope. The handwriting became scratchy and almost indecipherable at the end, as if he'd lost his train of thought and descended into scribbled madness.

Kyle phoned Nicole. "You guys need to get over here."

"What is it? What's wrong?"

"It's Daniel. He's gone."

"What? Where?"

"I don't know. I'm in his room right now, here at the dorm, but I can't find him."

Though the girls weren't allowed in here, Kyle figured that most everyone was at the gym anyway and they should be alright. "I want you and Mia to come over, help see if we can figure out where he might be."

"We'll be right there."

After hanging up, Kyle searched the room more carefully and finally located Daniel's phone under his bed.

The texts from this morning were there, along with a couple from Nicole last night telling Daniel goodnight. All of them were marked as unread.

The last one that'd been opened was from about half an hour after they'd dropped Daniel off here. It simply read: *Answer this call, Daniel.*

Kyle checked the recent calls.

It didn't appear that anyone had contacted his friend after that.

The last outgoing call was to Daniel's mom when he'd phoned her after they arrived at Sue Ellen's house.

While Kyle waited for the girls, he carefully examined Daniel's email and social media posts for any hint about where he might be.

CHAPTER TWENTY-THREE

Dr. Adrian Waxford walked out the back door of the Estoria Inn toward the forest.

Half a dozen cars of the workers currently at the facility sat in the shaded parking area nearby.

He hiked past them toward the maintenance building, and then continued to his favorite overlook near the perimeter fence that ran along the edge of the property.

From there, he could see through the trees and make out the next mountain over, the one that lay just beyond Little Bear Creek—which, with the recent rains they'd been having, wasn't really so little or even much of a creek right now. More of a river at flood stage.

He glanced back at the Estoria.

Stout poison ivy vines and unrelenting kudzu climbed nearly the entire eastern wall of the hotel, giving the old place an aura of mystery.

They'd renovated the building's interior but left the outside untouched.

The tales about this place being haunted might have attracted some curiosity seekers in the past, but even those stories had mostly faded from the collective consciousness of the area over the last two decades.

People said that a murder had occurred in room 113.

Adrian didn't believe in ghosts or the supernatural, but it was one of the reasons he'd chosen that room for the killer from Wisconsin. It just seemed fitting that a murderer of children should be in the most lurid room in the hotel.

Staring out across the valley again, Adrian tapped the screen of his satellite phone to put the video call through.

A few seconds later, the face of General Vanessa Gibbons appeared.

"I had a message to return your call," Adrian said.

"I'm coming down there," she replied in her clipped, efficient, military-esque manner. "I want you to show me around the facility."

"I can send you my latest reports. They should be enough to—"

"Adrian, our oversight committee has invested a *substantial* number of taxpayer dollars into this project and we've given you carte blanche to do as you see fit. However, this week I need to report back to them and they're going to be asking me some very direct, very probing questions about your progress, especially regarding this new drug you've been telling us about. Additionally, as I told you last month, one of the senators has been snooping around where he doesn't belong, and that concerns us—especially this close to our next budget meeting."

"Don't worry about the senator. I have a feeling that'll all blow over."

"We can't make policy decisions based on feelings. We need facts."

"I've made some significant strides recently. In fact, I have a new subject that we'll be able to track from start to finish. I'm almost ready to try out the Telpatine on him. Just give me a few more weeks to—"

"That's not soon enough. The committee members are pressuring me for answers now. The only way I can feel confident fielding their questions is if I verify things in person. How far are you from the Knoxville airport?"

"It'll depend on traffic, but plan on at least a ninety-minute drive."

"I'll contact you with the details concerning my arrival after I confirm my flight."

"Do you need someone to pick you up?"

"I'll rent a car."

"Alright, I'll make sure the main gate is open for you. I look forward to—"

But she hung up before he could finish.

So, then.

Admittedly, this put a bit of a wrinkle in his plan.

There were aspects of his research that he had not included in his reports, aspects that would be best kept confidential.

However, things could still move forward, especially if Henrik was able to deliver Zacharias before the general's arrival.

The renovations on the fourth floor weren't complete, so General Gibbons would have no need to tour that level. They could keep Zacharias up there until tonight's nine o'clock deadline.

Adrian pocketed his phone, returned to the Estoria, and told his assistants to prepare one of the rooms on the fourth floor.

Then, he went to finish the dosage calculations for the first human trial of Telpatine.

CHAPTER TWENTY-FOUR

The girls texted Kyle that they were at the dorm and he slipped outside to let them in.

Back in the room, he showed them Daniel's phone. "The last text he opened said for him to answer a call, but there's no record that anyone contacted him after that. It's like he just vanished after he read that text."

"Yeah, vanished without his phone." Nicole pointed to the desk. "Or his wallet."

"And look at this." Kyle pointed out the unfocused, disjointed writing in Daniel's journal.

"He did some weird journaling like that last winter too, remember? And now he's having his blurs again. This is not good."

Footsteps in the hall caught their attention. Kyle opened the door slightly, peered out, and then ducked his head back in.

"Quick—hide."

"Who is it?" Mia asked.

"The guy who checked Daniel in last night, the residence hall director. He might have seen you two come in."

Mia scrambled under the bed and Nicole disappeared into the closet.

Kyle snapped off the lights, dove under the covers, and drew them up to his chin just as the door opened.

When the lights clicked on, he groaned and rolled to his side. "Hey!"

The director consulted a clipboard. "Daniel Byers?"

"Yeah."

"Buddy, you're late. They started practice over in the field house half an hour ago."

"What?" Kyle pretended to be shocked. "What are you doing here?"

"Room inspection."

Kyle groaned again but did not climb out of bed. "A little privacy?"

The guy backed into the hallway again, shutting the door behind him.

Kyle waited a few moments, then stood and told the girls, "Okay. The coast is clear."

Mia emerged from under the bed.

Nicole stepped out of the closet. "We need to tell someone he's missing."

"Who?" Kyle asked. "If we call his parents, they'll just worry about him and there's nothing they can really do about it from Wisconsin anyway."

"The cops? Or campus security, maybe?"

But Mia shook her head. "We don't even know that he didn't just go for a walk or something and then lost track of time."

"I don't think that's very likely."

"Alright," Kyle said. "But before contacting campus security, let's have a look around, check the student center, the cafeteria, see if we can track him down. Maybe I just missed him earlier and he made it into the field house."

"His basketball shoes are still here," Nicole pointed out.

"Well, I should check just to be sure."

"Alright, then I'll get the cafeteria."

Mia was staring out the window at the broad, sweeping campus. "I guess that leaves me with the student center. Let's meet back as soon as we can at that fountain over by the library."

CHAPTER TWENTY-FIVE

Last night is fuzzy.

It's as if my memory is wandering through a thick fog and every once in a while something solid, something tangible appears, but then the mist covers it again and it's gone.

I remember returning to the dorm and sorting through the pictures from my mom.

Grandpa as a child.

Christmas photos of the family.

A picture from when I was five, just before he died.

Then there's the flicker of a memory about a phone call.

And then something about an SUV and—

Oh, yes

The driver.

Malcolm Zacharias.

Yes.

He texted you. He called you. He's the one who brought you here.

I sit up in bed and look around.

Nope. Definitely not in Berringer Hall anymore.

It might be a hotel room, but it's pretty Spartan. No wall hangings. No windows.

No TV.

No phone.

When I get out of bed, I see that I'm still wearing the clothes I had on last night when I returned to the dorm after leaving Sue Ellen's place.

Other than my shoulder sling, which is lying on the dresser near the door, I don't see anything else that belongs to me.

My shoulder is aching, so I gently ease my arm into the sling.

I wish I had some of the pain meds, but I don't see them anywhere. When I check in the dresser, I come up empty on the medication but find that the drawers are stocked with clothes that all look my size.

Weird.

And a little creepy.

Curiously, there's a mini fridge in the corner, and when I open it, I discover that it's filled only with bottled water and green apples.

It makes me think of forbidden fruit and fairy tales with choices that have deadly consequences, and I decide that, even though I'm hungry, I'll pass on the apples.

And the water too. Just to be safe.

I have no idea how long I've been asleep or what time it is.

There's no closet, just that door beside the dresser.

I try the knob.

It's unlocked.

An empty, cream-colored hallway stretches out in both directions. There aren't any windows, but the series of recessed fluorescent lights beside the ceiling offers a soft, ethereal glow.

As I walk forward it's almost like I'm entering a dream.

Maybe you are.

Maybe this is all just a blur.

If it is, it would be my most elaborate one yet.

But I can't dismiss that possibility.

It's too bad that I don't have a phone with me so I could record things and see if they're real.

However, blur or not, I need to figure out what all this is about.

A low, steady hum comes from the lights, but other than that, the hallway is quiet. I don't see any vents, but the air conditioning is cranked up almost high enough to make me shiver.

A security camera stares down at me from across the hall.

As I go left, it swivels, following my movement.

Maybe it's wired to a motion sensor—but it's also possible that someone is on the other end, manually controlling it, watching me.

The floor is tiled with geometric shapes that appear random, but when I study them more closely, I realize that there are ten different ones, and that each represents a number from zero to nine.

There are also other symbols that obviously correspond to mathematical operations. Together, their arrangement on the floor forms elaborate equations.

Whoever designed this place had to be a math genius—although, why anyone would put so much work into a floor's layout is beyond me.

I walk to another door, about forty feet away.

A camera identical to the one outside the room I came from picks me up as I approach it and tracks me as I try twisting the doorknob.

Locked.

Although for a couple seconds I'm tempted to call out to see if anyone's in there, honestly, I'm glad for the chance to have a look around before whoever's monitoring me through those cameras comes to find me.

For the next ten minutes or so, I explore the maze of hallways, mentally mapping them out, using the geometric shapes and the equations they represent to get my bearings so that, even though the intersecting hallways are confusing, I'm able to keep myself oriented.

Finally, I meet up with a T that I haven't come to before.

I'm debating which way to go when I hear a door bang shut somewhere out of sight around the bend on the left.

Sharp-sounding footsteps approach me.

I figure I'll get more answers talking to whoever this is than I will wandering around these halls.

However, I have no idea if the person will be happy to see me or not, so I brace myself for a possible fight, tightening my one good hand into a fist.

The stride is quick and firm.

Coming closer.

I wait, becoming more tense—but also more directed and focused—with every passing second.

At last, a man comes into view and stops when he sees me.

Malcolm Zacharias.

Though last night is still hazy, he looks just like I remember him from when we met in December: mid-thirties; straight dark hair; a piercing, intelligent gaze.

He's wearing blue jeans and a black turtleneck.

A scar he didn't have in the winter trails across his cheek.

"Daniel."

"What's going on here, Mr. Zacharias? What do you want from me?"

"It's time for you to meet the others—and we're going to be working pretty closely together. How about we just go by first names from here on out. You can call me Malcolm."

CHAPTER
TWENTY-SIX

"I know you must have a lot of questions," he tells me as he leads me down the hall.

"Why don't I remember last night?"

"I gave you a slight hypnotic."

"You drugged me?"

"I took certain steps to ensure plausible deniability for you."

"Plausible denia—what is this about?"

"Trust me, we're going to get you the answers you're looking for."

"Where's my phone?"

"I returned it to your dorm room for you."

A single elevator lies before us, the silver doors standing in stark contrast to the blank, monotonous walls surrounding them.

I study the patterns on the floor, visualize them mathematically, and commit this location to memory so I can find it again if I need to. "What is this place?"

"A training center. I'd show you around more, but time is of the essence."

We arrive at the elevator and he presses the "Down" button.

"Why is time of the essence?"

"We'll cover that in a minute."

"Last December you told me your job was recruitment, but you never explained who you were looking for, who you were recruiting."

"Those with the gift to see what most people miss."

"You mean when we have blurs?"

"There's a rare combination of factors that have come together in a fraction of a percent of the population. You're one of the few we've been able to locate."

The doors swish open and we step into a cramped, narrow elevator.

"So you want to study us?"

"Think of your blurs as a flashlight beam. Your subconscious is shining it through the darkness of all the distractions that are out there every day, all around you—all the untidy details of life—until it finds cohesion where there seems to be chaos, and then it draws your attention to it."

On the elevator's panel there's an upper level that appears to require a key card to access it. We're on B1. He presses B3, two levels down.

"So, like I said, you want to study us."

The doors close.

We descend.

"The agency I work with wants to help you focus the beam."

"I've read about the different aspects of schizophrenia. Is that what we have? Some sort of mental illness?"

"We're still trying to understand it," he says, which doesn't quite reassure me. "But we're going to have to put some of that on hold. A young woman is missing and we don't have a lot of time to find her."

"Who is she?"

"Senator Amundsen's daughter. She's like you. She has blurs. And we need to find her before nine o'clock tonight."

"Or?"

"Or her abductors are going to kill her, Daniel. But if they get what they want in their ransom demands, the very foundation of our justice system could be left in ruins."

I wonder if he might be exaggerating things, but the way he says it makes me believe him.

He doesn't elaborate.

The elevator stops.

The doors part.

Another hallway.

We walk for a few minutes in silence and, although the layout of the halls on this level appears to be identical to B1, the equations represented are different.

Well, at least if you get lost, you'll be able to tell what floor you're on.

Also different: All the rooms on this level require a key card.

Finally, we come to an unremarkable door in the middle of an unremarkable hallway and Malcolm waves the card in front of the reader.

With a slight whisper that reminds me of someone exhaling, the door whisks open, and he gestures for me to go inside.

CHAPTER TWENTY-SEVEN

It's a huge contrast to the austere room where I woke up.

One wall of the lush apartment is covered with a panoramic window. It looks like we're on the ground floor of a building in a dense forest.

Another wall contains an array of screens that display the security footage from the cameras that were in the hallways I was walking through earlier.

An imposing guy—maybe Hawaiian or Polynesian—stands beside the window. Near him, a fair-skinned girl is seated on a large, L-shaped black leather couch. They both appear to be about my age and when Malcolm and I step into the room and the door slides shut behind us, both of them turn our way.

The boy has me by at least thirty pounds, and it's all muscle. He looks street-tough and doesn't seem too happy to be here.

The girl's strawberry-blonde hair is trimmed into a neat pixie cut. She's almost as slender as Mia. Dark sunglasses hide her eyes.

"Daniel," Malcolm says, "I'd like you to meet Alysha and Tane. They've both agreed to help me." He sets his key card between an elaborate lava lamp and a vase on a table pushed up against the wall.

"With what? Finding the senator's daughter?"

"Petra. Yes. There's a man who's performing chrono-biology tests on prisoners. You'll remember him from last winter."

"Dr. Waxford."

"Right. My employer wants to stop him, and also wants to—let me back up for a second. As I told you upstairs, your subconscious is drawing meaning from the random data that passes by each of us all the time. It's the same for Alysha and Tane. We need to find a template for your conscious minds to interact with—"

His phone rings softly, with a distinctive, chiming ring-tone. He glances at the screen, and worry etches across his face. "I'm sorry. I need to take this. I'll give you a few minutes to get to know each other, then we'll have to get started. Please excuse me."

Tane silently watches Malcolm leave. As soon as we're alone, he strides toward me. I'm about to ask if he knows what exactly is going on, but before I can say a word, he cocks his fist back and sends it flying at me, connecting sol-idly with my jaw.

I can take a punch, but this guy has some serious heft to him and the force of the blow snaps my head around and almost sends me to the floor.

With my left arm out of commission, I don't really want to fight him, but I figure I'll do what I have to do.

Slowly, I turn and face him, wiping the blood off my lip.

I undo the Velcro strap on the sling and slough it off my arm, letting it drop to the floor beside me. "Hit me again and see how that goes for you."

I'm partly bluffing.

Partly not.

Tane opens his mouth slightly as if he's going to reply, but then closes it again.

He doesn't take another swing at me.

We both stand our ground.

"You'll have to forgive him," Alysha says in a soft, delicate voice. "We're both a little on edge here."

"How did Malcolm find you?" Tane asks me.

"Someone told him about me last winter. Why did you hit me?"

"Where are you from?"

"Wisconsin. I asked why you punched me."

"To see what you're made of. I'm from L.A."

"And I'm from Montana," Alysha inserts. "Do you see things that aren't there?"

"Hang on." I'm not satisfied with Tane's answer. "You wanted to see what I'm made of? That's not enough of a reason to walk up to someone you just met and slug him in the face."

"You can tell a lot about a person by how he reacts when you punch him."

"Really? And what could you tell about me?"

He leans over, picks up my sling, and hands it to me. "That I wouldn't want to fight you. Unless I had to."

The feeling is mutual, but I don't say that. I just put the sling back on.

The shoulder hurts, but I hold back from wincing as I strap the sling in place.

"So, do you see things?" Alysha presses me.

"You mean hallucinations?"

"Visions, revelations, whatever you want to call them."

"Yes. I do."

"When did it start for you?"

"Last fall. At a funeral. Do you see them too?"

"Well, not exactly." She removes her sunglasses and, although she's facing me, her gaze tips past me, her eyes cloudy and unfocused.

"You're blind?"

"Visually impaired," Tane corrects me.

"Let's just stick with 'blind,'" she says. "I hate all that stupid politically correct stuff. But to answer your question, Daniel, no, I don't see things. I hear them. And sometimes I feel them touch me."

"I see them. And I hear them too," Tane adds. "It's almost like other people are talking to me, right inside my head, even when there's no way I should be able to know what they're saying."

He seems more forthcoming than I would've expected.

Alysha is still turned toward me. "Do you have head-aches first?"

"I used to, but then, in time, they stopped, and I just started having the blurs without any warning. Look, how long have you two been here?"

"Blurs?"

"That's what I call them. When reality blurs along the edges and I can't tell what's real and what's not."

"Blurs." She nods reflectively. "Yeah, that makes sense. We'll go with that. Do you know what causes them? Your blurs?"

"I'm still trying to figure that out. So—how long were you saying you've been here?"

"Malcolm picked me up Saturday night," Tane tells me.

"And I've been here since last week," Alysha explains. "He told my parents that I was going to some sort of stu-dent leadership conference or something. I'm not sure. He's had me busy listening to 911 calls from missing persons cases."

"Why?"

"To see if I can notice things other people miss."

That was pretty much the same phrase Malcolm had used just a few minutes ago when he was explaining things to me.

Tane retrieves the key card that Malcolm left next to the lava lamp and studies it as if it might reveal clues about our situation. Then, once again he opens up more than I think he will. "I live with my mom. Dad's out of the picture. Well, he was never really in it. I don't know what Malcolm told her, but she was probably just glad to not have to worry about taking care of me for a while. She's not exactly a finalist for Mother of the Year. What about you?"

"My mom?"

"No. Does anyone else know you're here?"

"I . . . well . . . I'm not sure."

I realize that if they haven't already, my friends and my parents will be missing me soon.

Though my memory of what happened last night is still murky, I don't recall leaving any sort of note behind. It wouldn't have helped anything though, since I don't know where I am or how long I'll be here.

"Do you know why we're here?" Tane asks.

"Malcolm mentioned finding the senator's daughter."

"Petra."

"Yes. That's about all I know."

"You mentioned that someone told Malcolm about you," Alysha says. "That's how he found you?"

"Yes."

"Was he tracking your online activity?"

"Yes, actually he was."

"It's the same for both of us."

Tane is distractedly flipping the key card through his fingers. "He's looking for a convergence."

"A convergence?"

"Of knowledge and desire, of curiosity and ability. At least that's what he told me. Through algorithms and analyzing metadata, searches, interests, posts, and profiles. They look for people with certain, well, gifts."

I wondered if that might be connected somehow to the equations represented in the hallways.

Someone with the gift for solving equations just like me might have created them.

Tane glances at the window, then back at me. "Do you know what floor we're on?"

"The ground floor, I guess." A bird lands on one of the branches, chirps lightly, then starts to strut back and forth.

"Keep an eye on the bird," Alysha says. "Two more chirps and it'll fly away. Give it ten seconds or so."

I watch the bird and wait.

Within a few seconds it chirps once, then after a short pause, it does so again before lifting softly into flight.

Astonished, I turn to her. "How did you know that?"

"Every hour and five minutes it lands there. It's on a loop."

"A loop?" I walk to the window and put my hand against the glass. "This is just a video screen?"

"Yes."

"It's amazing. It's so realistic."

"So, do you have any idea where we are?" Tane asks. "The last I heard, Malcolm was going to bring me to Atlanta, but I'm not sure if that's where we ended up."

I'm still intrigued by Alysha's observation about the bird. "How did you realize the video is on a loop? I mean, I could see if it happened over the span of a few minutes, but you're saying it's over an hour?"

Tane gestures toward the monitors on the wall. "There's a time marker on the security cameras."

"But still."

"I heard it," she tells me.

"And you remembered it?"

She shrugs. "I just tend to remember things pretty well. That's all."

"That's incredible."

"Everyone's a virtuoso at something. It's just that some people haven't discovered their instrument yet. Mine is listening."

Everyone's a virtuoso at something.

Huh, I like it.

What about you?

Math?

I guess that would be my instrument.

As we wait for Malcolm to return, the conversation shifts from the gift of noticing what other people miss to how that affects the dreams we have.

Alysha starts talking about her nightmares, and I'm especially interested in what she has to say since she doesn't have visual dreams.

No images.

No colors.

"I was born blind so I've never seen anything, but I hear things and feel pressure in my dreams. Like, for example, I'm terrified of wasps. So I sometimes have a nightmare where I hear them circling around my head and I can feel them crawling on my face and my neck, but, obviously, I can't see where they are so I can't stop them or swat them away."

Then she asks us to tell her about our nightmares.

I go first, starting with that dream of the boy and the bats.

• • •

Kyle left the field house.

Nothing.

He'd even snuck into the locker rooms and wandered into the reception area of the office, where a bearded guy in his mid-twenties was filing the basketball camp registration forms.

He looked up at Kyle and asked somewhat brusquely if he needed anything.

"No. I'm just looking for someone."

"Well, no one's come through here."

"You've been here all morning?"

"I'm the receptionist. So. Yes."

"Right."

Although it was possible that the coaches would have noticed Daniel's absence, with so many basketball players, it would be easy for someone to slip through the cracks without drawing too much attention.

On his way to the fountain to meet the girls, Kyle texted them: *Nada. You?*

Mia responded first: *No.*

Then, Nicole: *He's not in the cafeteria.*

Nicole was waiting for him at the fountain and a minute or so later Mia walked up and asked, "What should we do now?"

"I guess we go to campus security after all," Kyle replied. "I'm not sure where else to look."

Using his phone, he pulled up a map of the university, located the security office on the far side of campus, and the three of them headed toward it.

CHAPTER
TWENTY-EIGHT

Malcolm still hasn't returned.

"He said he was only going to be gone for a couple minutes, right?" Alysha's concern is clear in her voice. "Where do you think he is?"

I study the bank of security footage monitors on the wall. "Tane, do you still have that key card?"

"Yeah."

I head to the monitors. "Swipe it on this reader to open up the files."

He does, unlocking the screen and allowing us to review the footage.

"I saw you earlier on here," he says, "when you were wandering the halls."

"I wasn't wandering."

"What were you doing?"

"Memorizing."

The interface is pretty user-friendly, so it's not too tough to pick up how to navigate through the current feeds, especially since the monitors all have touch screens.

I scroll through the various cameras, but don't see Malcolm.

As I review the hallways, I take a moment to explain to Tane and Alysha what I discovered about the equations represented by the arrangement of the tiles on the floor.

Before I can finish, however, Tane, who's swiping through files on the screen next to mine, cuts in. "What is this?" There's a mixture of anger and shock in his voice. "They've got archives here with our names on 'em. Some of these go back months."

"Months?" Alysha says. "That doesn't make sense."

"Yeah, I know, long before we ever got here. He has footage that was taken from, I don't even know . . . um—" He taps the icon for a file of his from Saturday night. "That's when I was still in L.A."

Footage comes up of him in a rundown apartment. By the angle, the video was evidently being shot from a phone that he's holding at his side: A woman is shouting at him threateningly, waving a half-empty bottle of whisky. He plucks a pack of cigarettes off the counter and clomps out of the room as she yells for him to bring back her smokes *now*!

"He hacked into my phone and turned on the camera," Tane mutters. "Maybe that's how he found me on that street corner. But I know I had my cell off when I got there . . . At least I thought I did."

There are both audio and video files of all three of us.

Although I'm curious to find out what conversations of mine Malcolm has been listening in on, I'm more interested in the video records of a boy named Liam and a girl named Jess.

"Did Malcolm ever mention any other kids to you?" I ask.

Both Alysha and Tane tell me no.

All of the footage appears to have been taken here at this facility.

I play the first one of Jess.

April 18, 7:17 p.m.

She's a dark-haired girl who looks a little younger than us. The video begins with her sitting on the couch, here in the apartment. Malcolm is standing beside her.

By their conversation it's obvious that she only recently arrived and he's trying to put her at ease.

"You have a gift that is very rare."

"I don't know anything about it being a gift. I'd call it more of a curse."

"Have you heard the story about the Chinese farmer's son?"

"Uh-uh."

"Well, there was a Chinese farmer whose stallion ran away one day across the border to where a group of nomads lived. When the people from the farmer's village tell him that he must be cursed, he says, 'Who's to say it's not a blessing?' So then, about a month later the stallion returns with a mare beside it. All of his friends comment on his good fortune that he now has two horses rather than just one, but he says, 'Who's to say it's not a curse?' Well, his son goes riding all the time on that new mare, and one day he falls and breaks his leg so badly that he can't walk anymore without a cane. Then when the people try to sympathize with the farmer, he says, 'Who's to say it's not a blessing?' So time goes by and war breaks out with the people from beyond the border, and all the men from the farmer's village who're able to fight go into battle, but since the boy has this disability he can't go. Most of the men die in that war but the boy survives and is able to care for his father even into his old age. And so, curses and blessings—who's to say which is which?"

"And that's the point of your story? That it's impossible to tell them apart?"

"No. We've brought you here to help turn what appears to be a curse to you into a blessing for others."

"Like with the son."

"Exactly."

"But he had to become disabled first."

Malcolm hesitates. "Yes. He did."

We check out a few more of Jess's videos.

Things do not end well for her.

She begins calling out to people who aren't there, then batting her arms through the air at something only she can see.

It's troubling to watch how quickly her blurs overwhelm her, until in her last video, Malcolm is standing by himself in the geometrically tiled hallway watching as someone in a white coat wheels Jess toward the elevator.

She's strapped down and shrieking something about someone named Sam.

Based on the patterns on the floor I can tell they're on B1. We pull up Liam's footage.

His mental deterioration happens even more quickly.

At the end of the second video, he breaks a lava lamp that looks identical to the one here in the apartment, grabs one of the glass shards, and starts going to work on his left arm with it.

A thin jet of glistening blood spurts from his wrist and sprays onto the wall.

Malcolm has to wrestle him down and twist his wrist backward to get him to drop the glass.

During their struggle, Liam rakes the glass shard across Malcolm's face, giving him the cut that turned into the scar I noticed earlier.

The whole time, Liam is laughing in a wild, unsettling way.

There are only three videos of him.

In the third one, he's being rolled away as well.

Though she can't see the images, Alysha can hear the guy's mad laughter as the video ends. "Is that what's going to happen to us?" she asks softly.

"No," I tell her. "Because we're getting out of here. Malcolm should have been back by now. Something's wrong. He told me that we needed to find the senator's daughter before nine o'clock, and that's never going to happen if we don't get moving."

She picks up her cane, a white stick about a yard long, and then asks me, "Do you trust him?"

"I don't know, but I believe him, and right now I think that's what matters most."

Tane brings the key card so we can get into the other rooms. "So, split up or stay together?"

"Stay together." Alysha is tapping her cane in front of her on the way to the door. "Bad things always happen to teenagers in situations like this when they split up."

CHAPTER TWENTY-NINE

The campus safety officer stared at Kyle over the top of his wire-rimmed glasses from where he sat on the other side of the counter. "So, how long has your friend been missing?"

"We don't know, exactly. He was supposed to meet me this morning for breakfast, but he didn't show up."

"Maybe he slept in."

"I checked. He wasn't in his room."

"Well, maybe he went for a walk."

"We looked all over."

"Does he have someone he knows in the area? Someone he might have gone to meet?"

"We're from Wisconsin. He's never been to the South before."

The cop shifted his gaze to Nicole and Mia. "You girls know of anyone?"

"No," Nicole said, but then backpedaled a little. "I mean, I don't *think* he knows anyone down here."

"You don't think he does."

"Right."

"Listen," Mia cut in. "This is serious."

"And so is you being here. Before I send out a car or dispatch officers to look for your friend, I need to make sure this isn't some kind of prank."

"It isn't a prank."

"Have you tried calling his phone?"

Kyle produced it from his pocket. "He left it in his room. The last text he opened was at 10:46 last night from someone telling him to answer a call, but there's no indication that one came in."

"Who sent the text?"

"No number shows up when you open it. You can check it for yourself."

"I'll take your word for it." He sighed heavily as if he was really going out of his way to do this, then shuffled through a stack of forms, pulled one out, and jotted a few things down.

He asked for Daniel's full name, date of birth, address, and a physical description. Kyle handed over Daniel's driver's license to save time.

"Where did you get this?"

"It was in his room. In his wallet."

"Along with his phone?"

"That's right."

The cop was quiet for a moment. "Let me ask you a question: Has your friend ever tried to hurt himself?"

"What?" Nicole said. "What do you mean?"

"Self-harm. Cutting. Suicide attempts. Anything along those lines."

"No. He would never do that."

"You're sure?"

"Yes. Absolutely."

"Alright."

To Kyle, it didn't sound like the officer necessarily believed her, but the man moved on and asked him, "You said you got this wallet from his room. What dorm is he staying in?"

"Berringer Hall. Room 303."

The man noted it on the form. "Is there anything else I should know? Anything else that might be helpful for us in finding him?"

Kyle wondered if he should tell him that Daniel sometimes hallucinated and ran in front of trucks as they sped down the highway, but decided that it probably wasn't going to help them locate his friend. He could always fill him in more later if he needed to.

When none of them spoke up, the officer agreed to contact the residence hall director and the coaches in charge of the camp to see if they knew anything, then ended by reassuring them, "I'm sure your friend is fine."

"What makes you say that?" Nicole asked.

"These things happen all the time. They never turn out to be anything serious. Maybe he just met some girl last night and—"

"That's not what happened."

"Alright, alright. Whatever you say. So, how can I reach you if I find out anything?"

She gave him her number and the three friends left the office.

Outside the building, Mia swore, and then began ranting about how much that cop pissed her off. "He didn't take anything we had to say seriously." But then her tone changed in a way that was hard for Kyle to read. "Unless you count him asking about if Daniel might have hurt himself."

Nicole folded her arms in defiance. "Well, we can't just sit around and do nothing. We have to keep looking."

"Do you think I should call my aunt? Tell her what's up?"

Kyle shook his head. "We still don't know what's going on, that's the thing. All we know is that Daniel isn't here. I don't want Sue Ellen or his parents to worry, especially if it's nothing serious. Let's just see if we can find him."

"Where else do you think we should look?"

"I . . . I'm not sure."

They all thought about it, and finally Nicole turned to Kyle. "You know how that cop in there asked if there was anyone in the area who Daniel might have gone to meet?"

"Yeah, but like I told him, Daniel's never been down here before."

"Right, but what if somebody went to meet *him*?"

"What do you mean?"

"Remember last winter? That guy Malcolm Zacharias? When we helped him out of that snowbank, his car had Georgia plates. Then there's this text message on Daniel's phone and the lack of a phone call. We already know that Zacharias was able to get in and delete records of calls—he did it with my phone in December. Plus, there's this anonymous person who paid for Daniel to come down and attend the camp."

"You think that was Zacharias?"

"I don't know, but whoever did that might be our link to where Daniel is now."

"So," Mia said, "you're thinking that if we can find Zacharias, he can lead us to Daniel?"

"I mean, it's worth a shot. I don't know what else to try at this point."

"But Zacharias didn't seem very excited about being found last winter. How are we supposed to track him down now?"

Nicole chewed on the side of her lip, deep in thought. "When we checked Daniel in, over in the dorm lobby last night, the director had all the basketball players' registration forms with him. Well, there must be a record somewhere of who paid Daniel's fee. I say we start with those forms."

Kyle nodded. "I might be able to help with that. When I was looking for Daniel earlier, I saw the receptionist in the field house office filing them."

"Okay." Mia looked back and forth from Kyle to Nicole. "So how do we get in there to have a look at them?"

"We'll need a way to distract him," Kyle replied.

Nicole's eyes lit up. "You know, I might have an idea, but first we'll need the name of one of the guys in the camp, and maybe where he's from." She started toward the cafeteria.

"Where are we going?"

"It's almost lunchtime. They'll all be standing around or getting in line. It'll be easy pickings."

CHAPTER THIRTY

Following the mental map that I formed earlier during my trek through the labyrinthine hallways, we begin to systematically search this level for Malcolm.

Tane uses the key card to access rooms.

We find a kitchen, a rec room, bathrooms, and more dormitory-type rooms similar to the one I woke up in. None of the rooms are labeled. All of them are empty.

Tane shakes his head. "Man, someone went to a lot of trouble designing and constructing this place."

"Yes," I agree. "They did. But why?"

"Your guess is as good as mine."

After checking two more rooms, I've had enough. "Listen, let's go back to the apartment and scroll through the footage from the moment Malcolm left. It should be archived. We can follow him camera-to-camera, see where he went. Track him down that way."

As we retrace our steps, I'm impressed that Alysha only has to tap her cane intermittently, and is still able to stay in the center of the walkway.

"Do you think this might be some kind of test?" she asks me. "I mean, him leaving us alone to see what we can figure out?"

"I don't think so. Not if there really is a tight deadline and someone's life is on the line." As we walk across the algorithms formed by the coded symbols, it gets me thinking. "Listen, does math come easily for either of you?"

"I've never really been too into it." Tane shrugs. "But, yeah. I'd say it does."

"Me too," Alysha replies. "Why?"

"I'm wondering if that analytical ability has something to do with our blurs. Maybe there's a part of our brains that takes the images or the sounds and makes sense of them. Malcolm mentioned cohesion to me. Order out of chaos. So, math. Logic. Maybe those are some of the skills we need for this to happen."

"That's possible."

We reach an intersection and Alysha begins to turn, just at the right time, remembering how many steps we'd taken since passing through here earlier.

"Do either of you sleepwalk?" I ask.

Tane tells me no, but Alysha says that she sometimes does.

He looks at her quizzically. "Do blind people sleepwalk? Really?"

"Sure, why not?"

"Well, I mean, they can't see where they're going, and—"

"And what? We *never* see where we're going. We have spatial understanding, though. I probably don't imagine things quite the same way you do, but if you were to describe where the furniture in a room is, I could make my way past it. I do the same when I'm sleeping. But now you've got me wondering—what's it like for you guys when you have a blur?"

"It's the same as experiencing anything else," I explain, "except the blurs are usually pretty shocking. I've seen dead bodies come to life, heard them speak to me, even had them reach out and clutch my arm."

"Have you seen any recently?

"Any?"

"Dead bodies?"

"I saw one in my attic last week. It looked just like me."

"Whoa."

"A couple days before that I saw a boy who wasn't there. He was standing in the road and I tried to save him from an oncoming truck. He disappeared at the last second and the truck hit me. That's how I dislocated my shoulder."

"What about your leg?"

"My leg?"

"You favor one leg. Did you hurt it in the accident?"

"Actually, my ankle. Yes. How did you know that?"

"When you walk. I can hear your gait. It's uneven."

Man, she's good.

We get back to the room and Tane and I immediately head to the monitors to see if we can get some answers about where Malcolm went.

• • •

Kyle waited outside the cafeteria as Nicole and Mia entered and got in the lunch line behind a bunch of guys from the basketball camp.

The girls had told him to give them five minutes.

"Should be more than enough time," Nicole had said, then smiled and motioned for Mia to walk with her. "Come on, Mia, let's go."

• • •

We discover that Malcolm stood just around the corner from this room talking on the phone for ninety-one seconds before leaving for the elevator.

As I'm trying to find footage from an interior elevator camera, or at least figure out what floor he might have exited on to, Tane grabs my arm and points to another screen. "Look."

Movement.

But it's not Malcolm.

"That's a live feed," he says.

"Level B1. That's the level where I woke up."

Alysha asks what's going on.

"There's someone here," I tell her.

"Who?"

"I don't know."

The towering man in the video walks stealthily down the empty hallway. When he pivots toward the camera, I see that he's carrying a handgun.

And I recognize him.

Last winter he introduced himself to me as Detective Poehlman, though he never mentioned what police department he worked for. He questioned me when my dad was attacked.

At the time, he'd acted somewhat suspiciously and even then I wasn't sure he was a real detective.

I'm even less sure of it now.

"We need to get out of here."

"Wait." Tane indicates the adjoining screen. "There's another guy."

"Who are they?" Alysha asks.

"Two men. Both armed."

"What!"

The second intruder is on our level and is approaching this apartment.

I study the screen, evaluate the direction and speed that he's moving and compare that to what I know about the floor plan of the two levels I've walked through. "I think I might know a way out of here. Follow me."

As we cross the room, Tane is by my side. Alysha is right behind us, gauging where we are by the sound of our footsteps.

At the door, I tell them, "Two rights, two lefts and a right and we should be at the elevator."

"How do you know?" Tane asks.

"It's my instrument."

Cautiously, we enter the hallway.

Clear.

I take the lead, with Alysha between me and Tane.

As we follow the route and make the turns, we don't see anyone—

Until that final hallway.

Just as I'm glancing around the corner to make sure it's clear, I catch sight of that second man coming this way.

I leap backward, grabbing Alysha's hand to pull her back as well.

"What is it?" She keeps her voice low.

"He's coming. He might have seen me."

"What do we do?"

"We need to get past him if we're going to get to the elevator. It's the only—"

Wait. What wouldn't he expect?

What—

There's a room right behind her.

"Tane, use the key card. Open that door. You and Alysha go in. I'll lure the guy in front of it. When I yell 'Now!' I want you to jump out and punch him as hard as you can. When you do, I'll go for the gun."

"That's your plan?" Alysha exclaims. "What kind of a plan is that? You'll lure the guy and—" She cuts herself off, listens. "He's close. We need to do something."

"Get in the room. Hurry."

Somewhat reluctantly, Tane swipes the card, the door opens, and they disappear inside.

Hurrying to the other side of the hallway, I drop to the floor and sprawl out, pretending to be unconscious.

I figure that the man might shoot at someone who was confronting him or even running away, but I'm banking on the fact that he won't shoot me while I'm lying on the floor.

His curiosity should play in our favor.

At least I'm hoping it will.

I hear him come around the corner.

His footsteps stop abruptly.

With my eyes open just enough to make him out, I watch as he studies me, assessing things, the gun aimed directly at my chest.

At last, holding his weapon in a tactical position, he edges my way.

As he does, I notice that Tane has cracked the door open slightly.

No, that wasn't the plan. He's supposed to wait. He needs to—

But then I have to close my eyes as the man arrives at my side, then nudges my leg with his foot.

I remain limp.

A moment later I hear him walk toward the door. "Henrik?"

Opening my eyes again, I see him press it open. As he enters the room, there's a flash of movement—Tane leaping out and punching him once in the gut and then landing a savage uppercut directly to his face.

The guy goes down hard.

By then, I'm on my feet.

Tane grabs Alysha's hand, rushes her out of the room, and we bolt toward the elevator.

"That wasn't the plan," I say.

"I got impatient."

"He still has his gun."

"Yeah, that part sucks."

We whip around the corner.

The elevator is about forty feet away.

"He's coming!" Alysha announces, obviously picking up the sound of his footsteps behind us.

We come skidding to a stop at the elevator doors, I hit the button to open them, and as they part, the man turns the corner and shouts for us not to move.

The doors slide apart.

We dash inside.

I hit the button for the next floor up as he starts sprinting toward us.

Tane pounds the button that's supposed to close the doors, but they don't respond.

"C'mon! C'mon!" He smacks it again.

The man pauses mid-stride, just as the doors begin to glide together.

He slings his gun forward.

Aims.

I step in front of Alysha as the doors close. The sound of gunshots reverberates through the air and four bullets rip into the metal.

"Use the key card," I tell Tane. "Swipe the top floor."

He slides it through the card reader and a blue indicator light blinks on.

"You stepped in front of me." Alysha rests her hand on my good shoulder. "Thank you."

"You're welcome."

And as the sound of more gunshots rings out below us, we begin to ascend.

CHAPTER THIRTY-ONE

We reach the top level and the elevator stops.

Tane and I stand ready, not sure what to expect when the doors open, but when they do, there's no one there.

Instead, we find an empty, wood-paneled room not more than ten feet long and six feet wide with a door on the far side.

Tane strides over and tosses it open. There's a sign emblazoned on the other side: "Authorized Personnel Only."

Beyond the doorway lies a parking garage.

"Talk to me," Alysha says.

"It's just a small room that leads to a parking garage," I tell her.

"Are there any steps? A stairwell to the lower levels? Anything like that?"

"No. Not in here."

She hands her cane to me. "Jam this in where the elevator doors close. If they can't shut, it won't go down and those men won't be able to get up here. It should at least slow them down, buy us some time."

"How are you going to get around without your cane?"

"You can be my eyes."

We wedge the cane in place to keep the doors from closing, then she takes my arm, holding it just above my elbow, and we leave the paneled room.

"So we're in a parking garage?" she asks me.

"Yes. There are seventy-two cars visible, so wherever we are, it's busy. It looks like we might be on the ground—"

"Hang on. I hear something. A phone." Her words are urgent. "That's the same ringtone from Malcolm's phone before he disappeared."

I can't hear anything.

"Don't you hear it? Either of you?"

"No," I say.

Tane shakes his head. "Uh-uh."

"It's . . ." She points ahead of us and slightly to the left. "Hurry! We need to find it before it stops ringing."

We run maybe thirty-five feet, but I still can't hear the phone. By the look on Tane's face, I can tell he can't either.

"Wait." Alysha pauses, tilts her head slightly to the side, concentrates, then points again, this time further left. "Go!"

We head in that direction and when we're about halfway to the cars parked along the wall, I finally hear the ringtone echoing faintly off the concrete.

But then a moment later, I don't.

"It stopped." She swears, something I don't expect, then gestures toward the wall. "It's somewhere over there. I can't tell how far. The acoustics in here are all screwed up."

"Malcolm?" Tane shouts. His voice echoes hollow and vacant through the garage. "Are you there?"

No reply.

Alysha tells us to keep looking. "I know that was the same ringtone. He might be hurt."

Tane and I scour the area, but find nothing.

I'm about to give up when he hollers that he's got it.

I lead Alysha over to him.

He's standing between a sedan and a white minivan holding Malcolm's phone, swiping across the screen to check the calls. "That was someone named Brad Amundsen. He's listed under Malcolm's favorites."

"I don't know the senator's first name," I tell them, "but Malcolm mentioned the last name of Amundsen. That might be him."

"The reception in here is gonna suck. Besides, we should probably take off before whoever was shooting at us finds a way out. C'mon."

He starts for the exit.

With Alysha and me by his side.

•　•　•

Kyle watched as Mia and Nicole emerged from the cafeteria.

Both were smiling.

"Benjamin Jameson," Nicole announced. "He's a junior from Athens, Georgia. Likes avocados, hip-hop, and zombie movies. Goes by 'Jamin' for short."

"How did you get all that?"

"We looked for a guy who couldn't keep his eyes off us. Then we just smiled demurely, giggled girlishly, peered at him with doe-like, wide-eyed innocence, and asked him what his name was."

"That's all it took?"

"At first he just told us 'Jamin,'" Mia explained, "but I winked at him and said 'We need your last name too if we're gonna be able to find you after camp tonight to party.' From there it was a done deal."

Nicole held out her arm. A phone number was written in pen on her wrist. "He could hardly write it down fast enough."

"You girls are good," Kyle said.

Mia scoffed lightly. "Guys are sheep."

"Come on." Nicole pointed toward the field house. "Let's go find that registration form."

CHAPTER THIRTY-TWO

Outside the parking garage, the day is bright and starkly hot, especially compared to the cool air of the subterranean hallways we just came from.

Traffic rushes by. Skyscrapers tower around us. Pedestrians hurry past.

"Where are we?" Alysha has her face upturned toward the sunlight.

"I don't recognize the skyline," I tell her. "It's a major city, though. We're downtown near a park. There are some fountains. A Ferris wheel."

A woman is walking toward us, and when she's about ten feet away, Alysha calls to her, "Excuse me, Ma'am. I'm a little bit turned around. Can you tell me what park this is?"

"Centennial Olympic Park."

"And what city would that be in?"

The woman stares at us strangely. "You're in Atlanta, dear."

"Thank you."

After she has gone on her way again, Tane says to Alysha, "You called her 'Ma'am.' How did you know it was a woman?"

"She's wearing high heels."

"You heard them on the sidewalk?"

"Didn't you?"

"Right, well . . ." He looks impressed and lets his eyes linger on Alysha for a moment, then studies the park. "Atlanta fits in with what Malcolm told me. Now that we know where we are, let's try to figure out where he is."

I ask him if I can see the phone. As he hands it to me he asks what I'm thinking.

"It's not just Malcolm we need to find, it's the senator's daughter too. Petra. I figure we call Brad Amundsen back and find out whatever we can."

The phone's screen isn't locked and I scroll to the recent calls, hit "Reply," and after one ring, someone picks up. A man's voice: "Malcolm, do you have them?"

"Is this Senator Amundsen?" I ask him.

"Yes. Who is this?"

"Daniel Byers. Something happened to Malcolm. We're not sure where he is. I'm one of the people he brought in to help."

"You're Daniel? From Wisconsin?"

"Yes." I'm not sure if I should be thrilled or not that he's heard of me. "We want to help find Petra—Malcolm told us she was taken."

"Who is *we*?"

"Alysha and Tane are with me."

A brief pause. "Where are you now?"

"Downtown Atlanta. Centennial Olympic Park."

"Alright. I have some people in the area. I'll send a car to pick you up. My house is about forty minutes from where you are. We'll talk more when you get here. Until then, I don't want to chance that someone might be listening in, so don't contact me. And whatever you do, don't call the police. The people who have Petra said they'll know if we do. They said they'll kill her."

"Okay."

He gives me the name of two streets that meet at an intersection nearby and tells us to be there in ten minutes.

"Don't be late."

"We won't."

CHAPTER THIRTY-THREE

12:00 P.M.
9 HOURS UNTIL THE DEADLINE

Flanked by Mia and Nicole, Kyle approached the field house.

"So, talk me through this one last time," he said.

"I go in first," Mia replied, with a somewhat impatient sigh. "I get the guy to leave, you two sneak in, find the info on who paid for Daniel's registration, and cruise before anyone sees you."

Through the windows, he could see that the same receptionist from earlier was still at work, now typing on his keyboard.

Kyle turned to Nicole. "Listen, you're better at computers than I am. While I look for the registration form, see what you can pull up from their system. There's got to be some sort of financial program or something that tells who paid for the players' tuition."

"Perf."

"I can *maybe* get him to go down to the locker rooms," Mia informed them, "but don't count on him being gone for more than three or four minutes, tops."

"And when he finds out Benjamin Jameson isn't hurt?" Kyle asked.

"I'll improvise."

Kyle and Nicole waited out of sight around the corner while Mia threw open the office door and rushed inside. "Hey, we need your help. My brother's hurt and they have to take him to the hospital!"

The receptionist looked up from the screen. "Your brother?"

"Benjamin Jameson, from Athens, Georgia. Get his medical release form. Now. Come on! Hurry! They said they need you to bring it over!"

The guy rifled through the drawer of forms, pulled one out, and then hustled after her down the hallway.

As soon as they were gone, Kyle and Nicole slipped inside.

Kyle thumbed through the papers looking for Daniel's paperwork while Nicole took a seat in front of the computer and clicked her way to the program registry.

"You gotta be kidding me," Kyle exclaimed. "How could these things not be in alphabetical order?"

"Are you serious?" She was scrolling through the files.

"There must be three hundred campers. How did that guy find Jamin's so quick—wait."

"What is it?"

"The forms are listed under the states where the guys are from."

He went to the back of the drawer.

And flipped to Wisconsin.

• • •

A black, impeccably polished executive car pulls up to the curb at the corner where Senator Amundsen had directed us to go.

Considering Tane's size, there isn't a whole lot of room in the backseat for all three of us, so he takes shotgun and Alysha and I climb into the back.

• • •

"Gotcha." Kyle snatched up Daniel's registration form and glanced it over for any info about who'd paid his fees. "Okay, so the payment came from the Marly Weathers Foundation."

"What's that?"

"No idea. Do you have anything yet?"

"This computer's a dinosaur. It's taking forever to—hang on . . . let me search under that name. You said Weathers?"

"Yeah, Marly: M-a-r-l-y. And Daniel's form is 178b. Maybe plug that in, or his room number in Berringer Hall—303."

Outside the window to the hallway, Kyle noticed Mia and the receptionist returning.

"Hurry, Nikki." He folded up Daniel's form and stuffed it into his pocket.

"Wait." She typed furiously.

"There isn't time."

"Hang on, just—yes. Okay."

"They're right outside the door. C'mon!"

Nicole whipped out her phone, snapped a picture of the screen, and quit the program. She leapt up, but before they could get out of the room, the receptionist started opening the door.

Kyle pulled Nicole toward him and they flattened their backs against the wall. He just hoped the guy wouldn't glance to the side or he'd see them just a few feet away.

Mia was walking beside him saying, "I don't know what happened. They must have gone on to the hospital already."

"Uh-huh."

When she saw her friends, her eyes grew large.

Quickly, she repositioned herself so the receptionist wouldn't look past her and notice them.

"Well," he said to Mia, "I'll give the head coach and the trainer a call. In the meantime, why don't you just wait in that chair right over—" He started to turn.

"Um . . ." She drew him close and kissed him on the lips, while gesturing urgently with one hand for Kyle and Nicole to get out of the room.

They crept past the guy—who didn't seem to be in too huge of a hurry to pull away from Mia.

As they were escaping into the hall, Kyle heard him say, somewhat breathlessly, "What are you doing?"

"Sorry." Mia patted his cheek, spun on her heels, and headed out the door, leaving him staring dumbfounded after her. "Wrong vibe."

They regrouped by a flowerbed around the side of the building.

"Kissing him?" Kyle said. "That's what you call improvising?"

"I had to think on my feet."

"He didn't seem to mind too much."

"Well, what's not to—wait. You're—are you jealous, babe? That is so adorable of you."

"But how did you know he'd close his eyes when you kissed him? Wait, lemme guess—guys are sheep."

"Now you're catching on. So, anyway, what'd you two get? Please tell me I didn't kiss that receptionist for no reason."

Kyle held up Daniel's registration form. "The camp fee and the debit card both came from something called the Marly Weathers Foundation—whatever that is."

Nicole pulled up the photo she'd taken of the computer screen. "I've got an address here from where the camp registrar sent the receipt. It's in Philly. And there's also an email address."

"So what now?" Mia asked. "It's not like we're gonna be able to go to Philadelphia. And Marly Weathers isn't Malcolm Zacharias—unless, who knows. Maybe he is?"

"I say we find out all we can about this foundation."

"Hold on a sec," Kyle held up his hand. "That's a good idea, but I'm still in my running clothes and I could use a shower and some food—I never did get any breakfast. Let's head back to Sue Ellen's house. I'll clean up and change, then we can grab some lunch and figure out where to take things from there."

"That'll work," Mia said.

As they started across campus toward the car, Kyle shook his head. "I still can't believe you kissed that guy."

"I'll make it up to you later."

"I can work with that."

"Stay focused, you two," Nicole chided them. "There'll be time for all that after we find Daniel."

CHAPTER
THIRTY-FOUR

I ask Senator Amundsen's driver if he can tell us anything, but he just explains that the senator will fill us in when we get there.

Now, as he maneuvers us through the hectic city traffic, I explore Malcolm's phone, but most of the apps, including the address book and email, are locked or password protected.

The camera works, though.

It makes me think of Kyle's hypothesis about being able to use photos to tell what's real and what isn't—but since I'm not having a blur at the moment, it's not exactly the ideal time to put things to the test.

I briefly consider calling my friends or my parents to tell them what's going on, but then I realize that wouldn't be a good idea—for all sorts of reasons.

After all, Malcolm remotely monitored our phones. Who's to say that someone couldn't do it with his as well? And not that long ago, a man was trying to kill us. The people he worked with could go after whoever I might call.

Also, it's possible that getting more people involved will put Petra's life at even greater risk, especially if her kidnappers were to suspect that someone had called the cops—and calling my dad would definitely fall into that category.

Yeah, best to hold off from calling anyone, at least for the time being.

"What are you thinking?" Alysha asks me.

"That we have a lot more questions now than we did earlier."

"Go on."

"Well, why the mathematical equations in the hallways and the video monitors? How long was Malcolm planning on keeping us down there? Who was shooting at us, and how did he and his buddy find that place?"

"And what happened to Malcolm?"

"Yeah. That's the big one. What happened to Malcolm."

I'm not sure how much I want to get into everything here with the driver listening to us, but I figure that if the senator can trust him, so can we.

Tane turns toward Alysha and me. "Let's talk this through. Malcolm tracks us down from all over the country and brings us to this secret, I don't know, base or whatever, hidden in downtown Atlanta. He tells us he wants us to save someone else who has blurs, that she was kidnapped."

"Petra Amundsen," Alysha says.

"Right. And we only have until nine o'clock tonight to do it."

"Okay. And?"

"And, why is all this happening right now? I mean, Malcolm first contacted me in November. Why wait until June to bring all of us together? Not to mention that suddenly, when he does, Petra goes missing. Doesn't that seem a little too convenient to you? Like too much of a coincidence?"

"Maybe." I consider that. "But I think it's safe to say that whatever's going on here, it's bigger than just us. Remember, Malcolm mentioned Dr. Waxford doing tests on prisoners. Why would he have brought that up unless it was related to everything else?"

"Yeah, what was all that about, anyway? He said you knew about him?"

I explain about Dr. Waxford and the chronobiology research. I also tell them that I recognized Detective Poehlman on the video monitor and that he'd showed up in Wisconsin around the same time Dr. Waxford disappeared.

Tane looks confused. "But how does that relate to Malcolm?"

"Last winter when I first met him, Malcolm told me his agency was trying to stop Waxford."

"And what agency is that?"

"Maybe the same one that built that maze of hallways under that parking garage."

• • •

Back at Sue Ellen's place, Kyle finished his shower, got dressed, and met up with the girls in the kitchen.

Mia's aunt had left some eggplant parmesan, watermelon, and fresh strawberries for them on the counter.

"All the fixin's are there," she told them pleasantly. "It's a do-it-yourself lunch. Go ahead and fill yerselves up, now."

They thanked her, heaped some food onto the china that she insisted they use, and moved to the dining room to do some research while they ate.

"When you were showering," Mia said to him, "Nikki and I looked up the Marly Weathers Foundation. Mainly they give scholarships, help with academic after-school programs, that sort of thing. It all looks pretty innocent and legit. There wasn't any mention of a Malcolm Zacharias in the staff directory on their website."

As they ate, they picked up the research where Nicole and Mia had left off, surfing on their phones and poring over the Marly Weathers Foundation website. When they were about halfway through with lunch, Nicole said, "Kyle, do you still have Daniel's wallet?"

"Sure. Why?"

"What about that debit card? The one from whoever was paying for the travel costs to get him down here?"

"What about it?"

"Could we use it to find out who he is? I mean, the person who preloaded the card?"

"How?"

"There's usually a phone number on the back for you to call if there's an emergency or if the card gets stolen or lost."

"Yeah, now there's a brilliant idea." Mia took a bite of watermelon. "Include a number on the back of a card for you to call when you longer have the card. Am I the only one who sees the flawed logic in that one?"

"But it might just help us this time, though." Nicole turned to Kyle again. "Zacharias is a guy so it'll probably be best if you make the call—in case it's his card. Pretend you lost it or something's wrong with it. See what you can find out."

"It's upstairs. Let me go grab it."

• • •

Dr. Adrian Waxford was at his desk studying the transcriptions of what subject #832145, the serial killer from Wisconsin, had been muttering to himself over the last few weeks, when Henrik called on the satellite phone.

Adrian picked up. "Yes?"

"We have him."

"Who? Zacharias?"

"Yes. He put up a bit of a fight, but we got him."

"How did you find him?"

"Tracked the SUV he was driving. It was purchased through Gatlinburg Holdings, which has connections to the foundation in Philly that we were looking into."

"Good work."

"The kids got away, though."

"Kids?"

"The video footage we found showed three of 'em. Byers, a blind girl, and an islander kid. Sergei confirmed it. He took a few shots at 'em, but they made it to the elevator."

"He shot at them?"

"If we have Zacharias and Petra, we have all we need, right? Wouldn't it be best to just get rid of any loose ends?"

"Perhaps. Hmm. I'll need to think that over. For now, bring Zacharias here to the Estoria. It'll give us a chance to get some answers before General Gibbons arrives."

"The general is coming down?"

"She wants to see the facility for herself in preparation for the oversight committee meeting."

A slight pause. "Do you think that's a good idea?"

"I'm afraid it's out of our hands. If the situation becomes unmanageable we can always move our base of operation. The renovations we made allow us that option."

"You mean use the rapid oxidation system. Burn down the Estoria."

"Only if necessary. We've had to start over before. It's not ideal, but I'll do whatever I have to do to keep this research going. Justice depends on it."

As he spoke, he made sure that the 9mm handgun in his desk drawer was loaded and had a bullet in the chamber.

"But the research depends on funding."

"True enough," Adrian acknowledged, sliding the drawer shut again.

"However, we probably won't have too much trouble finding other governments who would pay through the nose for your findings."

"That is true as well."

"Alright, I'm going to drop Sergei off at the house in Knoxville, but I should still be able to get to the Estoria by around five o'clock."

"We'll have a room waiting for Mr. Zacharias on the fourth floor."

After ending the call, Adrian looked at the bone-carved camel figurines on his desk and the vial of Telpatine that sat beside them.

Think outside the box.

Burn down the Estoria? Really?

Well, if necessary. Yes.

Sometimes unorthodox measures were required in the pursuit of doing what is right.

• • •

Kyle called the number on the back of the debit card and navigated his way past a series of automated prompts. When he finally got through to a real person, he said, in his best irritated adult bank-card-user-voice, "Yes, I'd like to report a problem with my card. It keeps getting declined but I think it should still have money on it."

"Alright." The woman didn't sound a whole lot more personable than the prerecorded messages he'd just finished listening to. "May I have the card number, please?"

He read it off.

"And the security code."

He gave it to her.

"And what's the billing address for the card's account?"

"The billing address?"

"Yes. To confirm the card's ownership."

"Oh, right. Hold on. We have, um . . . a couple different addresses we use. Let me just check which one this gets billed to."

He lowered the phone and said to the girls, "They need a mailing address. What should I tell 'em?"

"Here." Nicole used her cell to pull up the photo of the receptionist's computer screen and zoomed in on the address of where the receipt had been sent. "Try this."

Back on the line again, Kyle said, "Yeah, okay. Here's the one we have on file."

He told it to her and waited while she entered it.

"Is this Marly Weathers?"

"Yes."

"Ms. Weathers?"

"Mister."

"Oh, I'm sorry. It wasn't entered correctly here. Let me just fix that . . ." She typed. "There. All set. So, now, Mr. Weathers, how may I help you?"

"Right. Can you check the amount on the card?"

"According to our records, you still have $49,911 on that card. Will that be enough, or do you need to transfer more funds from one of your corporate accounts?"

He tried not to let his shock over the dollar amount come through in his voice. "Um, yeah. Maybe transfer some?"

"From which account?"

"How about the biggest one."

Yeah, okay, that was a stupid thing to say.

"The biggest one?" the woman asked curiously.

"Yes." He tried to regroup and sound confident again. "Precisely. And which one would that be, actually?"

"I'm afraid I'll need the email address associated with it to give you any additional information."

Maybe she was onto him.

"Just a sec."

He consulted Nicole's cell and read off the email address of the place in Philadelphia.

"So, Gatlinburg Holdings?" the woman on the phone said.

"Oh. Yes. Of course. Okay. Thanks."

"Did you still want to transfer any funds?"

"Naw. I changed my mind. Okay, have a good day, then."

"But you said the card wasn't working?"

"Um. Yeah. It started to."

"It started to—?"

"Just now, here—"

Okay, that's enough.

He hung up.

"Well?" Nicole asked.

"The card was issued to Marly. There's almost fifty thousand dollars left on it. And there's a company called Gatlinburg Holdings that's related to it somehow—I don't know how. It's another corporate account he has."

"I'm sorry." Mia held up a finger. "Did you just say fifty *thousand* dollars?"

"Yep."

"That could buy a *whole* lot of Fritos."

"Yes, yes, it could."

"So, then, we've got some things to look into." Nicole ticked them off on her fingers. "First: Who's Marly Weathers? Second: What's Gatlinburg Holdings? And third: What do any of these things have to do with Malcolm Zacharias?"

"If anything," Kyle said.

"Yes. If anything."

"Man." Mia was shaking her head. "We are talking a *lot* of Fritos."

"Focus," Nicole told her. "Remember? Daniel? Missing? Your friend? I'll take social media. Mia, you hit Wikipedia. Kyle, Google."

"A Dr Pepper to whoever comes up with the best stuff," Kyle told them.

"But you're the only one who likes Dr Pepper."

"Then I hope I win."

"How about if I win I get to keep that debit card," Mia suggested helpfully.

"Focus."

"Right."

CHAPTER
THIRTY-FIVE

As we drive, Tane tells us about his first blur.

It happened in L.A.

"So, the cops were looking for this guy from my neighborhood. It's, well, let's just say I don't live in a gated community. A drug deal had gone bad and a guy got shot. He was in rough shape."

"Did he make it?" Alysha asks.

"Yeah, he survived, but cops were searching everywhere for the shooter. I'd been following the story, you know, online. Also, this friend of mine had a police radio so we were listening in on that. And then suddenly it was like this voice in my head was telling me things I shouldn't have been able to know. I saw the guy who'd been shot. He was lying right in front of me in the road—I mean, I wasn't there, I was with my buddy in his room, but I saw it like

I would've if I was really at the site of the shooting. And everything became clear."

"Clear?"

"The voice told me to go to this one abandoned building we used to hang out in. I didn't have any idea what I'd find."

"But you went?"

"Yeah. Turns out, the shooter was holed up there. I ended up finding the guy and I had to decide whether or not to turn him in."

"What did you do?" I ask.

"I figured if he'd already shot one person, from there on out it would just get easier to shoot others. So in the end, I called the cops. And they got him."

When he was done, he asked Alysha to tell us about her blurs. "If you don't see anything, how does that work? Is it like your dreams? Your nightmares, where you hear or touch things?"

"I guess. Sort of. I hear people speaking, snippets of conversations, sometimes frightening noises, and then I have to piece it all together to make sense of it. That's how I helped find this girl from Billings who'd been kidnapped. She was twelve. Pandora Hutchinson. And she—"

"Hang on." I don't mean to interrupt her, but the girl's name catches me off-guard. "Did you say her name was Pandora?"

"Yeah. Why?"

"It's just that the myth of Pandora's box has been on my mind the last couple weeks."

"Weird."

"Another coincidence," Tane says.

"If coincidences even exist." Alysha shifts in her seat and her leg brushes against mine. "I think stuff always happens for a reason, even if we can't tell what it is at the time."

"Like with the story of the Chinese farmer's son?"

"Maybe. Yeah. So, well, with Pandora—she lived near me and I was listening to the news stories about her. I didn't go into a trance or anything, but it was like I could hear someone in a coffin and she was crying out and she said his name, the name of the guy who'd taken her, and then buried her. It was almost like I could imagine myself being there, trapped in that coffin, in her place. The scent of cedar. The sweat. The dirt falling between the cracks and landing on my face. Everything."

"Did they find her in time?" There's a slight chill in Tane's voice.

"Yeah. Thank God. I was at school when I had the blur. I started screaming. Freaked everyone out. The public safety officer came to help me. I kept repeating the kidnapper's name and the cop recognized it—I guess they'd already questioned the guy once but then let him go. He was a checkout person at the grocery store where Pandora's family shopped."

Alysha takes a deep breath, then lets it out as if she's trying to help herself relax. "They went to his house and found a shovel with some type of soil on it that led them to the part of the county where she was buried. They were able to use details from my blur to locate her. It was all over the news afterward. I think that's how Malcolm first heard about me."

"So that was your first one?"

"Yes. There were people who were saying I was psychic, but that wasn't it for me. It's not supernatural or paranormal—at least I don't think it is. It's just that my blurs, they help me hear things I wouldn't normally be able to hear and when I decipher them, there are answers embedded inside 'em that I hadn't even realized I'd pieced together."

I nod in agreement, but then realize that, of course, she can't see me doing it. "It's the same for me. So do either of you have any history of this sort of thing happening in your family? Any mental illness? Depression, or—"

Malcolm's phone rings, the same chiming tone as before. Senator Amundsen.

I answer. "Hello?"

"Everything alright with the driver? You're on your way?"

"Yes."

"Listen, I was thinking, is there anything I can do here that would help you out when you arrive? Maybe to facilitate the visions to help you find my daughter?"

"Well, it's probably the same for Petra, but we can't make the blurs—or the visions, whatever—come on command. We only experience them when our minds have images, sounds, details to work with. So as much as you can tell us about her would be helpful. Also, pictures, videos—and especially any info you have about what happened when she disappeared."

"I'll see what I can come up with."

When I'm off the phone again, Tane, Alysha, and I talk through our family histories. They know about a few cases of depression and even schizophrenia among their relatives, but we can't identify any one specific thing that all three of us have in common, other than the fact that we were all going through a stressful time when our blurs first began.

"Before you two came to the center," Alysha says, "Malcolm told me that he couldn't explain for certain why my hallucinations had started, but that adolescence is a time of tremendous change. I mean, obviously it is—developmental, physical, hormonal, all that. Our brain's physiology is developing at an astonishing rate and any of those factors, or a combination of all of them, could be the deciding one. He said he didn't know what was most important in causing the hallucinations. But he did mention what he called the honeybee factor."

"What's that?" I ask her.

"He encouraged me not to think of the hallucinations as being genetically caused, but instead that I was just genetically *predisposed* toward having them. Then, whenever I encounter the right environmental cues, they kick in. Like with a bee sting—you never find out if you're allergic until you're stung. Having a reaction, well, it's partly who you are, partly being at the right place at the right time—or the wrong one, depending on how you look at it. Some people are allergic but are never stung so they never find out. He said the hallucinations require a convergence of genetic predisposition and environmental cues. That's part of what makes all this so rare."

Huh.

Genetics. Family history. Environmental cues. Analytical thinking.

All pieces of the puzzle, one by one falling into place.

Along with pain and tragedy.

Rips in the fabric of reality.

The conversation trails off as we each take some time to process things.

After a little while, Tane yawns a few times, and not long after that, soft snoring drifts from the front seat.

While he rests, I quietly watch Georgia pass by outside the window and Alysha repositions her leg again, softly brushing it against mine.

CHAPTER
THIRTY-SIX

Dr. Adrian Waxford received word from General Gibbons that her flight would touch down at the McGhee Tyson Airport in Knoxville at 4:51 p.m.

That meant that, even with the time it would take to pick up her rental car, fight through Knoxville traffic, and drive up into the mountains, she would probably still arrive at the Estoria Inn by seven.

That should be plenty of time to show her around and then get her on her way to a hotel for the night before Senator Amundsen sent out the email at nine.

Now, as Adrian waited for Henrik to bring in Malcolm Zacharias, he went to see how the newest arrival was adjusting to life at the Estoria.

The man formerly known as Ty Bell was beating his chair desperately, yet futilely, against the one-way mirror.

Adrian watched until the subject finally gave up, collapsed in the corner, buried his face in his hands, and began to weep.

Hmm.

Interesting.

Perhaps he was a little too mentally unstable right now for the Telpatine test.

Zacharias, then?

That was a possibility.

But the more Adrian thought about it, the more he realized that the most profitable test, the most ideal candidate, would be one of the kids that Henrik mentioned were at that center in Atlanta.

With their hallucinations, it would be remarkably instructive to watch how they reacted to the drug. It could provide him with far more pertinent data than a test on someone who did not experience those altered mental states.

He decided to see how things played out, but if there was any way he could test the Telpatine on one of those teens before Sergei found and killed them, it might save him months of research.

• • •

"Okay," Kyle said to the girls. "What do we know?"

Mia went first. "If you believe Wikipedia, Marly Weathers is a reclusive billionaire who lives somewhere in upstate New York."

"Why wouldn't we believe Wikipedia?"

"No one really knows who Mr. Weathers is. There's speculation Marly is really a woman."

"That bank lady on the phone seemed to be confused that I was a guy. They had it listed as Ms. Weathers. So, who knows?"

"Yeah, well, anyway, the foundation is only a couple years old. Same with Gatlinburg Holdings—it was started two years ago. On the surface it looks like it's some sort of investment firm that also promotes—wait, let me pull it up." She went to the site and read, "'We support the community through peer-led education and advocacy programs that equip the next generation to make a positive impact on society.'"

"Does it say how the programs work?"

"It's mainly stuff for students in the Smoky Mountains. Field trips. Nature hikes. Like that. There's an educational center. But there's more: They also do work to stop mental illness in teens and abuses in the juvenile justice system."

"That's random for a nature center," Nicole said.

"Right—I thought the same thing, but all the money comes through this investment firm. I guess it fits, I don't know, but I think I win that debit card. I'm craving some Fritos."

"Didn't we just eat?"

"You can never be too full for a Fritos."

"Shouldn't that be singular? Like a Frito?"

"There's no such thing as a 'Frito.' Fritos is a brand name. Can I just see that bank card for a sec?"

"Not so fast." Kyle turned to Nicole. "What about social media?"

"Nothing so far on Malcolm Zacharias—which is sorta weird. I mean, I can't find *anything* on him—at least not based on what we already know he looks like from seeing him last winter. There's some stuff on that Gatlinburg educational center Mia was talking about and the foundation in Philly. Both seem to be pretty open about what they do, but not really into lots of publicity. What about you?"

"Basically confirmed what you two came up with, except I also found some more stuff on Waxford. Since Zacharias was interested in stopping him, I thought I'd look him up just in case he had anything to do with all this. Probably a dead-end, but there were rumors he was searching for a site in Tennessee to continue his research."

"Interesting."

"So where does that leave us?" Mia asked.

Nicole looked at them thoughtfully. "Well, like you mentioned earlier, Mia, Philadelphia is out of the question, but . . . Gatlinburg is what—only a couple hours away?"

"Probably more like three or four," Kyle answered. "Why?"

"Pull up the site for the educational center and check their hours."

Mia did. "It looks like they close at six thirty in the summer. Are you thinking what I think you're thinking?"

"See how far it is to Gatlinburg."

Kyle consulted his phone. "Almost two hundred miles."

"Wait." Mia flagged her hand in the air. "Slow down. And *why* exactly would we drive two hundred miles to this nature center?"

"Think about what else they do," Nicole said. "Research into mental health for adolescents—that fits with Daniel. And they also work for justice reform."

"And that fits with Waxford," Kyle said.

Mia shook her head. "It's a stretch."

"Also," Nicole added, "wasn't the group that Malcolm works for trying to stop Dr. Waxford's research on prisoners? I mean, that was one of his major deals when he showed up in Wisconsin in December, right?"

"What are you suggesting? We just pop up there to Gatlinburg and start questioning people?"

"We've got the debit card, the address in Philly, the email and the possible connection to Dr. Waxford. The center does educational programs for teens. We're teens. We want to be educated. Voila."

"Can't we be educated from here?"

"We're not going to find Daniel by waiting here or randomly driving around Atlanta. I know it's a little bit of a haul, but there's still time to get up there and make it back tonight—if we leave soon. This is the most solid thing we have."

Kyle wasn't sure exactly where he stood on all this yet so, at least for the moment, he sat back and let the girls sort things out.

Nicole started to pace. "Let's say we head out and maybe the campus cop guy calls us and tells us they found Daniel. So, awesome! Then we just turn around and come back. But if we wait, we won't be able to get up there today to check things out before the center closes. If there's anything we can do to find Daniel, anything at all, we need to do it."

"And a phone call wouldn't suffice?"

"How far do you really think that would get us if someone from there did take Daniel?"

"And contacting the cops?"

"With what we have here? Seriously? We can't even prove that Malcolm Zacharias exists."

Mia looked at Kyle, who shrugged. "She does have a point."

"I hate it when people have points," Mia muttered. "Alright. Lemme go talk to my aunt."

CHAPTER
THIRTY-SEVEN

Tane's snoring doesn't let up, even when we slow down and exit the highway.

"He must need to catch up on his sleep," Alysha whispers.

"I guess so."

"So you've been quiet for a while."

"Just thinking. Looking at the scenery."

"Hey." She pats my knee. "I've been meaning to ask you how you knew there were seventy-two cars back at the parking garage. There couldn't have been time to count them."

"I do it without thinking. Numbers. Math. It's like this constant thing going on in the back of my mind."

"Sure, no, I get that . . ." Our driver makes a turn, taking us onto a quiet country road lined with horse fields. "So, you said you were looking at the scenery. Describe it to me. What do you see?"

"Fourteen horses. Some rolling hills in the background. It all looks really peaceful. Blue sky. White clouds." Then I catch myself. "Wait. That doesn't make a whole lot of sense to you, does it? The colors blue or white."

"Not exactly. Tell me about the sky—not how it looks, but how it makes you feel when you look at it."

"Okay, so let's see. Think of warm sunlight on your face. Or maybe touching velvet or silk with your fingers."

"Okay."

"Now imagine listening to Rush."

"Rush?"

"The band."

"I don't know their music."

"How could you not know Rush?"

"Sorry."

"*Tom Sawyer? Fly by Night? The Spirit of Radio?*"

"Uh-uh."

"Alysha, we're seriously going to need to introduce you to some contemporary culture when all this is done."

"Sorry."

"Okay, well then, think of the most beautiful music you ever heard."

"Mozart."

"Oh. Well, okay. I guess."

"Not a fan of classical music?"

"Not so much, but we'll go with it. So, the sunlight, the silk, the music. That's what the sky is like today out there, only for my eyes."

"It's beautiful." Her voice is soft, almost reverent.

We ride for a couple of minutes in silence.

"Daniel, have you ever heard the story of 'The Country of the Blind' by H. G. Wells?"

"I don't think so."

"It was first published like a hundred years ago. When you said that about the colors not making sense to me, you made me think of it."

"What's it about?"

"Well, it's been a while since I read it—Braille, you know."

"Sure."

"As I remember, there's this mountain climber in the Andes Mountains. I don't know if this is exactly accurate, but I'll just tell it to you. One night he goes out to find some rocks for a shelter or something and ends up slipping down a glacier. He survives, but he discovers that on all sides he's surrounded by these sheer cliffs thousands of feet high. The only thing he can do is make his way down into the valley. Eventually, he comes to some llamas grazing there, and then, farther down, he finds a village. All the homes lie along a single road. Every one of them is windowless and awkwardly built with strange angles. Then he sees the people. When he waves to them, they don't respond. Finally, when they turn their heads, he realizes that they have no eyes—just shriveled slits of skin where their eyeballs should be."

"That reminds me of the type of story a couple of my friends, Kyle and Mia, might tell. For them, the creepier the better. But, sorry—you were saying?"

"Turns out, the climber had heard legends about this place before, but he didn't think they were true. According to the stories, all the people in the village, because of some birth defect or disease, are born with no eyes. It'd been going on for so long that everyone there had forgotten about everything dealing with sight, and even that there was any world at all outside of their valley."

"What happens to him?"

"A couple of the men feel his face, his eyes, and they're shocked—they think something is growing there that shouldn't be. When he tries to explain that he was climbing on the mountain, they have no idea what he's talking about. They think he's insane. Eventually, they take him to their elders to try to figure out what they should do with him."

"I'll bet he amazes them with his stories of life beyond the valley."

"That's the thing. He tries to, but it doesn't work. He tells them about sunlight on waves, and glowing clouds at dusk and the thousands of shades of green in the forest. He talks about sprawling cities and technology and civilization—everything—and they think it's all a fairy tale too strange to be true. The more he explains about what he sees, the more they think he's mad. Time goes by. Because of the cliffs, he can't leave the valley. Eventually he and this young woman fall in love. But the elders still think he's insane and they figure that the problem is the growths on his face."

"Oh. His eyes."

"Right. They talk it over and eventually tell him that he can only marry her if he'll let them remove the growths. And then, also, he needs to renounce all his stories and agree that there's no world beyond the valley. And he must never speak of those things again."

"So, basically, agree to live a lie."

"In a sense, yeah, although I never really thought of it like that. Huh . . . In any case, he loves her so much and he wants to be with her so badly that he decides to let them poke out his eyes."

The road we're on ends about a quarter mile ahead of us at an elaborate sculpted metal gate.

The horse fence also terminates there, and since we're starting to slow down again, I'm guessing that's our destination.

"On the night before they're going to do it, he steps out to look at the stars one last time. And as he does, he remembers the climb and falling into the valley and the old life he used to have. And there, in the starlight, he notices a crack in the rock face that he hadn't really paid much attention to before. And so he needs to make a decision: What's more important, being with the woman he loves but knowing that he would be living a lie, or pursuing the chance to be free?"

"And lose her forever."

"Yes."

"What does he choose?"

"The story ends with him starting to climb."

"We never find out if he makes it out alive?"

"We never do."

"But he decides to leave the one he loves."

"Yes, to be with the truth. Which he loves more."

As I'm contemplating that, our driver pulls up to the security gate.

At last Tane stirs, rubs his eyes, and looks around. "Where are we?"

"We're here," the driver tells him. Then the gate swings open and he takes us up a long curving driveway that ends in front of an expansive southern mansion.

• • •

Mia reappeared on the staircase and told Kyle and Nicole, "Alright, here's the deal: Sue Ellen's cool with us going, as long as we come back tonight. We have until eleven. We need to be careful, drive safe, you know, the whole routine, but we're good to go if you're still up for it."

"Let's do it," Kyle said. "Let's go."

"It's a good thing that I'm eighteen or this would never happen."

"And that you're so responsible."

"That too."

Nicole rose. "My purse is in the other room. I'll meet you two at the car."

CHAPTER
THIRTY-EIGHT

I figure that senators probably make a pretty good living, but this place seems like way more than I would expect from someone who's just a politician.

A distinguished-looking man who's maybe ten years older than my dad is standing out front waiting for us, hands clasped behind his back.

As we get out of the car, he greets us each with a brisk handshake and introduces himself as Senator Brad Amundsen. Once he has our names, he ushers us inside. "Come on. Let's see what you can do to help me find Petra."

His lavish living room sprawls the entire length of the house.

He scrolls across a tablet computer and an automated video screen lowers on the far wall as the blinds dial sideways. I assume it's to shut out the sunlight so it'll be easier to see what's projected up there.

"Has there been any word on Malcolm?" he asks me, probably because I'm the one he's been speaking with on the phone.

"No. And no one except for you has called his cell."

I fill him in on what little we know about the circumstances surrounding Malcolm's disappearance.

"Well, he trusts you," he says, "and that's enough for me. He said you've all helped find missing people through your visions, or whatever you want to call—wait, forgive my manners; I'm just anxious to get started. Before we move forward, can I offer you anything to eat or drink?"

The last meal I had was Sue Ellen's southern dinner last night, so I accept the offer, and I'm glad when Tane and Alysha do as well so I won't seem rude by being the only one eating.

The senator directs his cook to prepare some lunch for us, then as she leaves, he asks about my shoulder, how I hurt it. Leaving out the part about the blur, I explain that a truck bumped into me, but that I'm alright.

"Bumped?"

"With an attitude. Really, I'm fine."

"Okay, well . . ." He shifts his attention to the tablet again. "How much did Malcolm tell you about what's happened to Petra?"

"Very little," Alysha answers. "Just that she has visions too, and that she was taken."

"Okay."

He taps at his computer.

A college graduation photo of a young woman appears on the wall's video screen. Blond. Pretty. Somewhat lonely-looking.

"She was a double major in accounting and engineering."

"So, good at math?" I ask.

"That and logic. Yes. Extraordinarily good."

Okay. There it is again—analytical thinking, that trait we all have in common.

The senator points to the screen. "I wasn't sure what to pull up here, but I have links to her online photo albums, social media posts, and microblogs. I don't know all her passwords, but we should be able to at least review most of her profiles."

More pictures flow past us, and we describe them to Alysha as they do—some formal, some informal. Indoors. Outdoors. Selfies. Group photos.

In most of them, Petra appears content, but not especially happy, and I wonder how much of that is just her personality or how much is a result of her being troubled by her blurs.

Reviewing these pictures reminds me of looking through the photos of Grandpa that Mom sent me yesterday. My memory's clearer than it was when I woke up this morning, and now I can recall having the revelation that the boy in the road was really a blur of me as a child.

I'm caught in the middle of three mysteries.

Petra's kidnapping.

Malcolm's disappearance.

My own recent blurs.

Three completely different puzzles.

Yet, as varied as they are, I can't shake the feeling that they're all related, and that somehow each of them holds the key to unlocking the others.

"Petra's visions started soon after my marriage to her mother ended four years ago," Senator Amundsen explains. "Petra was seventeen at the time. My ex-wife was going through some difficult personal issues and Petra ended up in my custody. What else can I tell you? Petra hasn't had an easy go of it either. She takes antipsychotic meds."

He mentions the name of the drugs and I recognize them from when I was researching medications last year. The doctors had wanted me to take them too. Pretty powerful stuff.

"She needs them every day." He looks at us urgently. "I'm not sure how going without them for these last few days will affect her."

Alysha has put on her dark sunglasses. I'm not sure why. "Have there been any news reports about her disappearance?"

"No. The kidnappers were very clear—no media. No one else besides the driver that I sent to pick you up knows she's gone—well, and Malcolm. She was taken on Friday night. She'd just left the hotel where she works as an accountant. She was walking to her car when . . . Well . . ."

He loses his train of thought for a moment and stares off into space.

Obviously, thinking about his daughter's abduction is hard for him.

However, overall, he seems remarkably poised and clearheaded for a man who's going through something like this.

At last, he goes on. "I had one of my staff members obtain the security footage from the hotel's exterior camera.

The angle isn't quite right and the camera must be old because the image is grainy and black and white, but you can at least see what happens." He scrolls across his tablet. "Here, I'll pull it up."

Though Alysha can't see him, she sits directly facing him, no doubt zeroing in on where he is by the sound of his voice. "Is there sound?"

"I'm afraid not."

He finds the file and opens it.

In the footage, Petra approaches a car, then crosses the street to where a woman is standing beside a minivan. It looks like she's calming down a baby that she has in her arms.

The woman hands Petra the child, and while she's distracted, the minivan's side door whips open, and a man grabs Petra.

As he drags her backward and she struggles to get free, she drops everything.

The woman picks up Petra's purse, and what is now obviously a doll that was wrapped in the blankets, before closing the minivan's door.

Soon, the minivan pulls away and the woman takes off in Petra's car.

Because of the shadows and angles, it's impossible to see the face of either of the two kidnappers.

We watch it a second time and I explain to Alysha what's happening.

Suddenly, it hits me. "That's the same minivan."

"What do you mean?"

"The minivan they're using. It's the same one that was in the parking garage next to where Tane found Malcolm's phone. The plates. They match."

She gasps. "But you don't think they had Malcolm in it while we were there? I mean, do you?"

I don't know what to say.

It's a terrible thought—that we might have been that close and missed our chance to help him.

In anger, Tane smacks the arm of his chair.

I turn to the senator. "I know you're not supposed to contact the police, but do you have anyone who could check the parking garage to see if that minivan is still there?"

"Absolutely."

I verify that he has the correct location and he makes the call. When he's done, I ask him if he can rewind the video.

"To where?"

"To just before Petra was taken. I want to see when those people drove up, how long they were waiting for her."

He has to back it up ten minutes to find when the minivan rolls to a stop beside the curb. The woman gets out and wraps that doll in the blanket. A moment later, the man steps out as well and speaks with her briefly before climbing back in to wait for Petra.

This time, though, I can see the guy's face, and, apparently Tane notices the same thing I do. "Daniel, that's the guy who was shooting at us by the elevator, isn't it?"

"It sure looks like it."

Senator Amundsen glances at us curiously. "What are you talking about?"

"After Malcolm disappeared," I tell him, "a man—that man—came after us, tried to kill us. Senator, when did you first realize Petra had been kidnapped?"

"It wasn't until the middle of the night. I'd flown back from D.C. to do some work here at the house for an important Senate inquiry. I arrived home at just a little after ten. Rather than get her own place, Petra stays here at the estate, over in the east wing of the house."

He gestures toward where that is. "Since I haven't been home much in the last few months, I was hoping to say hi to her, but in the end, I was exhausted and went to bed around eleven. Sometime before dawn, my phone rang and woke me up. The call came from her number, but when I answered it, it wasn't her. A man's voice told me to check my email—that's it, that's all—then he hung up. When I opened my email, I found the video, the one with their demands."

As he explains all this, he begins staring at the screen on the wall, an empty look shadowing his eyes.

"I tried calling back to her number but no one answered. Her car is still missing. No texts. No messages. No more emails. I contacted the phone company and they told me there haven't been any outgoing calls from her phone since that one was made in the middle of the night. I tried to track her cell through one of those locate-your-phone apps, but I couldn't find it."

"Is it possible to see the video?" I ask. "The one the kidnappers sent you?"

"Of course." He taps at the tablet and an image of Petra seated on a cot appears on the video screen. "And for this one, there is sound."

He presses "Play."

And the video begins.

CHAPTER THIRTY-NINE

A strip of duct tape covers her mouth and her arms are drawn back behind her.

She looks frightened, but also defiant.

The blank cement-block wall behind her has a narrow window near the ceiling.

A man wearing a black ski mask that covers all of his face except for his eyes steps into the frame and says, "You have a lovely daughter, Senator." He trails his finger along Petra's cheek, but she draws back in revulsion. "I'd hate to see anything happen to such a pretty face."

Whoever he is, he must not have been too concerned about the senator recognizing his voice because he didn't try to disguise it in any way.

It's impossible to be certain, but it does sound a lot like the guy who yelled for us to stop as we fled into the elevator—right before he shot at us.

He goes on, "Here's what we want and how you can assure that Petra comes back to you healthy and happy and all in one piece. You're the head of the Senate's Judiciary Reform Committee that's set to begin a probe on Tuesday into some unaccounted for expenditures in the Defense Department. As the sitting chairperson, you have the authority—and the ability—to make sure that the inquiry never occurs. And that's what you're going to do."

Petra stares at the camera and tries to say something beneath her gag. I can't tell what it is.

The man chuckles, apparently amused by her failed attempt to communicate. "On Monday night at precisely nine o'clock you will send out an email to all of your committee members notifying them that the inquiry isn't going to happen. Once that's done, we'll return Petra to you. It's that easy. And one more thing: You'll make sure this inquiry never comes up again while you are serving in the Senate because now you know we can get to your daughter and we will come after her again if we need to. That all depends on you."

Then he gazes at Petra for a long moment, as if to underscore how vulnerable she is and how easily they could get to her in the future if they wanted to.

Finally, he faces the camera again.

"Do this and you can save her life. Fail to do it and we'll mail her back to you in a dozen boxes. We'll know if you call the police or the FBI. Don't risk your daughter's life by contacting the authorities in any way. The only person you may be in touch with is Sam. Don't leave your house until we email you again. Don't contact the media. We'll let you know when and where you can find your daughter."

Then he strokes Petra's cheek one more time as she recoils, trying unsuccessfully once again to say something.

With that, the video ends.

We all sit there in silence.

No one moves.

Finally, after a long moment, the senator says, "Besides sending it to Malcolm, I haven't shown this to anyone else."

When we were under Centennial Olympic Park earlier and saw that final video of Jess being rolled away on the gurney, she'd been yelling something about someone named Sam. It seems like too much of a coincidence that Sam's name would come up in the ransom demands too, unless all of this is somehow connected.

I'm about to ask the senator about it, but Alysha beats me to it. "Senator Amundsen, who is Sam?"

"My way of reaching Malcolm. But I couldn't get through and I was desperate so I contacted Malcolm personally."

A bit to my surprise, he leaves it at that.

Questions swarm through my mind: How would the kidnappers know about Sam? Why would they let the senator be in touch? How does this relate to Jess and what she knew?

However, the senator doesn't seem inclined to share any more about Sam and I figure that since he's desperate to save his daughter, he would certainly tell us whatever he even remotely thought would help.

As I'm sorting through all that, Alysha requests that he play the video again. "I think I might have heard something."

"What?"

"I'm not sure. I'll tell you when to pause it."

We all listen attentively as he plays the footage again, but even when Alysha says, "There—stop," I still have no idea what she might be referring to.

"Go back maybe five seconds," she tells him. "And turn up the volume a little."

He repositions the cursor and starts the video again, this time with the volume dialed up.

About two or three seconds later she stops him again. "Right there."

He pauses it. "What do you hear?"

"There's a train whistle in the background and a few seconds later, I can make out an ambulance siren. It's faint, but it's there."

He plays it once more. I'm barely able to hear the sounds—I never would've been able to identify them without her pointing them out first.

Tane leans forward in his chair. "Those are cement-block walls in the video. The sound of that whistle and that siren wouldn't have carried very far, would they?"

"So they're close," the senator concludes. "The ambulance and train were somewhere near her."

"It's very possible, yes," Alysha says. "Maybe if you can find out when trains were going through areas that also had ambulance calls at the same time of night, you might be able to narrow things down."

"I'm not sure I can pull that off without contacting the police, but I'll look into it."

It might be a long shot, but who knows? Right now we can use any lead we can get.

I figure that with Alysha's acute hearing, she might've been able to distinguish what Petra was trying to say. However, when I ask her about it, she tells me she couldn't make it out.

Tane looks a little confused. "Senator, this whole request about canceling the meeting—is it really that big of a deal?"

"It might not appear so at first, but I have reason to believe that someone in the Department of Defense is funneling money into black ops programs that aren't in the budget. This is the same type of thing that was happening when waterboarding was being used. I'm concerned that there might be torture occurring at some of our military's clandestine sites. If my sources are correct and I were to cancel this inquiry, dozens of people might be tortured. But if I do nothing, Petra dies. I don't want to give in to their demands, but I can't let them hurt my daughter."

"Alright," I say. "Then we just need to find her before nine o'clock."

The senator gets a message from his people that the minivan is gone from the parking garage. They weren't able to track it after it left Centennial Olympic Park.

I suggest that we take a look at the wing of the house where Petra lives, but before we can, there's a rap on the door from the kitchen.

It's the cook, bringing us a large tray of sliced fruit and chicken salad sandwiches.

I'd almost forgotten about the food, but when she drops it off, I don't complain.

The senator urges us to go ahead and eat while he makes a few calls regarding the possible link between the train whistle and the ambulance siren. "Then I'll walk you through my daughter's living quarters."

● ● ●

The blaring horn startled Kyle so much that he almost swerved into the car that was zooming past him on his left.

Mia was sitting beside him. "Babe, you alright?"

"Yeah." He shook his head. "Man, they've created synthetic chromosomes, made cameras small enough to fit in your bloodstream, and transplanted orangutan hearts into human beings. You'd think they could design a sideview mirror without a blind spot."

"So you're good, though? You're sure?"

"I'm good."

Nicole, who was in the backseat studying a map on her phone, announced that they were almost halfway to North Carolina.

Mia looked confused. "I thought we were going to Tennessee?"

"We are. We just need to scoot through a corner of North Carolina first. Don't worry, it's only a—"

Her phone rang, she glanced at the screen and immediately answered it. "Hello?" Then she said urgently, "So did you find him?" Leaning away from the phone, she exclaimed, "It's the cop from campus security!"

Back on the line, she told him that her friends were there with her. "Can I put you on speakerphone?"

When she did, they all heard the officer: "As I was saying, this is Officer Webster from the Northern Georgia Tech Campus Security Services."

"But you didn't find Daniel?" Nicole reiterated.

"Not yet. No. I'm calling to let you know that I've been in touch with the coaches running the camp this week and none of them have seen your friend. However, the Berringer Hall director does recall that Daniel was in bed right around nine this morning when he was doing room inspection. So that's a good sign. It means—"

"Um," Kyle interrupted him. "That was me."

"You?"

"I was . . . That's when I was looking for Daniel."

"In his bed?"

"I didn't want the dorm guy to know I was . . . Never mind. But it was me."

"Okay." The officer sounded annoyed that things weren't going to be solved so easily. "Has Daniel contacted any of you?"

"Uh-uh," Nicole answered.

"I'm going to need to give his parents a call. However, his registration form is missing from the files in the field house and it appears his emergency contact information was never entered into the system. Do you have a phone number I can use to reach them?"

"Um. Hang on." She muted her cell for a moment. "What should I tell him? If he calls Daniel's parents, they're going to worry. And they'll be mad too, that we didn't contact them earlier."

"I guess they have a right to know at this point," Mia granted. "I suppose we shouldn't really be keeping it from them that he's missing." Then she added somewhat morosely, "Especially if something bad has happened."

"What do you think? Should we call 'em or should I let the cop do it?"

"He's heading up the search back in Atlanta," Kyle replied. "Let him go ahead and contact them first. We can always follow up afterward."

Nicole pulled up Daniel's dad's number, got back on the line with the officer, and told it to him.

After he hung up, she said, "Now what?"

"Now we wait," Kyle said. "Give it some time, then we'll call them."

"They're not going to be happy."

"No. They're not."

• • •

After a quick lunch, the senator takes Tane and me to Petra's wing while Alysha stays behind in the living room with the tablet computer to re-listen to the videos.

Senator Amundsen explains that when Petra's visions started, he had her visit a counselor, and then a hypnotherapist in Gatlinburg, Tennessee. "Actually, the hypnotist was her idea," he clarifies. "He's one of the best in the country and it's not a long helicopter flight up there from here. But, well . . ."

"Did it help?" Tane asks.

"Hard to say. I believe he did help her tap into her subconscious more, but in her last session she had a pretty terrifying vision. She didn't want to see him again after that."

As the senator shows us around his mansion and I peer into Petra's room, I feel a little intrusive—especially since I don't know exactly what I'm looking for.

Nothing really jumps out at me, apart for the title of a book beside her bed: *Chinese Folk Tales for the Ages*. There's a bookmark in the middle of it, and when I flip to that page, I find the story about the farmer and his son, the one about blessings and curses, the one Malcolm told Jess when she first arrived at the center.

I'm not sure what to make of that, except that Malcolm might've heard the story from Petra.

Or maybe he gave her the book.

"So, anything yet?" the senator asks us hopefully.

I hate admitting it, but so far I have nothing—and that's what I tell him.

Tane says the same.

Discouraged, we follow Senator Amundsen back to the living room to finish reviewing Petra's pictures and social media posts, hoping for a cue, a spark, a trigger—anything that will bring on a blur.

CHAPTER FORTY

No.

This isn't working.

Not the photos, the posts, the videos.

None of us have any blurs.

We're not getting anywhere.

Before today, I've never tried to initiate a blur—only tried to get rid of them—so I'm not even sure how to go about doing it.

Earlier, when we were in the facility under the parking garage, Malcolm told us that we needed to find a template for our conscious minds to interact with—

Hang on.

Yes.

With our *subconscious* minds.

I turn to the senator. "You mentioned that Petra was seeing that hypnotist in Gatlinburg?"

"Yes. Dr. Carrigan."

"And you said that the last time she was there it actually caused her to have another hallucination?"

"That's right."

"Well, that's what we need to do right now, get ourselves to have some hallucinations. How long of a helicopter flight is it to get up there?"

"A little over an hour."

"From what airport?"

"My chopper leaves from here."

I didn't see a helicopter here when we drove up and when I ask him about that he tells me it's hangared nearby. "It can be here in fifteen minutes."

"We need to go visit that hypnotist."

He pulls out his cell. "I'll call my pilot."

• • •

Kyle's phone rang.

Since he was still at the wheel, Mia picked it up and checked the screen. "Okay, here we go. It's Daniel's dad. Should I answer it?"

"Yeah." He took a deep breath. "Go ahead."

She tapped the screen. "Hello, Mr. Byers. It's Mia. Kyle's driving. Do you—" She turned to Kyle. "He wants to talk to you."

He accepted the phone from her. "This is—"

"I want you to tell me exactly what's going on here, Kyle." The sheriff's voice was explosive. "I just got a call from the Northern Georgia Tech campus police telling me that my son is missing."

"We've been looking for him."

"And the last anyone heard from him was last night?!"

"We . . . I mean . . ."

"You mean what? Tell me."

"I'm sorry." Then Kyle quickly summarized their day, starting with the search for Daniel in the dorm room and talking through everything, right up to their trip to Gatlinburg.

When he finished there was a long pause.

For a moment he thought his phone might have dropped the call.

Finally he asked, "Are you still there, Mr. Byers?"

"I'm here."

Another pause. Then, at last, the sheriff said, "You called the number on the back of the debit card and pretended to be the card owner?"

"Just to see if it would help us find Daniel."

"By finding Malcolm Zacharias?"

"Yes."

"And have you?"

"Have we?"

"Found Zacharias?"

"No. We're hoping that maybe visiting this place in Gatlinburg will give us some answers."

"I want you to email me everything you have on Marly Weathers, Gatlinburg Holdings, and Malcolm Zacharias. Send it all. Even if you don't think it looks important."

"Yes, sir. And I'm sorry we didn't call earlier. We didn't want you to worry."

"That's not your decision to make."

Kyle didn't know how to reply to that. "What are you going to do?"

"I'll have some deputies follow up on what you send me. And I'm going to fly down to Atlanta and work with the local authorities to find Daniel. Contact me immediately if you hear anything at all."

"I will."

When the call was over, Nicole asked Kyle, "Well?"

"That went about as well as I expected."

"That bad, huh?"

"Truthfully, it could have been a lot worse."

"What did he say?"

"He's gonna fly to Atlanta."

"Did he tell you we had to turn around?"

"Hmm. No, he didn't. Maybe he was just too distracted and upset to think about it."

He gave the phone back to Mia and she said, "So, what next?"

"We email him everything we have. And then . . ."

"What?"

"I'm just thinking aloud here: He'll probably have to fly out of the Twin Cities to get a connection to Atlanta. But that's a three-hour drive from Beldon, so pulling that off today—I'd say it's unlikely."

"Okay. Where does that leave us?"

"The cops are looking in Atlanta, and now Daniel's parents know what's going on. There's really nothing we can do on any of those fronts. I suppose we move forward and see if we can learn anything in Gatlinburg."

He glanced in the rearview mirror at Nicole. "How much farther is it?"

She checked her phone's GPS. "It's saying we should get there at six eleven."

• • •

"It's all set," the senator informs us. "The hypnotherapist's name is Dr. Reginald Carrigan. He's apparently given up his therapy though, and now has a stage hypnotism show there in Gatlinburg. It's a tourist area, so there are lots of music venues and dinner theaters, that sort of thing. He's a little eccentric, but don't let that throw you off. He's smart and he knows what he's doing. The kidnappers warned me in that ransom video not to leave the house so I can't come, otherwise I would. My pilot is on his way. He should be able to get you up to Carrigan's place by five."

• • •

Still sealed in the cement-block room in the basement, Petra Amundsen watched the faces appear on the walls.

Her dad.

Her two kidnappers.

The concrete became liquid right before her eyes, then seeped down and pooled into a shimmering puddle at her feet.

She peered into it and all the visages merged into one, becoming a distorted reflection of her own face. Then, slowly, that became elongated, stretching in ways that could never happen in real life. It curled in on itself like it was caught in a whirlpool, but instead of waves circling around it, there were snakes.

The face's eyes closed, its mouth opened, and she heard her reflection murmur, "The handle. Take the handle."

Then, the image disappeared, the pool was gone, and the walls reformed. As the world organized itself around her again, her gaze landed on the bucket that her kidnappers had left for her to use as a toilet.

Its wire handle was sturdy, designed to support the weight of five gallons of water.

The ends were bent into small holes in the plastic, but if she worked at it, she might be able to get them loose.

But then what?

What good was a wired bucket handle going to do her?

She didn't know, but she *did* know that on the video the kidnappers had filmed for her dad, they'd told him that he needed to respond at nine o'clock on Monday night, and by now it had to be sometime in the late afternoon.

This voice just now in her vision told her to take the handle. Getting it off the bucket couldn't hurt, it might help, and she didn't have any better ideas at the moment.

Petra sat beside the bucket, tried to ignore the odor of the urine inside it, and began twisting the wire to work it free from the divots in the plastic.

• • •

As the helicopter comes in over the trees, it rotates clockwise, then descends onto the evenly trimmed lawn just south of the mansion.

"Call me when you get there!" the senator shouts to us over the sound of the rotors. "I'll do anything I can from here to help you find her!"

I nod, we climb in, buckle up, put on the radio headsets that the pilot has waiting for us, and then take off to visit the hypnotist in Gatlinburg, Tennessee.

CHAPTER
FORTY-ONE

We soar high over the Smoky Mountains.

I've been hiking with my dad in the Rockies before, and these mountains aren't nearly as rugged or majestic. They're densely wooded rather than bare-peaked and snow-covered like the Rockies, but they're still stunning as they cascade back magnificently, layer after layer, toward the horizon.

Right now I can't tell why they're called the Smokies, but I figure that as it gets closer to dusk, fog might settle into the rolling valleys and deep, river-etched gorges.

Although with the headsets on we can speak with each other, we're all quiet and I assume Tane and Alysha are deep in thought, just as I am, processing what's been happening.

Once again, I think of Grandpa and his death out on that road near where I saw myself appear as a boy.

How does that tie in with what's happening now?

Is it related somehow to Petra's disappearance?

The words from the dream that I had after being hit by the logging truck ring through my head: "He never meant to go. It all began right here. Follow the bats. Find the truth."

If it was talking about my grandpa's death, I could understand what "he never meant to go" referred to, and even the part about it all being "here," but what about the bats? What do they have to do with the truth?

My thoughts of Grandpa lead me to think about my mom. She must be seriously worried about me.

I'm sure that by now Kyle and the girls have found out I'm missing, and have no doubt let my parents know.

Which might not be good.

If my mom and dad sent out cops to search for me and the officers ended up somehow tracking things to Senator Amundsen's place, the kidnappers might think that the senator contacted the police—and they would kill Petra.

You need to make sure no cops are looking for you.

Petra's life might depend on it.

It strikes me that calling my parents at this point would probably not just be smart; it might be critical to protecting Petra.

However, I'm still not comfortable with the idea of using Malcolm's phone to make the call.

What about borrowing Dr. Carrigan's? There's no way the people who took Petra would be listening in on his line. You wouldn't have to say anything about her specifically, or the senator, or even Malcolm. Just tell Dad not to have anyone search for you.

As we skirt across the mountains, I make my decision.

As soon as we land, I'm going to ask Dr. Carrigan if I can use his phone. Then I'll call my parents and assure them that I'm alright.

• • •

Mia was at the wheel now, with Nicole beside her.

Kyle had kept Daniel's phone with him, and, throughout the day, a handful of texts had come in from some of Daniel's other friends. Other than that, things had been quiet.

While they drove, he spent some time going through the recent emails and saw that, last night, Daniel's mom had sent him more than fifty family photos. From what Kyle could tell they were all of his grandpa.

It made Kyle curious, and he told the girls about it, then handed the phone up to the front so Nicole could review the pictures.

"Do you think this might have something to do with his blurs?" he asked her.

"Possibly. Remember last winter? Those blurs of the girl from the 1930s were all tangled up with Daniel's memories of what happened when he was nine. The images, the pictures, they got lodged in his mind, but he repressed them. Trauma can do that."

"Well," Mia interjected, "I'd say that was some *serious* trauma—realizing that a kid had been killed in the barn while he was in there at the same time? Who wouldn't be affected by that?"

"And then, earlier in Daniel's life, there was the loss of his grandpa. After he died, that's when Daniel went sleepwalking for the first time."

"How old was he when it happened?"

"Five." Nicole looked up from the photos. "You know, all this kind of makes me think of the story of Cain and Abel. After Cain kills his brother, the Bible says that Abel's blood was crying out to God from the ground. That's sort of what's happened with Daniel all the other times when the blurs have occurred."

"How do you figure?"

"Well, dead people appeared to him. Their blood was crying out for justice, or, I don't know. Maybe not. It's just a thought."

"No," Kyle encouraged her, "keep going. You might be onto something."

"Daniel doesn't see ghosts, exactly, but . . . Well, when I was on the swing last night he was telling me about memory sparks. Maybe that's what he was trying to do with these pictures: help spark his memory."

"Wait—doesn't Cain say something about not being his brother's keeper?"

"Yeah. Cain said to God, 'Am I my brother's keeper?' But it was more sarcasm than anything."

Mia changed lanes and accelerated past a slow-moving RV. "I'm not thinking it's really the best call to be sarcastic with God. And if you ask me, we're all our brother's keeper."

"Good point." Kyle turned to Nicole. "So you think the blood of the dead cries out to Daniel?"

"I mean, it's one way to look at things."

"Is the blood of his grandpa crying out to him now?"

"Maybe."

Mia merged back into the right lane, and then said, in an uncharacteristically worried way, "Seriously, though, do you think Daniel's okay?"

"I'm praying that he is," Nicole replied.

"So am I."

"I didn't know you prayed," Kyle said.

"Normally, I don't. This time I'm making an exception."

• • •

Dr. Adrian Waxford was near the *Tabanidae* research room, planning how much of his research to share with the general when Henrik arrived, leading the handcuffed Malcolm Zacharias down the steps and into the hallway.

Zacharias's face was bloodied and bruised.

Henrik looked satisfied and sadistically pleased by the man's condition.

"Sergei's with Deedee and Petra," Henrik informed Adrian. "I dropped him off at the house."

Earlier they'd spoken about taking Zacharias up to the fourth floor, but Adrian anticipated that Henrik would want to spend some time down here with him first.

Adrian faced Zacharias. "I recognize you from the facility in Wisconsin. You're the one who helped Hollister escape last December."

Zacharias let his tongue glance across his swollen lip. "What you're doing with these men isn't right."

"I'm afraid that at this time in history, right must lie in the eye of the beholder."

"If that were true, there wouldn't be such a thing as good or evil. It would all just be opinion. That's not the world I live in. That's not a world worth fighting for."

"Mr. Zacharias, I'm trying to extend to these men the punishment that our government doesn't have the temerity to carry out. Would you really have our justice system continue to fail as it has, when we have the ability to correct it?"

"You mean corrupt it. Everyone who abuses power justifies themselves. They always have their reasons. Terrorist bombings, war, genocide—it's always done in the name of what the person in power claims is right."

"In August 2015, James Holmes, the Aurora theater shooter who killed twelve people at the opening showing of *The Dark Knight Rises*, was sentenced to twelve life sentences plus 3,318 years in prison. What was the point of that?"

"It was a symbolic sentence."

"But symbolic to whom and for what purpose? A three thousand-year sentence? Does that seem just to you? That's a mockery of justice. To give someone a sentence only to make a statement, but without any intention of having the person serve their time—where's the justice in that? Tell me and I'll stop this research right now."

"Adrian, where is Petra?"

"Ah, yes. That's right, you have ties to her father. Well, her whereabouts need not concern you. Now, we're going to be needing you to tell us the identity of the person who employed you. We know it's someone who goes by the name of Sam."

"Then you know as much as I do."

"And, see? I'm thinking there's more that you can bring to the table."

"Maybe there is, but I should tell you, I'm pretty good at keeping secrets."

At that, Henrik, who'd been standing by listening, scoffed. "And I'm pretty good at prying them out of people."

"Well," Adrian said to him, "I should leave you to it then."

Henrik led Zacharias down the hall toward the tattoo room.

Where he kept his needles.

• • •

The bucket's metal handle was proving harder to get off than Petra had anticipated.

She was able to pry one end loose, but the other was stubbornly refusing to let go of the plastic.

Night was coming, and with it, the deadline.

One thing was certain: She needed to get free and contact her dad to make sure he didn't cancel tomorrow's meeting. A lot was riding on it and, if he gave in to the kidnappers' demands, it could mean that some very bad people would get away with some very bad things.

In the video when her mouth was taped shut, she'd tried to communicate with him, but she wasn't confident that the message had gotten through.

With renewed focus, and as the chimeric snakes returned and slithered across her feet, she set to work again on the recalcitrant end of the wire handle.

• • •

We emerge from the mountains and soar over the city of Gatlinburg.

It's not huge, but there's a lot of traffic and I'm glad we're in this helicopter instead of stuck on the road down below.

As we reach the outer fringe of the city, the pilot points at an empty parking lot near a shabby-looking theater, and then takes us down.

A beefy man with crumpled clothes and a thick handle-bar mustache ambles out of the building to meet us.

CHAPTER FORTY-TWO

As the pilot powers off the helicopter and the blades cycle down, the mustached man introduces himself as the Great Carrigini.

"Actually, it's Reginald Carrigan," he explains with a wink. "But when you're in this business you have to have a good stage name. You understand, right?"

I'm not sure if it's a real question or a hypothetical one. "Sure."

When he realizes that Alysha is letting me guide her, he seems a little taken aback by the fact that she's blind, but he quickly recovers.

Before leading us inside, he suggests to the pilot that he enjoy a cup of coffee at the diner down the road while he waits for us.

"I should stay with my bird."

I watch to see if the Great Carrigini will do any hypnotic suggestions or Jedi mind tricks on him to make him go over there, but the hypnotist just shrugs. "Suit yourself. But it's good coffee."

"Can't drink coffee, actually." The pilot taps his chest. "Not with this ticker. I'm good to fly, but no caffeine. No strenuous exercise. Gotta take her easy."

"They have very fine desserts. Freshly made pies."

"Pies?"

"Yes. Freshly made."

"Apple?"

"And cherry."

"Hmm. Well, I do like a good apple pie. I suppose I could be tempted to wait at the diner."

He gives Dr. Carrigan his cell number, and then saunters across the street.

Huh.

Maybe there is something to the Great Carrigini after all.

"Follow me," he tells us, then turns toward the theater.

"Actually," I say, "before we get started, could I use your phone to make a call? I need to let the senator know we've arrived."

It's true.

Just not the whole truth.

"Of course." He draws out his cell and hands it to me, then the three of them head into the building.

First, as I promised, I contact the senator to let him know we're here. It only takes a few moments.

Then, I punch in my dad's number.

He picks up. "Hello?"

"Dad. It's me. Daniel."

"Daniel! Where are you?" He shouts to my mom, "It's Dan!" Then he's back, talking to me again: "We got a call from the campus police that you went missing. They're looking for you. I spoke with Kyle—no one knows where—are you safe? Are you okay?"

"I'm fine, but you need to get the campus police to call off the search. If you don't, a woman's life might be in danger."

"What are you talking about?"

"Trust me, Dad. I just need until nine o'clock tonight. Nobody can know what's happening. It's the only way to help her."

I hear Mom asking him what's happened, if I'm alright, where I am—too many questions for him to answer all at once. He tells her that I'm okay and asks her to give him a second, then he informs me that he's trying to arrange a flight down to Atlanta.

"No, no, don't do that. Really, I'm safe. I am. Can I talk to Mom? I don't have much time."

There's a shuffled silence as he hands her the phone, then she comes on the line. "Daniel, what's going on here?"

"Mom, I can't explain everything right now. I just wanted to let you know I'm alright."

"I shouldn't have let you go down to that camp. We never should have—"

"That's not it. I know it's hard to trust me right now, but you need to."

"Does this have anything to do with what we spoke about last week?"

"What we spoke about?"

"You asked me about my mother. About her suicide."

"No. It's nothing like that. Not at all."

"You're not hurt?"

"I'm fine."

"And you're not going to hurt yourself?"

"No, Mom."

Then, unexpectedly, she shifts to an entirely different topic, maybe just to keep me on the phone. "Did you get those pictures of your grandfather?"

Last night seems like a really long time ago. "Yes. I think the boy in the road was supposed to be me. But it seems like it's all connected with Grandpa's death too. I don't remember it. I was still pretty young when he died."

"You were five."

"Right. When I was nine and Grandma died, you didn't tell me everything about it right away. Is there anything about Grandpa's death that you haven't told me? I wasn't in the car with him, was I? When he crashed?"

"Goodness sakes, no. You were with me in my car. We were following him home when he hit the ice and went off the road. You were in your booster seat the whole time."

"But did I see him?"

"Maybe when they rolled him into the ambulance, but that would be all."

"Was he already dead?"

"Are you sure you're okay, Daniel?"

"I am. Was Grandpa dead?"

"Yes. Yes, he was. The impact killed him. A branch went through the windshield. It . . . well, the wounds in his chest . . . The doctors said he died instantly."

"Wounds in his chest?"

"Yes."

Then I hear my dad talking to her and she says to me, "Your father wants to speak to you again. I love you."

"I love you too."

Dad gets back on. "Daniel, I trust you, I do, but you ran in front of a truck just over a week ago because you thought that someone was in danger—but there was no one there. Can I trust that you're not going to do anything like that again?"

"I know what you're saying, Dad, I just—"

"Don't do anything that could endanger you or someone else. You need to assure me of that."

"Okay. I'll be careful."

"Kyle sent me some information earlier. Do you know anything about a Marly Weathers or an educational center in Gatlinburg?"

"No."

I don't tell him that I'm standing in Gatlinburg right now.

The same city in Tennessee? Really? That's way too much of a coincidence for this not to be connected somehow.

He goes on, "I'm wondering if it's involved with what's going on with you."

Don't tell him where you are. Don't jeopardize this.

"I don't know anything about a center in Gatlinburg."

"Call me if there's anything I can do for you. I still want to come down there."

"I don't think you should. Just wait to hear from me. And can you get in touch with Nicole and have her tell Kyle and Mia that I'm alright? I don't want to contact them."

"Are they in any danger?"

"I don't think so."

"I'll call her."

"Don't tell her that someone's life is on the line."

"I won't. Be careful and remember the fourth ground rule for your trip."

"Don't do anything stupid."

"Right."

"I have to go. I love you, Dad."

"You too."

After the call, I jog over to the building to join the others as the clouds coming in across the mountains begin to pile onto each other in the late afternoon sky.

CHAPTER
FORTY-THREE

I walk past the old-fashioned box office and enter the back of the theater.

The smell of stale popcorn mixed in with the faint odor of mold greets me.

I glance around and see that there are one hundred and eighty-four seats.

The cloth on most of them is ripped, stained, or faded. Some of the spotlights are burned out. The stage curtain has a long, uneven tear and hangs awkwardly from its runner.

This place has definitely seen better days.

Senator Amundsen told us that Dr. Carrigan was one of the best hypnotists in the country.

I wonder if he ever actually visited this theater.

Photos of the Great Carrigini on stage during his show, with people who are apparently hypnotized—and are acting ridiculous—line one wall. The other wall contains twenty-one exquisite prints of blown-up photographs of the nearby Great Smoky Mountains.

Dr. Carrigan is up on the stage right now, lining up three folding chairs. As I make my way toward the front row where Alysha and Tane are waiting for me, he notices me glancing at the mountain photos.

"I took all those pictures myself," he announces proudly. "Not available anywhere else, just a few prints for my friends. Lived here almost twenty years. I've hiked just about every trail in those mountains. I know 'em all like the back of my hand."

When I return his phone to him, he says, "The senator didn't explain everything to me, and I don't need to know the details. He just said that the photos and videos weren't enough and that you three have hallucinations similar to Petra's. Fascinating. I'd love to explore that more with you, but there isn't time for that right now. He told me you're here to try and conjure up those visions to help find Petra?"

I'm not sure I like the choice of the word *conjure* but I tell him, "Yes. That's right."

"I have a show at seven thirty and, from what the senator said, it sounds like you have places you need to be as well, so let's get started. My office is cramped and in a bit of disarray, so we'll do this here on stage, alright?"

We tell him that's fine, whatever will work best.

We each take a scat on one of the folding chairs.

"First of all, how familiar are you with hypnosis?"

He addresses all of us with the question, but Tane is the one to answer. "Not too much."

"So you've never been hypnotized?"

"No."

"And you two?" Dr. Carrigan looks my way. "Daniel? Alysha?"

Alysha says, "No."

I shake my head.

"Well, it's basically moving you into an altered mental state. Let's see . . . Um . . . Do any of you play sports?"

"I do," I tell him.

"Me too," Tane replies. "If boxing and jiu-jitsu count."

"Of course they do. So are you familiar with what it means when someone talks about being 'in the zone'?"

"Sure," Tane says.

"And how would you describe that?"

"It's like you don't consciously focus, or even try harder, but everything just flows. You kind of lose track of time. You just respond. Instinct takes over."

"And when you're in the zone, you play your best—or, well, do martial arts, or fight, the best. Yes?"

"Yeah."

"That's what we're shooting for with hypnosis. Think about your mind as having different levels of awareness. Your conscious mind is typically calling the shots, but, often, your unconscious—or what some people might call the subconscious—has solutions and resources that you aren't even aware of. We're going to see if, by tapping into those, you can enter a mental state where the solution will become clearer to you."

"Is that what happened with Petra?" Alysha asks.

"Petra is a unique case. I would rather focus on what we can accomplish here today than on what happened with her."

"And what is it, exactly, that happened with her?"

"She was my patient; I was her therapist. I'm afraid I can't share anything about our sessions because of doctor-patient confidentiality." Then he clasps his hands together in a definitive manner. "So, shall we proceed?"

"Okay," she says.

"Do all three of you wish to be hypnotized?"

It's our best shot at figuring out what's happened to Petra. "Yes," I tell him. "All three of us."

"Alright, well I should give you a small caveat then: Not everyone is able to be hypnotized. We're not sure why that is, genetics perhaps, but let's give this a shot and see how it goes. First, I need your permission. Do you agree to be hypnotized?"

I nod.

Alysha says, "Yes."

Tane's eyes are on the stage show photos—the ones of people acting like monkeys and grown men putting on makeup and teenagers lying on the floor trying to swim across the stage. "You're not going to make us do anything like that, are you?"

"No, of course not. In my show we take liberties. It's a comedy show. You understand."

"Uh-huh. And what about the power of suggestion? Mind control?"

"That's not what we're here for today. It is true that people are more open to the power of suggestion when they're hypnotized. That's why it can be used so effectively in therapy to help folks lose weight or stop smoking. But you need to trust me, and remember that while people are hypnotized they will never do anything against their moral code."

"Nothing against their moral code. Okay. Got it. I'm good. Hypnotize me." He looks around the nearly empty stage. "Do you need to swing a pocket watch or make us stare at a spinning pinwheel or something?"

"I prefer conversational induction."

Alysha, who has been following along quietly, speaks up. "What's that?"

"Well, we need to move you into a hypnotic state. There are a variety of different techniques for doing so. This one is nonintrusive. We just need to nudge the conscious mind out of the way. I use what's called imbedded suggestions. I just want you to focus on listening to me and then let your thoughts take you where they will."

Tane asks, "Do we need to close our eyes?"

"You can keep them open. It's okay. Now, I'm going to ask you to concentrate on the sound of my voice. I'll give you a series of instructions and I want you to follow them as best you can."

Then he starts talking to us in a sort of stream-of-consciousness way. "You're processing what's going on here. *You're in a safe place.* You can hear the soft hum of the air conditioner. *There's nothing distracting you.* You can feel yourself seated comfortably in your chair. *Leave your expectations behind.*"

He goes on like that for a little while.

His voice becomes calming, melodic.

However, though I do start to relax, I don't feel myself entering any kind of altered state.

"Now, I want you to imagine that you're on the top floor of a ten-story building that you're familiar with, one that you enjoy visiting. You see an elevator and press the 'Down' button. When the doors open, you step inside and begin to descend, floor by floor, to the basement—*nine*—As you descend you feel more at ease, more restful, more calm—*eight*—You can see the numbers counting down, and with each one you allow yourself to drift further into—*seven*—a state of relaxation. You feel yourself going deeper and deeper down with each floor—*six*—as you move to the lower levels. The further you go into the building, the safer you feel, the safer you become—*five*—You're leaving everything about this day behind you—*four*—There are no pressures down here, and—*three*—safer, safer, no worries and nothing that will—*two*—cause you any concern or—*one*—make you feel anything but open and free and—*now to the basement*—completely relaxed. And, you've arrived. The doors open and you're here, in a place where you feel welcome and comfortable, but a place you haven't visited before."

His steady, metronomic voice and the floor-by-floor countdown help calm me and center my thoughts, but I still don't sense that I'm in any sort of trance.

He starts talking about how our arms and legs should feel heavy, but mine don't.

When I glance at Tane, I see that he's staring oddly into space. Alysha appears transfixed as well.

I'm not sure if they're faking it or not.

I don't want to disrupt the mood or undermine what we're trying to do here, so I say nothing and just pretend that I'm under as well.

"Now," the Great Carrigini says, "let's explore what's down here in the basement."

CHAPTER
FORTY-FOUR

"You've entered a room with a giant movie screen. You take a seat and find a remote control in your hand. You can fast forward, pause, rewind. Tane and Daniel, you're going to watch the movie of all that you know about Petra. Alysha, you're going to listen for sounds that you haven't heard before. At any time, you can control the film, move it forward or backward, whatever you need to do."

All of us have our eyes open.

I don't see a giant movie screen, but when I stare past Dr. Carrigan, the boy from the road suddenly appears on the other end of the stage.

He's holding his hand out toward me like he did when I first saw him in Wisconsin.

Then he starts walking forward. With each step, he grows taller, more mature, until he becomes my age.

Now he's the figure that I saw in the attic—the corpse that looks just like me.

The torn fabric of his shirt hangs open, revealing a ghastly wound in his chest.

Blood drips onto the stage.

Dr. Carrigan continues, but with every word his voice fades further into the background: "I want you to start with the videos that the senator played for you. Review them, let the sounds and the images pass by you. You're not distracted by anything else. At any time you can pause or replay what you just experienced . . ."

Beyond the boy, the truck roars onto the stage and speeds forward, its headlights sweeping through the old theater.

It hits him.

Hits me.

I feel the impact.

It's bone-crushing and knocks the wind out of me.

I gasp. I can't help it.

Then the boy is gone and I'm just there on my chair, beside Alysha, catching my breath, trying to recover.

"Okay," the hypnotist says, his voice soft and coming from someplace far away, "now as you play the movie about Petra Amundsen, you're going to notice something you haven't noticed before. It's clear to you now. It's something that, when you were awake, you weren't even aware of. Daniel and Tane, you see the images and photos pass in front of you . . ."

I see images of Petra.

But then, as the pictures float before me, they're no longer of her.

But of my grandpa.

And of me with him when I was five, that year at Christmas. The year he died.

Dr. Carrigan's voice becomes nothing but soft, indistinguishable murmuring.

I hear the shattering glass in the hallway of Mia's ghost story.

See the deathly face outside the Blessed Virgin's splintered window.

Feel the coarse, wet tongue from the dog in Kyle's urban legend licking my hand.

It's all coming together.

Blessings.

Curses.

Prophets and dreams.

The glass shards on the monastery's stone floor turn into the ones from the lava lamp, the ones that Liam used to cut his arm and to scar Malcolm's face.

I see the wounds on the corpse from the attic, the one who was just here in the theater.

The same wounds Grandpa had.

The ones he died from.

Blood oozing across the floor.

Through the wood.

Dripping into my room.

Yes, the same wounds.

That's why he was bleeding like that.

That's why . . .

The years cycle past me, rushing by, a thousand memories covered by the dust of time flicker for a moment, then float away, until they're all gone and I'm sitting with my grandpa, alone, in the living room.

"Do you have any imaginary friends, Danny?"

"Yes. Two of 'em."

"Wow. Two! Are they nice?"

"Uh-huh."

"And what are their names?"

"Alfie and Fred."

"Are they here right now?"

"Uh-huh."

"Did you know your mommy and your grandma also had imaginary friends?"

"Were they nice?"

"Not always. You know, you can tell us if you ever get scared of Alfie and Fred."

"They keep me safe."

"They do?"

"From monsters."

"What kind of monsters?"

"They're like giant bats. But scarier."

"Well, then always keep Alfie and Fred close by. As long as they're protecting you, don't tell them to go away."

It's the last time you ever spoke with him.

Then you're in the car, watching out the window. You see his car ahead of you, spinning off the road. Its lights swish past you, making you dizzy.

There's a loud crash.

And your mommy starts screaming.

You want to go see if Grandpa is okay, but they make you stay in the car.

Then they put him in an ambulance and drive him away and tell you that he went to be with the angels.

And they don't let you see him again.

You wish they would. You want to say goodbye because you love him and he understands about Alfie and Fred and a lot of grown-ups don't, and he's nice to you and always brings you suckers when he comes to visit.

But they take him away and tell you they had to put him in the ground.

"That's where the monsters live!" you tell your mom.

"There's no such thing as monsters."

"Yes, there are! Grandpa knew it! We talked about 'em!"

Then they take you to a field with big rocks and give you some flowers and ask you to put them next to one of the rocks because it's where Grandpa's grave is.

"But I thought he was with the angels?"

"He is. But his body is down here."

And you don't understand, but you tell Alfie and Fred to stay and take care of him and make sure he's safe, and then take him up to be with the angels.

But the bats are climbing up from the ground out there, shaking the dirt off their wings, and grinning and flying all around you.

They follow you home.

And that night you get scared because Alfie and Fred are with Grandpa and not there in your room to keep you safe.

And there are the monsters.

Like giant bats.

But scarier.

All around you.

And you're worried they might go after Grandpa too.

You need to make sure he's safe.

That's when you get up and walk past your parents because you never got a chance to say goodbye and you want to, because the monsters live there by the grave and they're going to try to make Grandpa stay in the ground where it's cold and lonely and where he won't ever be able to leave and see the angels.

You need to help him.

You need to save him.

You need to say goodbye.

Goodbye, Grandpa—

Good—

"No!"

The voice scatters the images, the memories, the dreams.

They fold into themselves and slink back again into the hidden corners of my mind.

"Please, no!" It's Alysha. "No!"

The blur is gone.

And I'm here on stage, seated beside her.

Dr. Carrigan looks shocked.

She keeps shouting about some people named Deedee and Sergei.

"What's wrong?" I go to her, then call to Dr. Carrigan, "Something's wrong."

"She'll be okay. She's just—"

Alysha screams and starts frantically batting her hands in front of her like Jess did in the video we watched this morning.

"Wake her up!"

"I will," he stammers. "I—"

"Deedee!" Alysha shrieks. "Her name is Deedee and he's Sergei. She's—"

"You're on the elevator—" Dr. Carrigan sounds rushed, harried, afraid. "You're going to take it back up to the tenth floor as I count up to—"

"There's no time for all that." I shake her. "Wake up, Alysha."

"Don't do that!" Dr. Carrigan warns me. "It's not good to—"

Tane is still sitting there, staring blankly forward as if none of this is happening.

Dr. Carrigan clamors on, "Ride up safely to floor one, and then two—"

"Please!" Alysha cries.

"—You're passing three and four and five—"

I try to hold one of her wrists down to keep her still, but she has fierce strength in that slender arm and fights me off. "Alysha!"

"—Floor six. Getting closer. Feeling safer. Floor seven—"

She jerks to the side and throws her head back, almost tipping the chair over.

"—Eight and nine and ten. The doors open. You're here. You're safe. You can step out of the elevator now, leave everything from the basement far below you, far behind. You're back here in the theater, back in your normal, waking state."

Tane blinks, looks around vaguely, coming out of it, but Dr. Carrigan's elevator routine hasn't worked with Alysha. She stays under.

"Wake up," I say to her softly, hoping maybe by calming my voice it'll do the trick.

"Don't try calling Sam, Dad! Don't—" All at once she shudders and slumps to the side, but I manage to keep her from sliding to the floor.

Tane stares at us, confused, still orienting himself. "What's going on?"

"It's Alysha." I'm supporting her. "She's not waking up."

Finally, she moans slightly, then shivers again and tenses. At last she turns her head toward me. "Daniel?"

"It's okay. You're safe."

She leans into my arms and I hold her until she finally stops trembling.

Dr. Carrigan is standing there speechless.

"What did you do to her?" Tane rises. "What happened?"

"Nothing. I mean, she went under. She would have woken up by herself eventually. Sometimes people take a few minutes to return to . . . But I've never seen it happen like that . . . I'm . . . I've hypnotized thousands of people and I've never had them get so upset when they're under, not without more of a stimulus."

I'm starting to believe that this guy can't be nearly as good as the senator thinks he is.

Tane still looks agitated, but seems unclear about where to take out his frustration. "Were all three of us hypnotized?"

"I wasn't," I tell him.

Maybe you were, though. What about the blur? Is that what it's like to be hypnotized?

I ask Alysha, "What's the last thing you remember?"

"We were taking an elevator down. We passed the third floor. After that, I just remember it jolting to a stop, and I could feel the brush of air as the doors opened again and then you were holding me. So you weren't hypnotized?"

"I had a blur."

"About?"

"I don't think it has anything to do with finding Petra. It was more of . . . well . . . Some answers to some personal questions. It doesn't matter. All that matters is that you're safe. That you're okay."

She turns to Tane. "What about you? Were you hypnotized?"

"I guess I was. I don't know."

"What was it like for you?"

"Kind of like what you just said. I remember Dr. Carrigan talking to us about this elevator, but it wasn't so sudden for me when I woke up. It was like I felt light-headed, but I don't remember what happened when I was out."

"Neither do I."

"You don't remember crying out?" I ask her.

"No. What was I saying?"

"You were scared. You kept saying 'Her name is Deedee and he's Sergei,' and 'Don't try calling Sam, Dad!' You sounded terrified. Do you know what either of those things means?"

"Uh-uh."

"You were listening to the video of Petra when it happened," Dr. Carrigan tells to her.

"What?"

"While you were hypnotized, you said you had to listen to it again and I asked you, 'Listen to what?' and you told me, 'Petra. After she was taken.' That's all you said, though."

Alysha appears deep in thought. "I might know what it means. I think that's what Petra was trying to tell us when she had her mouth taped shut."

"I thought you weren't able to understand her?" I say.

"I wasn't—not consciously, at least. But maybe I identified it all subconsciously and didn't realize that until I was hypnotized."

Dr. Carrigan nods. "That is very possible. The conscious mind and the unconscious mind meet, merge, work together and affect our behavior in ways we still don't understand."

"So, if that's what Petra was trying to say, she might have been telling us the names of her kidnappers."

Okay, this might be something we could really use.

Tane looks concerned. "Did I say or do anything weird?" he asks me.

"Not that I could tell."

He faces Dr. Carrigan. "Put me under again."

"I'm not sure I . . ."

"Do it. And ask me about Malcolm."

"Malcolm?"

"Yeah. And film it. I want to know what happens." Then he turns to me and Alysha. "Just me this time. You guys wait here."

"What is it?"

"I think . . . I don't know. I sort of remember something from the trance, but . . . Well, I just need to be sure."

He presses Dr. Carrigan, until finally he agrees and motions for Tane to follow him. "Alright. Come into my office."

"Can we switch phones?" I ask him. "Let me use yours for a second and you can film him with this one."

Though he looks somewhat confused by my request, he offers me his cell. "Okay."

After we've exchanged phones, the two of them slip off to the office located just past the back row of seats, leaving Alysha and me alone on stage.

I put my hand on her shoulder. "Will you be okay here for a minute? I just need to call the senator and fill him in on what's happening. I'll see if those names you said while you were under mean anything to him."

"I'm fine. Yeah, go ahead."

I walk offstage to where it's a little more private and tap in Senator Amundsen's number.

CHAPTER FORTY-FIVE

"How did it go with Dr. Carrigan?" the senator asks me.

"I didn't end up getting hypnotized. Tane is trying it again because he might have seen something. Alysha heard some phrases that we're trying to figure out. She mentioned some names: Deedee and Sergei. Do those mean anything to you?"

"No."

"She also thought she heard Petra telling you not to call Sam, back when her mouth was taped shut in the ransom video. Do you know why?"

"I wasn't even aware she knew about Sam."

"Okay, did your people ever figure out where any passing trains and ambulance calls happened close together?"

"It wasn't easy, verifying it without being in touch with the authorities, but I called in some favors and from what we can tell, there were more than twenty occurrences that night, all throughout the South. It's just not as uncommon as you might think." Despite the fact that he seems to be trying to hide it, the strain from what's been going on weighs down every word. "So I'm afraid that doesn't do us a whole lot of good."

"But that narrows it down, though, right? I mean, if you take driving time into account from when she was kidnapped. Also, maybe you can check traffic cameras in those areas to look for that minivan entering or leaving the neighborhoods. There might be a Deedee or Sergei who has a minivan registered to their name, or who owns a house with a basement near those locations."

"Those are all interesting ideas, but I can't contact the police, remember?"

"I know someone who might be able to help you."

"Who?"

"My dad. He's a sheriff in Wisconsin, but he could go through his own law enforcement channels, say he's looking into an entirely different case. He could do the traffic camera and name searches, look into the databases. There wouldn't be any ties back to you."

"I don't know."

"I can call him if you want me to."

He's quiet, then says, "No. I can't chance it."

"Senator, I honestly don't know that we're going to be able to find Petra in time. I want to, I'll do everything I can to, but right now it's . . . This might be your best shot."

Another pause. "Can you make certain that none of this points to me or Petra?"

"I won't even tell him your name."

"Alright."

"Do you have a secure way that you can get him the info you pulled up on the ambulance calls and train whistle locations?"

"Yes. I'll have one of my people send it through my Senate account. It's encrypted."

I give him my dad's email address.

Then, as soon as he hangs up, I call Dad and tell him what we're going to need him to do. I finish by saying, "If it gets to be nine o'clock and you have a chance to call in help, do it. We might need it."

● ● ●

Adrian stopped by to see how things were going with Zacharias's interrogation.

The man was strapped to the chair in the tattoo room. Henrik was leaning over him.

Bloody tools lay on a tray nearby.

From this angle Adrian couldn't see Zacharias's face.

Henrik looked up. "Doctor."

"The general will be arriving at around seven."

"Our guest here isn't being entirely cooperative."

"But you're adapting?"

"I'm adapting." He cracked his knuckles. "I've done one of his eyeballs."

"Punctured?"

"No. Just tagged."

"I've never gotten a tattoo before," Zacharias said, unintimidated. "While we're in here why don't you give me a Celtic cross on my shoulder too?"

Adrian shook his head. "Mr. Zacharias, you can make this a lot easier on everyone involved if you just tell us how we can reach Sam."

"Sam wouldn't want me to do that."

Adrian assessed things, then said to Henrik, "How soon can Sergei and Deedee be here?"

"I'd say by eight. Why?"

"Alright. Have them bring Petra over. If Mr. Zacharias has decided that his own life isn't worth protecting, perhaps he'll be more willing to share with us when someone else is sitting in the chair."

● ● ●

Petra was still yanking at the wire, trying to get it loose from the bucket, when she heard heavy, clomping footsteps on the stairway leading down to her room.

Sergei.

But then, lighter steps followed.

Okay, so this would be the first time both of them had come down to check on her together.

She torqued at the handle—

C'mon, c'mon, c'mon.

All at once it snapped off the plastic.

She stared at it, dumbfounded that the wire was resting in her hand.

How long have you been working on this and it waits until now to come off?

Whatever. Hide it. Quick!

It was too stiff and curved to slide down her pants leg, so she stuck it under her shirt, then shoved the bucket to the corner of the room so her kidnappers wouldn't notice the missing handle.

The door popped open.

Deedee stood there holding a blindfold. "Hello, my dear."

Sergei had his roll of duct tape.

His nose was broken and he had a butterfly bandage across the bridge of it.

"What happened?" Petra asked him.

"The same thing that'll happen to you if you don't behave yourself."

"Don't make this difficult now," Deedee said. "We need to take a drive, and you can either be tied up or simply blindfolded with one leg cuffed to the floor. What'll it be?"

"Where are you taking me?"

"To get you ready to be reunited with your father."

"You're going to let me go?"

"That'll depend on him." Sergei held up the tape. "Now, are you going to struggle or are you going to behave yourself like I said?"

"I won't struggle."

"That's what I like to hear."

Petra let them put the blindfold on her and lead her up to the garage, and then into the back of the minivan.

When they got inside it, they didn't tie her up, but they did attach her ankle to a chain so she couldn't climb out.

She didn't fight them.

No, she did not.

And they hadn't noticed that the wire handle was missing from the top of the five-gallon bucket.

Alright, Petra. Let's see where things go from here.

PART III
CONVERGENCE

CHAPTER FORTY-SIX

I take a seat beside Alysha again.

"Any news on Petra?" she asks. "Do they know anything yet?"

"Not yet. No."

"How's the senator doing?"

"It's been tough on him. What about you? How are you?"

"Good." She takes a deep breath. "Better. Thank you for being there for me."

"Of course."

"And also, I never properly thanked you for stepping in front of me in that elevator when the guy was shooting at us this morning."

"You thanked me."

"Not properly. You might have been killed doing that."

"I'm just glad those doors closed in time."

"And that they stopped the bullets."

"That too."

"I like this habit of yours."

"What's that?"

"Looking out for me."

"Well, I don't know if I—"

"So, thanks. Officially."

"Sure."

"I owe you."

"Don't worry about it."

In the stillness that follows, I realize that I must be getting used to the smells of the old theater because they're not bothering me as much anymore.

That slipstream of reality.

Truth passing us by every moment while we only notice a sliver of it at a time.

"Daniel," Alysha says quietly, "you have me at a slight disadvantage here."

"What do you mean?"

"You can see me, but I still have no idea what you look like." She holds her hand. "May I?"

"Do what?"

"If you let me touch your face . . . if you're okay with that, it'll help me picture you."

Though it makes me a little uneasy, I don't like the idea that she thinks of herself as being at some sort of disadvantage around me, so I take her hand and place her palm against my cheek.

She moves her fingers slowly down to the line of my jaw, then pauses and lifts her other hand. "Is this alright?"

"Go ahead."

I close my eyes so she won't accidentally poke them.

Using both hands, she brushes her fingers lightly across my cheek, up to my forehead, then over my eyelids and my nose, and then down, momentarily grazing one finger over my lips.

At last, she trails her hands past my chin and down my neck, to its base, where she finally rests both of them.

"So how do I look to a blind person?"

"You're one of the cutest guys I've ever felt."

"Well, no one's ever told me that before."

She still has her hands on the downward slope of my neck.

I catch myself looking at her and I have the sense that, if she could see, she would be gazing at me as well.

Eye contact.

It's powerful.

I think of Nicole, and how—

"I'm guessing it gets weird after a while doesn't it?" Alysha says.

"What does?"

"Seeing me and not knowing what I'm thinking. I mean, most people get pretty good at reading other people's eyes, right? Or at telling things about them by how long they hold your gaze or how quickly they look away?"

"How do you know all that?"

"I may be blind, but I'm not stupid. And I am a girl." A tiny smile. "Besides, I do the same thing with words, with silences, with reading between the lines of what people say."

She lowers one hand to her lap, but leaves the other where it is. "Because of that, though, I'm afraid you still have me at a disadvantage, Daniel."

"How's that?"

"When it's quiet, when we're not talking, you can tell so much more about me than I can about you. But there's one way we can be on an even playing field."

"What is it?"

"Let me feel your heartbeat."

"Alysha, I, um . . ."

"Oh, don't be shy."

"It's just that I—"

"Trust me. It's okay. Let's see how well I do at reading between the lines."

After a brief internal debate, I position her hand on my chest, over my heart.

She presses her palm more firmly so that she can find the rhythm. "You can tell a lot by a person's heartbeat."

"What can you tell from mine?" Despite myself, I can feel my heartbeat quickening. Nicole comes to mind again. That and—

"Just a moment." Alysha slides her hand slightly to the side. "Hmm. I believe I've narrowed it down. You're thinking one of two things."

"And what are those?"

"First: You might be afraid."

"Of what?"

"Well. Me."

"Why would I be afraid of you?"

"Of being here with me right now."

"I don't—"

"Of where it might lead."

I'm not sure how to respond to that, but I start reaching up to remove her hand. However, it's almost like she can read my mind, because she pulls it back and rests it on her other one before I can touch it.

"Do you want to know the second thing?"

"Yes."

"That you aren't afraid at all."

"I don't understand."

"Do you trust me?"

"I . . ."

"Let me have your hand."

"For what?"

"Trust me."

She holds out her palm, and I place my hand on it.

"Now," she says, "close your eyes."

"Why?"

"Just close them."

"What are you going to do?"

"Trust me."

I close my eyes.

"Are they closed?"

"Yes."

She lifts my palm to her cheek. "Go ahead. See what I would look like to you if you were blind."

"Alysha—"

She gently flattens it against her warm skin, but lets her hand linger there. "It's okay."

But I open my eyes and draw my hand back. "Alysha, I have a girlfriend."

"And?"

"And this . . . I mean . . ."

"So you don't want to kiss me?"

"What?"

"Your heartbeat. It was either fear or, well, just the opposite, and I'm not sure what to believe."

"What do you mean?"

"Your heartbeat or your words. The first one is telling me that you do want to kiss me, the second, that you don't."

"I can't."

"But do you *want* to?"

It's a tough question.

Because despite myself, the answer is both no.

And yes.

"If you didn't have a girlfriend?" she says.

"But, I do, so I—"

The door to the Great Carrigini's office opens and he and Tane appear.

"So, we can talk about this later, then?" She is whispering so that only I can hear her. "Okay?"

I don't want to betray Nicole, but Alysha is right about one thing—this is not the time to sort this out.

"Okay."

All of this gets me thinking about Nicole again, and, though I'm tempted to call her and let her know I'm okay, I remind myself that Dad is taking care of that.

Tane has Malcolm's phone in his hand and is reviewing the video of what happened during their session.

"Well?" I ask him, glad to not be alone with Alysha anymore.

He looks up and studies the mountain vista photographs Dr. Carrigan has taken over the years, then walks to a picture of an old building with massive vines crawling up one side of it.

"This place," he says to the Great Carrigini. "What is it?"

"The old Estoria Inn."

"Tell me about it."

"Closed down in the fifties. You hear stories about it. I took that photo nearly a decade ago. Why?"

"What kind of stories?"

"The word 'haunted' gets thrown around. Supposedly, there's a malevolent spirit in room 113 that possesses anyone who stays in there for more than one night. People say a boy was murdered in that room. It's all just folklore, though. I don't think any of it's ever been verified."

"That's the place." Tane taps the picture. "That's where we need to go."

I look at him curiously. "Why?"

"That's where they're taking Petra."

"How do you know?"

"Malcolm told me."

"Malcolm? When?"

"Just now."

"What?"

He turns the phone's screen toward me and replays part of the session.

In the video, he's in a trance and Dr. Carrigan is asking him about Malcolm. Suddenly, he starts describing a building that sounds remarkably like that hotel.

"I don't understand," I say. "How is it possible that Malcolm could communicate that with you?"

Being psychic? Is that Tane's gift? His instrument?

But is it Malcolm's gift too?

"It only happened once before, when I was in L.A. Remember that story I told you about the drug dealer and how I helped find him? It wasn't Malcolm speaking to me then, but I heard something that there was no way I should have been able to know about that location. And the voice was right."

I give the hypnotist back his phone and Tane hands me Malcolm's, then he turns to Dr. Carrigan. "Can you get us up there?"

"I'm telling you, there's nothing there. It's just an old deserted hotel."

"No. This is it," Tane insists. "This is where we need to go." His firm tone leaves no room for argument. "What's the fastest way up there?"

"From here? It would take a while—there's no direct route. But I couldn't drive you anyway. I'd never make it back in time for my show."

"What about the helicopter?" I ask.

"I'm not sure there's really anywhere for him to land up there."

"You've hiked all over those mountains—you said earlier that you know them like the back of your hand. There must be somewhere with a flat enough field."

"Well, there are some meadows, but . . . wait . . ."

He hurries into his office and when he returns, he's carrying a large topographical map of the Smokies. He unfolds it on the floor and studies it, tracing hiking trails with his finger.

"This is Mount Dreyfus." He points to a peak on the map. "There was a forest fire there a few years ago. I think the area is still clear enough to get a chopper in. From there it's probably an hour-and-fifteen-minute hike along the ridge to the Estoria."

Alysha speaks up. "What if it's too overgrown to land?"

"Well . . . Then you'd need to fly to Spider Peak— maybe land at the base of it, here. It might be closer as the crow flies, but the trail is a little steeper and you'd have to cross Little Bear Creek. There should be a bridge, but it was pretty dilapidated the last time I was up there—and that was five years ago. I'm not sure if it's still even intact."

"Will flying a helicopter around draw attention if there are people at the Inn?"

He shakes his head. "It shouldn't. This is a tourist area. There are half a dozen companies that provide helicopter flight excursions and tours up in those mountains. Anyway, I'm not sure what you expect to find up there."

Tane taps the photograph one more time. "We're going to find the person we're looking for. Just like I did in L.A."

"Alright," I say. In the past I've had to trust the mysterious voices I've heard, now it was time to trust one of Tane's. "Let's go."

We find the pilot at the diner.

He brings a couple slices of pie to go and we return to the chopper.

The Great Carrigini speaks with him for a few minutes, pinpointing on the map where to drop us off. "If you can't land here on Mount Dreyfus, try the base of Spider Peak."

"So from there, how do they get to the Estoria?"

"The trail should be clearly marked. They'll cross the creek and then head uphill toward the Inn. It's not that far. I'm guessing it's about an hour-hike from the meadow where you'd be landing."

He offers me the map. "Here. Take it."

"We can use the GPS on Malcolm's phone."

"Oh, that won't work up there. No reception. Take the map. Believe me. If the trails are overgrown or that bridge is washed away, you're going to need it."

CHAPTER FORTY-SEVEN

Nicole Marten didn't know what to make of everything that was going on.

Ever since this morning when she found out Daniel was missing, she'd been worried and been praying—thinking about him pretty much the whole time.

The pit in her stomach felt sort of like the one she'd had last winter when he was seeing the blurs of the girl who'd died on that island in Lake Superior.

Was she concerned about him now?

Oh yeah.

Did she trust that God was in control?

Yes, she did.

So how did those two things work together—worry and faith?

Who knows.

But it was what it was.

Right now she was sitting in the passenger seat next to Mia, who was guiding them up further into the mountains.

They were almost to the Marly Weathers Great Smoky Mountains Educational Center, which was a lot more out-of-the-way than Nicole had expected. Kyle was in the back checking something on his phone.

Thirty minutes ago, Mia had swung through Rascal's Burger Hut.

They didn't serve veggie burgers, so Nicole had gone for a Mega-size Curly Fries, and then filled out her supper with some of the granola bars that were left over from the drive down to Georgia.

Kyle ordered the Mongo Burger, and Mia got a Western Rodeo Burger with extra bacon, and a "hand-spun" pineapple milkshake, which was taking forever to melt.

Now they'd all finished their meals, except for Mia, who was still working on her shake. She took a loud sip of it as they entered the educational center's parking lot.

There were so many cars that she had to park on the grass.

"Isn't this place supposed to be closing right about now?" Nicole asked.

Kyle looked up from his phone. "That's what I thought."

"I wonder what's going on."

Inside the center, people were lining up for trolley rides that departed from the back of the building.

Along the walls, Nicole counted sixteen glass-encased taxidermy animals showing the diversity of wildlife found in the Great Smoky Mountains—from black bears to timber rattlesnakes to different species of owls.

It sort of bugged her—animals are not on this planet for people to gawk at or be amused by—but she could understand that the center was probably just trying to help visitors appreciate nature more. She decided to give them a pass.

However, those animals weren't really the main attraction. The fireflies were.

The entire center was decorated with firefly stuff—from hats and jackets to stickers to cuddly stuffed animal fireflies with working lights.

A little boy was holding one of them, making the light go on by squeezing its tummy. "So why do their butts light up?" he asked his mom.

"It's their abdomen."

"What's that?"

"It's sort of, well, the part on the end, there."

"So, their butt?"

"Joey." She helped him put it back on the shelf. "C'mon. Let's go find your father. It's almost time for the trolley to leave."

Mia had brought her shake with her and kept trying to get the rest of it up the straw, but the pineapple pieces were too big and she ended up super-sucking the straw, lifting it out of the cup with the pineapple suctioned to the other end, then turning the straw around and biting off the hunk of pineapple.

Mia being Mia.

Kyle slipped off to use the bathroom and while he was gone, Nicole's phone rang.

At first she wondered if it might be the cop from campus security again, but when she checked the screen she saw that it was Daniel's dad.

What if something was wrong? What if Daniel had been found and he was hurt? Or worse?

Apprehensively, she answered, "Hello? Mr. Byers?"

"He's okay, Nicole. Daniel is."

"What? How do you know? Did the cops find him?" She grabbed Mia's arm and whispered to her, "Daniel's alright."

Mia almost choked on her pineapple chunk. "What? Who is that?"

"His dad."

Mr. Byers went on, "I spoke with Dan on the phone. He can't call you, but he's okay."

"Where is he?"

"Right now I just need you not to worry about him. He'll be in touch with you guys tonight around nine. How are you doing?"

"We're fine. So, but—you're sure?"

"Yes."

"I wish I knew where he was."

"Listen, it's important that you don't call anyone. Not the police. Not anyone else."

"Why would I call the police? Now you're getting me worried again."

"No, you're—look, I have another call coming in. I'm checking on some things here, so this might be important. I have to go. I'll talk with you later."

And then he was off the line.

"What is it?" Mia said.

"I don't know exactly. His dad says he's alright and not to call the cops."

"Not to call the cops?"

"Yeah. Weird, right?"

Kyle returned and they quickly filled him in.

"So now what?" he asked.

Mia looked around. "I guess since we're here we might as well try to figure out what's going on."

"Definitely," Nicole agreed. "Everything is just way too suspicious. Daniel's disappearance. All of this. His dad is gonna call us later. Until then, we should see what else we can learn."

A perky, twenty-something woman who was wearing one of the center's embroidered baseball caps approached them cheerfully. She sported a T-shirt with what looked like glow-in-the-dark fireflies and the words, "Light up the Night—Together!" emblazoned on the front. Her nametag read: "Tiff."

She tilted her head and smiled. "Do you have your tickets? I can get you on the next trolley."

"Tickets?" Kyle said. "No, we don't have any tickets."

Tiff looked genuinely disheartened. "I'm afraid if you don't have tickets already, you're out of luck. They're usually plucked up within a few minutes of going on sale."

"What exactly is all this? The trolleys? The fireflies?"

"You're not here for the firefly viewing?"

"We don't know anything about the fireflies. I thought your website said you closed at six thirty?"

"Oh. Well, this week we have special hours. It might not have gotten updated on the site." She spread out her arms in a welcoming manner. "We're open late all week for the Synchronous Firefly Event!"

"Which is, what, exactly?"

"The Great Smoky Mountains are home to nineteen different species of fireflies, but the most special of all are the *Photinus carolinus*. For one week of the year, here in nearby Cades Cove, they blink on and off—" As she said that, she opened and closed her hands in a blinky manner. "—all together, all at once. It's one of the only places in the world that it happens, and only during this one week."

"But how?" Mia asked. "How do they know when to blink?"

Tiff titlted her hands palms-up and smiled again. "No one really understands why it happens. They say it has to do with mating rituals."

"No, I mean, *how* do the individual fireflies know when to blink, if they all do it at the same time?"

"One of nature's great mysteries. And that's what everyone is here for . . . although tonight might not be the best showing. It's looking like rain, so our little friends might not be as active as they usually are."

"Actually," Kyle said, "that's all really interesting, but we're here because we . . . Well, we're looking for our friend Daniel Byers."

Tiff shook her head, still smiling. "Doesn't ring a bell."

"This may sound strange, but does a Dr. Waxford work here by any chance?"

Another head shake.

"Malcolm Zacharias?" Nicole asked.

"Well, yes, now that you mention it. I mean, he doesn't work here, but Mr. Zacharias comes by sometimes to pick up packages. We have one in the back for him right now, I believe."

"From Marly Weathers?"

Tiff stared at her, slightly puzzled. "How did you know that?"

"Because . . . Marly is my dad. He told me to come by and get it."

"He did?"

"Yes. I just—we just—flew in from Philly. Mr. Zacharias can't make it and Dad didn't want it sitting here tonight."

Tiff didn't quite look convinced.

"My dad has an unlisted number and he doesn't like me giving it out to anyone, but I can tell you his email address if you need to verify everything." She fished her phone out of her purse. "I have it right here, if you want to check."

"Um . . . well . . . that won't be necessary. Let me go get that package for you."

After Tiff stepped away, Mia asked under her breath, "How'd you know Marly Weathers's phone number wouldn't be listed?"

"I figured that a reclusive billionaire wouldn't want his number out there."

"Huh." Abandoning the straw, Mia tipped the cup to her mouth, gulped down the remaining pineapple globs and deposited the empty cup in a trash can nearby. "But he would let you give out his email address?"

"I wasn't sure about that part, but we got what we were looking for. Right?"

"Not yet, but—"

Tiff returned, carrying a sealed package about the size of two shoeboxes. "Here you go. Now, they need me to help corral people onto the trolleys, so . . ."

"Sure." Nicole accepted the box. "Thanks."

"I hope you do get a chance to see the fireflies while you're here in town. Somehow."

"Yeah. That'd be nice."

"It's a remarkable experience."

"Right."

Tiff swept off toward the trolley line, and Nicole led her two friends outside to open the box and find out what Marly Weathers had sent to Mr. Zacharias.

• • •

Dr. Adrian Waxford got a text from General Gibbons that she was on her way up the mountain.

He'd requested that she contact him when she turned onto Forest Service Road 141, since that was the last place where there was cell reception.

He directed Garrett Marion, the guard who was currently on duty at the Estoria, to drive down and unlock the gate so the general would be able to get through.

• • •

Nicole set the package on a picnic table nestled in a small copse of trees off to the side of the building.

Kyle offered to open it in case there was anything weird in it. She took "weird" to mean "dangerous" and didn't argue, but just slid it toward him.

He started working at the tape.

"It says to open the other side first," Mia pointed out.

"I'm living dangerously. Can I borrow your knife?"

She drew out her butterfly knife, skillfully flicked out the blade, and passed the knife to him, handle first.

"Man, every time you whip that thing around I think you're gonna cut off one of your fingers."

"Practice makes perfect."

"It also makes for nicknames."

"Nicknames?"

"Yeah. Like 'Lefty.'"

"Ha."

He carefully slit the tape, then tipped open the cardboard flaps, and removed the box's contents: a book about haunted places in Tennessee, a pile of overstuffed file folders, some maps of the mountains, and a stack of printed web pages with federal government letterhead.

"Divide and conquer," Nicole said.

They split up everything and got to work.

• • •

A storm is tracking toward us through the mountains.

Though the sun won't set for another couple hours, with the clouds mounting in the west, the evening sky is already beginning to darken.

"So Daniel, does it look like Rush out there?" Alysha asks me through her headset radio.

"More like Pink Floyd."

"Pink who?"

"Pink—never mind. Let's just say this is not a Mozart sky."

We fly over the peaks toward the fire-ravaged mountaintop that the Great Carrigini told us about, but as we get closer, it's evident that the area is too overgrown for a helicopter to land.

The pilot veers south and heads to the base of that second peak, the one that would be a shorter hike distance-wise, but that would require us to cross Little Bear Creek.

CHAPTER FORTY-EIGHT

Dr. Adrian Waxford watched as General Vanessa Gibbons's rental car rolled up the dirt road to the Estoria Inn.

She parked and stepped out, dressed in civilian clothes.

Adrian sent Garrett back down to ascertain that the gate was locked and secure once again.

Seeing the general out of her element like this, and not at the Pentagon, reminded Adrian of a time when he was a boy and glimpsed his elementary school teacher down the aisle at the grocery store.

It'd been such a shock to see Mrs. Reynolds in a place other than school, dressed in shorts, a T-shirt, and flip-flops. It seemed like the entire universe had shifted on some great, unseen axis.

His mom had been pregnant with his brother at the time.

His little brother, Jacob.

The one whose murder was the reason for everything here at the Inn.

General Gibbons removed her aviator sunglasses. "Adrian."

"General. How was your trip?"

"Endurable."

"Do you need anything?

"I do not. Let's begin. I'd like to accomplish as much as possible as promptly as we can. It looks like a storm is rolling in and I'm not excited about the prospect of driving down this mountain to my hotel while the roads are getting washed out by rain."

"Fair enough. Follow me."

Adrian placed his hand on the vascular biometrics vein recognition reader, the door opened, and he led the general into the Estoria Inn.

• • •

"Check this out." Nicole showed her friends the pages she'd been reading. "Marly's been monitoring everywhere Dr. Waxford travels around the country. There's a map to a place up here in the Smokies—the Estoria Inn. Kyle, you said there were rumors that Waxford was looking for a new research place in Tennessee, right?"

"Yeah. And this haunted sites book has that same hotel highlighted. Supposedly, it's haunted by a little boy who was murdered there. There's a blueprint of the place—it's got all the sightings marked, where they occurred, in which hallways and rooms—if you buy into that stuff."

It'd always amazed Nicole that for a guy who loved to tell stories about ghosts as much as Kyle did, he still didn't believe in them.

Mia pointed to the official-looking printouts in front of her. "This stuff is all about a Senate hearing tomorrow—an investigation into funds that the Pentagon seems to have misplaced."

"You think all this has anything to do with what's happened to Daniel?" Nicole asked. "Don't forget, it was Malcolm Zacharias who was supposed to pick up this box."

Kyle studied the papers and books strewn across the table. "Right now most of the arrows point to this Estoria Inn place."

"Does that book tell how to find it?" Nicole asked.

He consulted the appendix and then pulled up a map on his phone. "It looks like it's not too far from here. Maybe another ten miles or so around the other side of Spider Peak. Some of the roads are just for the forest service so it might be a little confusing, but we should be able to figure it out."

"We came all this way. It would be pointless to turn around and drive back to Atlanta without checking it out, right?"

None of them could come up with a good reason to leave Tennessee before at least seeing if they could get some answers, not if the hotel was that close.

"Do you need to call your aunt?" Nicole asked Mia. "Tell her we're gonna be a little later than we thought?"

"Probably a good idea."

Kyle gathered everything, jammed it into the box again, and they returned to the car. "If we get up there and anyone asks us what we're doing, we'll just tell 'em we're looking for ghosts—alright? We'll say we heard these stories about the hotel and maybe someone dared us to go up there, spend the night, something like that. We're teenagers. It's believable."

Mia cleared things with Sue Ellen, they piled into the sedan, and took off for the Inn.

• • •

As Adrian and the general neared the kitchen, he offered to find her something to eat.

"No. Thank you." She proceeded into the hallway leading toward the subjects' rooms. "I only saw three cars parked outside. How many staff do you have working tonight?"

"One of the cars is mine. Then, Henrik Poehlman is here—I think you've met him. We also have a security guard, Garrett Marion. Two other staff are on their way up. Our research assistants have all gone home."

"So, a skeleton crew."

"We value the funding that you and your committee provide. We try to stretch it as much as possible. It also helps to minimize the visibility of the center."

"How so?"

"The more guards, the more vehicles would be driving back and forth, and the more attention it would attract. But there are plenty of other security measures in place, I assure you."

He expected her to ask him to elaborate, but she said nothing.

They came to the first room.

A clipboard with the intake data about the subject hung next to the one-way mirror. The form listed the inmate's ID number, his crimes, his sentence, and the date of his arrival.

No names.

Just numbers.

It was easier that way, rather than being reminded that these men used to have a name, a life, an identity on the outside.

General Gibbons only glanced briefly at the form, then peered into the room and gasped—something Adrian had never before known her to do.

"What happened to his eyes?"

"We tattooed them."

"You tattooed his eyeballs?"

"Yes."

"That wasn't in your report."

"We do it to all of the subjects as a safety precaution."

"Explain to me how that's a safety precaution."

"The ink contains nanobot geo-trackers. In Wisconsin we had that incident in the winter with one of the subjects slipping away."

"Yes. I remember."

"Well, we didn't want to chance having that happen again here. This way, if anyone were to escape, we would be able to find him before he could even reach the base of the mountain."

"And if he did?

"If he did?"

"Reach the base of the mountain. I'm not familiar with this technology. What's the range for those trackers?"

"They're tied in to the defense satellite grid."

"So, global."

"Yes."

"Hmm . . . And what about the wounds on his face?"

"Those are from the *Tabanidae*."

"The flies."

"Yes."

"How long was he exposed to them?"

"I never leave anyone in there for more than fifteen minutes. The results after that would be . . . well . . . quite undesirable. And not productive for what we're trying to accomplish."

She was quiet.

"It's all in the name of justice. All for the greater good."

"Yes. So, regarding the geo-trackers: The subjects could be located wherever they go—unless they removed their eyeballs, I presume?"

"They haven't been told what the ink contains, so there's no reason to think they would take that step."

"Show me how to use it. How to track the men."

Adrian was a little surprised that she was so interested in this peripheral aspect of the program, but he decided that it would be best to do whatever was necessary to satisfy her curiosity as expeditiously as possible so she could get on her way before the nine o'clock deadline.

"The unit is in the security center just down the hall," he told her. "Follow me."

CHAPTER
FORTY-NINE

The pilot guides the chopper into the narrow clearing near the base of Spider Peak.

Because of the wind, his landing is a little rocky, but he obviously knows what he's doing and manages to rest the landing skids on the ground without jarring us too much.

He turns off the engine and indicates a trail entering the woods nearby.

"According to what Dr. Carrigan said, that's the one we want. We'll need to follow it past the creek, then up to that next rise."

"Wait," I say. "'We'?"

"I'm coming with you."

"What about your heart problems? You said earlier you couldn't do any strenuous exercise."

"I can't let you three go alone."

I shake my head. "No, really. We'll be okay. We can't take the chance that you'd have a heart attack or something."

"He's right," Tane agrees. "How serious are your heart problems?"

"Pretty much . . . I mean . . . I'll be okay."

"No," Alysha says emphatically. "You need to be safe."

Eventually, he sighs. "Alright. Yeah, I probably shouldn't come." He checks the time. "If the hypnotist was right, you'll easily make it to the Estoria by eight thirty."

"You should head back to town."

He shakes his head. "I want to be close by so I can get you out of here after you find Petra." He pulls out a hand-held two-way radio and gives it to Tane. "This'll be good for at least six miles. Even in these mountains, it'll cover you, no problem. Radio me. If I don't hear back from you by the time it gets dark, I'll go for help."

"What if the storm hits before then?"

"Well, if the wind picks up much more than this, I *will* need to take off." He rubs his jaw. "I can always call the authorities from town."

I shake my head. "Don't contact anyone until we radio you. Petra's life might depend on it."

"I'll just slow you guys down," Alysha says to Tane and me. "Maybe I should stay here."

Tane is studying the trail. "Honestly, it looks pretty smooth. I think you'll be okay."

"I don't know."

"We need you with us," he insists. "You hear what we can't—like when you noticed that cell phone ringing in the parking garage or the sirens on the ransom video. If we're in the hotel and people come after us, you'll hear them long before we do."

He does have a point.

"I don't have my cane," she notes. "What if the trail gets too narrow for you to guide me?"

"Well, if we need to, we can always leave the radio with you, keep going, and come back for you after we have Petra."

At last he convinces her.

The pilot finds a flashlight. "For your hike back here." He hands it to me. Then, as the storm clouds mount, Tane, Alysha, and I start toward the trail.

They're ahead of me, and just before I enter the forest, I glance one last time across the meadow at the helicopter pilot.

And I see someone standing behind him.

What?

I'm about to call Tane and Alysha back, but then I remember Kyle suggesting that I film things to try to discern whether or not I'm having a blur. And, since we're in the middle of the mountains and someone has suddenly appeared out of nowhere, this seems like a good time to test his theory.

I open the camera app on Malcolm's phone.

Switch to the video mode.

Hit "Record."

Peer at the image on the screen.

There's the pilot, just like he should be, beside the senator's helicopter.

All alone.

But when I move the phone aside, I see that other person.

And now I realize who it is.

The corpse from the attic.

The one who looks like me and has the same wounds Grandpa died from.

He gazes over the pilot's shoulder toward me, and it's disconcerting to see my own face staring at me like that.

I check things a few times with the phone, but it doesn't record him.

He isn't real.

But it sure looks like he is.

At last he raises his arms to each side, they morph into great black wings, and he takes off toward the churning clouds, making me think of my words to Grandpa about the monsters that I was afraid of when I was little: "They're like giant bats. But scarier."

The boy from my dream the night I got hit by the truck comes to mind, and I hear him tell me again that I should follow the bats, that I should find the truth.

But where? What does that mean to follow the bats?

I can't follow this one now because the boy is gone and the blur is over.

I glance at the pilot.

He's staring at me curiously, probably wondering what in the world I've been looking at.

After giving him a quick wave to reassure him that things are okay, I leave to catch up with Alysha and Tane.

I figure I don't need to tell them what just happened.

This was a blur for me, about my own issues.

It had nothing to do with finding Petra.

CHAPTER
FIFTY

In the security control room, Adrian finished instructing the general on how to use the portable tracking device to locate the subjects. The unit was about the size of a tablet computer.

"As you can see . . ." He pointed to the glowing dots in the virtual map of the Estoria. "Everyone's safely tucked in for the night."

She tapped the screen. "What's this on the fourth floor?"

One dot was blinking where no prisoners were supposed to be.

That must be where Henrik has Zacharias.

Reminding himself that, since it was in the service of justice, a slight lie would be excusable, Adrian said, "That's where we store the ink supply."

"I see." The general turned her attention to a nearby console with a panel of buttons and switches. It lay just beneath the reinforced window that provided a bird's-eye view of the hallway where the subjects were kept. "And this is where you, what? Control access to their rooms?"

"Yes."

"So, you have locked interior and exterior doors, vascular biometrics, armed guards, an isolated location, a global tracking system."

"As well as a perimeter fence and motion sensors in the woods."

"I would say that, given your resources, you are providing ample security."

"Thank you."

"Alright." She faced him. "I've read the reports, but I want to hear it from you. Talk me through your critical flicker-fusion frequency tests."

"Well, let's see . . . So, as you know, not all biological entities process the passage of time at the same rate. Even *Homo sapiens* of different ages process time differently. For example, time seems to speed up the older we get."

"And that's where the tests come in."

He nodded. "We flash a light at varying intervals and then study at what point, for that specific organism, the flickers of light appear to become constant."

"And how can you tell when flashing lights appear constant to, say, a fly?"

"By studying their reaction to the frequency of the flashes over a predetermined span of time."

The general evaluated that. "And by doing this you've confirmed that different species truly do perceive time to pass differently?"

Adrian's phone vibrated and, with everything that was going on, he decided to check it.

He found a text from Deedee: *Running late. Traffic is backed up. We'll be there as soon as we can.*

For a moment he considered replying and telling her not to bring Petra in, but he needed to control things and the best way to do that was by having her here at the Estoria. He could have them bring her in through a back entrance, keep the general away from her, especially at nine when—

"Adrian?"

"I'm sorry?"

"You were saying? The frequency of the flashes?"

"Yes. Right. Excuse me." He put the phone away. "Flies have been of particular interest to me since they process things four times faster than we do."

"So, to them, movement appears four times slower than it does for us?"

"Precisely." He thought about showing her the *Tabanidae* room in the basement, but decided that, to save time, he would only do so if she specifically requested it.

"And this new drug you've been telling me about, the one you've been wanting to test—it creates this same effect in people?"

"I believe it will, yes."

"Do you have any idea if it will alleviate pain?"

"Pain? No. It wouldn't serve to mitigate pain. Given the way it'll interact with the nervous system, if anything, it would intensify it."

She looked deep in thought.

He knew that the military was interested in his research for use in interrogations. He'd never probed into specifically how her people were going to utilize it, but now her questions made him curious. "I hope I'm not being out of line to ask this, but are you thinking of using Telpatine in lieu of waterboarding?"

She didn't deny anything. "We need interrogation methods that are just as effective but not as politically divisive."

"But I thought studies had found that waterboarding *wasn't* effective?"

"Adrian, you're a smart man. Do you really think that in today's political climate a government committee would come to any other conclusion?"

"Hmm. I suppose not."

"For example, can you imagine if the Senate Intelligence Committee would actually have come out and admitted how helpful it's been in our counterterrorism efforts? 'Yes, you know what? Waterboarding really does help us stop terrorist attacks. We're going to keep using it.'"

"The backlash would have been incredible."

"*Devastating* might be a better word. And so, it's no longer an option. That has left us searching for alternate techniques that will provide consistent, veridical, and reliable results during enhanced interrogations."

"And by making those interrogations seem longer than they are."

"When necessary."

"That's where the Telpatine comes in."

"Yes."

"As well as the other methods I've developed for the subjects under my care."

"Under your care?"

"Yes."

"That's an interesting way to phrase things."

"How would you have me phrase things?"

Rather than answer that, she said, "Do you have records of your tests with the *Tabanidae*? Video files? Anything of that nature?"

"Certainly. There's a conference room on the second floor, just down the hall from my office. We can watch them in there."

• • •

Nicole was driving. "We've gotta be close, right?"

"It looks like it," Mia answered from the backseat. Their phones had stopped getting any reception, so she and Kyle were studying the maps from the box they'd picked up at the nature center. "But what road are we on, again?"

"I don't think there was a sign. I thought you knew where we are?"

"I do. It's just . . . I don't know *exactly* where we are."

Half of the mountain roads were unmarked, some were just forest service roads. And, with the cloud cover, there was no way to tell where the sun was or which direction they were driving.

Nicole began to slow down. "Well, whatever road we're on, it ends up ahead. We need to decide whether to turn right or left."

"Is there a sign?"

"Nope."

"Of course not," Mia grumbled. "Why would there be a sign? If there was, people might actually be able to figure out where in the hell they are."

Nicole let the car idle at the intersection.

"It looks like we go right," Kyle said. "Then, in about half a mile, we should come to the road that leads up to the Estoria Inn—at least I think so."

Nicole noted the mileage. "Alright. Let's give it a shot."

Just shy of half a mile up the mountain, they came to a dirt road that led further uphill.

A metal gate blocked the entrance.

The road they were currently on was narrow, so to allow any other cars to get through, Nicole tucked her dad's sedan as far onto the shoulder as the steep, sloping embankment would allow, and parked.

Kyle climbed out and walked to the gate. "Sometimes these things aren't really locked, just made to look like it."

He rattled the chain and tried to unthread it, but it was secure.

"I'm pretty sure this is the place."

"How far to the hotel?" Mia asked.

"A couple miles."

"How many is a couple?"

"Two. Or so."

"Or so?"

"The road winds around a lot. From that map there's no way to tell the exact distance."

"And we need to walk."

"Yup."

"Uphill." Her overwhelming enthusiasm was clear in her tone of voice.

"Pretty much."

Nicole nodded. "We can make it. We need to have a look up there."

"Two miles isn't a big deal," Kyle said to Mia.

"Yeah, you run track. It's not a big deal for you. My sport is watching YouTube videos. Thus, for me, it would be a monumentalously big deal."

"Is that even a word?"

"It oughta be."

"Well, I could go on alone but—"

"No," Nicole objected. "I'm definitely coming. Daniel might be up there. I'm not just going to sit around here waiting for you to walk four miles."

"Oh, thanks for the reminder that we need *to come back two miles as well*." Mia sighed.

"But at least that'll all be downhill."

"There is that."

"If we're going to do this," Kyle said, "I think it's probably best for all of us to go rather than splitting up. So are we good?"

"Yeah. Okay, whatever. We're good."

He popped the trunk and began rooting around inside it.

"What are you looking for?"

"A flashlight. I'm not sure when it'll get dark out here, but I don't want to be caught on this road without some way of finding our way back to the car again, especially if it starts to rain."

He found a mini headlamp, tested it, then slipped it into his back pocket.

While the trunk was open. Nicole grabbed the first aid kit.

"Why are you bringing that?" Kyle asked.

"If Daniel's hurt. Or for bear attacks. I've got pepper spray in my purse, but—"

"Bear attacks?" exclaimed Mia.

"Sure. They're in this area, right? I mean—"

"Nikki, a few bandages, an Aspirin, and a roll of adhesive tape aren't gonna do us a whole lot of good if we get mauled by a bear." Mia went for the tire iron.

"Really?" Kyle said.

"Hey. You never know."

"Oh." Nicole opened the door to the backseat. "One more thing—that book about all the haunted places. If that's our cover story, we should have it with us. And also, Kyle, you said there was a blueprint of the building in it? Well, that should help us out while we're looking around."

After retrieving it, she locked the car, and the three of them began the trek up the road toward the old hotel.

• • •

Petra Amundsen sat on the floor in the back of the minivan.

The blindfold made it impossible to see where they were going, but she could tell they were driving uphill on a curvy road.

She recalled the first time she'd ridden in here, three days ago.

So, three days without her meds.

A long time.

Too long.

And now, in the darkness beneath that blindfold, the snakes appeared again, slithering and squirming and hissing before her.

She could see them, even though she couldn't see anything.

It was troubling.

The real world and the world of her hallucinations were overlapping.

Some of the snakes passed across her skin. Her arms. Her neck. Her stomach.

Then she felt something scratch against her right side by her ribs—*a snakebite!*

But no, it wasn't that.

It was just the wire from that bucket.

Hold it together, Petra.

Hold it together.

She repositioned herself so the wire wouldn't cut into her.

But even then, she could still feel the leathery, muscular bodies of the serpents that she knew were not real flexing across her body.

•   •   •

Dr. Adrian Waxford stood beside the general as she perused the videos of the experiments he'd done.

She finished with the fusion frequency tests and came to footage of one of the subjects in the room with the *Tabanidae*.

The man was strapped to a gurney, and he lurched and jerked, vainly trying to get free as the thousands of horse flies swarmed around him. Descended on him. Razored their mouthparts into his skin and lapped up his blood. Tried to crawl into his mouth and nose.

"Tell me, Adrian. How do you choose your subjects?"

"It isn't always easy. We want people who are in need of the kind of care I'm able to provide, but not so high-profile that their transfer from a traditional detention facility would attract media attention."

"On the phone earlier, you said you have a recent arrival."

"Yes. Just yesterday."

"Ty Bell."

"That's what he used to be known as. Yes."

"And he's from Wisconsin as well?"

"As well?"

"As well as your most infamous subject."

Adrian was quiet. He wasn't sure he liked the way she'd phrased that.

He waited for her to go on.

"I'm referring to the one who was never charged."

"He killed eight people."

"He was *suspected* of killing eight people. That was never proven."

"The evidence was overwhelming, General."

"The man was never brought to trial. He just vanished from that hospital in December."

"We thought it prudent to move things forward."

She produced a USB thumb drive from her pocket. "I'd like a copy of these videos. Then you can take me to him. I'm curious to see how he's been progressing. Under your care."

"You mentioned earlier that you might want to get to your hotel before the storm hits?"

"I'll make do." She handed him the drive. "Now, the files?"

CHAPTER FIFTY-ONE

We follow the trail toward Little Bear Creek.

It's well maintained and, with the switchbacks, not terribly steep, so the hike is going a lot faster than I thought it would.

Tane has taken the lead, leaving me to guide Alysha.

The path isn't wide enough for us to walk side-by-side, but as we proceed, she's right behind me.

After our face-touching encounter on the stage of the Great Carrigini's theater, I'm hesitant to lead her like this, but she says nothing about what happened in there and neither do I.

When we started walking together, she told me, "Just hold your arm behind you. I'll be alright. Tell me when the ground slopes a lot. And with trees branches or logs, just warn me to duck or to move to one side."

"Got it."

I went slowly at first, scared that she might trip or fall, but she told me to speed up and not to worry about her so much, so I did.

As we hike, I keep seeing that corpse from the attic rise up and fly into the coming storm.

Ascending and ascending until he disappears.

It looked so real. The blurs always look so real.

And then a series of questions comes to me unexpectedly: *What about back at the theater? When you were alone with Alysha? Did any of that really happen, or was that all a blur too?*

I'm not quite sure how to ask her about it, but I sense that I probably should.

Through the trees, I see the creek about a hundred yards ahead of us.

Even from here I can tell that the water is high.

$$\bullet \quad \bullet \quad \bullet$$

Nicole and Mia made their way steadily up the road.

Kyle was out front, keeping them moving at a pretty good clip.

"How much farther?" Mia called to him.

"I'd say we're more than halfway there. So, we're making good time."

"Whoever invented hills oughta be shot."

Nicole held up the first aid kit. "At least we haven't met any bears."

"And what exactly are we looking for up here again?"

"Daniel. Zacharias. Dr. Waxford. How they all fit together."

"Okay, I'm going to help us pass the time."

"How?"

352

"By telling you a heartwarming and touching story about a pet I used to have when I was a kid."

Kyle must have been intrigued because he stopped and waited for them to catch up. "I didn't know you ever had a pet."

"That's 'cause I never told you about Snookums."

"Snookums?"

"That's right."

The three of them continued on together.

"He was a turtle who lived in this little aquarium in my room. I had him for nearly two years, and then one day I wouldn't pick up my things and my mom made me go on a timeout. You know timeouts?"

"Sure," Nicole answered. "Sit off by yourself, think about what you did—but are you saying you had a turtle named 'Snookums'?"

"Uh-huh."

"Seriously?"

"What's wrong with 'Snookums'?"

"It's just . . . Well, it's more of a puppy name."

"Do I look like a puppy person to you? When I was little I heard the name 'Snookums' and I liked it. At first when I got him, I thought he was a girl. Ended up he was a boy. It's kinda hard to tell with turtles, but 'Snookums' is sort of a gender-neutral name, though, so I don't think he really minded."

"How *do* you tell with turtles?" Kyle asked.

"I'll talk you through it sometime. Now, do you two want to hear the rest of my Snookums story or not?"

They both told her yes they did and to please go on.

"So, my mom put me on this timeout and I started thinking about Snookums in his aquarium and I realized it was like he was always on a timeout, one that would never end. And I thought of how lonely he must be without any other turtles around to play with. So I decided to let him go."

The sky rumbled and Mia gazed up apprehensively. "Is that God telling me I shouldn't have set Snookums free?"

"No," Nicole assured her. "You're fine. Go on."

"There was this lake near where we lived. So, after I was done with my timeout, I told my mom I wanted to let Snookums go in the lake and she asked if I was sure and if he was going to be safe out there."

"What'd you say?"

"To this day I still remember: 'When you're a turtle, it's not about being safe, Mommy, it's about being free.'"

"That's a pretty insightful thing for a little girl to come up with."

"I guess." She shrugged. "I don't know. Anyway, we took Snookums to the shore and when we got there I picked him up and said goodbye and set him in the water—but he didn't go anywhere. He had this whole turtle paradise dream-lake right in front of him and he just sat there staring at me and not swimming away. It was quite moving, actually. Very affecting. Finally, after a couple minutes he did swim off, but it took a while."

"Did you ever see him again?" Nicole asked.

"Nope. Never did."

"Hmm. Well, I like it. There's deep truth in there, and no walls lined with skulls, so that's a plus. And no ghostly faces in the window or shrieks from the pits of hell."

"I'm working on a way to fit that stuff in the next time I tell it."

"Wonderful. So what made you think of that? Of Snookums?"

"Waxford. His research. It's like that's what he's trying to do with the convicts—put 'em on a timeout for hundreds of years. Solitary confinement to a degree that's almost unimaginable."

Kyle absentmindedly kicked a stone and it skittered off the road into the thick underbrush. "You know, your story reminds me of the Aesop's fable about Dog and Coyote."

"Does the dog lick anyone's hand?" Nicole asked.

"Nope."

"Okay, go ahead."

Thunder growled at them.

They quickened their pace.

"In the fable, Dog and Coyote, they're friends. Every day, Coyote would come in from the field and play with Dog, then at night he would return to the wild. One night, he invites Dog to join him, but Dog—" He paused. "Did you guys hear something?"

"Just some more thunder," Mia said. "Why? What is it?"

"I thought I heard a car."

They all waited. Listened.

Nothing.

"Okay, must have just been the thunder. So, Dog shows him this chain fastened around his neck. 'My master doesn't allow me to leave,' Dog tells him. 'But if you'll stay here tonight, he can put a chain around your neck, too, and then we can always be together.' But at that, Coyote trots away, saying, 'I much prefer the perils of freedom to the security of chains.'"

"That's a pretty insightful thing for a coyote to come up with," noted Mia.

"Right, so it was just like with your Snookums story there at the end when he finally swam off to—no, that's definitely a car."

"Okay. Wait—I hear it too," Nicole said anxiously. "It's coming up the hill."

"Get in the ditch. C'mon. Quick."

They leapt off the road and found places to hide in the tangled thicket bordering it.

Nicole had just finished getting into position when a white minivan came around the curve.

It jaunted up toward them, passed by without incident, and then continued up the mountain.

They waited until it was gone and then lingered for another minute or so just to make sure no other vehicles were following it.

Finally, they climbed out of the ditch.

Mia brushed the dirt off her jeans. "Whoever that was, they must have a key to the gate. And they most certainly saw our car down there—which means they might be on the lookout for us now. You think we should turn back?"

"Not until we have some answers," Nicole said firmly. "I mean, we've come this far. Besides, now we know for sure that something is going on up here. Let's at least get to where we can see the Inn and have a look around."

More thunder.

"Well, we better hurry then." Mia was eyeing the threatening sky. "Because that storm is definitely coming this way."

• • •

We're almost to the creek.

Tane is far enough ahead that he won't hear me, so, as I guide Alysha over a root in the path, I say, "I need to ask you a question and it's going to sound weird at first."

"What is it?"

We start down the trail again. "Back at the theater did we have . . . well . . . a moment?"

"A moment?"

"When you touched my face, when you felt my heartbeat."

"Daniel, why would you ask me that?"

"It's just that I'm not sure anymore what's real and what's illusion."

"I'm real. I'm here, right now, with you."

"I know that, but . . ."

We come to the place where the bridge is supposed to be. And there's nothing there.

CHAPTER
FIFTY-TWO

8:00 P.M.
1 HOUR UNTIL THE DEADLINE

Tane is staring at the remnants of the bridge's foundation. "It washed away."

The creek is bloated with brown water from the recent rains and has risen high on its banks, climbing halfway up the trees that would have lined it if the water were at normal levels.

It's thirty feet wide.

I watch the water rush past, maybe twenty feet downhill from us. "Well, we need to find Malcolm and Petra, and the only way to do that is by getting across this thing."

"How deep do you think it is?" Alysha asks.

"Too deep to wade across, and besides, the current's way too fast. We'd be swept downstream the minute we stepped into the water."

As Alysha shifts her weight to the other foot, the loose soil beneath her gives way.

She cries out as she tumbles sideways down the hill and slides toward the furious river.

I leap off the trail and race to get to her before she slips in.

Branches swipe at my face, but I fling them aside and lunge toward her, throwing my right hand forward. I miss her wrist the first time, but manage to snag it on the second try as her left foot plunges into the water.

Tane calls out to us and I tell him we're okay.

"I'm coming down!"

I help Alysha to her feet.

"There it is again," she says.

"What?"

"Your habit. Being there when I need you."

"So, we did talk back in the theater."

"Yes."

"And I told you I have a girlfriend."

"You did, and we agreed to discuss things later, when—"

Tane arrives before we can take this any further. "You two alright?"

"We're good," Alysha replies.

I assess things.

"So what's the plan?" Tane asks me.

"I'm working on one."

"I hope it's better than that one you came up with in Atlanta when that guy was searching for us in the hallway."

"You mean when I just lay on the floor and hoped he wouldn't shoot me?"

"That's the one."

"I hope it's better than that too."

The river churns and courses its way downstream.

A seven-foot-long branch goes by, dipping and rising as the muddy water carries it toward a channel that passes between two narrow, rocky outcroppings.

I trace the branch's movement, and watch it pass under a fallen tree that spans the river.

My plan emerges.

"See that tree, Tane?" I point. "I think it might be wide enough to walk across."

"Let's find out."

• • •

When Adrian finished copying the files for General Gibbons, he returned her USB drive to her, and then led her to the one-way mirror that allowed her to peer into room 113 at subject #832145.

"And he can't see us?"

"Correct. All he sees is a mirror."

"It's cracked on his side of the glass."

"That's from the chair."

"So he's tried to break out."

"Multiple times. Quite often, actually."

"And you let him keep the chair—why?"

"Part of his treatment."

He left it at that.

"I see."

To cut down on the chance of lice, Adrian's staff had shaved the man's head and beard while he was sedated. His tattooed eyeballs were completely black, making it impossible to tell what he was focusing on, but he was facing the mirror.

He looked wild. Savage. Barely human.

"And he's been 'under your care' since the end of December?"

"Yes."

"How much time has he perceived to have passed?"

"Based on our test results, I would say slightly more than forty years."

"All in solitary confinement."

"Yes."

"In white room conditions."

"Yes."

"And how long will you continue treating him?"

"If we work from the typical fifty-year sentence for each of his eight homicides, and then add in what he would serve for his related kidnapping offenses and other crimes, we still have, well . . . a considerable amount of time left together."

"What stops him from going insane?"

"That's always a risk, of course, but we do all we can to keep the subjects psychologically intact. Our results continue to improve as I refine my techniques."

"Alright, well, speaking of refining your techniques, I admit that I am more than a little intrigued by this new drug of yours. If it works properly, that might be enough to secure your funding for the foreseeable future."

"Let's swing by my office and I can show you the data I have. Then you can be on your way."

She didn't respond to that, but just walked beside him through the hall.

• • •

The minivan came to a stop.

A few moments later, Deedee unshackled Petra's ankle, led her outside, and removed the blindfold.

They were at an old building somewhere in the mountains.

A sheath of unchecked, sprawling kudzu covered one side of the structure, finding its way nearly to the roof.

Petra had grown up in the South, so she knew that plant—and she also knew the other one that entwined with it: the dense poison ivy vines that were anchored to the forest floor and extended up the wall. Some were as thick as her leg and made her think of great snakes writhing from a giant Medusa's head.

This building.

There was something about it.

Had she seen it before?

Part of her mind said yes, part was clouded by the way the world was fading into a dream.

And with that, she experienced it again—the hallucination she'd had the last time she visited that hypnotist.

The snakes.

All coming for her.

In her trance, she'd seen a wide stretch of broken glass before her, the shards slicing up the sunlight into little pieces and tossing jagged daggers of it back into the day.

Beyond the glass, a cliff dropped off into nothingness.

She wore only a swimsuit. Had bare feet.

When she turned around, she found herself facing barren sand dunes that drifted and blew back for miles.

Then, born from the earth, snakes began to emerge from the sand and slither toward her.

She glanced at the glass again, then back at the snakes.

A sea of serpents on the hunt for her, with no way for her to get past them on either side.

And so, the choice: run across the shards of glass and leap off the cliff into the unknown, or face the snakes.

She'd been transfixed, paralyzed, terrified as they came closer.

She tried to kick them away as they thrashed at her feet.

And then they began to scale up her legs.

She screamed and screamed and screamed and swiped at them until she lost her balance and tumbled backward.

Toward the glass.

And as she was falling, she awoke from the hypnotist's trance.

Now, as she stood here beside the building, she had a hard time separating what had happened in that hallucination from what was happening before her with those immense serpents squirming up the building. Interlaced. Interwoven. Frozen in mid-slither.

No. They're vines.

The snakes aren't real.

Sergei spoke to someone on a radio, interrupting her thoughts, bringing her back to reality. After the transmission, he said to Deedee, "Henrik is moving Zacharias to the basement. He wants us to use the west entrance and take Petra up to the fourth floor. There's a room already prepared. Waxford is keeping the general occupied, so we should be fine."

Zacharias?

They have Malcolm?

Petra processed that as they led her to a door and Sergei put his hand on some sort of reader.

The wall of serpents hissed at her in the gloomy, cloud-swallowed light.

Then the door opened and her two kidnappers pushed her inside.

CHAPTER FIFTY-THREE

We stand beside the downed tree.

"I should be able to make it," Tane says to me.

"You sure?"

"Yeah. You?"

"I'll be alright."

"How are we going to get Alysha across?"

"How wide is it?" she asks.

"It starts out at about a foot and a half," I tell her, "but by the time it gets to the other side, I don't know, maybe eight to ten inches."

She kneels and runs her hands across the log. "Is it covered with bark the whole way?"

"It looks like it."

"No moss?"

"I don't think so." I study the tree. "It's hard to say. Why?"

"If the bark is gone, the wood will be too slick. Also, if the bark is mossy, it'll be too slippery. If not, though, I can manage. I have pretty good balance."

She takes off her shoes and socks.

Tane watches her curiously. "What are you doing?"

"You ever see a tightrope walker wearing running shoes? This way, I can feel the log with my feet."

"Good point."

She stuffs the socks in the shoes, ties the laces together, and drapes them around her neck.

I offer to go first. "Alysha, you can hold onto my shoulders."

"You sure?"

"Yeah."

"Just one will be better. Then I can have one arm to help keep my balance."

"Alright. Remember, it's just like walking in a straight line on solid ground."

"Except," Tane adds, "this time if you lose your balance, you just happen to fall ten feet into a raging river."

"Oh, thanks. That's very helpful." Alysha turns to me. "You're an athlete, right? So you've got this?"

"I've got this."

I take off the sling so I can use both arms for correcting my weight distribution if I need to.

Then I face the river.

Alysha places her hand on my right shoulder. "Okay, let's go."

After taking a calming breath, I edge out onto the downed tree.

With every step, I remind myself of what I just told her: this is the same as walking in a straight line on solid ground.

But honestly, it doesn't do a lot of good—not when I see that ten-foot gap between the log and the roiling surface of the river.

It might've actually been easier if there was just empty space beneath me—if the tree were spanning a canyon.

As it is, the swirling water disorients me, and I end up having to stare straight ahead to keep my focus on where we're going rather than on what's below us.

I feel Alysha's grip tighten.

"You're doing great," I assure her. "We're halfway there."

After a few more feet, however, I see that I was wrong about the bark.

A section of it in front of me is sloughing off the log.

I freeze. If I step on it and it tears off, there won't be any way to keep from ending up in the river.

"What is it?" Alysha asks.

"There's some loose bark. We're going to need to step over it."

"How far?"

"Eighteen, maybe twenty inches."

A slight pause. "Okay. Talk me through it."

"First, get up right behind me because I need to get across and you'll have to reach my shoulder."

She nudges up close to me.

"Stay where you are until I get there. I'll tell you when to move."

"Careful."

"Always."

I gingerly step over the patch of rotten bark.

One foot.

Then the other.

It's not too bad.

"Okay, your turn." I look back over my shoulder to watch her. "You can do this."

She lifts her right foot and steadies herself. Her balance is extraordinary and I'm not sure if it comes naturally or if it's a result of compensating for being blind. Either way, it doesn't matter, as long as she doesn't slip.

She steps across the loose bark, squeezing my shoulder to steady herself, then brings the other foot forward.

"Are we good?" she asks breathlessly.

"We're good."

Even though the rest of the tree is narrower, it's not as tricky to navigate and it doesn't take us long to reach shore.

Tane, who's still on the other side of the river and has been waiting for us to get here before venturing onto the log, starts across.

I point to that dicey section of bark and yell for him to be careful. He flags a couple fingers to me that he's good.

He's moving smoothly, confidently, his boxing and martial arts training giving him poise and a steady sense of balance.

When he reaches the rotten bark, he agilely steps over it.

But then it happens.

Abruptly.

All in one terrible moment.

When Alysha and I walked across, we must have loosened up a larger section of bark, because as Tane puts his weight on it, a strip nearly four feet long rips off.

His foot shoots out from under him, throwing him backward. He smacks hard against the log and tries to grab it, but can't manage, and drops sideways toward the river.

As soon as he hits the surface, the water swallows him.

And he's gone.

CHAPTER FIFTY-FOUR

"What is it?" Alysha is holding my forearm. Her voice is urgent, and I realize that with the sound of the water rushing past, even with her acute hearing, she didn't catch the sound of Tane splashing into the river. "You just tensed up, Daniel. What's happening?"

"He fell in."

"Oh my God."

I'm staring anxiously at the water, but he hasn't come up.

"Can you see him?"

"No. Not yet."

I place her hand on the tree branch, then ease her leg forward to make sure she's on solid ground. All the while, I'm scanning the surface for any sign of Tane.

"Daniel, is he . . . ?"

"He hasn't come up yet."

Then, all at once his hand splashes out of the water halfway between where we are and the narrow chute that channels down fifteen feet deeper into the gorge.

A second later, his head appears, but then immediately goes under again.

It's enough to give me hope, though.

"I'm going to get him."

"Did he come up?"

"Yeah. He's alright."

"Don't lie to me." She's an expert at reading people's tone of voice. "Don't lie to—"

"Stay here. You'll be safe. I'll be right back."

Then I get moving, noting where I am so I can find her when I return.

With Tane.

When you return with Tane.

Using the sinewy rhododendron branches for support, I make my way along the riverbank, being careful that I don't slip in myself.

As I come to the place where the water funnels down, I'm forced to grab handholds in the rock face and downclimb a few feet. To keep from dislocating my shoulder again, I do my best to let my weight hang on the other arm, but still, the pain is fierce every time I move that bad shoulder.

Only then does it hit me that I left my sling back on the other side of the river, draped on a branch next to the log we walked across.

Deal with that later.

Just find Tane.

Wet and moss-covered, the route is dicey, but the out-croppings give me just enough purchase to keep my feet on the rock.

By the time I get to the bottom, I have no idea how far the current might have taken him.

I figure I need to look, though, at least for a few minutes. I can't just give up right away.

Yes.

With Tane.

You'll return with Tane.

• • •

After taking Petra to the fourth floor, Sergei and Deedee had shoved her roughly into one of the rooms and locked the door behind her.

She'd hollered out what she thought she should say. "Why are you doing this? Why did you bring me here!"

They hadn't replied.

She'd listened to their receding footsteps, and when the two of them were gone, she removed that wire handle from under her shirt.

And started looking for a way to get free.

Whoever owned this place was remodeling it and the room wasn't finished—but when she tried, she wasn't able to break through the exposed drywall.

An old metal radiator sat beside one wall, but she couldn't budge it.

She tried inserting the tip of the wire into the lock on the doorknob, but it didn't fit.

Her attention shifted to the window.

She studied the clasp that held it shut. It was screwed securely in place: When she tried to twist the mechanism, she couldn't get the latch to open by her grip-strength alone.

But maybe if she had more leverage?

There was a small hole at the top of it.

She passed one end of the wire through the hole in the hasp, bent it over, and tried getting enough torque to twist the latch and unlock the window.

● ● ●

I see something ahead of me near the shore in an eddy formed by a massive boulder.

A lump in the water.

Tane's back.

He's floating facedown.

No, no, no.

I scramble down the bank.

Though I don't really have any way of knowing how deep the water is here, I need to get to him.

If the boulder wasn't this close, I'd be out of luck, but the current is curling back toward the rock. That's what drew his body here. And that's what'll keep me from being swept downstream.

At least I hope it will.

I drop into the water.

Knee-deep.

With my first step, I almost lose my balance on the slick, rocky bottom.

Carefully, I move forward.

The water is up to the middle of my thighs now, but I'm almost to him.

I lean farther out and reach for him.

After a couple of unsuccessful tries, I'm finally able to snag his arm, but as I try to maneuver him to shore, the water tugs at him.

I lean back, and at last the current gives up its grip on him and he drifts toward me.

I'm not sure how I'll get him out of the water, but before worrying about that, I need to get some air into his lungs.

I've never been trained as a lifeguard so I'm not sure what I'm officially supposed to be doing, but I know that I need to get him breathing again as fast as possible. I know that much.

With his size, it isn't easy, but steadying myself as best I can, I roll him over so he's face-up.

His color has faded and his lips are blueish.

Just like the blur in the attic when you saw that body lying there, dead.

But then it came back to life—and he will too.

He will too.

Praying he'll be alright, I cradle him in my arms and give him a rescue breath.

Last winter you drowned in Lake Superior.

You went through the ice and Kyle had to save you.

Dead, then back to life.

First you.

Now Tane.

The river tries to draw him away from me, but I manage to keep him in place long enough to give him another mouthful of air.

I take a step closer to shore, pulling him with me, and I'm leaning down to offer him more air when I feel his body convulse.

His eyes snap open. He jerks and then coughs, spewing out a gush of water as he rolls out of my arms and tries unsuccessfully to get to his feet.

"It's okay! You're okay!" I almost fall over as I try to get him into the shallower water.

He manages to stand up, but can't keep his footing and ends up grabbing my left arm for support.

Pain thrashes through me.

"No! Tane!"

He immediately realizes what he did and lets go as I offer him my other arm.

Dizzy.

Control it.

Easy, easy, easy.

I'm just glad the shoulder didn't pop out of its socket again. With that much pressure, it easily could have.

We climb up the bank to where the ground is level.

While I let my shoulder recover, he slumps to the forest floor to catch his breath. Finally he says, "Man, that was not fun."

"I know the feeling."

"You've drowned?"

"Once. Yeah."

"And obviously somebody brought you back."

"My friend did."

"So did mine." He clasps my hand and I help him to his feet. "Thanks."

Thunder rolls through the gorge. "We should probably get moving."

As we start back toward Alysha, he suddenly pats his pockets and curses.

"What is it?"

"That radio the pilot gave me—it's gone."

"Forget it." I confirm that the flashlight is still jammed in my pocket, then I gesture upstream. "Let's go. If we hurry we can still make it to the Estoria in time."

● ● ●

At his home in Beldon, Wisconsin, Sheriff Byers evaluated things.

Although earlier in the day he'd looked into taking a flight down to Atlanta, it would've required a three-hour drive to the Twin Cities first, and right now it seemed like he was making more progress than he would've been able to while either driving or flying.

So he'd changed his plans.

Working discreetly through his law enforcement contacts, he'd been able to use the data that Daniel's source had provided regarding the convergence of 911 calls and the passing trains in the South to search for white minivans with that plate number passing through nearby traffic cameras.

Now, he received a call that a traffic cam in Knoxville had caught footage of the minivan in question, less than a quarter mile from a railroad crossing, not long before an ambulance was dispatched to the area.

A quick search told him that one of the addresses in a nearby neighborhood was listed under the name "Sergei Gorshkov."

"Sergei" was one of the names Daniel had told him to keep an eye out for.

Daniel had warned him about the deadline and about contacting the authorities, but if someone's life really was in danger, they needed to find her—otherwise what was the point of the search?

Time was running out.

Just thirty-six minutes until nine o'clock.

He called the Knoxville Police Department's chief, filled him in as much as he could about Sergei's possible involvement in a kidnapping.

He wasn't sure if it would be enough to convince him to send a car to check out the address.

But it was.

Sheriff Byers hung up.

And waited to hear back from the chief.

●　●　●

After we regroup with Alysha, the three of us find the trail that leads up to the old hotel.

Alysha does an amazing job of navigating along the path and we make up for lost time.

Around us, a heavy mist has started to form. Tendrils of fog wander among the trees, shifting and stirring in the breeze as if they were living creatures.

The Smoky Mountains.

Now I see why that name makes sense.

The shaded line of gray from the rain along the storm's front obscures the mountains that lie beyond it.

As the wind picks up, I see our chopper rise from Spider Peak and shoot across the valley.

"There he goes," Tane says. "I guess the storm is almost here."

CHAPTER
FIFTY-FIVE

The general sat at Adrian's desk studying the Telpatine analysis and data sheets.

Adrian excused himself for a moment and, taking both the radio and the satellite phone with him, caught up with Sergei and Deedee in the hall.

"Petra's upstairs," Sergei said. "She's secure—but there is one thing."

"Tell me."

"We saw a car parked by the gate, down at the base of the road."

"A car?"

"Yeah. A sedan. I didn't recognize it, but I did see that it had Wisconsin plates."

"What? Wisconsin?"

"Yes."

"Was anyone there?"

"No. We wanted to get Petra up here first before checking it out. I think one of us should go back and take a look, though."

"I agree. Deedee, why don't you stay here. I want you stationed outside Petra's room. Sergei, drive down, see what you can find. Get the license plate number and we'll run it when you get back."

• • •

Through the woods, Nicole caught sight of the Estoria Inn about two hundred feet ahead of them.

They crouched low and studied it.

"What does the book say?" Mia asked her.

Nicole flipped to the chapter. "Four floors. We definitely want to avoid room 113—that's the haunted one. There's also an old maintenance shed out back."

A burst of lightning slashed through the sky and thunder followed right on its heels, booming above them.

"Okay, that was close," Kyle said. "I say we try that shed, get some shelter and then figure out what to do next. Is it big enough?"

Nicole consulted the diagram. "Looks like it. But I don't think we should just walk up the road, even with our cover story."

"We'll cut through the woods. C'mon."

As they did, Nicole noticed the white minivan driving off again, away from the hotel.

• • •

Adrian tracked Henrik down.

"What is it, Doctor?"

"Where's Zacharias?"

"I moved him to the tattoo room so we could leave Petra upstairs. I was going to do the other eye."

"Is he secure?"

"Yes. Strapped in the chair."

"Leave him there for now. Sergei saw a car down by the gate. He's on it, but I want you to check the motion sensors. I sent Deedee to guard Petra's room. Garrett's manning the security center."

"And the general?"

"In my office. I need to get back in there."

"I'll radio you."

"Good."

• • •

As we reach the top of the hill, the old hotel, imposing and formidable, comes into view through the trees.

Just like the facility in Wisconsin, this one has a metal mesh fence running around the property.

Lightning spiderwebs across the sky.

Even the thunderstorms I've watched roll in across Lake Superior weren't like this.

Those were slower moving, with steady cloud banks powering in across the water, but here, there's a primal ferocity to the storm. The sky boils with layers of clouds all somehow moving at different speeds, the lower ones skirting ahead of the storm as if they're trying to get out of the path of the dark thunderclouds right behind them.

As the thunder explodes, it startles Alysha, and I realize it's because she can't see the lightning preceding it.

As we hurry toward the fence, I warn her every time the sky flashes.

• • •

Adrian was nearly back to his office when Henrik radioed him.

"The motion detectors have picked up something over on the west perimeter."

"What? Deer? Bear?"

"No. We have three blips and the way they're moving isn't like any deer or bear I've ever seen."

"Are all the subjects accounted for?"

"Yes. I believe we have some uninvited guests."

"Go check it out."

"Taser?"

"Take it with you, but if necessary, use something a little less ambiguous."

"Right."

When Adrian entered the office, he found the general studying the camel figurines on his desk.

"You like camels, I see," she said.

"It has to do with an old riddle my brother told me years ago. Look, I'm—"

"How does it go?"

"Um—"

"Adrian, I'm not driving down the mountain with the storm this close. You're stuck with me for now. Tell me the riddle."

He didn't like the idea that she would be around when the deadline arrived, but decided he would deal with that, if necessary, when the time came.

Outside the box.

Always be ready to think outside the box.

He explained the riddle to her. "It's a Sufi story. A teacher knew he was dying and he wanted his three students to find a worthy master after he was gone."

"Okay."

"He owned seventeen camels."

Adrian separated seventeen of the figurines from the rest.

"In his will, he dictated that, upon his death, the oldest of his students would receive one-half of the camels, the middle student would get one-third, the youngest would get one-ninth."

"One-half. One-third. One-ninth. Got it."

"After the master died, the three students tried to discern what to do with the camels. But no one could figure out how to divide them up."

"Do they cut up the camels?"

"Even then it wouldn't work."

She thought about it. "No, I suppose not."

"So, finally a caravan owner who was passing by heard about it and offered them the solution."

"And that was?"

"I—" A text came in from Deedee asking if he wanted her to confirm that Senator Amundsen sent his email at nine. They had a means set up to monitor his outgoing messages, but one of them needed to verify things.

"I'm sorry, General. There's a small matter that requires my attention. I'm afraid I need to step out again."

"What's going on, here, Adrian?"

"What do you mean?"

"These texts, carrying your radio around—is there something I need to know about?"

"Just some added security precautions in case the power goes out," he lied. "I'll be back shortly."

• • •

Mia and Kyle got to the shed first. As Nicole dashed across the road to join them, the rain began.

It started with large raindrops that seemed to be the size of dimes as they splattered onto the ground.

A few splashed against her arms, her head, her back.

Slow at first.

But growing in intensity.

She made it to the shed.

The overhanging roof would allow them a little protection, but whoever was in the Estoria would easily be able to see them if they waited out here.

Drop. And drop.

And drop.

Faster now.

Kyle tugged at the door, but it refused to open.

However, the nails securing the hasp that held it shut were loose and rusted.

He threw his weight into it, but it still wasn't enough. "If we could get that latch off, maybe I could—"

Mia snapped out her knife and handed it to him. "Try Lucy."

"You named your knife 'Lucy'?"

"Daniel named his basketball 'Alfie.'"

"That is true."

He inserted the blade in between the wood and the clasp and tried to pry it off.

• • •

Tane clambers over the fence and then helps Alysha climb down to join him.

Because of my shoulder, it's tougher for me to scale it, but I manage.

All around us, the wind is gusting through the trees. Almost as one, the branches bend before the storm as if they're bowing to allow it to pass.

The Estoria sits between us and an outcropping a hundred yards away.

• • •

As the raindrops began pinging rapid-fire against the metal roof of the shed, it became harder for Nicole to distinguish between the individual drops.

All at once, with a harsh, grating sound, the latch popped off.

"Got it," Kyle exclaimed.

He swung the creaky door open and the three of them ducked inside.

• • •

The heavens open up.

"Come on." I have one of Alysha's hands and I'm pressing her to go faster. "You can do it!"

But she keeps losing her footing on the slick mud.

"We need to get out of this storm," I yell to Tane.

"There." He points through the rain. "That shed."

• • •

Petra was getting nowhere with the window.

The latch mechanism was jammed too tightly, but if she could get the screws out, she might be able to jimmy the window open.

The wire was stiff and thick enough, but the end wasn't beveled at quite the right angle to fit in the screw head.

As she scanned the room, her gaze fell on the rough, gritty steel base of the radiator.

She rushed over and began scraping the wire's tip against it, using it as a file.

• • •

Sheriff Byers heard back from the Knoxville Police Department.

There was no one at Sergei Gorshkov's house.

However, when they searched the premises, they found evidence that someone had been kept confined in the basement.

They also discovered email correspondence with Henrik Poehlman, a former police officer who was wanted for questioning in the disappearance of a man suspected of eight homicides in Wisconsin.

And a map to the Estoria Inn, an old hotel in the Smoky Mountains, sat on the desk.

"Do you think we should send local law enforcement up to take a look?" the chief asked him.

Sheriff Byers considered the situation.

The kidnapped victim.

According to Daniel, her life was in danger.

It was closing in on nine o'clock.

They had to take action.

"What's the response time?" he asked.

"That place is remote. We might be talking forty, forty-five minutes."

"Dispatch some officers. Call me as soon as you know anything."

• • •

Henrik tugged a baseball cap down over his eyes to keep the rain out of them.

The strong wind turned the raindrops into darts that sheared past him, nearly parallel to the ground.

However, despite the diminished visibility, he briefly caught sight of movement near the maintenance building not far from the perimeter fence.

Drawing his gun, he went to check it out.

CHAPTER FIFTY-SIX

We get to the shed's door and I'm about to throw it open when Alysha grips my arm. "Wait."

"What is it?"

"There's someone here."

"How do you know?"

"I smell perfume."

I don't smell anything except the wet, forest-soaked scent of summer rain.

Tane moves into position on one side of the door. I take the other.

"You ready?" I ask.

He nods.

"Go."

He kicks the door open.

The inside of the shed is ruled by shadows.

Then they shift.

Alysha was right. Someone's in here.

"Hello?"

A menacing figure steps forward, holding a chainsaw high above its head. I instinctively throw my arm up to protect myself, but I then hear a familiar voice.

"Daniel?"

What?

"Kyle?" I can't see his face, but I know that—

"Put it down!" Tane orders him. "Now, or I'll—"

"It's okay," I assure him. "It's—"

"Dan!" Nicole rushes out of the darkness and throws her arms around me. She has a can of pepper spray in one hand and I'm glad she didn't fire it off at us before identifying who was at the door. "Are you okay?" she asks me urgently.

"Yeah. What are you doing here?"

"Long story."

"Kyle, what's with the chainsaw?"

"We heard noises and we . . . Yeah, I didn't really think that one through."

"What's going on?" Alysha asks and I realize she's still standing in the rain.

Kyle puts the chainsaw down, clicks on a headlamp, and we all crowd into the shed, tugging the door shut against the stubborn wind.

As quickly as I can, I introduce everyone.

"We need to get out of here," Mia says.

"No, we need to find Petra and Malcolm."

"Petra? Who's Petra?"

"A woman who was kidnapped."

I check the time on Malcolm's phone.

Eighteen minutes until the deadline.

"Alright. If what Tane learned earlier is true, Petra's in that hotel. We don't have much—"

Behind me, the door bangs open.

I whip around.

Poehlman, the man I recognized this morning when we were in that underground facility, is standing backlit by the storm, holding a gun.

He aims it uncertainly at the group, then seems to recognize me, and directs it at my head. "Nobody move."

But somebody does.

Alysha cries out, "Help me, mister!" She steps forward, feeling in front of her. "They're trying to—" She trips and falls headlong to the ground, barely throwing out her arms in time to break her fall.

While Poehlman's attention is on her, Tane goes for the gun.

Kyle leaps up to help him and the three of them crash into the side of the shed.

But Poehlman is a beast and he easily throws Kyle off to the side.

In the scuffle, however, Tane is able to get the handgun and as Poehlman tries to grab it back, Mia slams a tire iron brutally against the side of his leg, bringing him to his knees.

Tane tosses the gun to me, tackles Poehlman, and pins him with some sort of wrestling move.

It all goes down fast.

"Nice work." I can hardly believe he threw a handgun at me. I'm just thankful I was able to catch it—and that it didn't go off in the process. "Are you okay, Alysha?"

"When you're blind you learn how to break your fall."

"Did you know he had a gun?"

"Did not know that."

"Mia, where'd you get a tire iron?"

"I brought it with me from the car in case of bear attacks."

"Bear attacks? Okay, well . . ." I turn to Kyle. "You alright?"

"Yeah."

"Get his radio."

Poehlman is struggling fiercely to pull free, but Tane isn't about to let him go.

Kyle grabs his radio.

I glance around the shed. "Is there anything in here to tie him up with?"

"I saw some rope in the back," Nicole says.

I hand her the pilot's flashlight and she goes to find it.

We need answers, but I'm not about to point a loaded gun at Poehlman. While my back is turned to him, I remove the clip and empty the chambered round.

Then, I kneel beside him. "It's Poehlman, right?"

He spits at me.

"Where are Petra and Malcolm? Are they here?"

"You kids have no idea what you're doing. You're never gonna make it off this mountain alive."

Nicole reappears with the rope. Mia flips out her butterfly knife to cut it, and while Tane holds the guy down, she and Kyle start to tie his wrists tightly together behind his back.

He's putting up a fight, so I point the empty gun at him. "Easy."

He calms down, probably thinking it's still loaded.

"Nicole, keep watch." I point to the door. "Make sure no one else is coming."

I take Poehlman's Taser, and then check to see if he has a key to the hotel, but all I find is a set of car keys.

"Where are your keys to the building?" I ask him.

He just scoffs. "It's vascular biometrics. You need my palm on the reader, and that's not gonna happen. You'd have to drag me all the way over there. You really think you'd be able to pull that off?"

"We could cut off his hand," Mia suggests generously. "We do have a chainsaw."

"Wouldn't work," Poehlman tells us. I'm not sure how serious he thought she was being. "It needs to be attached to my arm. Blood needs to be flowing."

Yeah, with the size of this guy, getting him to the building would not be easy.

So.

Plan B.

While Kyle and Mia finish tying him up, I try to sort out what to do.

• • •

Petra tried the wire in the screw head.

It wasn't a perfect fit, not by any means, but it was good enough for her to turn it and start loosening the screw.

• • •

"We have a book that tells about the hotel." Nicole hands it to me. "That might help. The place is supposed to be haunted."

"Yeah, Dr. Carrigan mentioned that."

"Dr. Carrigan?"

"The hypnotist." I page through the book, past black and white photos of a family from Cades Cove, which must be pretty close by. Finally, I come to a detailed floor plan of the Estoria. "I'll tell you the whole story later."

I memorize the maze of hallways. "Okay, if this place is anything like Waxford's facility in Wisconsin, they have prisoners here. Some who might be seriously dangerous."

Tane, Mia, and Kyle step back from Poehlman.

He's secure.

I ask him how many people are in there and how many guards are on duty.

"I'm not telling you anything."

Since I figure Mia will be the one to enjoy using it the most, I hand her the Taser. "Stun him."

"Seriously?"

"Go for it."

She does.

Poehlman cries out in pain, but then just curses at us.

"Again."

She gives it to him again.

Still, he tells us nothing.

Alright, this isn't working and we don't have time to waste.

"Nikki, where's the car?"

"Two miles down the road."

"Was there cell reception down there?"

"Not at the gate, no. Not until you get further down the mountain."

I turn to Kyle. "How long will it take you to get there? I mean running flat-out, top speed."

"In rain like this? I don't know . . ."

"It's downhill," I remind him.

"Yeah, but it's a dirt road. It'll be muddy, slippery. I'd say maybe twelve minutes."

"Make it ten."

"That's pushing it."

"Then push it. Get to the car, drive down to where you can use your phone and call the cops. By the time they get here, the deadline will be past, but we're going to need help to stop Waxford—and I don't know how many guards are in there. Keep the headlamp. Use it to—"

"Wait!" Nicole exclaims. "That minivan. It's coming back up the road."

I join her at the door.

Down the overlook, a minivan is visible through the rain as it winds its way toward the hotel.

It's hard to be certain whether or not it's the same one the kidnappers drove, but it is the same color and right now, that's enough for me.

I'm guessing it'll get to the parking area within the next couple minutes.

Tane comes to my side.

"If we hurry," I tell him, thinking aloud, "we should be able to make it to the building. When the driver gets out, we jump him. He'll be near the door. We can use his hand on the reader."

"Then we go inside, find Petra and Malcolm, and get the hell out of here."

"Exactly."

"That's not any better than the plan this morning when we were trying to get away from that guy near the elevators," Alysha says.

She might be right.

But I can't come up with anything better and time is not on our side.

"Tane, you're with me. Kyle, wait for my signal, then run like mad to the car."

"What about us?" Nicole asks.

I give her Poehlman's car keys. "While we're in the hotel, see which one of the cars these open. We'll use it to drive out of here. Mia, you've got Poehlman. He moves, he calls for help, hit him with the stun gun again."

"I can do that."

But Nicole shakes her head. "Splitting up isn't a good idea."

"Never a good idea," Alysha agrees.

"Right now we have to. This is our best—"

Tane grabs my arm. "That van is coming. We need to go."

I hand Poehlman's radio to Alysha. "Monitor things. If it sounds like anyone is coming out here, I want you all to take off. Leave. Hide. Don't let them find you."

Then Tane and I sprint out through the rain toward the hotel and Kyle gets into position nearby to rocket down the hill.

• • •

Adrian still hadn't heard from Henrik since sending him out to see who was setting off the motion detectors.

In the hallway now, he tried radioing him.

No answer.

A moment later, though, Sergei's voice came through: "I'm almost there. I've got the plate numbers. And you're gonna love this—there's a sticker on the back of the car for a fishing permit for Waunakee Lake back in Wisconsin. Isn't that up where you used to do your research?"

"Yes. It is."

Adrian sorted through the implications.

Daniel Byers lived in that area and was at the center in Atlanta earlier today. Was it possible? Could it be his car?

If it is, you could test the Telpatine. That would work out perfectly.

"Alright, as soon as you arrive, get in here. We'll run them. Then I want you to help Henrik search the woods."

As he ended the transmission, Adrian turned and saw General Gibbons standing in the doorway to his office, glaring at him.

"Adrian, you're going to tell me exactly what's going on here and you're going to do it now."

• • •

Tane and I hide behind one of the cars as the minivan's driver maneuvers into a spot beside the building.

Parks.

Opens the door.

A man steps out and raises one arm to shield his face from the rain.

As he hurries toward the door, we're right behind him, using the sound of the storm to cover the sound of our footsteps.

Once he's beside the building, Tane taps him on the shoulder, startling him.

He spins, a look of surprise on his face.

It's the same guy who was shooting at us when we escaped into the elevator in Atlanta.

Tane starts punching him and doesn't stop.

Five, six, seven times, I'm not sure. It's hard to tell.

But it does the trick.

The man goes down.

Knocked out cold.

Tane is proving to be a handy guy to have around.

Kyle's watching us from near the shed and I motion for him to go.

Immediately, he takes off down the road.

Tane and I drag the unconscious driver to the door and place his hand on the reader beside it.

It only takes a moment to verify his identity.

The lock clicks and the door opens.

"What should we do with him?" Tane asks me. "We can't just leave him here. He's gonna wake up."

I hadn't really thought that far ahead.

Tane retrieves the minivan keys from the man's pocket, and that gets me thinking.

There's no trunk in his minivan.

But all the other cars do have one.

Nicole's got Poehlman's keys.

"We'll lock him in a trunk." I slide a rock in place to keep the door ajar. "Go back. Get the keys from Nicole. I'll watch this guy while you do."

• • •

From the shed's doorway, Nicole watched as Tane left the Estoria and started running across the parking area back toward the shed.

What's he doing? Why's he coming back?

"So," Alysha said to her, "are you the one Daniel was telling me about?"

"What? What do you mean?"

"The way you greeted him when we got here. I'm guessing you're the girlfriend."

"*The* girlfriend? What's that supposed to mean?"

"Yeah," Mia spoke up. "What's that supposed to mean?"

"He just mentioned it, I mean, that he had a girlfriend. That's all. You should feel lucky. He's quite a guy. Cute too."

Tane was halfway to them.

"How do you know he's cute?"

"He let me feel his face."

"He let you *what*?"

"It's how I get to know people."

"You haven't asked to feel my face," Mia noted.

"I—"

Tane arrived and told Nicole, "We need Poehlman's keys."

"I'm coming with you."

"That wasn't the plan."

"Screw the plan."

CHAPTER FIFTY-SEVEN

Nicole is with Tane when he returns.

As soon as they get to me, I ask her what she's doing.

"I'm gonna help you."

"Nikki, I don't think that's a good idea."

"I have pepper spray."

"I know, but still, it's . . ."

Tane hits a button on the key fob and the trunk of a Ford sedan parked about thirty feet away pops open.

With Nicole beside us, we start dragging the man toward the trunk.

"Tell me about the face thing with Alysha," she says.

"What?"

"She thinks you're cute."

"Oh, right. No, that was nothing. I had her at a disadvantage—wait, I don't mean . . . That doesn't sound right. I'm just saying, I could see her, but she couldn't tell what I look like."

"Okay."

"She's the cute one," Tane mutters under his breath. "I'd let her feel my face anytime she wants to."

Hmm.

I didn't see that coming.

At the car, because of my shoulder, he insists on doing most of the heavy lifting.

"So nothing happened?" Nicole asks me.

"No. Trust me."

Once the guy's inside, Tane slams the trunk door. "Think that'll hold him?"

"Let's hope so."

He pockets the keys and we hurry back to the Estoria.

I say to Nicole, "Whose phone number is that on your wrist?"

"Just this guy from the basketball camp, but, I mean—no, no. That's not what it seems like."

"I believe you." We get to the building. "So believe me."

"Okay."

"We cool?"

"We're cool."

Before we go in, I try one more time to dissuade her from coming along, but her mind is made up.

"Keep that pepper spray ready."

She pulls it out of her pocket.

Cautiously, I press the door open and peer inside.

Beyond the lobby, an empty hallway stretches before us.

It's relatively dim, with only a few ceiling lights on. The rest of the light bleeds out from windows to the rooms.

The storm rages behind us.

After a short internal debate, I decide that since there are prisoners housed in here, this door might be set to lock from the inside as well. So, I leave the rock in place to make sure we can get back out.

As we enter, I ask Tane if he has any idea where Petra might be. "Did Malcolm give you any specifics when you were in the trance and heard him tell you that she was here?"

He shakes his head. "Uh-uh."

Okay.

Plan C.

I mentally review the layout of the hotel. "We might as well start on this floor. Let's go."

Together, we cross the lobby and, after passing the stairwell, we come to the first room.

A man with black-as-night eyeballs is in it. Despite his bizarre appearance, I recognize him immediately.

Ty Bell.

"Daniel, is that Ty?" Nicole whispers.

"Yeah. It is."

"What's he doing here?" Her voice trembles. "What happened to his eyes?"

"I don't know. Come on, we—"

"Wait." Tane grabs my arm. "Someone's coming. Get in the stairwell."

• • •

"I'm done with this, done with the lies," General Gibbons said to Adrian as he attempted to bluff his way past her suspicions. "This has to do with the senator and his daughter, doesn't it?"

He blinked. "What?"

"You left me alone in here earlier. I work for the Department of Defense. How long do you really think it took me to get past the password prompt on your computer? Your brother's date of birth? Really? That's touching, Adrian, but hardly secure."

She spun the laptop around on the desk to face him.

The ransom video that Deedee and Sergei had filmed was paused on the screen.

"Well," Adrian said. "Look what you found."

"Blackmailing a United States Senator after kidnapping his daughter? Are you *insane?*"

"Sometimes justice requires bold and decisive action."

"Bold and decisive action? That's what you call this? Where is that young woman? Is she here? Did you bring her here?"

He stepped around to the other side of his desk while the general leaned over and snatched up the satellite phone. "I'm shutting this down."

Adrian opened the drawer and reached inside. "I'm afraid I can't let you do that."

"Ex*cuse* me?"

He pulled out his 9mm handgun and aimed it at her.

"Oh. Are you really going to shoot me?"

"I would prefer not to." He gestured toward a chair by the window, then took out a pair of Henrik's handcuffs. "Sit down over there by the radiator."

"I'm not sitting anywhere. Where is Petra Amundsen?"

"Please sit down, General."

But instead, she took a step backward toward the door.

He squeezed the trigger.

He'd never shot anyone before.

And now, seeing the dismay on her face, and the red stain spreading across her stomach, he found that it did not bother him as much as he thought it might.

No. It didn't bother him at all.

• • •

We left the stairwell door open a crack, and Tane is staring through it down the hall.

"Yeah, there's a guard. I don't think he saw us—but I don't think we should stay on this floor."

"Alright," I say. "Let's hit the basement. Work our way up."

As we descend, Tane asks us, "So you recognized that guy in that room back there?"

"He's from our hometown," Nicole explains.

"How did he end up as one of Waxford's test subjects?"

"That's a good question."

We arrive at the basement door and I whisper, "We'll figure it out later, when all this is over. Right now we need to find Petra. They've obviously remodeled this place since that book came out, but according to the floor plan, there should be nineteen rooms down here."

Tane offers to take the left side of the hall.
Nicole and I take the right.

CHAPTER
FIFTY-EIGHT

Adrian stood beside the general and watched her bleed.

She'd collapsed near the desk and was crumpled on the floor now, leaning against it.

The bullet had hit her in the lower abdomen and, based on his knowledge of anatomy, Adrian didn't expect that she was going to die immediately. He was curious what it would be like to watch her fade away, though, so he didn't shoot her again.

"If you keep pressure on that," he told her, "it'll buy you a little extra time."

Then he radioed his team. "Deedee, bring Petra to my office. There's been an unforeseen turn of events. Garrett, go find Henrik. The last I heard, he was out by the shed. And keep an eye out for Sergei. I haven't seen him come in."

Then Adrian went online and typed in the code that would allow him to confirm when the senator's email went through.

Just ten minutes to go.

•   •   •

"They're sending someone named Garrett out here," Alysha, who was monitoring the radio, told Mia. "We need to leave."

Mia grabbed the flashlight Daniel had brought in earlier.

Before passing out the shed door, she used the Taser on Poehlman once more. "That's for making me walk two miles."

And then again. "And that's for it being uphill."

She took Alysha's arm and hurried her outside, then around the back of the shed behind a downed tree.

•   •   •

In his estate on the outskirts of Atlanta, Senator Amundsen thought this through for the millionth time, still unsure how to solve things.

If he didn't cancel the inquiry, his daughter would die.

If he did, others would suffer.

He needed a way to both save her and save them. A third option.

But he still couldn't come up with what that might be.

•   •   •

Petra finished with the screw, tossed the clasp aside, and yanked the window open.

Rain blasted in, drenching her shirt.

It was nearly dark outside, but light from her window allowed her to see partway down the building.

The kudzu wouldn't support her, but the poison ivy vines were thick enough. From walking through a patch of it last year she knew she was allergic, but she didn't really have a choice. She could deal with any sort of reaction later.

But as she stared at them, the vines stopped being vines and became snakes again, scaling the building, coming toward her.

No, no they're not. They're just vines. You can get out of here.

Poised to strike.

Go. You have to!

Rain pelted her as she peered down.

Serpents.

They're serpents.

It had to be close to nine.

She needed to go.

Leaning out the window, Petra grabbed the stoutest vine she could reach. As she swung her left leg out, the lock of the door behind her clicked loudly enough to get her attention.

She paused.

Turned.

And saw Deedee standing in the open doorway.

"Where do you think you're going, my dear?"

"Don't come any closer or I'll jump."

"Well, if you want to die, I'm sure that can be arranged, but I'm just here because it's almost time to see how valuable you are to your father. I'm going to need you to come with me."

"You want me? Come and get me."

CHAPTER
FIFTY-NINE

So far we haven't found anyone in the basement.

We've passed a window to a room filled with thousands of swarming flies, and another room set up for surgery, outfitted with strange wired caps and brain electrodes.

This hotel is like something straight out of a nightmare. It doesn't need to be haunted—it's horrifying enough as is.

No sign of Petra.

Tane is ahead of us and when he peers into the next room, he shouts for us to get over there, then disappears inside.

"What is it?" I call, as Nicole and I sprint toward him.

He just yells for us to hurry.

Petra? Is it her?

Nicole must be thinking the same thing, because she exclaims, "Is she okay?"

I enter the room.

A man is strapped to what looks like a dentist's chair.

Bloody utensils and grim-looking tattooing equipment lie beside him.

Nicole is right behind me and I tell her to wait in the hall. "Nikki, you don't need to see this."

"What is it?"

The man has been beaten and his face is pulpy and swollen. One of his eyeballs is colored completely black, just like Ty Bell's were.

At first I don't recognize him.

But then I do.

Malcolm.

He's unconscious.

Tane is working to undo the straps holding him in the chair.

"Daniel?" Thankfully, Nicole is still in the hall. "What is it? Tell me."

"It's Malcolm. He's hurt."

I shake him gently to wake him up.

It takes a few moments, but finally he stirs.

"Malcolm? Can you hear me? Are you alright?"

Tane finishes freeing his ankles and wrists.

"Daniel?" Malcolm's voice is raspy and weak.

"Yeah."

"I heard them talking. Petra is upstairs. Fourth floor." Every word sounds strained and full of effort. "Third room on the left. Forget me. Just get her out of here."

From the shape he's in, I doubt he'll be able to stand on his own, let alone get up the steps without help. With my recovering shoulder, I'm not the best one for that job. "You two help Malcolm. I'll get Petra. We'll meet you outside by Poehlman's car."

I still have that gun with me, and as I head toward the steps I start wishing I hadn't unloaded it.

• • •

Mia and Alysha crouched behind the deadfall near the shed.

"What's happening?" Alysha asked her.

"A guy left the hotel. He's coming this way."

"What should we do?"

"I'm not sure."

"Do you know what time it is?"

"No. Why?"

"Petra's deadline is at nine. It's gotta be close."

"Alright. That's it. I'm going to help them—but you can't stay here."

"What are you thinking?"

"Maybe someone left their keys in their car. Let's get you to safety." She placed Alysha's hand on her elbow so she could lead her. "C'mon."

• • •

I take the stairs two at a time.

Past the second floor.

Third.

Thunder booms outside and the lights flicker.

To the fourth.

I push open the stairwell door.

Another poorly lit hallway.

By the looks of it, this level is still under construction.

The door to the room Malcolm told me to check is partly open.

With the empty gun out so that I can bluff if I need to, I approach it. "Petra?"

No reply.

I ease it open the rest of the way.

"Are you here?"

The room is empty.

Rain splatters in through an open window.

I cross to the sill.

Though it's not completely dark yet, it's tough to see very far—but then a thread of lightning illuminates the area and I make out a woman's body lying on the ground four stories below me.

She isn't moving.

But there is movement along the side of the hotel, about ten feet below the window. Someone is clinging desperately to the vines.

Thunder from that last lightning strike peels through the night.

"Petra?"

She looks up and there's just enough light for me to recognize her from her college graduation pictures.

"Help!" Her voice is filled with terror. "They're all around me!"

"You'll be okay. You're okay. Climb back up here. You can do it."

"It's the snakes. Please! I'm gonna fall!"

"There aren't any snakes. Relax. You can make it. Come on."

"Who are you?" The words tremble with a mixture of hope and fear.

"Daniel Byers. I'm here to help."

"Daniel?"

"Yes."

"I know about you."

"Malcolm told me about you too. I met your dad."

"My dad?"

"He's really worried. You can do it. Come up and we'll get out of here."

With her arms shaking, she begins to climb.

• • •

In the darkness of the shed, Henrik raged against the ropes biting into his wrists and ankles, but they were too tight.

Then the door swung open and he heard Garrett's voice. "Henrik? Are you okay?"

"Cut me free. Now!"

• • •

Nicole walked down the hallway beside Tane, who was supporting Mr. Zacharias, with one arm slung around him.

"I'm not sure how I'm gonna get Malcolm up the steps," Tane said. Then, with his free hand he dug Poehlman's keys out of his pocket. "Get the other girls from the shed and get out of here. We'll follow you in the minivan. I have the keys to it. Go."

• • •

Petra's almost to me.

She keeps worrying about snakes getting her and I keep telling her that she's going to be alright.

Earlier today, her dad had mentioned that she takes antipsychotic meds, and that he wasn't sure how well she would do if she had to go three days without them.

Well, here was the answer.

Hallucinations that don't stop.

Listening to her reminds me of the videos of Jess and Liam—how they lost it.

I hope it's not too late for her.

Finally, she reaches the windowsill and, gripping her wrist firmly, I help her into the room.

"She was trying to hurt me," she gasps. "I didn't mean to push her. I didn't try to make her fall."

"It's okay."

"Her name's Deedee. I think she might be dead."

"We need to go, Petra."

"Did they bite me?"

"No, they—"

"I know they did." She starts examining her arms and legs. "I know—"

"You're okay." I put my hand gently on her shoulder to calm her. "Listen. Let's go."

She shakes her head. "Malcolm's here. They said they have him. We can't leave. We need to find him."

"My friends are with him. They're going to meet us outside. C'mon."

• • •

Because of the slope of the road and the slick mud, Kyle hadn't been able to find his stride, and now, for the third time, he wiped out.

After scrambling to his feet, he checked the phone just in case.

No signal.

Drawing in a quick breath, he raced down the mountain toward the car.

• • •

Senator Amundsen read through his resignation letter.

It wasn't a guarantee, but it was something. Yes, he would cancel tomorrow's inquiry to satisfy the kidnappers, he would do that, and he would also resign from the Senate.

Then later, he could always fight for justice, for truth, as a private citizen, once his daughter was safe.

• • •

Mia didn't find keys in any of the vehicles.

Alysha was with her, and Mia was trying to figure out what to do when she heard a man hollering. "Stop right there!"

Poehlman.

He stood twenty feet away, holding a gun—probably from the guy who'd gone out to the shed, and was now by his side.

Poehlman moved closer to her. "Drop the Taser. I know you have it."

She didn't.

"Drop it or I will shoot you where you stand."

She got rid of the Taser.

He took another step toward her.

"And that knife you carry."

After a short hesitation, she tossed Lucy into the mud.

He was right in front of her now. "I oughta use a Taser on you four times too, just for fun."

"Oh, is that how many it was? I guess I lost track."

Poehlman backhanded her harshly across the face, then took the radio from his partner and told him, "Get the blind girl."

The man grasped Alysha's arm.

Mia brushed her finger across her bloody lip.

Poehlman hit the "Transmit" button and said, "Doctor, we've got two of them out here. We're bringing 'em in. The others are inside already."

The man that Tane had locked in the trunk earlier must have heard them out here, because he began crying out and beating against it.

Poehlman found a way to get it open, freed the guy, and then the three men led the girls toward the door.

• • •

Nicole rushed outside on her way to find Mia and Alysha, but as she burst out of the building, she almost ran into Poehlman, who had a gun aimed at Mia.

"Oh." He grinned. "And what have we here?"

He gestured toward one of his men, and he started toward her, but Nicole drew out the pepper spray and blasted it in his face. He cried out and clutched at his eyes, but then the other guy wrenched it away from her and shoved her back into the hotel.

CHAPTER SIXTY

I'm leading Petra out of the stairwell when I see them in the hallway.

Nicole. Alysha. Mia.

And three men.

Mia yells, "Run!"

But Poehlman grabs Nicole and sticks the gun to her head. "Move and she dies."

I freeze.

"You took my gun earlier. Hold it out nice and slow and set it on the floor."

As I do, Petra, who's standing beside me, starts muttering, "Malcolm. We need to find Malcolm. And we have to call my dad. We have to—"

"Where's Deedee?" The guy that I'm assuming is named Sergei cuts her off.

"Forget Deedee," Poehlman says to him, then turns to me again. "Kick the gun over here."

I do.

Then, he has the man whose eyes are red and bloodshot and is dressed as a security guard collect everything from our pockets, including our phones and all the keys to the vehicles.

While Poehlman directs us toward the room where Ty Bell is, he sends his two men to the basement to find Tane and Malcolm.

By the time we get to Ty's room, they're returning with Tane, who's coming along more willingly than I would've thought.

"Where's Zacharias?" Poehlman asks him.

"I don't know. I couldn't find him."

"I don't believe you."

"Yeah," Tane says, "you know what? I wouldn't believe me either."

Poehlman's face reddens. "The condition he's in, he won't get far." He sends the guard to the end of the hall to some sort of security room to unlock Ty's door, then tells us, "From what I understand, this young man is an old friend of yours. Let's see how well you can all get along."

But before the door clicks open, a man in his sixties with a tangle of unkempt hair appears down the hallway.

I recognize him from the research we did on the chrono-biology facility in Wisconsin: Dr. Adrian Waxford.

He approaches, and then studies us, one by one.

In the end, his gaze lands on me.

"Daniel Byers. Young man, you've been on my radar screen for quite some time now. Yes. You and the others like you." He eyes Tane. Then Alysha. Then Petra.

What? How has he even heard about us?

"We know what you're doing here," Tane exclaims. "About the prisoners you're torturing."

"Well, *torture* is a loaded word, isn't it? Justice is all we're after. What is the point of handing out a sentence that we don't expect someone to serve? There will never be justice when people are sentenced to time simply to make a statement or to be symbolic."

Then he says to his men, "I want Daniel with me. Bring him to my office. Lock the others in with #556234, then go find Zacharias."

• • •

Kyle shot around the final curve and came to the metal gate at the base of the dirt road.

Unlocking the car, he climbed in and gunned the engine, but the loose soil along the roadside was too washed away and the wheels spun uselessly in the mud.

He tried the phone.

Nothing.

Still too far up the mountain.

He pounded the steering wheel in frustration, got back out and started running down the road again, hoping to finally get a cell signal so he could call for help.

CHAPTER
SIXTY-ONE

When we enter Dr. Waxford's office I see a woman on the floor, slumped against his desk.

Blood covers the bottom half of her shirt.

Her breathing is shallow and quick.

"Daniel, meet General Gibbons." Dr. Waxford is holding a gun and points the barrel at her as he tells me her name. "She was being uncooperative. I trust that I won't have that problem with you?"

This guy is a complete psychopath.

After going to his desk, he tosses me a pair of handcuffs. "Cuff your left wrist to that radiator pipe."

"Let me help her."

"I'm no expert on gunshot wounds, but I think it might be too late for that. Go on. The cuff."

I hesitate, but finally do it.

My left arm

My bad arm.

At least it leaves my good arm free.

He begins to prepare a syringe. "Who's Sam?"

"What?"

"Sam. The person who's been trying to stop my work. The person behind you being here. I'd rather not have to go through setting all this up again. The time spent doing so is too much of a distraction from my research."

"Is that what this is about? The blackmail? The ransom video? *Finding Sam*?"

He asks me again, but I have no idea who Sam is so there's nothing to tell him.

"Why are you doing all this?" I say.

"Justice." He checks the drug level in the needle, then looks at the time. "Within the next two minutes the senator is going to send his email, but . . ." He glances at the dying general. "Things have become a bit more complicated. I acknowledge that."

I'm trying to figure out what to do, how to get out of here, but I've got nothing.

"This drug," he says, "I've been wanting to see how it affects people. With your hallucinations, I'm anticipating that the effect will be enhanced. It's a chronomorphic drug. That means it'll affect the way you perceive the passage of time."

Carrying his gun, he comes toward me. "I'm going to inject this into your arm. Considering my job here, I've had to learn to do this one-handed, but if you struggle, if you try anything, I'll have to consider that being uncooperative and I'll be forced to take unwelcome steps. Do you understand?"

I'm still not clear on why he's doing this, especially now. *He's crazy. That should—*

"Daniel?"

"Yeah. I understand."

"Slide your shirtsleeve up."

After I do, he positions the tip of the needle against my vein.

"Be assured," he says, "this is all for the greater good."

Then he jams it into my arm.

And depresses the plunger.

CHAPTER
SIXTY-TWO

Senator Amundsen hit "Send."

There.

It was done.

Now, at least, Petra would be safe.

Then, he sent the second email.

Resigning his seat in the Senate.

• • •

Nicole stared at Ty Bell, who was standing just five feet from her.

He was dressed in white.

All in white.

Tane, Mia, and Alysha were beside her. Petra sat crouched in the corner, trembling and mumbling to herself about how the snakes were after her, how they would get her, how they had to be stopped.

"Don't come any closer," Nicole warned Ty, even though she had no weapons, no way to fend him off.

She did have Tane, though.

Ty, who hadn't said a word since Poehlman and the other guards locked them in here, finally spoke. "I'm sorry, Nicole."

"Okay, and why are you sorry?"

"For what I did last year. For when I tried to hurt you."

"Oh, well, I'm glad to hear you're a changed person."

She was a little surprised by how genuinely contrite he sounded, but also, not that surprised. Being tortured here probably gave him a lot to think about.

"And for threatening all of you," he went on, "Daniel too. It wasn't right."

"Wonderful. Good for you. Now—"

"What can I do?"

"What are you talking about?"

"To help. There's no way they'll let you go. Not anymore. You know too much. I don't think they'll let any of us go. When they were processing me, I heard 'em talking about being able to burn this place to the ground. It sounded like when they renovated it, they designed things so it would go down quickly."

"Do you really think they would do that?"

He was silent.

She took that to mean *yes*.

Tane grabbed the steel chair and headed to the one-way mirror.

"That won't work," Ty said. "I've tried."

"I haven't."

And he hurled it at the glass.

• • •

The drug doesn't take long to kick in.

Somehow, everything is beginning to move in slow motion.

I blink, trying to orient myself.

"So, the senator has sent the email." Dr. Waxford's words are thick and slower than they should be, as if they're moving through liquid rather than air. "The inquiry has been called off. However, now with the general here, it looks like we're going to have to take additional steps."

"What's happening to me?" My voice sounds slurred, almost like people do when they're drunk.

"It's the Telpatine. What's it like?"

My left shoulder is weak, and it's that wrist that's handcuffed, so I reach around with my other hand and try to yank the cuff off the pipe, but it's secure.

Dr. Waxford sets the handcuff key beside a small propped-up photograph of the mountains on a shelf not too far from me. The photo looks vaguely familiar.

"I'll tell you what." He goes to type on his computer. "You solve the riddle of the camels and I won't move your friends into room 113 with the man who tried to burn you alive last winter. You remember him? Killed eight people? He's been deteriorating mentally ever since I brought him here."

His words stall in the air, falling toward me one at a time.

The general—she's going to bleed out. She's going to die.

Time stretches out, like it did when I was in the air flying toward that ditch after the truck hit me.

That night, as I landed, time caught up with itself.

I'm still waiting for that to happen now.

I reach for the key, but it's a few inches too far away.

Dr. Waxford watches me try to retrieve it and smiles.

He's mocking me. Toying with me.

"Well," he says, "what do you say about the riddle?"

I don't understand why he's taking time to do this.

At least you can help your friends if you figure it out. Do that much.

"Tell it to me."

• • •

"It's an old Sufi story."

Adrian typed in the code to wipe the server, then walked over to the general.

Kneeling beside her, he started relating the ancient puzzle as he shuffled through her pockets until he came up with the USB thumb drive.

• • •

"Ah, there it is," he mutters, then continues with the riddle about seventeen camels, about how they were supposed to be divided three ways after a guy's death—

I try for the key again.

Fail to get it.

Man, if I could just make it another couple inches I could reach it!

I try sliding the handcuff farther over, but it's already as far as it'll go.

Focus on what he's saying, Daniel. Help your friends.

So, one-half of the camels go to the first student, one-third to another, and one-ninth to the third. Then a caravan owner comes along and solves things.

The more I lean toward the shelf, the more fire rages through my injured shoulder and I have to ease back to catch my breath and try to quiet the pain.

Even though this drug seems to drag out everything else, it's jacking up the pain, making it more intense.

Just a few more inches.

That's all I need.

But it's not going to happen.

"So, my riddle?"

Poehlman appears at the doorway, "Doctor, there's something—"

"Just a moment, Henrik. He's trying to solve it."

"But—"

Seventeen can't be divided by half, by thirds, by ninths. It's—

"A caravan owner shows up?" I say to Waxford.

"Yes."

"So he has camels too?"

"Yes, yes. He does."

"It's eighteen."

"What?"

"The answer is eighteen."

And then as I hear myself give him the explanation, my words are so drawn out from the effects of the drug that I hardly recognize my own voice. "The caravan owner offers them one of his own camels. Then when there are eighteen, the first student gets nine. The second student gets a third of eighteen: that is, six. And the last student gets two camels—or one-ninth of eighteen."

"Then what?"

"When you add that up, it's seventeen, not eighteen. So they just give the caravan owner's camel back to him. Everyone gets their camels, no one is out anything, and the riddle is solved."

"You hear that, Henrik?" Dr. Waxford says proudly. "I told you before that this young man was clever."

"That you did."

"And see how he solved the puzzle?"

"He did a fine job. Now, Doctor, I came here to tell you that I've received word that local law enforcement has dispatched two units. They're on their way up the mountain, but there's still time for us to get out of here."

Adrian peers at me with what might be a look of admiration. "Was that your doing, Daniel—or was it your father's, perhaps?"

It might have been Kyle. Maybe he got down and was able to make the call.

The general is getting weaker.

Hurry. Help her!

"You said you'd let my friends go if I solved your riddle."

"No, I said I wouldn't lock them in with a murderer. And I won't."

•   •   •

Adrian assessed things.

It was similar to the riddle he'd just told the boy: Sometimes the solution is right in front of you, but your preconceptions cloud your thinking. You need to consider all possible options, use your assets, think outside the box.

Options. Assets. Solutions.

He thought of his phone conversation with Henrik earlier in the day, when the topic of the hotel's rapid oxidation system had come up.

Yes.

"Burn it down," he told Henrik.

"What about the subjects?"

"Leave them."

"Burn them alive?"

"It's true that they won't be getting the justice they deserve, but at least they'll be getting the full extent of the justice that we can, in this moment, provide. If we let them live, they'll be returned to traditional incarceration. We can't let that happen."

"So we kill them in the name of justice."

"We do what is necessary to serve the greater good. Start the oxidation."

"The kids too?"

"I've been thinking about what you mentioned earlier about loose ends—you were right. We should get rid of them all."

"Yes, Doctor. The controls are in the basement. I'd suggest you get going. Once it's started, we'll have less than five minutes before this place is fully engaged."

Adrian turned to Byers. "I would've liked to spend more time with you to see the Telpatine's effects. I wish I could be here to record your progress for posterity, but it looks like the circumstances have ruled that out. Good night, Daniel. Goodbye."

• • •

He and Poehlman leave.

I yank at the cuff again.

Useless.

Dark shapes begin to circle through my vision. At first I'm not sure if it's the drugs, or shadows, but then I realize what they are.

Bats.

And then the boy from my dream appears right here, by my side—

But no, it's not him. This boy is a little older, nine or ten, maybe. He's pale and ghostly and dressed in old-fashioned clothes.

I don't recognize him. He doesn't look like I did when I was younger.

"Who are you?" I hear myself ask.

"You need to leave." His voice is hushed and coarse. "You all need to leave."

It sounds like both a warning and a threat.

When I reach out to touch him, my hand passes through him.

A blur?

A ghost?

He faces the key and reaches for it.

Just like the boy on the road reached out for my hand as the logging truck roared toward him.

Just like the girls in my earlier blurs reached out to me so I could save them.

So—

My dreams.

My blurs.

My reality.

The girl last autumn in the casket.

The girl in December bursting into flames.

All those blurs merging together.

Bats flapping around me.

Nearby, the general watches me, her breathing becoming more and more ragged.

Follow the bats.

But how? Where?

The boy stretches his arm out longer than it could ever go, all the way to the shelf, all the way to the key.

But I can't reach it.

I can't—

Oh.

Unless.

Unless my shoulder was dislocated.

Then I could get those extra few inches.

He says to me, "This is going to hurt. But it's going to help."

When I was at the hospital after getting hit by that truck, the doctor warned me that I ran the risk of pulling it out of socket again unless I was careful. Earlier today that almost happened at Little Bear Creek when Tane grabbed my arm.

It's been just over a week. It's probably still loose enough.

Propping my leg against the wall, I take a deep breath.

Then push as hard as I can.

Fire splinters across my shoulder.

The drugs make it seem to last forever.

Those flickering shadows open their hungry mouths to devour me.

Like giant bats.

The shoulder rages with pain, but stays in place.

It's not going to come out if I go slowly like this. I need to create enough force to pop it out of its socket.

I scoot closer to the wall, scrunch up both legs, and then throw myself backward.

The shoulder dislocates and a wash of dizziness spreads over me, through me, overwhelms me.

The boy, the bats, they all slip into the background, fold back into the air.

Stretching out as far as I can, I nudge the small picture aside to get to the key, and the photo tips off the shelf.

I see it falling slower than it should through the air, a mountain vista angled and dropping to the floor. Then its glass shatters, and as it comes to rest I recognize it from Dr. Carrigan's theater. A print of one of his photos.

The key.

Get the key.

My fingers find it.

I don't want it to drop to the floor, so I pinch it carefully as I draw it off the shelf.

Everything still seems slow and prolonged as I unlock the cuff and, with my left arm now hanging useless by my side, I start toward the general.

As much as I'd like to get that shoulder back in place, it's probably too messed up right now. I'm going to need help with it this time.

Everything is bleary, dreamlike.

I make it to her side. "If I help you, can you get to your feet?"

She shakes her head weakly.

"We need to go. He's gonna burn this place down."

"I can't." She uncurls one of her hands and a USB drive drops to the floor.

"I thought he took that?"

"It was the wrong one." She smiles faintly. "Everything's on here. Post it online. Get the truth out."

I pick it up.

She coughs and a thread of blood dribbles from her mouth.

With my one good arm, I try to lift her, but she cringes and shakes her head so I stop.

"Leave me."

Smoke begins curling out of the vents along the wall.

This is happening.

It's happening now.

Go, Daniel. You need to leave.

"Listen," I tell her urgently, "they locked my friends in one of the rooms. Do you know how to get the doors open?"

"The security center on the first floor." Her voice is soft now, barely audible. "Open all the doors. These men don't deserve to die in here—but they can't go free. Get the geo-tracker."

"What's that?"

"Looks like a tablet computer. It'll find the ink in their eyeballs."

I don't know what she's talking about, but then she stares past me, her eyes glaze over, and her body goes limp.

I shake her, call her name.

No response.

It's too late.

You have to go.

More smoke seeps into the room.

Poehlman said there'd be less than five minutes to get out after the fire started.

Pocketing the thumb drive, I head to the hallway.

The hall seems to waver somewhere between time and space. Taking an unsteady step forward, I lose my balance and lean my right arm against the wall for support, then stumble toward the stairs.

CHAPTER
SIXTY-THREE

Kyle was cornering a bend when he saw the pair of head-lights cut through the storm.

Maybe the driver had a phone that got reception up here.

He took off the headlamp and waved the light to flag the car down.

It stopped in the middle of the road.

As he hurried toward it, the driver swung the passenger door open and Kyle took it as an invitation to climb in and get out of the rain.

But before he did, he bent and looked inside.

The man spoke first, "What are you doing out here? Are you okay?"

"Yeah." Kyle was still breathing heavily from his run. "I need your help. Can I use your phone?"

"Sure. Yeah, yeah. Get in."

Kyle got into the car and tugged the door closed. "I'm Kyle."

"My name is Reginald Carrigan. Now, you were about to tell me what you're doing out here in the middle of this storm."

• • •

It took Henrik a little longer than he anticipated to remotely open all the vents and start each of the conflagration units in the basement.

Now, he was on his way toward the stairs when a figure emerged from the shadows near the fly room at the end of the hall.

Zacharias.

"So, there you are." Henrik drew his gun.

"You won't shoot me."

"Oh? And why not?"

"You're not a coward. Come here. Come closer."

Henrik did.

This place is burning down. Just kill him and get out.

No, you're not a coward. He's right. You can't just shoot him. Kill him. But do it with your hands.

Henrik holstered the gun. "Okay, but I'm afraid even then this won't be a fair fight. You can hardly stand."

"I'll hardly need to."

Ten feet separated them.

As Henrik approached him, Malcolm didn't step aside, just drew his shirt up over his mouth.

Henrik couldn't help but scoff. "What are you doing?"

"It's so they don't get in my mouth."

"What?"

But then it was too late.

A sudden dark realization.

Malcolm threw open the door.

Releasing the ten thousand *Tabanidae* into the hall.

• • •

As the flies swarmed forward, Malcolm made his way to the stairs, breathing through the fabric.

He heard a brief shriek, but it was cut short as a wave of flies poured into Henrik Poehlman's mouth.

Malcolm entered the stairwell and closed the door behind him.

As the smoke creeping through the ventilation units thickened, rose, and gathered along the ceiling.

• • •

I find the security center on the first floor.

The console is easy enough to figure out, with numbered switches corresponding to each room.

I flip them all.

Open every door.

The general said to get the geo-tracker.

There's only one thing in here that looks like what she described, so I grab it. Then I leave to find my friends.

• • •

Nicole watched as Tane tried to smash the mirror.

Ever since the smoke had started to invade the room, he'd become more desperate, but the glass didn't break.

However, all at once, she heard an electric click. The door's lock.

Curious, she pushed against the door and it opened.

"Hurry!" she cried. "Let's go!"

Flames were licking up through narrow slits in the floor along the wall. Prisoners from the other rooms were venturing into the hallway. Some seemed disoriented—maybe from their torture and sleep deprivation, maybe from the smoke and the fumes. Some looked suspicious that all this was some type of trap or another one of Dr. Waxford's twisted treatment strategies.

Tane stood beside her. "We need to get these people out of here!"

• • •

One of the prisoners rushes toward me.

In slow motion, I can see him rearing back to take a swing at my face, but I'm able to lean to the side and get out of his path before he can land a punch.

It doesn't feel like my reaction time is faster than usual. It just seems like everything else is slowed down.

The effects of the drug.

Confused, he staggers past me.

I don't see the girls, but Tane yells and waves.

The lights flicker like they did earlier and I'm not sure if it's from the storm or from the fire destroying the wires.

I start toward Tane.

• • •

The smoke was in Nicole's eyes and she wanted to help get people out, but she could barely see.

She moved forward and ran into a wall.

The overhead lights blinked out.

All around her there was smoke and flames and confusion.

"Over here!" Alysha yelled. "Walk toward my voice!"

Nicole hobbled forward and almost ran into her.

"Mia!" Alysha called. "Petra!"

"Where are you?" Mia shouted.

"Here! Hurry!"

A moment later, they were all together.

"I'll get you out of here," Alysha said to them.

"How?" Nicole asked.

"I remember how many steps it was. Grab my shoulder. I'll be your eyes."

• • •

Tane finds me. "Your arm!"

"I'm okay. Where are the girls?"

"They were near the door when the lights went out."

A burning beam tilts from the ceiling and as it falls, I shove Tane to the side.

With a burst of flame and sparks, it crashes to the floor where he'd been standing only a moment earlier.

Ty joins us and we point prisoners toward the door.

As we pass room 113, the one Waxford threatened to put my friends in, I see that it's empty.

• • •

Outside the hotel, Nicole watched flames shoot out the windows and claw at the night.

The rain only managed to calm down the fire a little, and not fast enough to save the building.

As the prisoners burst out the doors, she silently prayed that everyone would get out alive.

Where's Daniel? Where are the others?

Please, please, please let them be okay.

Please.

Some of the men stopped near the hotel and stood staring at the blaze, mesmerized by it, as if they were caught in some bizarre dream and hadn't woken up yet.

Others fled into the storm, scattering and escaping into the night.

Please!

Then they appeared.

Tane first. Then Ty.

And, finally, Daniel.

Oh, thank you. Thank you. Thank you!

But when she saw that Daniel's shoulder was out of socket, she gasped.

• • •

Nicole hurries toward me and asks about my arm. I assure her that I'm okay, then confirm that the rest of our friends are out here too.

All the cars are still in the parking lot and I wonder what happened to Dr. Waxford and his staff.

Was there another way off the mountain?

Since they took the keys from us earlier, we can't drive out of here, but Poehlman said that cops were on their way up. We just need to hold out until they get here.

As I'm thinking of that, headlights appear on the road.

But then, all at once, from near the building, someone shouts my name.

I turn.

Dr. Waxford emerges from the shadows with his gun aimed at me, and stands between me and the hotel, his back to the blaze.

I don't know why he hasn't left the area yet. It seems like he should have, like there was enough time.

And then, behind him, the man from room 113 appears— the serial murderer who killed a boy in the same barn where I was playing when I was nine.

Now he stands, hulking, in the doorway with the flames raging around him.

He stalks forward.

"Run," I tell my friends. "Go, go, go."

They back up, but Dr. Waxford warns me to stay where I am. "Do not move." He doesn't see the killer that he's been tormenting and torturing for months coming toward him. "I've only shot one person in my life up until now, but—"

I hold up my hand to warn him. "Dr. Waxford, you need to—"

"Quiet!"

Then two giant bats appear to my left and begin to skirt along the ground.

Follow the bats.

The words resonate through my head. Call to me, won't let me go.

And my dad's saying, "Nothing is mundane if everything matters."

Everything matters.

Follow them.

Ever since my dream when I first heard those words I've wondered what they mean.

Maybe this is it.

This is where everything was pointing.

Leading.

I trust the moment and take off after them.

Dr. Waxford hollers at me, shoots.

Misses.

And is distracted enough by my movement that he doesn't notice the killer.

I glance back and see the man grab hold of Waxford's hair, yank him backward off his feet, and start dragging him toward the hotel.

"Come on, Doctor," he says, his voice more of a snarl than anything. "Let me show you my room."

The bats disappear and I watch what's happening with Waxford.

He cries out and struggles to get free, but it does no good.

As he's pulled through the mud, he twists his arm and fires at the man.

It looks like he hits him, but it doesn't stop him, and the killer hauls Waxford into the blazing hotel.

For a long moment I hear his screams echo out the door. And then I do not.

This place where Waxford had handed out his own twisted form of justice had now handed it back to him.

The only sound is the crackling flames devouring the building.

As I'm standing there listening to the sizzle of the blaze in the rain, the car that was coming up the hill arrives.

CHAPTER
SIXTY-FOUR

The drug that Dr. Waxford gave me still makes everything seem slower and more deliberate than it should be.

Kyle leaps out of the passenger seat.

Dr. Carrigan climbs out the driver's side.

"Are you guys okay?" Kyle shouts. "We called the cops, but they were already on their way up."

He's right—beyond the sound of the rain and the fire, the echo of police sirens comes rolling up the mountain.

Seeing Dr. Carrigan makes me think of the photograph I saw in Dr. Waxford's office—the same print from the theater.

Carrigan said he took all those pictures himself.

He said he didn't sell them, just gave copies to his friends.

Does that mean that—

"It's you!" Petra shouts at Carrigan, then shudders and backs up.

"Petra?" He looks shocked.

"What are you doing up here?" I ask him suspiciously.

"The helicopter pilot called me. The guy who likes apple pie. He told me that you needed help, so I cancelled my show. What's all this about? What's happening here?"

"How did you get past the gate?"

He doesn't answer that. "What happened to your arm, Daniel?"

"The gate. It was locked. How did you get past it?"

He's in on this.

He's part of it.

The sirens are closer now.

Kyle answers, "He tried it. It was unlocked. Someone from up here must have unlocked it."

"Did you see him?" I ask.

"What?"

"Did you see him try to unlock it?"

"I—No."

He has a key.

He has his own key to the gate.

"You weren't coming up here to help us," I tell Dr. Carrigan. "You were coming up here to help the doctor."

"Why would I help Waxford?"

"No." I shake my head as the first police cruiser pulls up. "I never told you his name."

"What?"

"Not here. Not at the theater. I never mentioned Waxford's name."

"I didn't either," Kyle says. "How did you—?"

The Great Carrigini begins easing back toward his car.

Then, as an officer gets out of the squad car, Dr. Carrigan produces something from his waistband.

A revolver.

"Watch out!" I yell to the officer, who pulls his own gun and directs it at Dr. Carrigan.

"Stop! Hands up!"

A second cruiser arrives.

Staring at me with cool, steely eyes, Dr. Carrigan slowly raises his hands.

"Drop the gun!" the cop orders him. "Now!"

He does.

Then the officer comes forward, has him kneel, and handcuffs him.

Excellent timing.

When the prisoners who'd remained near the hotel see that the police are here, they all disperse into the woods. Although, in this storm I'm not sure how far they're going to get.

Mia is on her hands and knees near the hotel, searching for something in the mud.

What is she doing?

The officer from the second squad sees the way my arm is hanging from my shoulder and radios for an ambulance. Then he asks us what's going on up here while the other cop takes care of Dr. Carrigan.

"Do you have a way to make a phone call?" I ask him. "A satellite phone? Anything like that?"

"No, but we can radio down to dispatch. Why?"

"We need to get a message to Senator Amundsen from Georgia and let him know his daughter is alright."

I'm not sure who to trust, or if these officers will know what to do with the general's USB drive. However, there's one person in law enforcement who I know I *can* trust to do the right thing.

My dad.

As soon as I can, I'll get it to him and we'll let the world know what Dr. Waxford was really doing up here.

We would get the truth out there. I would honor the general's dying wish.

"Aha!" Mia reaches into the mud and comes up with her butterfly knife. "There you are, Lucy!"

I hand the geo-tracker to the officer. "General Gibbons told me that you can use this to find them."

"General Gibbons?" He looks confused. "Find who?"

"All of the escaped, crazy, tattooed-eyeball prisoners," I tell him. "From the top-secret, government-funded torture site," Kyle adds helpfully.

"Oh."

As the officer radios dispatch to get word to the senator, Nicole asks me quietly, "Any sign of Malcolm?"

"No."

"Do you think he's alive?"

"He can take care of himself. I'm sure he made it out."

But I'm really not sure about that at all.

Wondering if the bats will reappear, I study the fringe of darkness surrounding the fire.

But maybe they've finally served their purpose because they don't emerge.

However, the boy with the old-fashioned clothes does appear again, standing beside the hotel. He nods once toward me, turns to vapor, and merges back into the night.

CHAPTER
SIXTY-FIVE

We step off the trolley.

Evening mist circles through the cool, twilit forest.

The park rangers limit the number of people who can visit this valley, the only place in the United States where the synchronous fireflies congregate. However, even though the tickets for tonight were sold out, they found a way to fit us in.

Nicole points toward some of the rangers who are cheerily directing people where to go. "They look so happy in their Smokey Bear hats and uniforms. And so pleased to have all these people here in their park."

"Warms my heart," Mia mutters.

Kyle takes her hand. "Mine too." In his other hand he's carrying his energy drink concoction. "Do you know what time it is?"

"Give it up, babe. You're never gonna break your record."

"No, I'm serious, if I can make it through until midnight I'll hit thirty-nine hours and forty-two minutes."

"You'll probably fall asleep before the fireflies even come out."

Just behind us, Tane is leading Alysha, who hasn't had a chance yet to get a new cane.

Yesterday, she and I talked through things regarding the "girlfriend issue," as she put it. I made it clear that I was taken, and later I saw her sitting with Tane. She had her hand on his cheek feeling his face and I took that as a good sign. Who knows where it might lead?

My shoulder is back in place.

Thankfully.

A new sling.

Still hurts, but not as bad as when it was dislocated.

And this time, despite the fact that I'm missing the basketball camp, I'm going to rest it. Sometimes it just takes time for things to heal, and there's no way to hurry the process along.

The doctors are still going to do a few more tests on me, but so far it looks like Dr. Waxford didn't give me enough of his chronomorphic drug to have any long-term effects.

Nearby, my parents are talking with Kyle's mom.

The three of them flew down yesterday morning—compliments of Marly Weathers.

Still haven't met her.

Or him.

At least not that I know of.

Mia's and Nicole's parents couldn't make it. Neither could Tane's mother. Alysha's mom and dad will be arriving tomorrow morning.

Sue Ellen drove up from Atlanta this afternoon with homemade fudge for everyone, and now ambles along beside Petra and Senator Amundsen. He may have resigned, but Petra told us that once you've been a senator it's a title you get to keep for life.

Earlier tonight, at supper, she mentioned that she'd started taking her antipsychotic meds again and, though they hadn't totally kicked in yet, she was beginning to feel better.

She even solved some of Kyle's math and logic problems. A kindred spirit. She was at least as good at them as I am.

The doctors gave her a shot of some type of steroids to calm down her reaction to the poison ivy, and she's recovering.

Senator Amundsen got a note from Marly Weathers telling us to cash in the debit card and split up the money between our families. He and Petra declined accepting any, but it would sure help the rest of us, even provide me with some cash that I could put aside for college in case I don't end up with a scholarship.

Together, we move with the throng of several hundred people toward the expansive picnic area.

With the touch of fog wisping through the towering trees, it almost seems like we've entered another, slightly magical world here in the Smokies.

The crickets chirrup at us as we pass.

A park employee with an infectious smile motions us forward. "Just go off by yourself, find a boulder or a log to sit on—there are plenty of them out here. We have some historical cabins in the area, so let's avoid going into those. As it starts to get dark, the fireflies will come out. Don't disturb them and you'll see what you came here to see!"

"That's Tiff," Kyle tells Tane and me. "She's the one who gave us the package from Marly Weathers the other day."

"So does she work for the park service or the educational center?" Tane asks.

"Dunno." Kyle takes a slurp of his drink. "That's a good question."

Tiff continues with her instructions by reminding everyone not to use flashlights unless they have a red cellophane filter over the lens. "Otherwise, it can disrupt the activity of the fireflies." She sweeps her arms to the left. "For complimentary red filters, please line up over here." And then to the right. "If you're all set, c'mon this way. Remember to pack out your trash and enjoy your time at Cades Cove! The fireflies await!"

When she sees us, her eyes light up. "So, you got some tickets after all!"

"We did," Nikki replies.

"I'm so glad you could make it."

"So are we."

"When do you fly back to Philly?"

"Sorry?"

"Back home to your dad, Mr. Weathers."

"Oh, right. We're hoping to enjoy the South for a few more days first."

We move to the right and join the people who are picking out viewing spots throughout the valley.

"Your dad?" I ask Nicole.

"I sorta fibbed to her the other day."

"I'm sure you had a good reason."

"Sure I did. Finding you."

It's been an eventful couple of days.

My dad posted the videos from the USB drive that General Gibbons gave me and they went viral. Dr. Waxford's secret research is all over the Internet.

Even though the senator's committee meeting was cancelled, now the FBI is involved and there's going to be a full investigation—not just on the proper use of Waxford's findings, but also on the role of consciousness in punishment to examine what is ethical and what isn't.

His research might be beneficial someday—like maybe to help alter the perception of how much time someone spends in pain after surgery, to make it seem shorter. Or for drawing out positive experiences so they seem like they last longer: prom nights, birthdays, graduation parties. First dates and sunsets and fishing trips and roller coaster rides.

Or maybe, it'd be better if we left things as they are.

Maybe we're meant to just experience every moment as is, taking it for what it's worth, nothing more, nothing less. I guess that's something to consider too.

As far as Dr. Waxford, neither he nor the serial killer who dragged him back into the building survived the fire.

The other convicts were all located through the tracking unit and U.S. Marshals were returning them to the prisons they'd originally been transferred in from.

Henrik Poehlman never made it out of the hotel. They found his body in the basement, his lungs filled with smoke, his throat with dead flies.

As it turns out, Deedee didn't die when she fell from the fourth-story window, but she did break her leg, and the fall knocked her unconscious. Her partner, Sergei, was picked up by state troopers after trying to hitchhike near Gatlinburg. Both are in custody and being guarded by the police.

Waxford's other staff members and researchers have been arrested as well. Depending on how much they participated in his work, they're each facing a whole list of charges.

For helping save the other inmates, it looks like Ty Bell is going to get some leniency in his sentence.

I'm not sure how I feel about that, but my dad said there comes a time to trust the justice system and I figure, after all that's happened, he probably has a point.

We still don't know where Malcolm is. No one has seen or heard from him and, although the fire investigators are still going through the charred remains of the hotel, so far they haven't found his body. Though his eyeball was tagged, he didn't show up on the tracking unit.

And Dr. Carrigan?

The police are trying to figure out what to do with him. Evidently, he'd been hypnotizing Dr. Waxford's prisoners over the last few months and implanting destructive suggestions while they were in their trances. It wasn't ethical, but it wasn't clear if it was an actual crime or not.

He said that when he drew his gun he was just trying to protect himself from the prisoners, but I doubt that. The last I heard, he was in custody, but his lawyer was trying to get him free and I'm not sure they'll be able to hold him with what they have.

The trail we've been taking through the picnic grove fingers off into a series of more overgrown paths that meander through the valley.

Initially, my mom and dad were pretty upset with my friends for not telling them that I was missing the other day, but they've had some time to process what happened and it doesn't seem like they're going to hold a grudge.

So that's cool.

Now, I tell them that we're going to head down by the stream where it looks like there's a clearing.

"So you can see more fireflies?" my mom says.

"Exactly."

Over the last few days we've talked more about the shadows she sees out of the corner of her eyes and the bats that have been haunting me—or helping me. At the hotel, the monsters from my childhood turned out to be not so monstrous after all.

Maybe these things do run in families.

So maybe, as a family, we could learn to deal with them better.

As I turn toward the creek with my friends, I see her reach over and take my dad's hand.

Tiff was right about there being plenty of places to sit.

We all locate logs or boulders surrounding the stream.

Not too many other people have found their way down into this part of the cove.

"Have the fireflies come out yet?" asks Alysha, who has positioned herself on a massive log near the water.

"Just a couple here and there." Tane is sitting beside her. "So this is for real, though? Thousands of them are supposed to just blink on and off, all together?"

"That's what they say," Nicole replies. "On the trolley ride over here, the guy next to me mentioned he's been coming for five years. He said to just give it some time. There need to be a bunch of them first before they start blinking synchronously."

Tane shakes his head. "That's impossible, though. The whole synchronous thing. I don't get it."

Alysha smiles. "And this coming from a guy who hears people who are miles away talking to him in his thoughts. I'd say lots of impossible things happen every day."

"It doesn't make any sense," Mia says. "*How do those little buggers know when to blink?*"

"I say God designed them that way," Nicole tells us confidently. "And he's an expert at making impossible things come true."

"Not to change the subject." Kyle clears his throat slightly. "But, Alysha, I've been meaning to ask you something."

"Yes?"

"How do you spell your name?"

"A-l-y-s-h-a. Why?"

"It's crazy, but Alicia is The Thing's blind girlfriend in the Fantastic Four comics. It's spelled differently, though: A-l-i-c-i-a."

"Well, I can definitely tell you that The Thing is not my boyfriend." But then she adds, "Although, I have had guys about as interesting as a rock ask me out."

"But you have to admit it's kind of a cool coincidence, though. I mean, you weren't blinded in a laboratory explosion by a vat of radioactive clay, but you do have the same name as her."

"Maybe it's not a coincidence at all. Actually, I don't believe in them."

"Neither do I," Nicole notes. "I think there's a bigger reason that we can't always see, directing the things that we can."

Her words make me think of the Chinese folktale again.

Curses.

Blessings.

Turning the first into the second.

Blurs and clues, glimpses of the future through the lens of the present.

I guess a lot depends on your perspective and whether or not you trust those reasons that you can't see.

And maybe that's something I'm finally ready to do.

The darker it gets, the more fireflies begin to emerge.

A few dozen flicker around us now.

They're still blinking on and off intermittently.

Not in sync quite yet.

"Okay," Kyle speaks up. "I just thought I'd mention that no one has solved my riddle yet."

"Which riddle is that?" Tane asks.

"The one I made up on the drive from Wisconsin—I guess I never told it to you guys. So: 'What's the largest thing you'll ever see, yet smaller than a pin? You're looking into history, so let the guessing begin.'"

Tane stares thoughtfully into the distance. "Is it a problem—that's something that can be small but seem big, right? Or maybe a riddle?"

"Nope."

"A blur?"

"Nice try, but no."

A little boy who looks about seven years old starts walking toward us.

"I think I might know the answer," Alysha tells us.

"What is it?" Kyle asks her.

"A star."

After a moment of shocked silence, Kyle exclaims, "That's it! You got it!"

My attention is split between the riddle conversation and the boy coming this way.

Nicole looks curiously at Kyle and Alysha. "How's it a star?"

Though I don't know the boy, he seems to recognize me as he angles my direction.

I'm not entirely certain that he's real.

He might be a blur.

"Because you'll never see something bigger than a star," Alysha answers, "but when you see it in the sky—"

"Oh." Nikki catches on. "Right, it looks smaller than a pin."

As discreetly as I can, I take out my cell phone and tap the video recording app.

"Yes. And you're looking into history because the light from the star takes thousands or even millions of years to get here, so some stars might have already burned out, but their light is still traveling through the universe."

"Wait. How do you know all that?" Nicole says, as it dawns on her that all this is coming from a girl who was born blind.

No one else seems to have noticed the boy.

Maybe because they're focused on solving the riddle.

Maybe because he isn't there.

I tilt the phone toward him.

"I've heard a lot about stars over the years," Alysha explains. "I hear they're beautiful."

"They are," Nicole tells her.

The boy shows up on the screen.

So, real after all.

"You didn't solve it Daniel," Kyle says to me. "I finally got you."

"Right." I'm still distracted.

I remember looking at the stars when we were at Mr. Schuster's house on our way down to Atlanta. Also, when Alysha told me the story of "The Country of the Blind," she mentioned that the mountain climber looked up at the stars and found his freedom from the valley.

It seems like there really is something at work here in my life, something that's lacing coincidences and blurs together in an intricate and remarkable way.

Synchronicity.

The boy stops a few feet from me.

"Hey there," I say.

"That ranger wants to talk to you." He points behind him.

Wondering if it might be Tiff, the only ranger we've met, I glance toward where he's pointing.

The ranger stands about fifty feet away from us, facing the other direction. Definitely not Tiff. He's using his red-filtered flashlight to direct people.

"He sent you over here to tell me that?" I ask the boy.

He nods, hands me a small tile, the same kind that was used to create the geometric patterns on the floor of the hallways beneath Centennial Olympic Park, and then darts away and joins his parents who are waiting by the trail and offer me a friendly wave.

Okay.

Weird.

I stare at the tile, then tell my friends, "I'll be back in a minute. I need to check on something."

Then I leave to go talk to the ranger.

CHAPTER SIXTY-SIX

Though it's getting dark, there's just enough light for me to pick my way along the trail without having to turn on my flashlight.

"Excuse me." I walk up to him and hold up the tile. "Did you ask a little boy to give me this?"

He turns to face me.

A patch covers his right eye.

A scar marks his cheek.

The bruises from when he was beaten are still visible.

"Malcolm?" I gasp. "What are you doing here?"

"Walk with me."

He takes off briskly down the trail but I'm able to keep up with him.

"Your eye patch," I say, "that's the eye they tattooed, isn't it?"

"It was."

"What do you mean 'was'?"

"There's only one way to make sure no one can locate you when you're marked with those nanobot trackers, and

I couldn't have someone following my every move, now, could I?"

"Are you telling me that you . . . ?"

"Yes. As they say, 'In the Country of the Blind, the one-eyed man is king.'"

"Wait—what?"

"It's a line from a philosopher back in the sixteenth century, Desiderius Erasmus of Rotterdam. H. G. Wells referred to it in one of his stories."

"I think I might know which one."

He must have found out that Alysha told you that story. But how?

Well, he communicated with Tane during that hypnotism session. Maybe he can tell what other people are thinking too.

"How's your shoulder, Daniel?"

"Honestly, it's pretty sore."

"Give it some time."

"I will."

"It's good to see your parents could make it."

"Marly Weathers paid for them to fly down."

"That was generous."

"Yes," I say. "It was."

He uses his flashlight to point out a few thick roots bulging across the trail and we step over them.

"Do you know who Marly is?" I ask him.

"Not for certain."

I hold up the tile that the boy handed to me. "What about Sam?"

"I'm not so sure they aren't the same person."

I let that sink in.

The more I think about it, the more it makes sense. Maybe I'd suspected it earlier, at least subconsciously, but either way, it could help explain how everything fits together.

He goes on, "I have my suspicions. It would need to be someone with money, influence, and an agenda."

"But to pull all this off? How?"

"When you have enough money, you don't need to be good at everything. You just need to be able to afford the people who are."

"Like you, with recruitment?"

"I suppose."

We have to duck under a tree branch that forks out above the trail.

I still don't know where he's taking me.

"Malcolm, there's something I've been wondering."

"Yes?"

"Yesterday, Tane told me about how you fought that man in L.A. He said he'd seen the guy fight before and he was good, but that you handled him no problem."

"Okay."

"So how did Poehlman and Sergei capture you at the facility in Atlanta?"

"I thought it might lead me to Petra."

"You thought—wait. So you let yourself get taken?" I process that. "But you let them torture you for the rest of the day."

"I needed to find Petra before I could let Tane know where she was. When they first brought me in they wouldn't tell me. So, I had to let them . . . well."

"So, letting Tane know about her—are you one of us?"

"Everyone's a virtuoso at something," he says, echoing what Alysha told me the other day.

I wonder if he taught her that saying.

Or if she taught it to him.

"Are there more of us out there?"

"Probably. And as long as the right environmental cues come along, we'll find them."

"The honeybee factor."

"Yes."

I still have a lot of questions, but two top the list: Is all of this paranormal or just the interplay of nature and nurture—a simple scientific explanation we haven't been able to decipher yet? And, of course, will the thread snap for good?

"Are we going crazy, Malcolm? Are we going to end up like Jess and Liam?"

"Even Jess and Liam didn't end up like Jess and Liam. At least not forever. Not for sure."

"What do you mean?"

"Gatlinburg Holdings. Their work in helping stop mental illness in adolescents. They're making huge strides. The future isn't as bleak as it used to be. I think a lot of answers lie just around the corner."

"So, what do we do now?"

"That'll depend a little on your parents. A little on you, on how involved you want to be. There are plenty of people who can be helped by your gift."

Gifts.

Curses.

Blessings.

"In one of my blurs," I say, "it seemed like someone was pulling on the other end of the sling while I was trying to get it in the attic. Is there any reason you can think of for that?"

"Not off the top of my head."

Great.

Maybe the thread has already snapped.

Ahead of us, on the edge of Malcolm's light, I see the outline of an old log cabin. It looks small. Maybe only one room.

Tiff mentioned something about cabins in the area.

Malcolm tips his light toward it. "That's it. That's where we're going."

"So, when my grandpa died back when I was five, it really affected me. Is that what started all this? The trauma? Is that what planted the seed for my blurs? The bats chasing me all these years?"

"There's still a lot we don't know. Life is mystery and not equations. When you think you've got something pinned down, well, then, you can be pretty sure something else is going to come along pretty quickly and unpin it."

"I didn't get to say goodbye."

"Goodbye?"

"To Grandpa."

"Well, maybe all this was a way of telling you that that's okay."

He stops at the porch.

The park service has posted a warning out front not to enter the cabin, but Malcolm ignores it and presses against the door, which protests with a creak but finally opens.

I follow him inside.

The air is thick with the smell of old wood and dust.

"What is this place?"

"C'mere." He walks to the fireplace where an old black and white photograph hangs askew on the wall. "There really was a boy who died up there in the Estoria Inn. It was back in the 1940s. You see that photo?"

A boy, maybe ten years old, is standing beside a stern-looking woman. The Estoria lies in the background.

"Look carefully."

I do.

And I see that it's the boy who appeared to me in Waxford's office. The one who showed me how to reach out and get the handcuff key—which ended up being the secret to saving us all.

"Have you ever seen this photo before?" Malcolm asks.

I remember the book of haunted places in Tennessee. The photos in it.

"I'm not sure. Maybe. How did you know it was here?"

"Research," he says somewhat cryptically.

"What happened to him?"

"It's not completely clear, but from what I've been able to uncover, he was staying with his mother in room 113 when he died."

"Died or was killed?"

"I'm still trying to figure that out."

"Dr. Carrigan told us it was just a folk tale."

"Sometimes the truth turns into a folk tale. Sometimes it's the other way around."

"So when I saw him earlier, was he a ghost or a blur?"

"He may have been both. I'll be in touch." He winks with his remaining eye. "Enjoy the fireflies."

And then he slips out the door, turns off his flashlight, and disappears into the night.

It's dark now and I have to use my cellophane-filtered light to follow the trail.

Fireflies are all around me.

Starting to find their rhythm.

As I make my way back to my friends, I try to process things.

How does Malcolm's story tie in with mine? How did my mind know, on the night when I was hit by the truck, that I would need to follow the bats there at the Estoria?

Maybe it's that bigger plan Nicole talks about.

Paranormal. Supernatural. Maybe even God giving me a glimpse into the future.

Mystery and not equation.

We want the second, we're handed the first.

As I get closer, I hear Mia and Kyle talking about Snookums and a coyote and the perils of freedom versus the security of chains. I don't quite follow.

"I still can't believe you called your turtle 'Snookums,'" he says to her.

"Just be glad I don't call you 'Snookums.'"

"Believe me, I am."

Nicole notices my light. "That you, Daniel?"

"Yeah."

Alysha mentions that the guy in the story of the Country of the Blind faced the same choice as the coyote and Snookums and someone asks her to tell the story, but she says later might be better.

I enter the circle.

"Everything okay?" Nicole asks. "Who was that?"

Right now doesn't feel like the right time to get into everything.

"Just a ranger showing me around."

"Oh. Well, come here." She pats a spot beside her on the boulder. "Sit down and watch the show."

• • •

Sam watched the fireflies blink on and off, all together, all at once. Thousands of them communicating in some mysterious, unseen, inexplicable way.

To Sam—who also went by the name "Marly Weathers" when necessary—the fireflies seemed to represent what'd been accomplished over the last few years: the center in Tennessee, the firm in Philadelphia, the facility in Atlanta.

All in sync.

All the pieces coming together at once.

Searching for a way to turn the hallucinations into something positive.

Designing the tile patterns of the hallways of the facility under Centennial Olympic Park as a way of testing and connecting with the people who were brought there.

And, of course, stopping Dr. Waxford.

Like the Chinese farmer's story.

Curses into blessings.

It'd been difficult to accomplish it all in such a short span of time, especially keeping things a secret from friends and family, but dedication had paid off. That, and the passion to make great things happen.

So that Jess and Liam could be helped.

And the others too.

And you.

A familiar voice called from beside the stream, "Hey, are you coming?"

"I'll be right there," Sam replied.

So now, things could move forward once again.

They still needed to figure out exactly what caused the hallucinations, and how better to interpret them to use them for good.

And then there was the ongoing search for more virtuosos.

A new chapter.

New beginnings.

Sam went to join the others and took a seat on the boulder next to the senator, the one who'd unwittingly provided the trust fund that had paid for everything.

"It's good to have you back," the senator said.

"It's good to be back, Dad," Sam told him.

Then Petra leaned her head against her father's shoulder and they sat together just upstream from their new friends and watched the fireflies blink in synchronicity with each other.

On.

And off.

And on once again.

Bringing brilliant symmetry to the night.

THANKS TO

Courtney Miller, Anna Rosenwong, Eden Huhn, Alex McReynolds, Katrina Johnson, John-Phillip Abner, Justin Cockrell, Tate Luck, Annie Park, Dr. John-Paul Abner, Dr. Clay Runnels, Pam Johnson, Trinity Huhn, Liesl Huhn, Dr. Paul Kelley, Cleon and Joyce Glaze, and Dr. Todd Huhn.

Photo: Emily Hand © 2014

ABOUT THE AUTHOR

Steven James has worked as a professional storyteller, camp program director, wilderness guide, and museum educator. Over the years he has taught storytelling and creative writing around the world. These days he enjoys being a full-time novelist.

Quick trivia: He has never owned a turtle named Snookums or a basketball named Alfie. He lives in eastern Tennessee and has seen the synchronous fireflies in the Smoky Mountains.

And yes, they are remarkable.